Fate of the Unknown

Magic of the Realm
Book Three

Kimberly Marraffino

Fate of the Unknown
Magic of the Realm ~ Book Three

———◦✕◦———

Cover by Stefanie Saw (www.seventhstarart.com)
Copyediting by Enchanted Ink Publishing
Proofreading by Dennis Doty
Map by Kimberly Marraffino
Symbol designed by Kimberly Marraffino and made by DRIVEN Digital Services

First Edition December 2022
Printed in the United States of America
Published in Nacogdoches, Texas

ISBN: 979-8-9861792-1-6 (Paperback)
Library of Congress Control Number: 2022921804

www.KimberlyMarraffino.com

To those who are broken . . .

KILUEMAR
North Shores
Lunar Cave
Werewolf Highlands
Forbidden Coast
Demetrius Desert
Arista Bay
Dragon Cove
Full Moon Forest
Midnight Ridge
Dead Man's Bay
Elf Beach
Centaur Forest
Dwarf Ridge
Lucien Valley
Cursed Cave
Siren Sea
Forsaken Bluffs
Raven Lagoon
Enchanted Hills
Casteya Castle
Stoweward
Shadow Forest
Sunset Cliffs
Valley of the Giants
Maevis Mountains
Mystic Woods
Drolnogard Peak
Nymph Grove
Guardian Lake
West Shores
Muse Meadow
Kitra Forest
Emrys Cave
Caerwyn Village
Cassil Cabin
Sunrise Mesa
East Shores
Cavern Beach
Half Moon Harbor
Dryad Forest
Grotto Bridge
South Shores
Ember Cliffs
0 1 2 3
Miles
N
W E
S

Timeline

—◦✕◦—

Events from Book One and Book Two

<u>Mid-January</u> –

~ The twins, Pavian, Kavana, and Aidan return to Kiluemar

~ Karramis wakes up at Château Rouge

<u>Mid-February</u> –

~ Lucas and the others return to Kiluemar

~ Attack at the cabin

~ Tressa convinces Merrick to leave Kiluemar

<u>Mid-June</u> –

~ The twins celebrate their sixteenth birthday

<u>End of June</u> –

~ Rhiannon finds out Ryan is a werewolf

<u>Early July</u> –

~ Rhiannon visits Casteya Castle during a new moon to find out why Merrick and the others have gone quiet

<u>Mid-July</u> –

~ Pavian and James meet Rhiannon, Karramis, and Will at the cabin to practice summoning the twins' Guardian magic

~ Another verse of the prophecy is foreseen

Note from the Author

<u>Content Warning:</u>
I want my readers to be well-informed of any possible triggers
or content that might not be appropriate for some.
If you would like to know if this book contains any elements
that might be of concern to you, please check the back of the
book or my website for more details.

I would also like to point out that even though this series is
classified as young adult, it is also considered coming-of-age
and contains mature content.

Read at your own discretion.

<u>Pronunciation and Translation Guide:</u>
Both are provided in the back of the book.

<u>Appendix:</u>
This is provided in the back of the book to help refresh your
memory of previous characters and creatures already
introduced in the series.

Table of Contents

Chapter 1

Trespassing

The present
Mid-December

Will appeared midair within the early-morning sky, free-falling toward the earth as a misty portal ejected him over a dense forest. The crisp and brittle air sent cold shards prickling against his exposed skin. Fresh cuts sliced into him as he plummeted through the bare low-hanging trees, the thinner shoots snapping clean off and various parts of his body thudding against the thicker branches. A gasp erupted from him as he collided with the hard snow-covered terrain, sending soft flurries rising up around him as he rolled uncontrollably a few feet before crashing into the base of a tree. A silent inhale tore through him, the air sucking into his bruised and lacerated body.

A quietness filled the forest as thick gray clouds hovered within the winter sky, the light of dawn trapped behind the lingering storm. There was nothing—no birds, no wind nor the rustling of leaves, just an eerie stillness, as if the forest itself waited in shocked silence for the scene playing out to unfold.

Trails of blood spattered about and soaked into the ground, broken and bright red against the newly disturbed snow, traces of brown grass and uprooted underbrush now visible beneath the flattened muddy slush. Twigs and branches scattered across the ground, and fragments of dry leaves, dead bark and moss, and dirt fell from the sky, landing without a sound as they disappeared within the blanketed ground.

A cough and muffled groan echoed through the forest, the sound bouncing off the trees as Will took a few hurried breaths and pulled his body back into full consciousness. He pushed himself up, his body shaking as blood trailed down his arms and dripped from his face. Cuts lined both arms, his right bicep displaying the worst injury, while various rips sliced through his jeans and bloodstained shirt. He forced himself to his feet but stumbled into a tree as the world around him spun. Pain shot up along his spine, his back arching as agony shredded through his muscles, slashing and burning as the bruise developing on his back from his impact with the tree began forming around another wound gnawing along his side. Shapes and colors blended together as his head pounded in sync with his hurried heartbeat. Warmth trickled down his face as he lowered his eyelids, the discoloration along one cheek and the dark crimson against his beige complexion bringing out the blue in his eyes. Adrenaline and rage rose inside him, surging as he fought against the pain and irritation burning through him.

"Dammit, Karramis," Will groaned under his breath through gritted teeth as he pushed himself off the tree, grasping his side and limping through the snow. "When the bloody hell did you learn to do that?"

His heart raced, each beat bringing a heaviness to his chest as he scanned the area. The ragged exhales billowed from his mouth, the condensation like thick smoke. Fresh blood pooled from the deeper lacerations on his arms but froze, the freezing air acting as a bandage against the wounds along his cold-kissed skin. Cradling his midsection, he ignored his bruised muscles and potentially broken ribs, analyzing his surroundings. He had no clue where Karramis had sent him, but he had to get back to her. He had to help her. Protect her.

"Terramina!" he called telepathically to the Earth Dragon.

Nothing.

"Raeth! Oakley!"

Pushing aside shrubs, he panted, each step more painful than the last. His limbs were numb, the cold piercing through his wet, tattered clothes, but with each nip from the winter air, the discomfort surrounding each injury sent a wave of soreness squeezing every nerve throughout his body. He trembled, the coldness and pain taking control of his muscles.

"Ignara!"

His mind remained silent.

"Dammit, can any of you hear me?"

Frustration rose as he leaned against a tree, the frost-covered bark seeping through his thin shirt and searing into his injured back like a hot iron. He forced his eyes shut and let out a muffled groan behind his clenched teeth.

Shoving from the tree, he blew out an ear-piercing whistle, hoping his winged horse, Callie, was nearby.

Nothing.

He did it again.

Again, nothing. She was too far away.

"Anyone!" he pleaded loudly, his gravelly voice traveling through the trees.

Only silence—an eerie and unsettling silence—remained as his voice faded, aside from the shuffling of snow under his feet.

"Hello? Is anyone out here?"

Will scanned the dense canopies of partially bare branches overhead and glanced around the heavily wooded area. He was certain he was still on the island, but with the nearly barren trees and snow-packed ground, he could not determine which forest he had ended up in, which side of the island he was on, or even which direction he was headed. A mountain range rose not far from him, the monstrous rich chocolate stone disappearing into the sky. But with the sun hidden behind the clouds, he did not know in which direction the peak lay. So, he kept moving forward, hoping once he broke free from the tree cover he would know where he was and be able to get help.

A tightness wrapped around his gut, a soul-wrenching agony tearing through his insides, but not from pain. No, this was far worse. Will had to get back to her. He had to help Karramis before it was too late. She had saved him by sending him away, and he was not going to leave her in the hands of those seeking to take what they wanted from her, even if it meant killing her in the process.

If any of them touched her, he was going to kill them all.

Will's legs grew heavy as he trudged through the snow, his limp and pain becoming harder to fight. Leaning against a tree for support, he took a few controlled breaths.

"Hey!" Will yelled, disregarding the potential threats of the forest as he continued forward, his voice growing louder. "Is anyone out here?"

He picked up his pace, wincing and groaning with each step. His pulse hammered harder in his head as his chest ached, the hurried pounding sending jolts of pain through his injuries.

"Hello?"

The word echoed through the forest, the sound resonating as it reached the mountainside.

Then silence.

"Terramina!" he said, pleading for a response as tears of helplessness filled his eyes.

A sharp pain throbbed under the hand pressing against his side as he picked up his pace. He wrapped his other arm over his chest, trying to trap the remaining heat his body had left. He had to find help. The desperation was taking over, the sheer determination to get back to Casteya Castle driving his every step. Karramis was in danger, even more so after saving him.

A rush of regret, resentment, and rage pooled in his gut, masking his pain. Regret for not being able to stop it, not being able to fight and save her instead. Resentment toward Karramis for choosing him and not herself. And rage for who she was now trapped with, alone.

"Goddammit, Karramis," he snapped, guilt and frustration at what she had done to protect him twisting his stomach into knots. "I'm the one who's supposed to protect you, you stubborn woman."

His staggering, unsteady stride turned into a shuffling jog, the crunching snow growing louder with each hurried step.

"Hello?" he yelled again.

Footfalls ricocheted, growing louder and pounding with a steady rhythm, the sound seeming to come from all directions.

Will halted, delight and uncertainty tugging at his insides as he scanned the area.

He swallowed down the hesitation. "Help!"

The pounding steps, louder and more chaotic as another set joined in, advanced closer and stopped beyond the trees, a ghost now lingering out of sight.

Twisting around, Will searched the area, but there was nothing, only silence again.

"Who are you?" a deep, stern voice asked. "Why are you on our lands?"

Will cautiously stepped around a thick tree, his bloody hands up in surrender.

A large creature came into view, a set of intimidatingly unkind brown eyes staring down at Will. Standing a few feet away, the half man, half horse was over eight feet tall, with a rich chestnut coat covering his lower half and slightly lighter skin on his naked upper body. His black hair was pulled back into a loose ponytail and matched his tail and the silky fur wrapping around his ankles. The creature radiated elegance and power and reminded Will of the magical flawlessness of dragons.

A cold mist blew erratically from Will's gaping mouth as his arms hung lazily. He fixated on the centaur, unable to take his eyes off the superior creature in front of him. He had somehow landed in Centaur Forest on the northwest side of the island, a section of Kiluemar no other creature, animal, or human ever dared enter.

Years ago, Will had learned centaurs were very antisocial creatures, refusing to associate with anyone or anything outside their collective species. They were untrusting of the outside world, especially humans, and extremely territorial. With the body of a horse from the waist down and the upper half section being human, centaurs were part of the first round of creatures who had escaped to the realm after the barrier had gone up. Hunted for centuries for being an abomination in the eyes of those in the non-magical world, centaurs had fled to Kiluemar and taken refuge among the trees just below Dwarf Ridge. Over the years, many of the centaurs had disappeared after falling victim to the various hungry creatures on the island. Many hid, never coming out unless absolutely necessary, and they were eventually deemed extinct both in Kiluemar and the non-magical world. But now, Will stood face to face with one, and it was clear the centaur did not welcome his presence. He was in the creature's domain. Will knew he was in dangerous territory, for he was an intruder.

"I didn't mean to trespass," Will said wholeheartedly, hesitant to move, "but I need to—"

The centaur raised a hand and cut him off. He stared at Will for a moment with a fierce gaze, crossing his arms and establishing his dominance.

"What business do you have here?" the centaur asked, holding his gaze. "And why are you drawing attention to yourself? That is a good way to get yourself killed."

"You can talk." Not a question.

The centaur narrowed his eyes, his tone tight. "Of course I can talk. I am not some mindless beast."

"I meant no offense. It's just, I was unaware your kind could. My apologies." Cradling his abdomen again as he leaned back into a tree, Will declared with a pained inhale, "I need help."

The centaur took a few steps closer, his voice turning predatory. "You will not find it here, so unless you are wishing for the latter of my previous statement, I suggest you leave."

"No," Will said, shaking his head. "I do not wish that."

"Then I will tell you again. Leave. Now. Before I change my mind by giving you the option."

"No," Will said, calm, steady, and firm as he pushed himself back onto his feet, his legs unstable beneath him. "I need help. I need—"

"We do not help humans," the centaur declared indignantly.

"Please. Please help me. I've got to—"

A branch snapped behind Will, and he twisted, groaning as a shock wave of pain ripped through his side and back. He let out a deep, guttural yelp as he fell to one knee. Grasping his side as he forced himself to breathe through the sudden jolt, he glanced up.

Another centaur stood a few feet away, standing statuesque as he stared at Will. This one was taller and more muscular than the other and appeared older. Regal and wise. A leader. With a black coat and silver hair and tail, his olive skin along his human body clashed with his horse half. As the centaur moved closer, his long silvery tresses, thick and wavy, brushed across his bare chest, the silken mane flowing past his biceps and covering most of his extremely muscular midsection.

The black-and-silver centaur made his way over to his companion as he kept a watchful eye on Will. "Who is this human?"

The brown centaur faced Will. "Who are you?"

Rising to his feet, he answered, "Will."

"And *what* are you, Will?" the darker centaur asked, the olive skin of his human half gleaming against the white-and-gray backdrop surrounding them.

"He is a human," the brown-coated centaur stated matter-of-factly. "That is all we need to know."

"I'm a Drolnogard," Will added.

The two centaurs exchanged puzzled glances.

"I thought your kind was extinct," the older centaur said with a husky tone lined with an unfamiliar accent.

"Same," Will said with a bit of irritation in his voice. "Listen, I don't have time for this—"

"You are in our territory, human," the brown centaur interrupted in a sharp, bitter tone.

"Yes." Will stepped back, keeping his eyes on them. "Yes, but it was not by choice. I have to get out of here and find help." He retreated, slow and cautious, each movement careful as he continued backward. "I'm leaving. My wife is in danger, and I need to get back to her."

The brown centaur hurried around behind him, stopping Will's retreat, and puffed out his chest. "You were not given permission to leave."

"Racentu!" the black-and-silver centaur said fiercely, proving he was the one in charge. "He is not a prisoner, nor is he a threat to us."

A flash of uncertainty flickered in Racentu's eyes. "How can you be so sure, Marcellus?"

The centaur ignored the question as he locked eyes with Will. "How did you get here? No one can get in or out without the wards alerting us."

"Please, I don't have time to explain right now." Will was polite but anxious. "I need to get to Stoweward. If you can please help me, I will answer any questions you might have along the way."

Marcellus thought for a moment. "We cannot help you."

"All right," Will said with a sigh. "Then please let me pass."

Marcellus stepped aside and pointed southeast. "Stoweward is in that direction."

Will shuffled past the centaur and forced a smile up at him, the dry blood on his face pinching his skin. "Thank you."

The two centaurs monitored as Will limped away, dragging his feet through the thick blanket of snow.

Racentu folded his arms across his chest. "You are making a mistake by letting him go."

Marcellus took his silvery waves into his hands, exposing his chiseled stomach and chest and tying back his hair. "And what makes you think that?"

"Because he will tell the others about us." Annoyance lined Racentu's tone.

Smiling, Marcellus patted Racentu on the back. "I do not believe he will."

"How can you be so sure?"

"Well, first of all, he's a Drolnogard."

"And what does that have to do with anything?"

Marcellus pressed his lips thin and scowled at him. "Well, if you would stop interrupting me, I could explain myself."

"My apologies," Racentu said genuinely.

"Drolnogards are one of the most trustworthy humans to all magical creatures. They value loyalty, honesty, trust, and integrity."

"And again, what does that have to do with letting him go?"

"Well, it has everything to do with it. Not to mention, my dear Racentu, I know something about him that you are apparently unaware of."

Racentu turned his gaze from Will over to Marcellus. "And that would be?"

Marcellus smiled. "Will Drolnogard is the father to the ones the prophecy spoke of."

"And how do you know this bit of information?"

"Quinian. He has met the young boy, James."

"Do you really believe the prophecy is right and they will stop Merrick? And we can finally come out of hiding?"

"I believe anything is possible. But first, we must help him."

Marcellus galloped after Will before Racentu could object, jumping over bushes and roots peeking up from under the snow. Footfalls pounded after him as Racentu followed closely behind. Racing in front of Will, they forced him to a stop, the abrupt halt sending Will's hands into the side of Racentu. Quickly pulling away, Will tossed the centaur an apologetic glare.

"We will help you," Marcellus announced, tucking the now-loose silvery strands behind his ears.

Will let out a sigh of relief. "You will?"

"Yes, but there are a few conditions we must agree on first."

Will grinned. "Anything."

"First, you have to promise you will keep our encounter a secret. No one must know we are alive."

"I give you my word, I will not tell anyone about either of you."

"Great," Marcellus said. "Now, if your children really do stop Merrick, then we will come out of hiding. No more living in fear. But until then, our existence is only privy to you and the dwarves."

"Anything else?" Will asked restlessly as time dragged on.

"Yes," Racentu said. "We can only take you to the edge of the forest near Stoweward. We do not leave the protection of the trees." He paused, scowling down at Will. "And you will *not* be riding me."

"That's not a problem." Will made his way over to Marcellus. "Thank you. I'm utterly grateful for your help."

Marcellus lowered himself to the ground, and Will struggled as he climbed on top of the centaur.

"What do I grab hold of?" Will asked as Marcellus stood up, his body unbalanced on the creature's bare back.

Racentu leaned over and whispered with a chuckle, "I do not recommend grabbing anything."

"Just wrap your arms around my waist, Drolnogard," Marcellus said as he took off. "And hold on!"

~

Will climbed over the fence on the west side of Stoweward as the two centaurs observed from the trees.

"Terramina?" Will called again through his mind as he stopped to listen. *"Raeth? Ignara? Can you hear me?"* He

waited before resuming his trek toward the center of town. "Dammit!"

Will was freezing. Even the pain was masked behind the numbness taking over his body. It had been a welcome reprieve at first, but as he forced his legs forward, the cold slowed him down. His muscles stiffened. He could barely feel his hands or feet. The blood along his pale skin was frozen, and the temperature remained unnaturally cold despite the sun most likely being high above him beyond the clouds by now. The bruises along his back, arms, and face darkened as the chilled air swept past him, tiny prickles of snow brushing across his exposed skin as he made his way closer to his destination.

Stoweward appeared to be a ghost town, completely deserted and eerie. Silence filled the area, the quietness veiled behind a lingering darkness. An ominous sense of doom and a gut-wrenching fear loomed around every corner as Will made his way farther into town, making his way to Pavian and Raina's place.

Smoked billowed from a single chimney, a lone house resting in the center of town.

"Pavian!" Will yelled, pushing himself to move faster. "Raina!"

His urgent call echoed all around and bounced off the empty houses, amplifying his voice.

Louder, he called again, "Pavian!"

The front door flung open, and Raina rushed out onto the porch, wrapping her arms across her chest to shield herself from the cold.

"Will," she mumbled to herself, her shaky breath billowing in front of her face.

Liam exited the house and stopped next to his mother, the crisp air bringing him closer to the warmth coming from her.

As Will limped closer, Raina took in his slowed saunter and the blood coating his clothes, arms, and face.

Raina twisted and ushered Liam inside, following closely behind him. "Get inside, sweetie." She hurried to grab a blanket from the couch and gave her son a peck on the cheek. "Stay inside."

Closing the door, she bolted toward Will. She ran, supporting her protruding stomach as her bare feet pressed footprints into the snow. The sight of him sent a rush of fear crashing through her.

A large black-and-blue bruise covered the left side of his face, accompanied by a clotted gash—a clean slice diagonally across his cheekbone. His lip was split in two places. Cuts littered his arms, and a deep laceration appeared beneath his ripped sleeve along his right bicep. Dry blood, a deep shade of reddish brown, was caked against his abnormally pale skin. He clutched his midsection, and his haggard breath told her he was struggling to fight whatever damage lay beyond his grasp.

"Are you mad?" Will asked as she reached him, observing her thin pajamas and lack of shoes. "You're going to freeze."

"I'll be fine," she reassured him calmly. "Pregnancy makes me run hot." She flung the blanket over his shoulders and examined him. "Oh my gosh, you're the one who's freezing. Come on, come inside. I need to clean these off, and we need to get you warmed up. Where else are you hurt?"

"I'll be all right," Will said unconvincingly, still draping his arm across his stomach as he winced, moving again causing the pain to shoot through him.

Raina glanced down at him clutching his ribs. "Are they broken?"

"I don't think so." There was discomfort in his soft declaration.

She grabbed his wrist, lowering his arm to his side. "Let me take a look."

Will winced again and pulled in a hissing inhale through his teeth. "Don't worry—"

"Let me take a look, Will," Raina insisted adamantly as she carefully lifted his shirt.

The lower half of his rib cage was badly bruised, a mix of purple, black, and blue along the upper part of his abdomen.

Raina gently examined the area, and he gasped. "Sorry." She pressed again, softer but still feeling each bone carefully. "I don't think any have dislodged—at least what I can feel. But I think a few are bruised for sure, maybe even fractured." Releasing the shirt, she asked nervously, "How did this happen?"

Will returned his hand to his side, grimacing as he answered with a pained tone. "I rolled into a tree."

"That injury is not from a tree. I've been a nurse long enough to know the difference between a single blunt trauma and a series of them. You were in a fight, weren't you?"

Will did not answer as he gripped the corners of the blanket draped over his shoulders with one hand and continued toward the house.

"Will," Raina said behind him, hesitant to ask the next question as she swallowed, stepping closer to him. "What happened?"

"Where's Pavian?" he asked instead.

"He's not back yet. I figured he would go see Zarrius first."

"Of course." He dropped his gaze, avoiding eye contact but realizing she was still barefoot. "We need to get you inside." Turning toward the house, he added, "Get you warmed up. And I need to find a way to reach the dragons."

She followed but asked again, her tone nervous and trembling, "Will, what happened? Is everyone okay?"

"No." He cleared his throat and faced her. "Listen, I need your help. I've got to get back. Karramis needs my help. Merrick and the others have her."

"Okay." Standing tall, she blew out a misty breath and regained her composure. "What do you need?"

"Do you think you could travel to the cave for me and get one of the dragons to come here?"

Raina shrugged and shook her head. "I mean, I could try, but my magic has been harder to control the further I get into my pregnancy. But I don't think it will do any good. They won't understand me."

Will bowed his head. "I know. I'm just unsure how to get them to come to me."

Raina considered. "I could go to the cabin—"

"No," Will said in a panic. "No, don't go there."

Concern pinched her expression. "Why?"

He did not answer.

Raina stepped closer, the bitter air not the reason for the chill racing up her spine. "Will, what happened?"

"I don't have time to explain right now." Will placed his hand on her shoulder. "Something happened last night, and . . ." He faltered. "Raina, listen, I really need to get to Karramis. But you can't go to the cabin right now, and I can't let James and Rhiannon know what is happening. It's . . . I just can't explain it right now. Please. Don't make me."

"Okay." Raina nodded solemnly. "What about Callie?"

"What about her?"

"Do you think she'll listen to me if I go to her?"

"Yes," Will said enthusiastically, grimacing at his foolishness of moving too fast as he hugged her. "I do believe she will." He pulled away, grasping her shoulders and leaning into her. "Why didn't I think of that?" Forcing a smirk to cover up his pain, he added, "Brilliant idea."

"Thanks." Raina pushed open the front door as an uneasiness settled in her features. "Let's go inside and get warmed up. I'll go to Callie while you change into something warmer and clean those wounds." She paused, giving Will a stern glare. "No argument."

Will nodded. "Yes, ma'am. But we have to hurry."

~

Callie arrived moments later. The black-and-white winged horse stood regally with her wings pressed firmly against her sides as the pewter clouds darkened overhead.

Will strained as he attempted to mount Callie, unable to jump onto the back of the horse. His loyal friend lowered herself to the ground, and Will eased onto the creature. Dressed in a thick robe and tall boots that disappeared beneath the fluffy material resting along her calves, Raina slid her hand along Callie's neck, petting the creature as she peered up at Will, who was now dressed in some of Pavian's clothes—a thick long-sleeve sweater and dark denim jeans. The shirt was a tad too small for him along his broad shoulders and muscular arms. Butterfly bandages stuck to his bruised cheek, and the cuts along his lip were now clear of all remnants of blood.

"Wait," Raina said, racing back into the house.

Pushing open the door, she disappeared, returning seconds later with a stool. She held her stomach as she placed the stool on the floor near the threshold and climbed up the two steps, reaching over the doorframe. A sword came into view, the gold hilt gleaming in the flickering firelight coming from inside the house.

Hurrying back outside, she handed it to Will. "Here, you might need this."

The leather-bound sheath was black with intricate gold inlays around the edges. The golden hilt had a red leather grip and a slightly curved guard with the symbol of the prophecy embedded in the circular pommel.

"Thank you," Will said, drawing the sword halfway from the sheath and examining the double-edged blade, the words *Kill or Be Killed* engraved down the center of one side.

"You're welcome," Raina said, her voice soft.

Will met her worried gaze, placing the sword across his lap. "He'll be back soon."

She gave a single nod. "I know. Now go."

Will leaned forward, bracing for takeoff as Callie outstretched her wings.

"Will?" Raina called, sadness lacing her expression.

"I'm getting her back, Raina. Even if I have to die trying."

"Be careful," was all she said.

Chapter 2

Failed Attempt

The late afternoon sun was hidden behind the clouds hovering above the eastern-most part of Caerwyn Village. A lone gray two-story stone building sat in the middle of an open field, the massive solitary building resting perfectly in the center of the trees circling around the old structure. The edge of the village lay a few yards away, the dense line of trees, vines, and bushes along the outskirts acting not only as a fence but as a reminder that only those permitted were allowed through the protective wards. A thick layer of freshly fallen snow lay across the quiet field, but footprints of both humans and creatures were scattered near the front of the aged building, creating a trampled, muddy path leading to the stone steps beyond the front archway.

Three dragons circled overhead, their tiny shadows barely noticeable against the snow-covered ground. Raeth, Oakley, and Terramina patrolled high above the area as smoke billowed from two of the three chimneys sitting atop the roof. Light shone through square-pane windows on the first floor, the bright illumination of modern electricity and the flickering of flames both evident behind the frosted glass.

A frigid breeze blew through the stone colonnade along the east side of the building as James leaned against a pillar, his attention drawn toward the tree line to the northeast. He did not seem to mind the icy blast despite only wearing a thin jacket over his short-sleeve shirt and a pair of worn-out jeans. The swirls of air drifted with the small flurries in a flawless magical dance around him, caressing him with a crisp winter touch against his warm complexion.

Rhiannon opened the door, the hinges creaking as she closed it behind her.

"James?" Sadness lingered in her voice as the coldness of his magic glided across her face and hands.

The plumes of snow fell against the stone floor in a silent slumber, but he did not face her.

Rhiannon's eyes were red, and her cheeks were flush as she rubbed her hands along the soft material of her long-sleeve sweater. "Anything?"

James kept his eyes on the peak of Maevis Mountains. "No. No sign of them." He tilted his head, the concern pinching his features matching his tone. "How's she doing?"

Rhiannon let out a sigh as she came up beside him, the warmth of her breath clashing with the cold air. "She's still sleeping."

"Is she going to be okay?"

She lowered her eyes. "Alfina and Nina think so."

"What about you?" he asked earnestly, reaching out and taking her hand. "Are you okay?"

"I'm fine," she answered, flat and sharp, trembling from the cold.

Standing in front of her, he announced firmly, his sister's eyes still lowered to the ground, "No, you're not. Don't do that. Don't shut me out again."

"Fine," she let out with a soft but shaky breath. "I'm not okay."

He wrapped his arms around her upper body and hugged her. "Neither am I."

The door creaked opened, and the twins turned as Aidan stepped outside with a bundle of cloth draped over his arm.

"Here," Aidan offered, handing the twins each a thick oversized blanket. "You two are goin' to freeze out here."

The dark green pullover hoodie and light denim jeans Aidan wore were covered in dry blood. His face was flushed, and the bright emerald in his worried gaze clashed with his bloodshot eyes.

Rhiannon grabbed both blankets and handed one to James. Unfolding the other, she stood on her tiptoes and flung the blanket over Aidan's shoulders. "Maybe you should go get some rest." Gathering the corners of the material in her hands, she gave him a weak smile. "I promise I'll get you as soon as she wakes."

Aidan shook his head, refusing to take hold of the blanket she had wrapped tightly around him. "No. I will rest once we get them back."

Rhiannon lifted his hand to where she held the blanket and made him take hold of it. "What if . . ." She hesitated, the trepidation magnifying inside her and slowly consuming her as it spread like slow-moving fire through her veins. "What if they're . . . What if it's too late?"

James opened the blanket in his hands and covered Rhiannon's shoulders, the material nearly touching the floor. "Merrick can't do anything with them until the next full moon. That's the one thing I'm holding on to right now. He needs the full moon to do the ritual." His brown eyes shifted to Aidan. "Right?"

Aidan gave a single nod. "Yes."

The door opened again, the hinges emitting a long-winded squeak.

Nina exited, her long coppery hair pulled back into a messy bun. The light blue scrubs she had on were clean and smelled of fresh laundry.

"She's awake," Nina said tiredly, her beautiful green eyes dull behind the sorrow plaguing her expression.

Aidan dropped the blanket as his eyes widened, and he rushed toward his sister, who still stood by the threshold.

Nina held up her palms as he nearly collided with her, stopping him in his tracks. "Aidan."

He huffed, the wildness in his gaze frantic. "What's wrong?"

"She's still out of it."

"Did she say anythin'?" He shifted on his feet, the urge to push past her rising to the surface.

"No. Alfina told her she was injured and at the infirmary, but nothin' else."

"I want to see her."

"Aidan," Rhiannon said, stepping closer to him as he faced her. "She's okay." She slid her arms around his waist and hugged him, the warmth from him erasing the chill creeping through her body as the blanket glided down her shoulders. "She's okay."

Closing his eyes, Aidan released a shuddering breath and relaxed into her arms, resting his cheek against the top of her head as he returned the embrace.

"Do you want to see her?" he asked, his eyes meeting hers.

She smiled weakly. "I'll be right up."

Aidan twisted away from her.

"Aidan?" Rhiannon called softly.

Following Nina, he paused in the doorframe and faced Rhiannon.

Grief lined her features, and her voice fell to a whisper. "Don't mention—"

"I know. I won't."

And the door closed behind him.

Rhiannon lowered her eyelids as she faced the empty space by the door. A swarm of emotions stirred in her core—fear, defeat, anger, worry. Her stomach tightened, her nerves tingled, and her skin flushed. She wanted to scream and cry. Anything and everything to release the overwhelming mix of feelings taking control of her.

"Breathe," James's voice said in her head as he came up behind her.

He could feel everything she felt—every emotion, every heartache. She allowed him in, her mind wide-open. She did not want to feel alone again. He was the anchor keeping her grounded. Focused. With him near her, she was not so out of control.

"Breathe," he repeated, his inner voice soothing, taming the anxious beast trying to take over his sister.

She opened her eyes and slowly exhaled through her mouth. "Thank you." She twisted around, sliding the blanket back up over her shoulders.

"You would've done it for me," he said with a dismissive shrug.

"No, thank you for always understanding me. I don't think I thanked you before. So, thank you for never giving up on me. And . . . for making me feel like I'm not alone. Like I can do anything, as long as I have you by my side." She chuckled under her breath. "Or in my head. Thanks for reminding me how to regain my control."

He smiled. "Anytime." Reaching for the other blanket on the floor, he added, "Let's go check on Aunt K."

Heading inside, they halted abruptly.

Voices filled their heads, all three dragons alerting them of who was coming. They jerked around and bolted down the stone steps as Callie came into view. The winged horse swooped from the air, landing with a heavy thud as she cleared the trees, galloping closer to the infirmary.

Shock rose on the twins' faces as they raced after her, the winged horse carrying their father and a limp figure in his arms.

"Dad!" they called after their father.

Callie slid to a stop, and James faltered as shock filled his chest, squeezing the air from his lungs. Rhiannon slowed as she came up behind her brother, the shuddering exhale of disbelief interrupting her heavy panting.

Will held their mother, who was lifeless and covered in blood. "Get help!" The frantic plea was choked with anguish as tears slid down his bruised and bandaged face.

Rhiannon rotated around and yelled, "Aidan! Nina!" She ran toward the building, a lump rising in her throat. "Alfina!"

Refusing to let go of Karramis, Will dismounted and fell to his knees, cradling her as he tried to stand. "Please." His eyes never left her, his hand trembling as he pushed back the strands from her ashen and bruised face. "Open your eyes." Leaning back onto his heels, he pulled her body close to him, the coldness from her seeping through his clothes. "Not yet, darling." His voice was barely audible as he placed his lips close to her ear. "You hear me? I'm not ready to let you go. Please." He closed his eyes, more tears falling as he drew in a shuddering breath. "Please stay. Don't leave me."

"Dad," James whispered as he knelt in the snow in front of his parents, his voice cracking as he took in his mother's injuries, tears filling his eyes.

Karramis was covered in blood. Her shirt had soaked up most of the brownish-red fluid that had seeped from the various injuries littering her body. Dry blood trailed down her neck from two puncture wounds and another set on her wrist. A fresh bruise lay along the old scar on her face, the deep blues and purples clashing with the paleness of her skin. There was so much blood all over her body that James could not tell where it was all coming from.

"Dad?" James said helplessly, taking his mother's limp hand, the blood sticky under his trembling fingers.

She was so cold, and her lips were tinged with blue.

A burning sensation pinched at his nose, the emotions escaping down his face as he squeezed his lips together, the effort to control his sobs making his chin tremble.

Lifting his gaze from Karramis, Will moved his glossy eyes over to his son's troubled expression. "I'm so sorry." His voice was weak and unsteady. "I didn't get back to her in time."

Rhiannon shuffled to a stop, her heavy pants followed by hurried footsteps as Aidan raced behind her.

"No," Rhiannon breathed, shaking her head and covering her mouth as she spotted Karramis. "No."

Staring at his mother, James traced his fingers along her uninjured wrist. His hand shook so hard he could not steady them against her ice-cold skin.

Kneeling beside him, Rhiannon held his other hand.

His hand stilled, and he pressed his fingers into his mother's wrist. He waited, praying he would feel something. Anything.

Nothing.

"James," Aidan said, standing behind him and placing a hand on his shoulder, "she's gone."

James ignored him as Rhiannon began crying silently next to him.

He focused and waited.

And waited.

Still, there was nothing. No condensation billowed from her mouth against the cold air. Her chest remained still. Her limbs were limp, and her body was rigid. There were no traces of anything left in her lifeless body. No color. No warmth. No magic.

Not even a heartbeat.

She was gone.

Karramis was dead.

Chapter 3

Arrival

Five months ago
Mid-July

Discovering Merrick had potentially been trapped in the non-magical world, James and Rhiannon were anxious and uneasy about tonight and even more determined to drive their Guardian magic to the surface. But they worried if it would matter—if having those abilities would be effective against what was coming. No one knew when Merrick would return, or if he even could. But if he was, in fact, biding his time before returning, what was he waiting for?

With the other Guardians' magic fading, the twins needed to summon their own dormant powers—a sure sign they had the ability when James could hear the distant voice of his Messenger. Even if the Guardian magic was faint, even a sliver of it present, James and Rhiannon could possibly sense if Merrick, or any other threat, entered Kiluemar tonight. Or if anyone came through at all.

But yesterday had taken a toll on the twins. After hours of training, the only Guardian magic James could pull to the surface was the voice of his Messenger in his head, speaking to him in a muffled, distant voice he was unable to understand. And Rhiannon could sense the portals, the tingle tugging in her gut, but she could not pinpoint them. She was not even sure if what she was feeling were the portals or her own nerves of tonight rising inside her. Something deep down told her tonight was not going to bode well, and she did not need magic to send her instincts firing on high alert.

~

The glow from the full moon burst from behind the dark horizon, lighting up the canopies of the trees as shadows hid within the forest. A cool ocean breeze blew in from the east, the blazing heat of summer now gone as the sun disappeared far behind the western horizon, making the night both a blessing and a curse as the celestial wonder inched closer to its magical peak.

"This is ridiculous," James said, annoyed, opening his eyes. "We've been at this forever."

Pavian checked his watch, letting out an exasperated sigh as he fought back the urge to roll his eyes. "We've only been doing this for forty minutes."

James plucked a piece of grass from the ground and tossed it before letting out a frustrated groan. "And all day yesterday."

"Not all day," Pavian corrected. "Just a few hours."

James groaned again and leaned back onto the grass, tucking his arms under his head and peering up at the clear star-specked sky.

"What exactly are we supposed to feel when it happens?" Rhiannon asked, playing with the hem of her dress as she sat next to her brother.

"You'll feel it first," Karramis answered, sitting on the steps of the cabin's porch, her arm interlocked with Will's as he sat next to her, "then hear it soon afterward. But you'll have to focus on the feeling aspect of it first."

Rhiannon pulled her attention inward, as if trying to listen, then quickly blinked. "I don't hear anything. What's it supposed to sound like?"

"Do you feel it again, though?" Will asked, the tips of his fingers gliding subconsciously along the back of Karramis's hand as her arm rested on his thigh.

"Yeah, but it's not any stronger than yesterday. It's more like a hunger pang, nothing remotely magical or anything."

Pavian strolled back and forth a few feet from the twins with his arms folded across his chest. "Well, something is better than nothing."

"Right." Rhiannon shifted her eyes between her mother and uncle. "What am I supposed to be listening for?"

Pavian dropped his arms and slowed his pacing. "The portals release vibrations at all times, but they're faint." There was an informative lilt to his tone and demeanor—a confident, serious, and disciplined persona only a skilled and knowledgeable leader could convey. "Only a fully developed Guardian can sense them at any given time. But when they open, those vibrations magnify, making your entire body fully aware of them. All of them. And once you turn your focus toward that sensation, you hear a buzzing in your head."

"Actually, mine is more of a humming," Karramis corrected, leaning into Will, her cheek resting against his shoulder. "And Kavana and Meadow hear a ringing. It's different for everyone."

"Okay, so . . ." James sat up. "If we can't hear all that until they open, then why are we trying this now? What's the point of all this?"

"The point is, James," Pavian said, stopping and glaring down at him, "Guardians can sense the portals at all times, like I said before. They just have to focus on them to do it. The portals inside are always open and have less power, but the ones on the outside have stronger magic linked to them—to control them. And that sound, those vibrations emitting from them, only gets stronger the closer the outside portals are to opening. It's like a security alarm, alerting us that the doors are about to open. Then, when they finally do, that alarm pulls our attention, and we are then able to focus on those coming through."

Karramis peered up at the night sky. "And at this point in the evening, the noise should be somewhere in the back of your mind, creating that unique vibration and slowly rising, kinda like an underwater beacon drifting closer to the surface."

"Can you hear it right now?" Rhiannon asked her mother and uncle. "Sense it at all?"

"No," they both said, disappointment and worry coating the word.

"Not anymore," Pavian added, plopping down next to James and leaning forward, resting his arms against his bent knees.

"My Guardian magic has never been very powerful," Karramis said, "or accurate for that matter. Sensing magic has never been my strong suit. But being able to feel the portals when they opened or when anything came through was something I was always able to do without any major issues. Even if I didn't know the exact magic most of the time, I was still able to sense when the portals were open and when they were being used. Kavana and Pavian always had the strongest connection to the Guardian magic, though, even more so than our dad. I mean, it probably had a lot to do with the fact that was their only power and they were the oldest of the new generation and received their magic so young, but it still made me jealous of them sometimes."

Pavian forced a smile as he met his sister's gaze. "At least you still have your portal magic and other powers. Mine are almost completely gone, and Kavana is even weaker than I am. We're both pretty much powerless right now. Everything linked to our Guardian magic is almost gone. Only our trained skills remain."

Rhiannon ran her fingers along the hem of her dress again, her eyes tracing her slow movements. "What if we don't hear anything? Or what if what I'm sensing is as good as it's going to get right now? Then what?"

Pavian thought for a moment. "Then we wait until next month and try again, or—I don't know . . . Just figure it out as we go, I guess."

"One step at a time," Karramis said to her with a wink.

Rhiannon flashed her a quick grin before asking her uncle, "What makes you so sure James or I even have Guardian magic in us? Maybe the Messenger thing is a fluke. Maybe what I'm sensing isn't really anything significant."

"Yeah," James added, locking eyes with Pavian. "I mean, you said before that the realm's magic is weakening, so if that happens, wouldn't Guardian magic cease to exist?"

"I have to believe that won't happen and that all the magic of the island will hold on long enough to be saved and restored to its original strength."

"Is it even possible?" Rhiannon asked doubtfully.

"Anything is possible," Will said with a grin as he slid his hand into Karramis's and interlocked their fingers. "Magic is an extraordinary force. It is the definition of miraculous. I mean, look at you two. Look at your mum. You three are literally walking miracles."

"Miracle, huh?" Karramis said adoringly with a smile. "I like the sound of that."

Will grinned and winked as he leaned over and kissed her forehead.

Leaning back, James rested his palms against the lush ground, his fingers disappearing into the grass. "But what happens if the magic can't be restored? Does another ritual have to happen, sacrifices and all? Does someone else have to be cursed again like the first Gatekeeper?”

A screech and heavy flapping of wings echoed overhead as a honey-and-amber-colored bird swooped down from the sky, its sharp taloned feet stretching out toward the ground and morphing into fully clothed legs and feet. Its wings shrank, transforming into arms as silky feathers slid inside porcelain skin. More clothes seemed to grow, and the remaining bird features faded as a fully clothed human stood before them.

Straightening his hunched body, Aidan pulled his broad shoulders back as he tugged on the bottom of his white shirt, adjusting it over the leather belt holding up his dark blue jeans.

“That’s so cool,” the twins said together, directing their attention over at Aidan.

“I don’t think I’ll ever get tired of seeing that,” Rhiannon added with a smirk as she got to her feet.

“Thanks,” Aidan said proudly with a coy smile. “How’s it goin’?”

“Fine.” Rhiannon hugged him. “I didn’t know you were coming.”

“I didn’t intend to be here either.” He tossed his gaze between Pavian and Karramis. “Yer sister sent me. She won’t be able to make it, as I’m sure you already guessed. She planned on comin’ to help, but she’s with yer father.”

“Is something wrong?” Karramis asked tightly, sliding her hand from Will’s as she unhooked their arms and leaned forward.

"Oh, no." Aidan's tone was unconvincing. "No, I believe it's just a precaution."

Pavian drew his brows together. "What is?"

"Tonight."

"Is something supposed to happen tonight?" Rhiannon asked, worry pinching her features. "Should we not stay here?" Her voice was quick and low. "I knew this was a bad idea. Bad things happen here on a full moon."

Aidan placed his hands on her shoulders and gently squeezed. "Don't fret, lass. Like I said, it's only a precaution."

Rhiannon fixed on him with a skeptical scowl. "Why do I not believe you?" She paused and analyzed his eyes, attempting to spot any signs of deceit. "Are you lying?"

Grinning, he said with an overexaggerated Scottish accent, "Nah, lassie, I wouldnae tell ye no lie, for I fear the wee powers in ye may rise up tae burn my arse."

She pinched her lips together, stifling a grin. "Oh, hush." Playfully pushing him away, she added, "You know, it's not nice to tease a witch."

Everyone laughed except James, who was staring at the group with a perplexed expression on his face. "I don't get it. What'd I miss? And what the heck did he even say?"

"You should know the phrase, lad," Aidan said lightheartedly, squatting next to James and patting his back. "Liar, liar, pants on fire."

James arched a brow. "I still don't get it."

"He's making fun of me," Rhiannon admitted, her demeanor now relaxed. "You know . . . because of my fire magic." She waited a moment before asking, "Get it?"

A fake snickering snort came from James as he announced, "Right, okay. Yeah, I get it. But what's with the weird accent?"

Rhiannon avoided Aidan's gaze as her cheeks grew warm and turned rosy. "Well, I made the mistake of telling him I found his accent attractive the other day and how I like that I can understand him more than other Scottish accents I've heard before. So, now . . . now he likes to tease me because of it."

Aidan grinned bashfully at James as he pointed his thumb over at Rhiannon. "She thinks I'm sexy."

"Eww! No, I never said that," Rhiannon argued, embarrassed. "I said your accent was attractive. And I never used the word *sexy*, and nowhere in that little conversation did I mention you specifically."

"Eww? Did you just say eww?" Aidan gave her an exaggerated pout. "You don't find me attractive then?"

"Well, no, I—I didn't say that exact—"

"So, you *do* think I'm attractive?" His voice was boyish and teasing.

Rhiannon blushed, her cheeks even more flush. "No—I mean yes. Wait! I mean no! Shit!" She took a breath, composing herself. "I mean yes. Yes, you are *very* handsome, Aidan, but you're . . . old." She panicked at Aidan's mischievously offended expression. "No! That's not what I meant. It's just . . . you aren't . . ." She faced James and pleaded telepathically, *"Help me out here, please."*

James pressed his lips together, trying not to laugh. "So, Aidan . . ." He snickered and cleared his throat. "So, why *do* you and Nina sound so . . . not so Scottish anyway?"

Aidan winked at Rhiannon and threw his arm over her shoulder. "That was fun, lass." He turned his attention to James. "Well, Nina and I have lived here most of our lives, and not havin' other Scots here on a regular basis, the accent kind of faded a wee bit."

"It's a good thing too," James confessed candidly, rising to his feet, "because I didn't understand a word you said before."

Aidan laughed, dropping his arm from around Rhiannon and making his way over to James. "No worries, lad. Most people don't understand the thicker Scottish accent. It's a language in and of itself. But most Scots don't talk like that."

James lowered his voice and leaned into Aidan. "By the way, nice transition there."

Aidan matched his tone and said sarcastically, "Whatever do you mean?"

"Distracting her—making her forget about being scared."

Aidan winked at him. "A wee trick I discovered over time with her."

"I'll have to remember that for future reference."

"Definitely." Aidan faced Pavian and asked in a normal tone, "Do you want me to stay? I know nothin' about Guardian magic, but I can help in any way you see fit."

"It might be a good idea," Pavian answered. "You never know, you might be able to help. Plus, if my father is taking precautions, then it might be in our best interest as well to have some extra bodies here. Each full moon presents uncertainty with Merrick being gone."

"Yeah," Karramis and Will said together.

"Could we please not use the word *bodies* right now?" Rhiannon asked, her words more bothered than worried.

"I think it's a good idea," Karramis continued. "Strength in numbers, right? It'll better our chances if any unwanted visitors show up and start trouble again."

"Okay." Rhiannon swallowed loudly, clearing her throat. "That didn't sound any better."

Will made his way over to Rhiannon. "You'll be all right." He grabbed her hands. "Nothing is going to happen to us as long as we stay on the porch."

"Yes," James said with a stern demand in his voice, glaring at his parents, "as long as *everyone* stays on the porch."

Karramis lifted her arms with her palms facing out. "Hey, look, I'm not the one who left the porch first." She pointed at Will with her thumb. "That was him."

"Yeah," Will mocked, giving her a cheeky grin, "but that git had it coming. Just seeing that arrogant bastard made me mad for a split second. I couldn't help myself. Plus, in my defense, I wasn't the bloody fool who decided to go completely mental and taunt the bloke for letting a werewolf run wild."

"So, I'm a bloody fool now?" Karramis gave him a teasing scowl as she folded her arms. "What happened to me being a miracle, huh?"

"Yes, you're a miracle." Will wrapped his arm around her waist and tugged her against his body. "But you are also a bloody fool at times." He leaned down and kissed her before slowly pulling away, his eyes meeting hers. "But only when your family is involved. That's one of the things I love most about you—your selflessness. Your love and loyalty to us. Your willingness to fight for us."

Karramis unfolded her arms, which were still pressed against her body, and slid her hands up to his face and kissed him again.

"Not that I don't love this wonderful, and slightly gross public show of affection," James said, interrupting them, "but I think it's best if we get inside and focus on why we actually came here. Plus, I'm hungry."

Rhiannon chuckled, strolling past her parents as they continued to kiss. "You're always hungry."

James followed behind her. "Nuh-uh."

"Yes, you are."

"Am not!" James said with a childish and playful retort.

Rhiannon rolled her eyes. "What are you, five?"

"Nope. Six, actually."

"You're a pain in the ass, you know that?"

"I know you are, but what am I?"

"Hold up!" Rhiannon halted before reaching the front door.

James crashed into her. "Ow! Jeez, Rhiannon."

Rhiannon twisted around, her wide eyes glaring into his.

"What's wrong?" he asked, his body tensing.

Rhiannon's response filled his mind. *"Werewolves."* Her inner voice was tight and shaky.

"What about them?" James asked out loud.

"What about what?" Will said behind his son, stepping onto the landing.

Karramis stopped beside Will and spotted her daughter's grim expression. "Rhiannon, what's the matter?"

"Stupid!" Rhiannon closed her eyes and clutched a handful of her flowy dress in a tight fist. "I can't believe I never thought to ask this before." She blew past her brother and started to pace along the porch. "How could I be so stupid not to ask?"

"Uh, hello?" James idly waved a hand in her direction. "Wanna fill us in, Rhiannon?"

James focused on her thoughts, her inner monologue chaotic and rapid, but a single word filled his mind, her voice repeating it over and over.

Werewolf, werewolf, werewolf.

"Again, what about them?" James asked softly, concern rising as panic flooded his sister's mind and body.

She ignored him.

"Rhiannon!" he called into her mind.

She halted, her deep blue eyes jerking between her parents and uncle. "How do they get here?"

"Who?" Karramis asked, her features narrowed with confusion.

"Werewolves." The word shuddered as she said it. "How do the werewolves get here?"

"To Kiluemar?"

"Yes," Rhiannon said sharply, her chest heaving. "If the portals only open on a full moon, and werewolves are only in their cursed form during that time, then how do they get here? How are they contained?"

Plainly, Pavian answered, "They aren't."

Worry flashed in Rhiannon's eyes as panic filled her stomach, twisting and churning with each panting exhale. Tightness squeezed her chest, and a burning sensation coated the back of her throat.

Wrapping her arms across her midsection, she held tight, fighting against the ache bubbling in her guts. "I think I'm going to be sick."

"Relax, Rhiannon," Karramis pleaded. "Let us explain."

James took her hand. "Yeah, it's going to be—"

"Don't say fine!" Rhiannon snapped, trepidation taking over. "Do *not* say fine. It's not going to be fine. I mean, what if there are werewolves out there right now waiting and—and they shift and come through? What then, huh? No one can sense the magic coming through anymore, so what if they just come in and roam free? Someone could get hurt, or worse. What if Haydrin comes back tonight?" Her eyes widened. "Oh my gosh, what if he can sense me because he's tasted my blood? What if he comes back to finish me off?" She faced her mother. "Can werewolves smell their prey?"

Karramis hesitated but answered with careful consideration. "Not from miles away."

"But they can?" Rhiannon continued, pacing again. "I—I should've stayed away. I knew this was a stupid idea. What if he comes for me? What if he—"

"Then you do what you did last time and set his ass on fire," James interrupted with a comforting but unyielding tone louder than hers.

Rhiannon exhaled. "But I don't—"

"No buts!" James gripped her shoulders. "Rhiannon, you need to calm down." His eyes met hers. "You are *not* helpless. And you sure as hell aren't defenseless. Not to mention you have all of us here."

Rhiannon glanced over at her parents, uncle, and Aidan.

James loosened his hold on her. "When are you going to see just how powerful you really are and how much *more* powerful you could be?"

"He's right," Karramis said proudly.

Will, Pavian, and Aidan nodded in agreement.

"Hey," Aidan said, his voice filled with kindness, "if you'd like, I can go patrol for you. Make sure the coast is clear."

"No, that's all right." Rhiannon shook her head. "I don't want you out there tonight either."

"That's very kind of you, but I've been out at night many times before, lass. Flyin' adds a wee bit of protection from the beasts around here."

"I just wish the damn portals would open already," Rhiannon declared. "I want this over with. This whole situation makes me nervous."

"Not much longer," Pavian admitted, checking the position of the moon.

Will said to Rhiannon, "I'm surprised you were even comfortable enough coming here at all during a full moon after last time."

"Honestly, I'm not." She exhaled, attempting to release the uneasiness settling in her core. "I didn't even want to come, but Aunt K and Ryan told me I needed to face my fears. Personally, I think this whole idea is insane, and you all are just as crazy for staying here. That's why I want this night over with already. I'm here—I'm facing my fears. And now I want it to be over. I'm still not comfortable being outside the village, *especially* on a full moon."

Karramis tilted her head, arching her dark brow with an amused glare. "But you went to Casteya Castle by yourself at night. Now that was rather foolish, if you ask me. So, what made that different than this?"

"Well, first of all, I had Ignara with me. I figured she would protect me or, if nothing else, get me the heck out of there if anything came after us. Second, I didn't go on a full moon, so I figured I was safe, or *safer* at least. I guess I wasn't really thinking everything through that night."

A loud electric buzz filled the air outside, followed by a low rumble—both lasting a few seconds.

"What the hell was that?" James asked as everyone instinctively made their way down the stairs, searching the area.

Rhiannon stumbled off the bottom step and clutched the railing as she gasped, her eyes going wide and her face twisting into a contemplative frown.

Everyone rotated in her direction as she hunched over.

Reaching her side, Karramis asked tensely, "What's wrong?"

A subtle tightness rose from her core, filling her body with comfort and ease. Her nerves tingled, warm and energizing. Her heart thumped rhythmically and delicately in her chest, and every thump spread the sensation throughout her body.

Karramis cupped her daughter's face. "Rhiannon, what's—"

"Shh," James breathed, raising a finger to his lips, his eyes lost in an unblinking trance.

Karramis, still holding Rhiannon's face, shifted her worried expression over to Will, Pavian, and Aidan. "What's wrong with them?"

All three men shrugged and remained quiet, dumbfounded and concerned.

"James?" Karramis said cautiously, dropping both hands from Rhiannon and grasping each child's wrist. "Rhiannon?"

Rhiannon blinked, her eyes landing on her mother. "I can feel them."

"And I can hear them," James finally said calmly.

Whispers of Mother Nature filled his mind with the soft melodies of her soothing songs: the sea sloshing against the shoreline; the gentle wind dancing among the trees, swaying as rustling filled the air; raindrops crashing against rocks with a harshness of beating drums; a crackling fire, roaring and snapping with a comforting fierceness.

"They're open," James and Rhiannon said together.

"Can you sense where they are?" Pavian asked, stopping behind Karramis and peering at them from over her shoulder.

Rhiannon and James closed their eyes and focused.

Taking a deep breath, Rhiannon asked, "What are we searching for exactly?"

"The portals," Pavian answered in a sarcastic tone.

Rhiannon opened her eyes and rolled them. "Well, duh."

"He's such a smartass," James said secretly to her, smiling and trying to focus again.

"I know that," Rhiannon went on. "I mean, how do we pinpoint them?"

"I don't know," Pavian said. "It's never been separate with Guardians before. We usually feel *and* hear them."

Karramis directed her attention to Rhiannon. "Try this. Try to force whatever sensation you are feeling inside you into different sections. Separate them. See how many pieces you are able to make." Her attention shifted to James, and she touched his arm. "And with you, whatever you are hearing, try the same thing. Imagine it as a sound wave and divide it into separate lines. How many do you see?"

"Brilliant," Will said next to James, grinning at his wife.

She returned the gesture with a quick flick of her brow, mouthing the word *miracle* and pointing to herself.

Everyone waited as the twins concentrated on the magic coursing through them.

Minutes passed, but nothing happened

Rhiannon grabbed her brother's hand and focused harder. James squeezed, drawing himself further into his mind.

The twins opened their eyes, both plagued with fear as they said, "Four."

"Four?" Pavian repeated. "Four doorways from the outside? Or four total?"

Observing the terror pinching the twins' faces, Karramis added, "What is it? What else did you sense?"

James narrowed his eyes and peered over at Rhiannon before facing his mother. "Someone came through."

He and Rhiannon pushed past the others and stared at the tree line to the southwest, both refusing to blink as he announced, "And I think they're coming this way."

The others walked over next to them and followed their gazes. A massive dark figure soared over the trees through the dimness of the night with large muscular wings gleaming in the moonlight and flapping thunderously as it flew straight toward them.

Grabbing Karramis's hand, Will demanded, low and serious, "Get on the porch."

Chapter 4

Broken Curse

A creature of monstrous proportions landed with a loud thump, straightening at the waist as it pulled its broad muscular shoulders back. Marching with a heavy foot, it glided over the grass with power and grace. The twins watched in awe as the dark figure advanced closer, the shadows fading with each step. The moonlight gleamed along its chiseled muscles and coarse skin. A quick flap sent its massive wings tucking behind it, sticking out above its bald head and hanging inches from the ground.

Rhiannon retreated from the railing as the creature's steps sounded across the field. Fear rose in her stomach and chest, pulling and twisting as a numbness shot along her lower abdomen. She halted when she brushed against James's arm.

Taking his sister's hand, James squeezed, reassuring her he was there. His warm and dry grasp sent a calm through her as she focused on settling her hurried pulse, matching the steadiness of his own body.

"Breathe," he said through their connection, encouraging and with ease.

"It's Viktor," Karramis announced, both relief and worry biting her words.

James squinted and took in the sight of the seven-foot-tall gargoyle as he came to a stop a few feet from the bottom step, his perfectly chiseled body gleaming brighter in the glow of the full moon and porch lights, the brightness bouncing off his rough dark gray skin.

James's grip loosened as Rhiannon let out a relieved breath.

"What are you doing here?" Pavian asked, direct and serious. "Is everything all right?"

"Is my dad okay?" Karramis added, an uneasiness causing her gaze to scan the area.

"I came with word from your father." Viktor's voice was low and gruff, a sound pulling from deep within his extremely beefy chest with a thick Italian accent.

Rhiannon was unable to blink, her eyes fixed on the massive creature in front of her—his torso was as wide as hers was long. "Jeez." Her tone was smooth with pure awe. "He's . . . *huge*."

"Shh," Will and Aidan breathed quietly as they held back a laugh.

Karramis gave her a quick sidelong glance with a sparkle of humor flickering in her eyes. "Rhiannon."

Rhiannon lowered her voice and shrugged apologetically. "Sorry, but I've never seen a . . . a . . ." Her words were even quieter when she asked, "What exactly is this thing?"

"I am *not* a thing," Viktor said firmly, his solid black eyes glaring over at her.

Meeting his shadowy gaze, she stepped back. "Oh, I'm sorry, I—I didn't mean—"

"I am a gargoyle," Viktor announced, not a hint of arrogance in his tone. "And I, my child, am at your humble service." Placing his hand over his chest, he bowed. "It is a pleasure to meet you."

Dumbfounded, Rhiannon stared as a wave of comfort washed over her. She had not expected that kind of response from this beastly creature.

Viktor squared his shoulders and stood tall. His body moved with ease despite the illusion of his extremities weighing him down and the ground sinking beneath his hefty body. He took a step closer, and the lights along the porch illuminated his coarse stony skin along his humanoid form.

Viktor pulled his gaze away from Rhiannon and stopped on James. "Both of you."

Reaching out a hand, Viktor raised the corners of his narrow lips, which sat below a wide nose and along a square jaw. His smile made Rhiannon tense as he strolled up the stairs and revealed four canines resting along two rows of flat teeth, but his outstretched hand slammed into an invisible wall just below the threshold. The gargoyle jerked his hand back, confusion erasing his friendly but unnerving grin.

"Oh, sorry, Viktor," Karramis said, her voice laced with guilt. "Boundary spell. If we'd known you were coming—"

Viktor raised his hand and cut her off. "Nonsense. No need to apologize. You did not know I was coming. Nonetheless, it is best to limit access to your home. Keeps the magic stronger."

"Well, Viktor . . ." James reached his hand past the barrier. "It's a pleasure to finally meet you. I've heard a lot about you."

"Oh?" Viktor smiled at Pavian, Rhiannon again flinching at his sharp teeth. "All good things, I hope."

"Absolutely," Pavian said, flashing him a grin. "I don't think anyone would ever say a bad thing about you."

Karramis gripped the railing, her voice serious. "Not that we aren't glad to see you, Viktor, but you don't usually show up without some kind of news."

"Ah, yes." Viktor stood at attention. "I am afraid I have some interesting and potentially dire news to report."

"Go ahead," Pavian said with stern authority.

"Zarrius has received word that Merrick will be returning this evening. Apparently, he has been lying low in the non-magical world for the last six months, and he is to return tonight."

Will arched a brow in concern. "How did he come by this news?"

"The brother of one of Merrick's followers notified Zarrius as soon as he got word. His brother lives in the castle."

"A brother of one of Merrick's guys?" James asked suspiciously. "Can we trust this guy? I mean, it seems like a conflict of interest, don't you think?"

"No," Pavian admitted with certainty in his voice. "I have a feeling I know who this is, and if I'm right, he is not a threat to us."

Leaning against the railing, Aidan asked Viktor, "Does Zarrius know why Merrick left in the first place?"

"No, he does not. That information was not revealed to him." Viktor shifted his black eyes to Pavian. "But that is not all."

"Go on," Pavian said, serious and composed.

Rhiannon's heart sank into her stomach. "Please tell me it doesn't involve werewolves."

"No." Viktor shook his head. "I have not spotted any this far south."

Rhiannon blew out a controlled breath.

"Then what?" Karramis asked, taking her daughter's hand.

"A shock wave of energy blasted through one of the portals moments ago."

"Yeah, we felt *and* heard it," Pavian said. "Do we know what caused it?"

"No, but we are looking into it."

Pavian's attention shifted to the twins. "You mentioned four portals, but did you mean four total or four doorways from the outside?"

"From the outside," James answered, glancing at Rhiannon as he scanned her face for confirmation.

"I can't be too sure, but . . ." Rhiannon nodded. "Yeah, I think he's right."

"Good." Pavian squeezed their shoulders. "That's good. We can work on confirming it at a later time. But you two did well tonight."

"Has anyone come through that you are aware of?" Viktor asked the twins.

"I think someone came through right after that shock wave happened," Rhiannon answered.

"I do too." James gave a quick nod. "I can't be certain, but there was this disturbance in the sounds I was hearing."

"Yeah," Rhiannon added. "Something was yanking at the sensation I was feeling, almost like it was pulling me toward it."

Pavian glanced up at the moon and checked his watch. "They should be closed by now. Can you feel or hear anything anymore?"

James and Rhiannon concentrated.

"It's fading, but I can still feel it." Rhiannon rubbed her stomach. "It's like the lingering tingle of when my foot falls asleep, but it's deep inside my core and inside my veins."

James sat on the top step and leaned back, turning his eyes upward to his uncle. "Why isn't the Guardian magic working right? Why are Rhiannon and I doing it differently than the ones before us?"

Rhiannon joined her brother on the stairs. "And why did that portal send out energy like that?"

"I have no idea," Pavian said, shrugging. "I've never heard of this happening before. I mean, the only time portal magic ever went wonky before was when Merrick broke the Gatekeeper curse. But even then, the portals didn't disappear or malfunction like this."

"What happened to them?" James asked, leaning into his legs.

"When the curse broke, Adalaide's magic exploded into the island, drawing all the portals inside the realm together. And for a very brief time—I mean, it was a matter of minutes—the portals in the non-magical world and here combined as one large vortex, opening up the two worlds to each other. It created this powerful magnetic force, sucking everything, even magic, within thousands of miles from it into it and spitting it all out again in random locations near the massive portal. The magic from that strange event still lingers even today in the non-magical world, causing strange events to occur without warning."

There was a moment of silence.

"Wait . . ." Rhiannon paused and examined his words. "Are you talking about the Bermuda Triangle?"

Pavian lifted his brow. "The what?"

"The Bermuda Triangle You've never heard of the Bermuda Triangle before?"

"I have," Will said, raising a hand. "Learnt about it in school."

"We know nothing about it," Karramis admitted.

"Yeah." Pavian lifted his shoulders dismissively. "Never heard of it."

"I've heard stories," Aidan added, "but I thought it was folklore. Just made up in stories."

"Really?" Shifting her puzzled expression over to James, Rhiannon asked, "Have you heard of it?"

"Yeah," James said flatly, "in movies. I didn't know it was a real place, though."

"Didn't you go to school?" Rhiannon said patronizingly.

"Yeah," he said mockingly, "but I guess I missed the lesson on magical vortexes while I was learning the square root of pi; that Sirius and Bellatrix are actually stars, not just characters; and the difference between sedimentary and metamorphic rocks. Oh, yeah, and trying to figure out why the heck potassium is the letter K on the periodic table."

"It's Latin," Rhiannon explained.

"What is?" James asked with an arched brow.

"The K on the periodic table is because the Latin word for potassium starts with the letter K."

"Oh. Yeah, well, you know what, smarty-pants, I can spell Micropachycephalosaurus and Archaeornithomimus." He stuck out his tongue. "And," he added, drawing out the word, "I can speak three languages."

Rhiannon tilted her head curiously with an uplifted brow. "You can?"

"Yeah, but only the bad words and enough to order food."

"Anyway," Rhiannon said with an amused scoff, drawing out the word and rolling her eyes as she faced the others. "The

Bermuda Triangle is this large area around Florida and Bermuda where strange and sometimes unexplainable events happen."

"Oh"—Pavian snapped his fingers—"you mean Stoweward's Abyss."

"Stoweward?" James lifted a brow. "Like the town we live in?"

"Yes. They're both named after Adalaide."

"She's the person who broke the Gatekeeper curse, right?"

"No, *she* didn't break the curse. Merrick broke the curse *on* her."

"Sorry to interrupt," Viktor said, "but I must leave. I have to patrol the island and make sure no dangers came through." His eyes stopped on Pavian. "Your father's orders."

"Be careful," Rhiannon called out with a slight wave.

Viktor unstretched his long charcoal-colored membranous wings. "Thank you." He winked. "You as well, my child."

With one powerful flap, Viktor shot into the air, sending a sweeping blast of wind crashing down. Then he was gone.

"Can you feel that?" Rhiannon asked James, her eyes open but distant.

"Yeah." James nodded, his head tilting as he concentrated. "What is that?"

"What is what?" Will asked.

"A feeling," James and Rhiannon answered, both still focused.

"What kind of feeling exactly?" Karramis wondered, gripping Will's hand.

"Uhm," Rhiannon said, placing her hand over her midsection. "It's like when the portals sent the vibrations before, but it's . . . hot."

"Yeah," James added, "like when you drink something too hot and it burns deep in the pit of your stomach, but there's a strange tingling with it."

Karramis smiled. "That's magic."

James met his mother's gaze. "What do you mean? This isn't like anything I've felt before."

"It's not *your* magic. It's ours. You're sensing our magic. All of ours."

Rhiannon remained quiet, and James joined her as they both drifted inward, their consciousness diving into the deepest parts of their minds, concentrating on the warmth and the tingling vibrations rising from the core of their bodies.

"Were you able to sense who came through earlier?" Pavian asked. "Their magic, I mean."

"No," the twins said.

"Sorry," Rhiannon added. "I wasn't feeling this before when the portals were open."

"Sensing people coming through is the easy part," Karramis said, "but pinpointing the type of magic linked to that person is the hard part, especially if a lot come through at once. It will take time to master it. All of it."

"At least they can sense the portals and magic," Aidan said, his arms folded over his chest. "And people comin' through."

"He's right." Will smiled and squeezed their shoulders from behind in a congratulatory manner. "You ought to be extremely proud of yourselves."

"It's not enough, though." Rhiannon frowned. "We couldn't sense if any danger came through. And if the rumors are true, then Merrick will—"

"Rhiannon," Will said with a tender yet firm voice, squatting next to her, "don't look a gift horse in the mouth. You should be proud of your accomplishments so far, even if in your mind they're trivial or insignificant."

"But—"

"We will cross that bridge when we come to it." Will grinned. "Now, accept the fact you did something absolutely brilliant, and relish it for a moment."

"Hey." James cleared his throat, directing his attention at no one in particular. "Can I ask you all something?"

"Sure," said everyone except Rhiannon.

He shifted his eyes between Pavian and his mother. "How was the curse broken?"

"The Gatekeeper curse?" Pavian asked.

"Yeah, the one with this Adalaide person you were talking about earlier. I remember you mentioned the Gatekeepers before, but you never told me how the curse was broken."

Rhiannon turned, facing her uncle. "What are Gatekeepers?"

"Those are what the Guardians were before they were Guardians," James answered.

"Oh." Rhiannon pondered. "And they were cursed?"

"Yes," Pavian, James, and Karramis answered in unison.

"Why? And how?"

Aidan leaned over, pressing his arms against the railing. "Before you go into all that, I think it's best if I join Viktor with patrollin'. It might be a good idea to have as many eyes out right now as possible." He winked at Rhiannon. "Just in case."

Rhiannon gave him a grave expression.

"I'll be fine, *piuthar beag*." The corner of his mouth lifted. "I promise."

Aidan headed down the steps and lifted his arms.

Rhiannon hurried to her feet, the words meaning little sister lingering in her mind and making her chest squeeze. "Aidan, wait!"

He blinked his bright emerald-green eyes at her.

"Be careful, please."

"Aye." Aidan flashed her a quick smirk. "But you best be takin' yer own advice there, lass. Don't get into trouble, you hear me?"

Hugging him, she muttered into his chest, "I'll try."

"Well, please try really, really hard, eh?"

"I will."

"Good." He gripped her shoulders and gave her a nod. "I'm goin' to hold you to that."

Her mouth twisted into a grin. "Okay."

Aidan waved and closed his eyes as his fingers morphed into feathers, the rich honey and amber colors spreading along his arms and over the clothes pressed to his body. Thin scaly limbs and talons transformed from his legs. His nose and mouth elongated as a smooth beak formed, and deep green eyes peered back, sparkling and competing with the moon as they seemingly glowed in the dark. Spreading his golden eagle wings, Aidan jumped into the air and flew into the night sky.

~

Rhiannon sat on the couch and rested her head on her brother's shoulder, fighting the urge to fall asleep.

Outside was fading into pure darkness as the full moon inched closer toward the horizon. A cool breeze blew through the open windows—continuous, soft, and gentle—laced with a mix of sea mist, varying scents of green foliage, and wildflowers.

"Do you think it will get worse?" Will asked Pavian, leaning against the wall next to the front door. "With the portals, I mean."

"I really have no idea. When the portals malfunctioned with Adalaide, it only happened that one time, but it was a fluke. In that very moment, magic was so strong—she was strong. She was extremely powerful when the magic of her curse, the magic of the spell, and the magic of the island bound together inside her. And by some miracle, she was even able to control it, all of it. But it didn't last long."

Rhiannon lifted her head. "Why?"

"Curses can't be broken—that's not how they work. They're supposed to be permanent, hence why they are a curse. But with the Gatekeeper one, some believe because it was given to a willing individual and bound to the magic of the realm and not a sacrifice in the usual manner, it didn't have the same magical binding as regular curses."

"I don't understand," Rhiannon said.

"When Zacharia accepted the duty as the first Gatekeeper of Kiluemar," Pavian continued, "he agreed to a curse that would end his life with the birth of a third member of his bloodline— whether it be a sibling, another child, or a grandchild. Curses require a sacrifice. Always. However, sacrifices are a form of dark magic, and the witches who performed the Gatekeeper curse didn't want to suffer the same consequences as the witches who had participated in the initial ritual of the island. So, with careful planning and wording, the witches recited a spell that would curse Zacharia and his family as long as they possessed the Gatekeeper magic."

James tilted his head in thought. "What did the spell say?"

"I don't remember."

Sitting on the floor, Karramis let out a heavy sigh. "Magic of the island come undone, borrowed powers given to one. Rise above and soon disperse, a bloodline faced with a deadly curse. Powerful magic will flow within, a lineage now fated with this darkest sin. Power divided but bound to the realm, gifted magic to lead the helm. Doorways forever protected, portals and family now connected. Death will come to a third Gatekeeper, for more than three will bring the Reaper."

Pavian glared at his sister, shocked. "You memorized it?"

Karramis nodded. "Yeah."

"Why?"

"After I found out about the prophecy, I wanted to find out more about my lineage, both sides. I wanted to know why I was supposed to be this special person to help save magic. Why I was chosen and not someone more . . . qualified. So, I spent all my free time researching Fire Witches, Guardians, and the Gatekeepers."

James stifled a yawn. "Did you find anything useful?"

"No, not really. But at the time, most of the archives and books were at MUSE, and the ones here were scattered all over Kiluemar. I'm pretty sure Randolyn is still finding them here and there and trying to get them cataloged and organized in the library."

"She is," Rhiannon confirmed with a nod. "She has boxes of them all over the place."

James rubbed the heaviness pulling on his eyelids. "So, how was the curse broken? How did Merrick do it exactly?"

"Curses work by plaguing the blood of an individual," Pavian answered, "and in some cases, an entire bloodline."

"Like werewolves," Rhiannon said.

"Exactly. When Zacharia was cursed, it was magically linked to his blood. But when Merrick tried to take Adalaide's magic, he unlinked it, and the magic became part of her instead—no longer linked to just her blood. The curse was lifted, and she then possessed the magic itself. And when that happened, the magic became stronger and grew. Then a new line of magic was born—Guardians. But the magic was bound to Kiluemar, and it still is. Our magic only works here within the boundaries of the realm or on the outside near a portal, our bridge between the two worlds."

"But how?" James rubbed his brow. "How did he break it?"

Karramis shook her head and shrugged. "We don't know."

"No one does," Pavian went on. "That part is still a mystery to all of us. But after that, Merrick never tried stealing Guardian magic again, and Adalaide became the only key to the portals, being able to control them completely inside the realm."

"So . . . so, she was no longer the Gatekeeper, but rather the . . ." James paused for dramatic effect and chuckled. "The Keymaster?"

Pavian, Karramis, and Rhiannon stared at him, and Will smiled, holding back a laugh.

Karramis shifted an arched brow between her son and husband, her face scowling in confusion. "What's so funny?"

"Really?" James said, his tone comical and animated. "You know, Gatekeeper? Keymaster?" He paused, glaring between the others. "You know! Who ya gonna call?" The last sentence lined with a singsong tune before letting out a disgruntled groan. "Do you people not watch movies?" Spotting Will, he said enthusiastically with a grin, "Dad gets it."

Will broke into laughter, shaking his head at his son's sense of humor.

"No, we do not watch movies," Pavian said, glaring at him blankly. "We don't have televisions here."

"Yeah, I'm aware." James slouched and folded his arms. "By the way, could we please enter the twenty-first century and get one? I mean, we have electricity here."

Facing Will, Karramis asked, "Anyway, what is our son talking about? What do Gatekeepers have to do with movies?"

Still chuckling, Will said, "It's from a popular movie from the eighties."

A knock pounded at the door, and everyone turned.

"It's me," Aidan said in a hurry from the other side. "You better get out here."

Pavian rushed to the door and flung it open. "What is it?" He stepped onto the porch and noticed Aidan's worried expression. "What's the matter?"

The others joined Pavian and Aidan on the porch.

Aidan glanced over his shoulder at the tree line to the south, then back at the others. "He's comin'."

"Who?" Karramis asked as Will's hand rested on her lower back.

Aidan hesitated when Rhiannon tensed and gasped.

Rhiannon's heart skipped a beat as it grew heavy in her chest, her heaving, unsteady breaths echoing in her head. She knew the answer; she had sensed it all night. She had somehow known coming to the cabin was a bad idea—and not just because of the fear from the attack months ago following her around like an all-consuming shadow. No, it was something much deeper.

Maybe it had simply been a gut feeling, or maybe it was the memories and uneasiness Rhiannon had felt after visiting Casteya Castle still lingering in her thoughts. But she was not the only one who had known he would return tonight. Even though Rhiannon was unsure what had been said, she was certain the woman she had watched through the window a few weeks ago had been either worried or scared. But if Rhiannon had to guess, it was probably both.

"Merrick," Rhiannon said for Aidan, her words hoarse and shaky. "Merrick's the one who's coming."

Chapter 5

Impending Return

Ten months ago
Mid-February

Tressa gripped the railing as she descended the stairs of the tower, the smell of Camille's rotting corpse fading with each step. She tiptoed cautiously down the creaky wooden slats, making sure her bare feet avoided the sharp splinters and rusty nails. Exiting the arched entryway, she paused as an intense set of eyes surveyed her every move, sending a bone-chilling surge crawling up her back. She shifted her head upward, and her dark brown eyes stopped on Merrick's demonic outline in the large stone-arched window. The monster surveyed her as if she were prey, his unyielding gaze cold and lethal. Viciously, he tore a piece of flesh from the bloody leg clutched tightly in his oversized hand. The skin and muscle ripped from the bone without a hint of resistance, the sounds of fleshy sinew tearing and a low growl filling the silence within the night sky overhead.

Tressa drew in a long breath and released it with a huff, turning her back to him and continuing into the castle. "What a waste."

Camille's magic may not have been rare, but even Tressa had believed Echoes were a myth—a fairy tale fabricated to create an even more enticing magical world. The Echo's ability would have enhanced the magic already inside Merrick, but the power-driven and bloodthirsty man was too stubborn to admit he needed more power aside from Will's and his children's. Merrick needed the power of all four elemental witches if he wanted to take on the power the prophecy foretold, and Karramis was the only Fire Witch they had been able to find since her mother.

Tressa was certain if she had not convinced Merrick to leave tonight for a few months, his feral instincts would have ruined everything they had worked for, thus throwing away years of careful planning and hard work. Now, all she had to do was tie up a few other loose ends, giving her more time to come up with a plan to restrain the faltering patience Merrick was now exhibiting.

~

Theseus trailed behind Tressa, the muscular half man, half bull mimicking her steady stride as she swayed down the dimly lit hallway a few hours later, the stone walls amplifying their unmasked footsteps. She pulled her shoulders back, poised and confident. Her eyes beamed with purpose while her lips puckered together in a cunning grin. The material of her purple velvet cloak flapped as her stiletto heels clacked against the tiled floor. Rich dark waves bounced against her back, the lush tresses glistening with the glow from the candles placed in the sconces along the walls. Stopping outside a large arched wooden door, she reached for the bronze handle, but it swung away from her.

"Well, hello there," Leif said amorously, bare chested as his brow twitched upward and his blue eyes flickered with approval. "Fancy seeing you here." He slowly drew one corner of his mouth up and winked. "Is there something I can do for you at this ridiculously late hour?"

Tressa let out a breathy scoff, her face like stone. "That is not why I'm here."

"Too bad." He winked again, pulling open the door. "Come in."

Theseus stepped forward but halted as Leif's hand slammed against the minotaur's hairy chest.

"Not you," Leif demanded as he scowled up at Theseus. "No pets allowed."

Both sets of eyes were full of an unwavering dominance. Theseus growled as he leaned into Leif, the towering beast exceeding the vampire's six-foot-four stature by half a foot.

"It's fine, Theseus," Tressa said, slightly annoyed. "Leif isn't going to hurt me."

The minotaur backed away in a huff before planting himself outside the door, folding his arms, and glaring at Leif standing under the threshold.

"That is, of course," Leif said, his tone arrogant and carnal, "not unless she wants me to."

Leif winked at the fuming beast and closed the door.

"You're an ass," Tressa admitted matter-of-factly. "Why must you get him all riled up?"

"Well, I would much rather get *you* all riled up, but since you aren't here for that, I have to find my entertainment elsewhere." Leif leaned his pelvis against her body, gliding a hand down her back. "Though you should really reconsider. You seem a little tense. Are you sure I can't help . . . alleviate some of that for you?"

Tressa eased out of his hold, smooth and graceful. "Would you focus? This isn't a social call."

"All right then." He threw himself on the bed, lounging with his arms behind his head. "So, why are you here then?"

Tressa folded her arms over her ample chest and drummed her fingers against her biceps. "Did you kill her?"

"That's a rather vague question for a vampire. You're going to have to be a bit more specific."

"Camille. Did you kill Camille?"

"No. Well, not entirely." His lips arched into a wry smirk as he flicked an eyebrow up playfully. "I simply . . . helped. And she was rather delicious too, if you ask me. Better than I had expected. I do love the blood of other magical creatures. They taste so much better than regular mortals."

Tressa sighed, her hands now gripping her hips. "I thought she was your friend?"

Leif let out a half-hearted laugh. "Hardly. I simply tolerated her for the sake of Merrick and him possibly wanting her magic . . . among other things." He chuckled, the sound low and deep, as a side smirk played across his lips. "Let's just say she wasn't completely useless all those years stuck in that godforsaken place. The poor child was so hung up on Lucas that it was quite entertaining to play on her drunken emotions." His eyes became shadowed behind a momentary daydream. "Man, I'm definitely going to miss her. She was rather fun to play with."

Tressa cleared her throat. "I'm really not interested in your vile, not to mention disturbing, love life."

"Oh, I would hardly call it a love life. I merely enjoy satisfying a different kind of hunger."

"Either way, you can keep that to yourself."

Leif snickered. "Jealous?"

"Absolutely not." She dropped her arms to her sides and stormed over to the bed, placing her hands on the black silk sheets and leaning over him, her face inches from his. "We needed her magic, Leif." Her voice was thick and bitter. "With her powers, Merrick could've doubled his abilities with a single sacrifice."

He drew his body closer, his nose nearly brushing hers. "That's not up to you." He sat up farther, and she backed away, their eyes never leaving each other as he rose from the bed and stood up, his demeanor and voice shifting as he glared down at her. "You're not the one in charge around here. Or did you forget that while we were away? And I don't take orders from you, witch."

Tressa blinked, her expression radiating a dismissive and careless glare as she stepped back, heading over to the door. "Merrick's leaving tomorrow for a few months."

"Why?" Leif asked as he trailed behind her, his tone bored but his strut predatory.

"He's been trapped in here too long, so he's going to get away for a bit. Go back to Ireland and enjoy an unlimited source of food."

Leif twisted his expression, both approval and consideration lining his features as he inched closer, the smell of her awakening his carnal hunger. "Hmm, sounds fun. I could use a good game of cat and mouse." He towered over her and pulled in a long, slow inhale. "I sure do miss the stimulating pleasure of a good hunt."

Tressa peered up at him through thick black lashes. "You didn't have that when you were stuck on the outside?"

"No. Unfortunately not." His fingers caressed the top of her wrist and trailed up her arm, his voice low and smooth. "Lucas was a bit of a stick in the mud when it came to that. He insisted we had to stay off the radar since Haydrin had already caused us some grief a few times, not to mention having a damn ogre around." He slid a palm over her shoulder and cupped the back of her neck, their eye contact never faltering. "So, I was forced to drink from blood bags or go weeks without eating. I did leave to feed occasionally, but I haven't actually killed anyone in a long time." Leaning down, he whispered, "That is, of course, until a few hours ago." He released his gentle hold and twisted around, a devilish grin playing on his lips as he lounged back on the bed, letting out a sigh of disappointment. "My only regret is I didn't get a chance to enjoy her company one last time before killing her. I mean, she *was* good for something."

Rolling her eyes, Tressa said, "If you don't mind, could we please get back to the point as to why I'm here?"

He cocked his head. "And why are you here, if not to welcome me home?"

"To inform you that you and Lucas are leaving as well. Again. Merrick agreed you both deserve a break from your duties. You know, to go clear your heads and whatnot. Take a holiday. Do as you wish for a bit."

"Lucas is coming? With me?" Leif let out an annoyed grunt as he said sarcastically, "Now, that should be fun."

"I doubt you'll have to worry about him thinking he's the boss with Merrick around. Plus, I don't believe you are obligated to stay with them."

Leif smiled. "That's good, because I have some fun things planned while I'm away." He winked.

"Right. Then I'll leave it up to you to tell Lucas." Tressa turned to leave but twisted back around. "Six months."

His fair-haired brow quirked up.

"You are both to stay away for six months. Then, when you all come back, we'll decide the next steps to take with Karramis and her family."

Leif sat at the edge of the bed, his brow now creased with a pondering and suspicious expression. "What's in it for you?"

Tressa's head flinched back in mock surprise, her tone quick and casual. "What do you mean?"

Leif lifted himself from the bed and folded his arms across his lean, muscular, bare chest, staring at her with an unblinking gaze. "Why do you want us gone?"

"Stop being so damn paranoid," Tressa said dismissively. "I just need a break from him. I need a damn break from everything. Clear my own mind and figure out the next steps. It's not as simple as Merrick is making it seem. There needs to be a strategy—a clear-cut plan. He's become unstable in the past few years. Insane almost. Well, more than usual. He's more unpredictable. More dangerous. I mean, do you know what it's like being cooped up with a raging lunatic for eight years?"

"Well, I've lived with Haydrin, Gastell, and Lucas for the last eight years, so . . . yeah. They are all certifiable in some way."

"Ha! That's the pot calling the kettle black. You are a natural-born killer, Leif. You're the king of crazy when it comes to the four of you."

"Hmm," he drawled almost seductively, "as much as I love hearing you call me king and the idea of you kneeling before me, I don't know about that. I think Lucas is catching up." Pausing, he added in a more serious tone, "So, what exactly are you planning, Tressa?"

"Nothing," she said plainly.

"Right. And what will *you* be doing while we are all gone?"

Swaying her hips as she made her way over to him, she said casually, "Hmm, I don't know. Maybe I'll read a few books. Or organize my panty drawer." She pressed her upper body into him, her cleavage drawing his attention. "Or maybe I'll just dance around completely naked." She trailed her fingers down his chest. "Ooh, or maybe I'll take a nice, long, hot, bubble bath."

Leif leaned into her, aroused. "What else?"

She lifted her sultry gaze, gently pushing herself away as his hands trailed up her waist. "Wouldn't you like to know?"

"Yes." His tone was soft and husky. "Yes, I would actually."

Tressa released herself from his grip and winked. "Don't miss me too much while you're gone."

Leif ran his tongue over his lower lip and gently bit it. "I've been away eight years. What's another six months gonna do?"

"Right. Well, I guess we'll just have to wait and see about that." Tressa gave him a quick grin and flick of a brow as she opened the door. "Have fun, Leif."

"Trust me," he called as she slowly slid the door closed, "after that, I will."

Tressa's heeled shoes clanked against the floor as Theseus pounded behind her, both turning the corner and disappearing.

Tressa was convinced her plan to get rid of Merrick, Leif, and Lucas would work in her favor, giving her enough time to figure things out without having to deal with the trivial interruptions of a lovesick Telematra and a restless, vindictive, lustful vampire. The years away from Lucas and Leif had proven to be beneficial for Tressa. They had allowed her to focus her attention solely on Merrick and his unsavory desires, using his limited food source as a way to control his lust and hunger—tame him in a way one does with a caged beast. She had been able to reprogram his mind and body, giving him control over himself. However, with Lucas's and Leif's return, Merrick had veered off their planned course of action with the news those children—the foretold creations of magic—were, in fact, still alive. Skeptical of her ability to convince Merrick it was not the right time to take their powers, Tressa worried about the opportunity of losing out on the unlimited and unknown powers flowing inside James and Rhiannon. Having been away from Kiluemar their whole lives, many of their powers were surely still dormant, their full potential hidden behind emotions and adolescent immaturities. Not to mention concealed magic was impossible to steal and unbind—a safeguard created by magic.

Six months. Tressa only had six months to formulate a plan to stop Merrick from acting on his impulses, his rage, and his desire to prove no one was going to stand in his way. Six months to prevent him from making a mistake and ruining everything.

~

Five months ago
Early July

The moonless sky was scattered with flickering stars against the blackened backdrop as a hot breeze blew across the quiet and desolate mesa, the dirt gliding silently along the smooth stones. Eerie shadows swallowed the island as waves crashed against the cliffs resting miles away, washing over the stones on the forbidden side of the island.

Casteya Castle was dark and still except for the glow coming from a single window pane gleaming through the darkness, the curtains left open to welcome the night. The stale, damp, unnaturally hot summer air intensified the odor emanating around the grounds. A warning filled the silence—a lingering danger as the emptiness blanketed the area.

Tressa paced around her room with her arms folded across her chest, the wooden floor creaking beneath her bare feet as they kicked out from under her long black dress.

The immaculate chamber was fit for royalty. An oversized mahogany four-poster bed with heavily draped dark purple curtains rested in the center of the room. Black marble lined the large open fireplace nestled along dark cedar walls, and a black-skinned rug sat on the wooden floor by the foot of the bed. A single picture hung over the fireplace: a full moon, bright and welcoming, among a star-kissed midnight-blue backdrop with colorful swirls of rich greens and light blues flowing together as luminous fireballs zoomed through the sky.

A quiet knock sounded against the door, and Tressa hurried over to answer it.

"It's about time," she said with a soft voice to a muscular, pale-skinned man on the other side of the threshold.

The man, who appeared no older than thirty, replied with a low tone and Russian accent, "Sorry, madam, I was preoccupied."

The man entered as Tressa swung open the door. Theseus came into view and followed behind him, ducking to avoid hitting his head on the low-hanging doorframe.

"With what?" Tressa closed the door and faced him. "No, never mind, I would rather not know." She sat down in a chair next to the bed and crossed her legs, her poised, statuesque figure majestic in the lavender velvet-lined wingback chair. "Damn vampires and their insatiable eating habits."

"My apologies," the man said. "Did I do something to upset you, madam?"

"No, Niko," she said apologetically. "I'm the one who should be sorry. I'm just a bit on edge these days, that's all."

"Is it due to Merrick's early return?"

"Yes." The word was flat and filled with concern.

"But we have done everything necessary to prepare." Niko stood feet from where she sat with his arms tucked behind him, his shoulders pulled back on his tall frame. "The tower has been cleaned." His tone was precise and informative, his accent clear and pronounced. "The Keep is full. And thanks to Lucas, we will even be able to give Merrick a thorough report on that family. Merrick should be pleased by this, should he not?"

"There's no telling," she admitted with a shrug, her eyes expressing concern. "It depends on what kind of mood he returns home in." Tressa folded her hands across her lap. "Speaking of Lucas, where is he?"

"I do not know, madam. He was not in his chambers."

"Of course not," she said under her breath. "That son of a bitch can't seem to follow directions and stay put."

"Though Lucas has been helpful, no?"

"Yes, Niko." She lifted the corners of her mouth, flashing him a quick smile. "And so have you. Your loyalty has been admirable."

He gave her a terse nod, no emotion showing on his face but pride gleaming in his green eyes. "Thank you, madam."

Nikolai Lescan was not a typical vampire. When he was not hungry or in full monster mode, he was shy, compassionate, kind, and unrealistically and unnaturally obedient for an apex predator. Niko was young, both physically and magically. He was a new vampire, having only been plagued with this curse since the late nineteenth century. His traits were rare when it came to new vampires since many embraced their new life after being reborn as an immortal creature. Blood, lust, and murder were all vampires knew—hunting for the pleasures linked to all their wild cravings.

Tressa, however, never questioned his ways. In fact, she took comfort in them. More than any other vampire, she trusted Niko. Even Leif, despite their unusual relationship, rendered her cautious and tense when he was around, especially when Merrick was present. The two fed off each other's desires, encouraging the other to satisfy their needs. Although her instincts about Leif made her question her mindset when it came to him, he was, at least, good at some things. Really good. And she, too, had cravings to satisfy. But even then, she could not trust Leif with her life, or anything else.

"Then why . . ." Niko said, his eyes searching as he sniffed the air. "Why are you so upset?"

Tressa rose from the chair and paced the room, the floorboards creaking with each casual step. "We do not have all the information we need. If we don't give Merrick ample details about all of them, he may do something stupid."

Niko opened the door and peeked his head out, his attention pulled in another direction but still listening to her every word. "What details are we missing?"

"The girl and Karramis. Lucas may have been able to help a little with the boy and Will, but we still know nothing about that damn girl. Unlike her foolish brother, she never leaves the village, and Lucas's powers can't penetrate the spells warding it. Or if she does, Lucas must not be trying to track her. But every time he has tried to sense her, he's turned up with nothing. And Karramis is still able to block his telepathy."

"How is she able to do that?" Niko asked, closing the door, his eyes narrowed as he scanned the room.

"It's not that hard to block telepathic powers," she stated, her face pinched in deep thought. "Honestly, it's a pretty weak power. Most telepaths have to work really hard to enter someone else's mind. And not everyone has an inner monologue. But Lucas's Telematra powers are strong, one of the strongest when he can control them, just not strong enough to get through the barrier around the village."

"Why does he not just go into the village then?" Niko patrolled the room, his eyes and ears fully alert as he sniffed again. "You know, just search for her inside the barrier."

Tressa continued to traipse back and forth throughout her considerably large room with her arms folded across her chest, passing Niko multiple times. "It wouldn't matter anyway because he can't read her mind or the boy's. Like Karramis, his telepathy is blocked somehow with them. We don't know how much of their magic has surfaced without being able to do that. Lucas's power to read minds is completely useless when it comes to that family."

"But what about Will?"

"Lucas has made it a point to stay out of Will's mind as much as possible lately."

"Why? If it will help us."

Tressa breathed a chuckle. "Well, let's just say being in Will's head at a completely inappropriate time when he's with the woman you are in love with isn't exactly a good idea."

"Oh," Niko noted with a snicker as he continued searching the room, his nose scrunching occasionally.

"Yeah. After that, Lucas has kept out of Will's mind and decided to focus on only sensing him, Karramis, and their children, then trying to break whatever magical barrier those children have on his powers."

Niko stopped at the window and peered out into the darkness, but there was nothing.

"Niko," Tressa called, her dark brow up after observing his strange behavior. "What the hell are you doing?"

He remained facing the window, his perusal still focused on the darkness outside. "I believe we were being watched, madam."

Tressa walked over to the window. "By whom?"

"I do not know for sure, but I could smell someone. A human. A magical human. But the smell was masked behind something else, another creature of some kind."

"Did you recognize it?"

"No, madam. I did not see anything, and the smell was unfamiliar to me."

"Did you hear anything?"

"Just a heartbeat. A very loud heartbeat. Too loud to be a human."

"Hmm." Tressa considered. "Maybe some of the others are out hunting tonight." She faced the minotaur standing quietly in the corner of the room. "Theseus, go patrol outside. See if you can find anything. I give you permission to kill anything that doesn't belong on these grounds. I have enough to worry about. Oh, and go check the Keep. I don't need any of them getting away."

Theseus gave a single nod and exited the room.

"Would you like me to go too, madam?" Niko asked, heading over to the door.

"Thank you, but no. You are free to leave, though."

"Are you sure?"

"You are free to do whatever you see fit for the rest of the evening, Niko. I will go find Lucas and see if he has any updates for me."

Niko stopped in the threshold, his hand resting on the doorknob. "Are you sure it's safe for you, madam?"

Narrowing her eyes, she said with irritation in her voice, "I'll be fine, Niko. Leave."

"Good night, madam."

Tressa waited as his footsteps retreated down the hallway before swinging open the door and heading down the hall in the opposite direction toward Lucas's room.

There were only two weeks left. Only fourteen days before he was scheduled to return—a month earlier than she had expected. Just two weeks before she had to endure the unpredictable plan Merrick had formulated while he was away.

Tressa had experienced his impulsive nature many times in the past, but she feared she would not be able to control him this time around. He was not only a determined man, but he was calculating, cunning, smart, impulsive, and vicious—and answered to no one. Merrick was not going to wait around any longer, his exact words before he left. And when he made up his mind, there was no changing it. He knew what he wanted, and he was certainly going to get it, one way or another.

Tressa had to convince him to control his urges and stick to the plan, focus on what he originally wanted from all of this— enough powers to control his transformation and truly be immortal.

The full moon was looming, and in a matter of days, Merrick would be back in Kiluemar, and there was no telling what would happen once he returned.

Chapter 6

Five months ago
Mid-July

Glints of light gleamed atop the trees as the moon kissed the horizon to the west, the darkness slowly swallowing up the night. The forest was motionless, and shadows lingered among the obscurities beneath the lush branches. A warm breeze whispered across the open field, but a chill nipped in the air, an undeniable ghostly presence. Silence beyond the gently moving grass spread, the quietness deafening with each moment as an unwanted guest stalked closer.

Merrick. Merrick was coming.

Words remained unspoken as everyone waited and searched for any signs of movement across the vast, still, quiet area.

Interrupting the silence, Will reached for the weapons he had leaned against the pillars the day before.

"What are you doing?" James asked as he eyed the meticulously placed weapons scattered along the porch. "Are these really going to help us against him?"

"Nope," Will answered plainly as he leaned a sheathed short sword against the wall by the door, "but it sure as hell makes me feel better having them."

Fear rose in Rhiannon's chest, crushing her lungs and making it hard to breathe as she monitored her father's swift movements distributing the weapons. Tightness wrung in her lower abdomen, twisting and pinching as if searing fingers had taken hold of her insides.

James took her hand, her dread making his body warm. Worry coursed through him, fluttering like fiery butterflies in his stomach. His skin tingled with prickling numbness as his heart hammered in his ears, the pounding echoes masking the unnerving silence.

Rhiannon tensed and drew in a shaky breath as she spotted movement. She squeezed James's hand as his gaze angled over to where she was staring.

A slow-moving silhouette prowled closer through the darkness, silent like a predator hunting for its prey.

Will moved closer to Karramis, ushering her slightly behind him, the back of his arm brushing the front of hers as he gripped her hand. Everyone's gaze shifted toward the figure strutting with such suave casualness it was as if it were taking a leisurely stroll. Inch by inch, the shadows faded from the dark outline as the beam of light from the porch trailed up and gradually erased the darkness.

Karramis guided the twins behind her and Will. "Stay behind us." Her voice was barely above a whisper.

Will tilted his head and leaned back, aiming his attention at Rhiannon. "And don't call the dragons."

Rhiannon blinked in shock as her head snapped in his direction, the matching blue gaze peering back at her. "What?"

"Don't call the dragons," he repeated in a whisper as the figure eased closer.

"Why not?"

His voice lowered even more. "We don't want to give him a reason to attack. Bringing them could escalate the situation."

"Let's just see what he wants," Aidan added from behind her, matching her father's tone as the four adults angled their bodies around the twins.

A set of dark denim-covered legs came into view, followed by a torso clad in a white shirt and a black leather jacket fitted perfectly against the lean body. A pale neck and perfectly trimmed beard were revealed as a handsome and not-at-all dangerous face came into view with a wickedly warm and cunning grin plastered across it.

James scoffed dismissively, sliding his hand from his sister's grip and peering over his mother's head. "This is him? This is Merrick?"

James could not believe that the man right in front of them was the all-powerful, magic-stealing, evil and demonic creature he and the others were supposed to be afraid of. No, there had to be some mistake. This had to be someone else, because this guy was so . . . normal, so unintimidating. There was nothing remotely terrifying about him. If anything, this man radiated a more domineering persona, making James want to take orders from him, not run in the opposite direction.

"James," Pavian said, scolding his nephew under his breath. "Shut up."

Rhiannon examined the man before her, analyzing his physical characteristics and focusing on his eyes sparkling behind a narrow and deep-set gaze. She struggled to connect the heaviness of nerves filling her chest and the unease of fear squeezing her stomach. With his side smirk, light brown hair, and neatly trimmed beard resting against his flawless alabaster skin, she found him pleasant, attractive even—for an older man. But there was still something off about him, something not quite right. Something that made her insides churn with dread—an alarm of some kind in her gut shooting off warnings about his true and unpredictable nature, which seemed to hide behind the charm radiating from him.

The man casually strolled a few feet closer and slid his hands into his jacket pockets. He examined each and every person on the porch with careful consideration.

His gaze stopping on James, he said smoothly in a soft Irish accent, "I am, in fact, he whom you speak of. I am Merrick, and it's a pleasure to finally meet you. It's been a long time comin', has it not?"

Merrick moved closer, his steps calculated and smooth as he drew in a steady breath, deep and with purpose. The corners of his lips twitched higher, a hint of pure delight flashing in his eyes.

Instinctively, Rhiannon crept backward but halted as her body pressed into Aidan.

Merrick's eyes narrowed, and his grin faltered as his gaze ignored Karramis and Will and landed on Rhiannon, the smile quickly returning as he took her in. "Well, hello there." His face lit up as he drew in another deep breath through his nose. "You must be the other half."

No one said a word.

Closing the distance between him and the stairs, Merrick lowered his eyelids and gently rotated his head, cracking his neck. He sniffed the air, and a soft moan vibrated through him as he licked his lips.

A gleam of predatory intrigue lined his face, and his eyes shot open, his gaze landing on Karramis. "I almost forgot how delicious you smell, love."

Cringing, Karramis blurted instinctively, "Don't call me that, please."

"So polite." Merrick licked his lips again, giving them a little bite and eyeing her with ferocity. "It's wonderful to see you again, Karramis. It's been a while."

Confusion flashed across Pavian's face as he angled his head toward his sister. "You two have met before?"

Karramis nodded, her eyes never leaving Merrick.

"When?"

Her voice was quiet and tense. "A long time ago."

"Seriously," James interrupted with a patronizing scoff, pointing at the man at the base of the stairs, "*this* is Merrick?"

Merrick glared at him, unblinking, his face like stone.

"Yes," Aidan answered, sharp and raw, a hand resting on Rhiannon's arm with a comforting and protective grip. "Yes, this is Merrick."

Merrick turned his attention to Aidan, giving him a real, genuine smile. "It's been a while. It's lovely to see you. Ya look well."

James flinched in surprise and directed his bemused gaze over at Aidan. "You two know each other too?"

"You could say that," Aidan said, hostility pinching his tone.

"Aye, it's true." Merrick placed a foot on the bottom step, keeping his eyes on Aidan. "You could say he and I have a . . . mutual acquaintance." Sniffing, he stopped his hungry gaze on Karramis. "My, you smell utterly divine. Just as delectable as ever. So potent . . ." He took another step. "So unique . . . and yet so very strange." Stopping, his eyes moved between the twins. "However, they smell even better." The predatory gleam shifted as he focused on Rhiannon, a pondering expression lining his relaxed features. "Are you frightened, sweetheart?"

Rhiannon remained still. Her eyes fluttered in an unnatural blinking fit as trepidation squeezed in her lower abdomen, turning her skin pale and cold as icy shards of alarm trailed up her spine. The fear intensified as his unblinking beautiful blue eyes observed her—analyzing her, studying her.

"You stay away from her," Will said boldly, moving in front of the others. "You will not touch my daughter."

"Oh, I won't, will I?" Merrick arched a contemplative brow at Will. A stimulating flash shot across his face. A challenge. His eyes landed back on Rhiannon, and their gazes locked.

Silence filled the area as Rhiannon drew herself inward, the fear rising to the surface. Her voice rang out in her head, the words muffled and distant. It was her voice, but she could not understand it.

James whipped his head sideways, his eyes settling on the darkness to the east.

Will eased back, being mindful not to draw Merrick's attention as he tapped James's arm.

Shifting his eyes back to Merrick, James turned his inner attention to his sister. *"Rhiannon?"*

Silence filled James's mind as Rhiannon's blank stare fixed on Merrick, the man refusing to pull himself away from watching her. Fear rose inside James like tendrils of smoke and seeped into his muscles, making his body tremble. He lifted a hand, gliding it into his sister's shaky palm as the four adults remained around them, still and quiet. He had to get inside her head. He had to get her to stop.

Merrick cocked his head as he fought back the twisting of the corners of his mouth.

"Rhiannon," James said again, his internal tone tight in warning. *"Stop."*

The word echoed in her mind as confusion pinched her brows together. *"Stop what?"* Her inner voice was sharp and bitter.

Her face fell as realization sank in. She was calling the dragons to her. It was the one thing her father had told her not to do.

"It's okay," she quickly called out to the dragons. All of them. She had sent out a plea for help, and every single dragon was headed their way. *"It's okay,"* she repeated frantically. *"I'm okay. Turn back. We're all okay. False alarm."*

A few moments later, Rhiannon, James, and Will relaxed, the tension in their shoulders easing.

Returning to the conversation, Merrick eyed Will with a grim expression. "Well, fortunately fer your children, they are not who I want at the moment." Something flashed in his eyes. Something devious and deliberate as he lifted his chin to Karramis. "Now, her on the other hand."

A brazenness sparked to life inside James, his protective nature taking over as he pushed his way through the adults, stopping near the top of the stairs. "And you think we're just going to allow you to take her?"

"Over my dead body," Will said gallantly as he reached for his short sword resting against the pillar, shielding his wife and unsheathing the blade.

Merrick did not flinch as he stared at the weapon and back over at Will, his face emotionless and tone foreboding. "Such a noble gesture. So brave. So fearless. And yet . . . so powerless."

Will clenched his jaw as the sword jerked forward in his hand, the sudden pull forcing him to brace himself as his shoes slid against the smooth wooden boards along the porch. With another yank forward, the sword slipped from Will's tight grip, and the others dodged out of the way as the sword flew through the air and into Merrick's hand.

Merrick's eyes were dark and maniacal, a finger tracing the length of the blade with careful consideration. "You know, Will, if ya truly wish to be as heroic as you would like to believe you are, that little statement you just made can definitely be arranged."

Scoffing, James said with a snarky tone, "You can't touch us here."

A dark gaze fixed on James as Merrick tossed the sword with a powerful thrust into the ground over the railing, the bare hilt the only part remaining above the ground. Climbing the few remaining steps, he stopped on the top of the stairs just short of the magical wall.

"Hmm . . ." Merrick examined the threshold diligently. "Boundary spell, eh?" His eyes stopped on Karramis. "Well, I see there's a wee clever witch in our midst. Fair play, Karramis." His attention was cold and unyielding as it shifted to James. "As for you, young fella, you, on the other hand, are a wee thick eejit fer yappin' your beak before thinkin'. Ya really ought to mind your tongue before it gets you killed."

Behind the others, Pavian asked sharply, "What exactly do you want, Merrick? And if it's my sister, you better be damn sure we won't let you take her without a fight."

"Well, well," Merrick said with a cocky grin, "if it isn't the eldest heir of the Guardian bloodline. How is your father, by the way? I haven't seen him in a while."

Pavian ignored the question and stopped at the landing of the stairs, standing eye to eye with Merrick, who was just a step down. "You really need to leave."

"Leave?" Merrick asked with a cruel smile. "But I was just gettin' started."

"Leave, Merrick," Aidan declared, coming up next to Pavian and James.

"No," Merrick announced matter-of-factly, his attention pulling to Aidan, "*you* need to leave. Your presence is extremely distractin'."

"I'm not goin—"

"That," Merrick said sharply, the word deep in his throat and serious, "was not a request." He slowly turned his head, eyeing Pavian with a heavy scowl. "And take him with you."

Pavian mirrored Merrick's expression. "No, I think you need—"

Blackness swelled in Merrick's eyes as he shot his arm outward and clasped his fingers around Pavian's neck, grasping tight and choking him. He pushed Pavian back as he took a step onto the porch.

"What the hell?" Shock and terror laced James's voice as he and the others retreated back a few steps.

Karramis pulled Rhiannon behind her, and Will hurried in front of them both.

Pavian lifted his hand upward and curled his fingers around Merrick's wrist, pulling with everything he had as he struggled to breathe.

"How's . . . ?" Rhiannon's words faltered as her face paled. "How's he able—"

Merrick tightened his hold on Pavian's throat and chuckled, Rhiannon's words cutting off as she gasped.

"You ignorant fools still underestimate me." Merrick squeezed harder as Pavian's hand slacked against his wrist. "Did ya really believe a boundary spell could stop me?" He clicked his tongue against his teeth. "Shame. Now your mistake will cost him."

Pavian silently gulped, and his eyes rolled back.

Karramis bolted forward. "Stop! You're killing him!"

"Karramis!" Will grabbed her around the waist and forced her back against his body.

"That's the point," Merrick admitted candidly.

Aidan clutched Merrick's wrist and tugged, Pavian's weakened body jerking with the movement. "Stop!"

Rhiannon gasped and drew her hands over her mouth.

Merrick's gaze snapped to Aidan, the shadows in his eyes disappearing. His hand slacked, and Pavian took a deep breath as he slid from Merrick's grasp and crashed to his knees, panting and rubbing his neck.

A warning lined Merrick's cold expression as he glared at Aidan. "I will say this one final time. Leave. Now. And take this sorry excuse of a Guardian with you. He is useless to me. His life is not one I want, nor is it mine to take."

Lifting Pavian to his feet, Aidan said to him, "We have to go."

"No," Pavian said hoarsely, still rubbing his neck. "I'm not leaving them to fend off this—"

"Choose your next words wisely, Mr. Ward." Merrick stopped inches from Pavian's face. "Whether you survive the night depends highly on my mood. And right now, my generosity is fadin'."

"No," Rhiannon said with a harsh tone, shaking her head, "they can't go out there tonight. You're freakin' crazy if—" She halted, instantly regretting her outburst.

A distant darkness loomed in Merrick's eyes as rage and desire burned closer to the surface, the blue in his eyes now black. He drew in a breath and angled his head.

Rhiannon swallowed, her eyes terrified and pleading. "I-I'm sorry. I just mean—"

"Come here," Merrick demanded a bit too casually, signaling with a finger for her to come closer as the volatile shadows lingered in his gaze.

"No," Karramis said flatly, shielding her daughter.

Merrick stood motionless, his unblinking gaze on Rhiannon as he gave her a taunting grin.

"Come here," he said again, the demand feral and deep.

Rhiannon did not move from behind her mother.

Karramis collapsed to her knees as an inaudible gasp fell from her lips, desperately trying to pull in more air.

Rhiannon leaned over her mother, the panic in her voice tight. "Mom?"

James and Will buckled, and Pavian and Aidan dropped, all matching Karramis's plea for oxygen as they clutched their necks and chests.

"Stop it!" Rhiannon yelled, twisting frantically as she watched the others seizing in desperation. "What are you doing to them?"

"Killin' 'em," Merrick answered simply, not a hint of regret in his statement.

The color drained from all their faces as they collapsed to their backs and sides, inaudible chokes heaving in their chests.

James struggled to breathe, the strangling gasps mixing with silent retching as he reached out for Rhiannon. A plea.

"Please!" she begged as a rush of something cold and empty ripped through her. Darkness filled her veins, the blood in her slowing as her pulse grew weak. A pain burned her chest, and each breath felt as if no amount of air was enough. "Stop it!"

"Come here," he drawled, calm and amiable, holding out a hand for her, "and ya have my word I will stop hurtin' 'em."

Rhiannon hurried around the others and slid her hand into his. Fear slammed into her like a raging bull as his surprisingly warm fingers took hold of her with a crushing force—hard and painful. His magic shifted toward her with ease, and she could no longer breathe, each shallow inhale catching in her chest and crushing her lungs. Her knees crumpled under her own weight as her limbs turned to lead. Every ounce of warmth was swept away behind an icy wave of pure horror. Numbness filled her veins, but her nerves and guts ignited with piercing alarm. Tears burst from Rhiannon's eyes as his bore into hers—dark, cold, and hungry.

Then, it all faded away.

The others gasped for air, taking in deep hurried breaths as Rhiannon coughed and pulled in a ragged inhale before panting with hurried determination, feeding her starved lungs.

"Next time . . ." Merrick cupped Rhiannon's chin gently and met her eyes as he tucked a loose strand of brown hair behind her ear. "Next time, I might not be so easily persuaded to show mercy, so it would serve ya well to do as you're told the first time in the future."

Rhiannon nodded.

"Pardon me?" Merrick leaned in. "I didn't quite hear ya."

Swallowing, Rhiannon choked out, "Okay."

"Okay what?"

Panic flashed in her eyes. "Sir?"

Merrick gave her a wide, devilish grin. "Well, it would seem you do have manners. Such a lacking quality in today's society. Now then, let's see how well ya listen." He lifted a palm. "Give me your hand."

Rhiannon hesitated but finally did as she was told, lifting a shaky hand and sliding her fingers across his.

Shuffling sounded as Aidan rose to his feet, rushing to Rhiannon's aid, but he halted as Merrick yanked her into him and flipped her around, pressing her against his body.

"Rhiannon!" James and Will called through uneven pants.

"Leave her alone!" Karramis pleaded, following Aidan's faltering approach.

James gritted his teeth and clenched his hands into fists, still trying to catch his breath. "Let her go."

Stepping after them, James was quickly pulled back by his mother and father. Aidan and Pavian stood beside them, a few feet from Rhiannon and Merrick, who remained by the stairs.

"James," Karramis said as she held his wrist, "you're going to get yourself killed."

Merrick cocked his head. "I'd listen to her, James."

With a calm voice, James repeated firmly, "Let her go."

Tugging Rhiannon tighter against his body, Merrick smelled her hair. "Nah, I think I'll have a wee bit of fun first."

James balled his hands as rage erupted deep inside his body, the power surging as his nerves shot electric jolts under his skin. Strength rose from deep inside his core, and his veins burned hot, pushing the magic rapidly through his body.

The still, quiet summer air churned to life around James, blowing outward and crashing over the others. Everyone's hair blew wild. Dust and dirt swirled together. Blades of grass from the field rose into the night sky, joining the wind storm blasting across the porch.

Unfazed, Merrick lifted a hand and curled his fingers, smothering the element and crushing the power rising from James. The wind slowed, fading gradually into a soft breeze before disappearing completely. The leaves, dirt, and grass dropped back to the earth, and silence fell across the area again.

"Impressive," Merrick said, pleased. "Your powers are strong. Unfortunately, not strong enough."

"Give me a few more months, asshole, and we'll see who's stronger."

Merrick released a low rumbling laugh. "My, aren't we a rather arrogant fella. Bit of a chancer, if ya ask me." He stared at James. "Challenge accepted."

James did not waver from meeting Merrick's gaze as his anger continued to boil inside him, fuming from the fear and pain flooding Rhiannon's body. James wanted to protect her, save her, but how would he overpower a man with limitless and unmatched abilities?

Karramis tugged on her son's arm, coming between him and Merrick. "James, what are you doing?"

James shrugged. "I don't know. I couldn't help myself."

"You sure are a brave one, I'll give ya that," Merrick said with a smile. "I commend ya on your vigor." He pressed his mouth against Rhiannon's ear. "You should take note of this."

"Enough with the bullshit, Merrick," Aidan said candidly as he leaned against his upper thighs.

Merrick grinned in his direction. "My, my, Aidan, aren't we bold? Must run in the family. But . . ." He let out a disappointed sigh. "But a tad foolish, especially since I already ordered ya to leave. You should take up my offer before the sliver of mercy I still have left fades completely."

"Fine," Aidan said flatly, turning to Pavian. "We need to get out of here."

Pavian hesitated. "No—"

"We can't help them if we're dead." Aidan's voice was low as he gripped Pavian's arm and headed down the stairs.

"Oh, and Mr. Ward," Merrick called after them as they stepped onto the grass.

Pavian glanced over his shoulder.

"Ya might want to send someone to go check on that school of yours—the one you all tried so hard to ward. I fear somethin' terrible might've happened there." There was no concern in his tone.

Pavian's shoulders sagged and his eyes widened as Aidan ushered him into the shadows along the side of the cabin.

Rhiannon watched as Aidan and her uncle stepped out of the illumination of the porch lights. "You can't do this." Her body tensed when Merrick's grasp tightened around her even more. "They're going to get killed out there."

"Don't worry, sweetheart." Merrick lowered his voice and leaned in again, stroking her arm. "I do believe Haydrin is busy elsewhere tonight."

Rhiannon's eyes widened, and her body went rigid. "How did you—"

"Oh, you silly girl," he crooned, slow and taunting, "I know all about your encounter." His voice fell to a whisper. "And trust me, you should be more worried about yourself when it comes to Haydrin, not anyone else. He has claimed you. And he *always* gets what's his."

"What do you want with us?" James asked, trying to pull Merrick's attention away from Rhiannon.

Easing his hold on her, Merrick gripped her wrist and forced her behind him, his focus now on James. "I simply came to talk. To see how the magic trainin' is goin'. To assess the status of my magic."

"*Our* magic," James corrected with a hostile tone, but Merrick went on.

"But I was distracted by the allurin' and delicious scent of all the magical blood surroundin' this place."

"You're sick and twisted, you know that?"

"James!" Karramis and Will reprimanded under their breaths.

"Aye." Merrick narrowed his eyes at James, neither one refusing to break their focus. "You really are quite thick, boy." There was a daringness to his statement, a push to see how far the young man would take his pride.

"You don't scare me," James said arrogantly, the flicker in his eyes immediately showing the regret in his declaration. Fear rattled through him as his sister winced from behind Merrick, his grip on her tightening. *Shit.*

"Well then," Merrick challenged as he twitched his mouth into a half smile, "let me fix that fer ya."

Chapter 7

Merrick seized Rhiannon by the throat in one swift movement, so fast it was barely registered by her and the others before it was too late.

Lifting her onto her tiptoes, he snarled and revealed two rows of pointed teeth and four razor-sharp canines, two on the top and bottom along the outside rows. His blue eyes disappeared behind solid black, pools of darkness flowing within the sockets. Red and black veins rose along his face and pulsed, making his skin even paler. Cuts erupted along the exposed parts of his body, tiny slivers ripping apart the skin on his face, neck, and hands, exposing leathery black muscle and torn tissue. Merrick tensed as he closed his eyes, stifling the pain of his transformation searing throughout his body. A growl roared from his chest, rising and reverberating through his arm and against Rhiannon's neck as his grip loosened.

Grabbing her shoulders, Merrick plunged his face into her neck, his four sharp fangs piercing through her skin with ease.

The teeth stabbed through her like fiery-hot spikes, searing and carving deep into her neck as her flesh ripped. Warmth coated her neck as his mouth pressed harder, the squeezing of his cheeks driving more blood to the surface. His tongue glided across the wetness seeping along her skin as the smell of blood, strong and coppery, filled her nose. A hand gripped the back of her neck, grasping with a painful hold as it drove her closer to the mouth pressed against her clammy skin. Blood trailed down her neck, the steady stream cooler than the heat radiating from the tightly clasped lips sucking at her nape.

Her name echoed in her head, muffled and distant as the others screamed for her. She gasped as a scream caught in her throat, the pain searing through her as blood dripped between her neck and his lips.

Terror and helplessness flooded her, rising from deep inside her core and taking control of her body and mind. But it was wrong. It was misplaced. Foreign. Far away but not. And it hurt. It hurt so bad. Not the pain from what was happening, but the emotions swallowing her whole. It was like being pulled under water with nothing but darkness. No air. No light. No life. Nothing. She closed her eyes, focusing on it and driving it away, shoving everything into a distant place deep inside her mind.

Power surged from Merrick as the others advanced toward him, and he continued to ravenously suck the blood from Rhiannon's body while creating a magical barrier. The three others flew back against the wall with a crashing force and tumbled to the porch.

Rhiannon's knees buckled, and her body went limp as she crumbled against Merrick's fully clothed half-demonic form.

Her eyes rolled back in her head as her muffled cries grew quiet, and the grip she had on his leather jacket loosened.

Will grunted and rose to his feet, but a heavy weight forced his back against the wall and pinned him against it. The magic surging outward from Merrick pressed against him, Karramis, and James, the force slowly starting to crush them.

Fighting through the pain, Will shoved against the magic, but he could not move it or weaken the hold compelling them harder against the side of the cabin.

Karramis screamed as Rhiannon's body sagged in Merrick's grasp, the tendrils of flames sputtering in her hands flickering in and out, her powers faltering as she watched her daughter growing lifeless. Summoning her telekinesis, she fought against the invisible force, easing some of the strain crushing them.

"Rhiannon!" Karramis yelled.

Wind swirled around as James called forth his air magic again and pushed against the wall of power.

"You've made your point!" James shouted as a low rumble quaked under them, the power of earth warming his insides.

Merrick removed his teeth from Rhiannon, his eyes closed and blood dripping down his face. Exhilaration twitched his mouth into a grin as his blue eyes flicked open. His hands tightened around Rhiannon as his skin sealed and the veins faded. Holding back another roar, he retracted his canines. He lowered his eyelids and twitched his neck as his body returned to normal, no signs of damage lingering on his flesh and a set of human teeth resting in his mouth.

Rhiannon regained her footing and opened her watery bloodshot eyes. Her face and skin were colorless as blood trailed down from the open wound in her neck and over the front of her dress.

"Interestin'," Merrick said, drawing out the word with amusement. He examined her wound. "You shouldn't be conscious, let alone standin'."

"Let me go," Rhiannon choked, her tone shaky and not at all as fearless as she had hoped.

"Makin' demands now, are we?"

"If you killed me now, you'd never get my powers." Rhiannon could not meet his gaze as she stared at the blood— her blood—on his chin. "So, let me go." Glancing over at James, she repeated his words. "You've made your point."

"Have I now?" Merrick angled his head with an evil gleam leaking across his features. "Nah, I do believe I'm just gettin' started. I'm not finished with you yet." He slid his hand up her neck, holding her in place as he leaned into her, his cheek brushing against hers. "Do me a favor, sweetheart." There was a softness to his words, a calm and enchanting plea. "Run for me."

Dread shot up her spine, the icy chill zooming into her stomach and sending a shiver through her body. "What?"

Standing tall, he tilted his head and gave a sinister chuckle as his pupils dilated, focusing on the unsteadiness of her rising and falling chest. "Run." There was no humor in his voice, only pure, undiluted demand. "Now."

Without a second thought, Rhiannon bolted, her bare feet slipping on the grass as she ran.

"Rhiannon!" her mother yelled from the porch, the sound of shuffling feet echoing around.

Without giving her a head start, Merrick slowly stalked behind her. The smell of her blood filled the air as her pulse quickened, the wound still seeping the sweet-tasting elixir of her living essence. The faster she ran, the easier it would be to find her.

Karramis and Will were on their feet as James raced after Merrick and Rhiannon.

Merrick turned on his heels, and James slid to a stop. A mocking grin appeared on Merrick's face before he zipped out of sight and appeared in front of Rhiannon a few yards away. Pulling her closer, he stopped her face inches from his as he drew in a slow, deep inhale, taking his time to breathe in the entirety of her scent. She whimpered as his body quivered, his gaze fixed on the drying blood resting under his grasp. Letting her go, he leaned forward and licked her neck—unhurried, tender, and with a carnal want behind his animalistic gaze. As he drew back, his eyes met hers, hunger glaring within his ravenous blue eyes.

Footsteps hurried closer, and the muffled pants of the others neared as Rhiannon's heart pounded. She jerked and twisted, trying to escape his hold, but Merrick snatched her back against him as a wall of rushing liquid shot up from the ground and reached into the sky, encasing them inside a magical room of four reverse waterfalls. Raging but quiet. Thick and solid.

James reached the wall and pounded against it, water splashing in his face. "Rhiannon!"

Karramis and Will circled around it, searching for a tear in the magic as the ground turned soggy beneath their hurried steps.

Merrick focused on Rhiannon's heartbeat, the magic of his stolen water powers dividing them from the others as he concentrated on her blood pumping through her veins—warm, sweet, and inviting. Tracing the backs of his fingers along her arm, he caressed her clammy, smooth skin. His hand moved to her face, examining every inch of it, wiping away her tears. His gaze settled on her lips as she panted. Closing his eyes, he leaned in, inhaling and placing the tip of his nose against her cheek.

Rhiannon's body trembled, cold and frozen in terror. His breath was hot against her face, and the lingering metallic scent of her blood made her queasy. She was no longer in control of her breathing as her chest heaved and burned. Panting, she forced herself to swallow the dryness coating her raw throat. Her neck ached with her hurried heartbeat, but the pain from the bite was fading. A sudden rush filled her mind, either from blood loss or the fear taking over, and the world around her began to spin. She allowed her thoughts to fade away into nothing as she closed her eyes.

Whipping her around, Merrick compelled her closer against him as he slipped his arm under hers and trailed his fingers down along her side, gliding his hand over her waist and resting it atop her hips.

Squeezing her eyes tighter, she focused on her breathing as she pulled herself inward, fading deep into her mind with each controlled inhale and exhale. *Control.* She breathed again, slow and steady. *You are in control.*

Merrick's face leaned into her bloody neck, the beard along his face scratching as his warm breath blew against her skin.

Her body recoiled, the disgust sending acid burning up her throat. *Focus. Don't let it take control. Breathe.*

Emotions swarmed her. Shock. Defeat. Regret. Panic. It all engulfed her, swallowing her whole, along with the hopelessness as the tip of his tongue glided across the puncture wounds healing along her neck.

Merrick moaned, the deep growl vibrating against her skin. "I wonder if your brother and mother taste as good as you do."

Rhiannon flung her eyes open as his arms rested across her midsection, urging her closer against his taut body. Revulsion rose in her stomach as anger and fear collided, billowing higher from deep in her core. The water around them instantly stilled, completely immobile as it floated in midair.

"So," he drawled with an amused chuckle as he observed the watery wall, the one he no longer had full control over, "you finally decided to allow some magic to come out and play."

Rhiannon threw her hips back into him and twisted away, but Merrick snatched her wrist. She yelped, tensing and flinching as she spotted his solid black eyes and fanged teeth again.

"Let me see more," he said calmly, his face transforming back to normal. "Show me what ya can really do."

Rhiannon ignored him as she steadied her breathing.

"Rhiannon!" she heard over and over again on the other side of the water wall.

"Let her go, you fuckin' bastard!" James yelled from the other side, his voice muffled.

"Well, that was rather rude." Merrick tilted his callous expression down at Rhiannon and circled around her with his hands behind his back. "I can feel it, ya know. Smell it."

Rhiannon did not say a word but held his gaze, turning as he walked casually around her.

"It's in you. Raw. Untamed. And powerful." He continued circling, his voice a bit too calm and pleasant. "The magic—your magic—I can feel it. It's strong. Very strong." His eyes remained on her, monitoring every step, every breath, every beat of her heart. "It's ragin' deep inside ya, but it's trapped. Stuck behind an unbreakable and impenetrable wall. And do you know what that wall is built entirely out of?"

She still remained quiet as the power she had on the water faded, returning the upward flowing of the solid wall of liquid to its previous state.

"Fear." His voice was low and husky and thrumming with smooth tautness. "It courses through you. Your heart." He halted, inching closer to her. "Your soul. Your blood. It's part of you 'cause ya give in to it." A low groan rumbled as he angled his head down and placed a whiskery cheek against the side of her smooth, tear-soaked face. "And it tastes *so* sweet." Pulling back with a disappointed sound clicking against his teeth, he mocked, "Such a waste. All that potential . . . All that power completely wasted on a pathetic, scared, worthless little girl. Your weaknesses will be your downfall, sweetheart. Oh, but . . ." He met her gaze, a gleam of pure evil in his eyes as he smiled. "But the things I will do with your magic once it surfaces and I finally get to tear it out of your fragile young body."

Wind swirled, and Merrick shifted his attention toward a misty vortex forming behind him. Yanking Rhiannon around in front of him, he held tight to her arm. Karramis appeared as she exited the portal, narrowly missing them as she stepped into the small enclosed area inside the wall of water around them.

"Well," Merrick said, impressed, "this is unexpected."

Karramis ignored him, her concerned gaze landing on Rhiannon, the fear evident behind her daughter's blank expression. "It's okay, sweetie." A comforting statement, a voice of reassurance only a mother could give. "You're okay. Look at me." She waited, and Rhiannon's watery blue eyes met hers. "Good. Just keep looking at me." A smile appeared, real and soft. "Focus on me. Only me. Nothing else. Okay?"

Rhiannon gulped and gave her a quick nod.

"Let her go, Merrick," Karramis demanded, the shift in her gaze and voice unlike anything Rhiannon had ever witnessed before from her mother. There was a fire there—a rage of intense power behind her simple demand. "Let her go. Now. She's just a child. I know you have no humanity, but do you have no morals as well?"

Merrick glared at her, calculated and wild. "Nah, I do. I most certainly have morals. Strong ones, in fact. But ya see, Karramis, you have not taken into consideration the slight misconception in your declaration there." Tilting his head down, he gave Rhiannon an arrogant but almost genuine smile as an animalistic desire filled his expressive eyes. "This precious mortal here is no child. Not to me. Not when it comes to the beast ragin' inside of me. Nah, it does not see age. Nor does it see male or female, skin color, or societal status. It does not care if one is rich or poor. And religion and politics are trivial. Nah, all mortals and immortals are the same—magic or no magic. Ya see, in the end you are all one thing to the hungry beast inside. Food. And you, my sweet, delicious Karramis, are all at the bottom of the evolutionary food chain, whereas I am at the top. I will always be at the top. In life, you all have but one certainty—death. It's only a matter of when and how. And lucky fer me, I have control over those things, fer I see ya all only as my prey. And I do fancy a good hunt."

Karramis squared her shoulders. "She is of no use to you right now, so let her go."

"Now, why would I do that, love?"

Karramis flinched, her face tight with irritation.

Merrick gave a malicious grin as he raised a brow. "Why do you detest that name so much?"

Ignoring the question, Karramis said, "What if I offer you something else? Something you won't want to turn down."

Merrick considered. "You dare enter a deal with me." Not a question, but a challenge. "Rather audacious, if ya ask me. Because from where I'm standin', you are at quite a disadvantage. I have somethin' you want, and you lack anythin' in exchange."

"I guess that's a gamble you'll have to take then, huh?"

Loosening his grip around Rhiannon's arms, Merrick said, "I'm listenin'."

"No," Karramis declared calmly as she shook her head. "Let her go first, and we'll discuss it."

"Mom. No." The words were strained behind the tightness in her throat.

Giving Rhiannon a quick reassuring smile, Karramis said to her daughter, "It's okay, sweetie. It's going to be okay." She lifted her gaze to Merrick. "Let her leave here without any more harm coming to her and allowing her to safely return to her brother and father, and we can come to an agreement."

Silence.

A palm glided up Rhiannon's arm as Merrick trailed a hand up to her neck, running his fingers over the tacky blood caked to her heated skin.

Merrick narrowed his gaze. "This better be worth it." He lifted a hand and licked his fingers, savoring every remaining drop before lowering his lips to Rhiannon's ear. "Until we meet again, sweetheart."

In the blink of an eye, Rhiannon was shoved through the water paused in midair, the rush of cold liquid drenching her and sending her into a moment of shock before she tumbled onto the grass on the other side. The wall of diluted magic thickened and began flowing again, raging in silence as Rhiannon sputtered behind choking coughs and spewing water.

James and Will hurried over and knelt beside her.

"What happened?" Will asked, worry lacing his words as he pushed back her wet strands and examined the two deep puncture wounds on her neck. "Where's your mum?"

Staring with a frozen gaze at the magical wall of water, she winced as her father gently wiped away the now wet and smeared blood along her skin with the hem of his shirt. "She's still inside . . . with him."

Chapter 8

A Deal is Made

The wall of water vanished without a trace of its presence lingering along the ground, every drop drawing back into the soil and evaporating in the cool night air.

Merrick and Karramis stood staring at each other, neither one easing the superior stances they both possessed.

Reaching out a hand, Karramis asked firmly, "So, do we have a deal?"

Merrick gave her a curt nod but did not take her hand. "You have my word."

He nodded again, rotating around and leaving.

"Merrick," she called with an authoritative inflection in the simple word, her hand still outstretched.

He twisted back toward her, not an ounce of emotion on his face but a flicker of satisfaction in his gaze.

Raising her hand higher, Karramis said, her tone sharper and more dominant, "It is customary to shake when a deal is agreed upon."

"Is my word not enough?" Merrick asked, amused and poised.

"I've always been told you're a man of your word, as I am a woman of mine, but this . . . this is simply a sign of good faith. You know, a little peace of mind to help me sleep at night."

"As you wish." Merrick slightly bowed his head and took her hand. "Now, ya not only have my word, but you also have any additional reassurance that those words will remain true and honest." Turning and strolling away, he added over his shoulder, "Until we meet again, Karramis."

Releasing a deep exhale through her nose, Karramis made her way closer to the others, her expression sullen with a forced smile.

"He's leaving?" James asked, his eyes wide with surprise. "Just like that? Wh-what did he say?"

Karramis watched Merrick as he meandered farther into the darkness, allowing a good distance before she twisted to Rhiannon. "Are you okay?" She examined the wounds on her daughter's neck. "How are you standing right now? You lost so much blood."

"I'm fine," Rhiannon said, her voice low and raspy, her blue gaze empty and distant. "It doesn't hurt that much anymore."

"Are you sure?"

"I'm fine," she repeated.

James wrapped an arm around her and gently squeezed her shoulder. "Her healing abilities must be getting stronger."

His eyes stayed on his sister as she stared in her mother's direction, but her gaze peered at nothing. He pulled his thoughts deep into his mind and tugged on her inner consciousness, her emotions.

Nothing was there. Only emptiness.

He focused harder, his inner voice calling to her, begging her to answer. *"Are you really okay?"*

Silence.

"Please, Rhiannon, talk to me."

Rhiannon felt his eyes boring into her. "I'm fine."

James lowered his arm and faced her. "Are you—"

Cutting him off as she gently clutched his arm, Karramis uttered, soft and sympathetic, "Give her a minute, James. She just suffered through something very traumatic, and her mind is trying to process it all." Turning to Rhiannon, she asked, "Do you want to go inside and get cleaned up?"

"No," she blurted flatly, blinking back into full awareness and peering at her mother. "I want to hear this. I'm fine." There was a sharpness in her tone. "Really. I'm fine, just tired."

"Understandable," Will said, his hand resting on the small of Karramis's back. "You lost a lot of blood."

James took his sister's hand, smiling when she gladly accepted it. "So, Mom, what happened?"

"What kind of deal did you make?" Rhiannon asked tightly as emotions pinched her throat.

Will slid his hand along her back as he stepped around, taking in the whole of her face, her eyes. "I would like to know that as well."

Reluctantly, Karramis answered, composed and proud, "I got him to agree to give them more time."

Will raised a brow. "More time for what?"

"To prepare themselves."

Will folded his muscular arms over his chest, a lingering concern lining his features. "How long do we have before he comes back for them?"

"Less than a year. Until their next birthday."

"But why?" Rhiannon asked, her rough voice cracking. "Why did he agree to this? I mean, he clearly had other plans for tonight. Why just stop everything and allow us to go—just like that? Why give us more time to learn to fight him? It doesn't make sense."

"Yeah," James added, "he was so hell-bent on showing us just how powerful he was, why not just take us now?" He pointed a hand at Karramis. "Or you?"

"Because," Karramis said with a sigh, "Merrick is not only a prideful man, he's also a very arrogant and sadistic man who likes playing games. He gets off on his victims fighting him. On their fear. Their pain. It's far more . . . pleasurable for him."

Rhiannon shivered, trying to erase his touch from her.

"Ugh!" James scrunched his nose. "That's sick."

"Yes, it is," Karramis said. "But I used it to our benefit. I played off his ego and narcissistic tendencies for self-gratification, and it worked."

Rhiannon rubbed her neck and smeared the remaining blood along her wet skin. "So, we have a little less than a year to bring all our powers to the surface, master them, and stop him from overpowering us, stealing our abilities for himself, killing us, and destroying all magic."

Karramis nodded. "Yes." It was a simple but indignant response.

"Great," Rhiannon said sarcastically, "no pressure." There was hostility in her voice, something strange and detached.

"Sounds easy enough," James added even less enthusiastically, the shift in her demeanor making him uneasy.

Karramis slid her hands into theirs. "Well, at least we don't have to worry about him tonight. Or anytime soon." She gave Rhiannon's hand a gentle squeeze. "Now, let's get you inside and get that wound cleaned up."

Rhiannon shook her head. "No, it's fine. It will heal on its own. I think I'll just go take a shower and go to sleep."

"Yeah," James agreed, "it's been a long night."

Rhiannon pivoted away from them, her loose grip pulling from her brother's as she headed for the cabin.

Lowering his voice as he rushed up next to her, James asked sympathetically, "Are you sure you're okay? You blocked me out."

Rhiannon halted, her sharp gaze landing on him. "I didn't block you out."

"You didn't?"

"No." That was all she said as she continued forward, her sluggish steps ascending the stairs of the porch.

Stopping at the base of the steps, James called softly after her, "Rhiannon? Talk to me. Please."

Rhiannon hesitated, stopping at the door as she took hold of the handle, bowing her head and dropping her gaze.

"What is it?" James asked, now nervous about his inability to sense her emotions as he met her on the porch.

"Why?" Her pained eyes met his. "Why is it always me?"

Rhiannon did not need an answer because she knew why—why she was always the one targeted and attacked. She just could not bring herself to admit it out loud.

James did not reply, the guilt and concern rendering him speechless.

Rhiannon sighed as she entered the house, and James followed, Karramis watching as he closed the door behind him.

"What are you not telling them?" Will asked from behind her, caressing his hands down her arms before gently grabbing a wrist and turning her to face him.

She leaned into him and wiped away a tear pooling along her eye. "I offered him a deal."

Easing her away from his chest, he curled a finger under her chin and lifted her rich brown gaze. "What kind of deal?"

She cupped his face with both hands and kissed him.

Opening his eyes, he asked, "Should I be worried?"

Karramis kissed him again, slow and passionate.

Smiling as he leaned away, Will flicked a mischievous brow at her. "Are you attempting to distract me, darling?"

"Who? Me?" she asked, giving him an innocent grin. "Never."

Will opened his mouth to say something, but Karramis placed her lips against his again.

"Fine, you win." He playfully wiggled his index finger at her. "But just this one time."

Karramis let out an amused snort and patted his chest. "Right. Keep telling yourself that, Dragon Lord." She headed for the cabin, giving him a flirty grin over her shoulder, her voice sultry. "I always win, and I always get what I want. I'll prove it later."

"Karramis," he called after her with a teasing grin, catching up to her and swinging her around as she giggled. "You're such a tease, you know that?"

She pecked his cheek, smiling. "You like it."

"Yes, that's true." The corner of his mouth rose with a quirk of his brow. "Especially when I get something out of it."

"And who says you won't?" Grasping his hand, she persuaded him to follow, but he remained still and held her tighter, forcing her to halt. "What?" Her smile faded. "What's wrong?"

His voice and face were serious. "Are you trying to distract me or yourself?"

Karramis heaved a deep sigh. "Both."

"What was the deal?"

Hesitating, she answered, "I offered a trade."

"You for them?" He already knew the answer.

She blinked and gave a single nod. "Yes."

"Are you mad?" Will protested, sliding his fingers through his dark brown hair, a flash of panic sparking in his blue eyes at her confirmation. "What were you thinking? He's going to kill you, Karramis."

"I know that, but—"

"But nothing!" His voice grew louder, the irritation and fear rising to the surface. "Being a martyr isn't going to protect them forever. You aren't saving them by giving yourself over to him. No, you're only buying them more time before the inevitable happens." He took a few steps back, the realization of her actions settling inside him. Advancing closer, he continued, his tone strained with worry. "He's still going to come for them. And when he does, they are going to need you. I am going to need you. You need to be there to fight with them. With us. I'm not losing you again!"

"Will, listen to me," she pleaded, reaching for him.

"I know! I know what you're going to say, Karramis. I knew what I was getting into, but . . . but you can't do this. You can't go willingly into the lion's den. They *will* kill you. And there isn't anything that can bring you back this time."

"Will," she begged again, trying to get him to listen to her.

But he ignored her, the tension building in his voice, his posture. "You don't always have to be the one saving everyone else, you know?"

The corner of her mouth quirked, and she said playfully, "But I'm the savior."

"This isn't a joke, Karramis. I'm serious. You don't have to be the one doing everything by yourself. We're a team. Partners." He sighed. "I just got you back. Please . . . please don't do this. You can't. I'm not willing to let you go again. I won't. Not yet. And now you're just going to give yourself over to him. Just like that. For what, more time?"

"Yes," Karramis answered simply with a bite in her tone. "If they can just have more time to bring all their magic out and train and control it, they might have a fighting chance. *We* might have a fighting chance."

Will began to pace, his voice rising with each stroll past her. "There's no *we* if you're dead. And if you go with him, you will be."

"I can handle this. I know I can."

"I know you can too, but you don't have to—you shouldn't have to."

"It's my duty to protect them, to save them. And I would rather die than lose them. Or you."

Will did not say anything for a moment as he halted, his eyes and face seeping with sadness. "What about them losing you? What about me? You were dead, Karramis. Dead. At least I thought you were. I mourned you." He choked back his emotions. "I already lost you once. I don't—I can't—lose you again."

Karramis stared at him, fighting the burn in her eyes and the lump in her throat. "Will, you knew from the—"

"I don't care!" he snapped, pacing again. "It doesn't make it any less painful."

Karramis glanced over her shoulder at the cabin, stepping closer to him and lowering her voice. "Would you please calm down before the kids hear or see you traipsing back and forth like a caged animal."

Will made his way over to her. "Wait, you're not going to tell them?"

"Not yet. Not until I'm certain of everything that could go wrong."

Understanding settled in him as he remembered Karramis was usually always one step ahead of everyone else. "I'm sorry." His eyes were apologetic, but his voice was concerned as he took her hands. "I know what you told me, but . . ." He could not bring himself to finish, and his gaze dropped to the ground. "That doesn't make this any easier."

Karramis removed her hands from his and cradled his face, her hopeful gaze meeting his. "I'm not giving up. This will not be the end of me. You won't lose me. Not yet. I know what I'm doing."

"Care to fill me in then?"

"The deal was, if he allowed them more time to train and prepare themselves to go against him in a fair fight, then I go with him willingly."

"What?" Will said sharply.

"But I *never* said I'd stay," Karramis declared without delay, trying to ease the tension in his voice and worry on his face.

"And I never agreed that I wouldn't fight like hell once I got there. I simply said I would go willingly."

Will considered for a moment, his tight expression easing a bit. "Do you really think it will work? He's smart and powerful."

Karramis dropped her arms to her sides. "Then I'll just have to be better than him when he comes for me. I'd like to think I can outsmart them, but even I have no idea if, in the end, it'll work. But I'm damn sure going to try. For them. And you. For us. Even a few extra months of training and practicing their magic might help them. Merrick is powerful, but I know they are too. All we can do now is prepare for the worst and hope for the best."

"What if you fail? What if this doesn't work and they take you away from us again?"

Karramis kept her gaze on him as sadness lingered in her eyes, unable to answer the question.

Finally, Will said somberly, "Then we train. Together. No holding back. We make sure we don't fail and your plan works."

Karramis kissed his cheek.

His voice dropped even lower as he traced the scar on the left side of her face with his thumb. "How much time do we have?"

She swallowed and cleared the tension building in her throat. "Like I said, until their next birthday."

He gave her a wry smirk as a deep crease formed between his brows. "You know that's not what I mean, Karramis. How much time do *we* have?"

She drew in a deep breath and let it out slowly. "He's coming for me in a few months."

He traced his hands along her neck and slid them under her hair, cupping the base of her head. "Then let's make every minute count. Always and today, right?"

Karramis nodded as she lifted onto her tiptoes, wrapping her arms around the back of his neck as he pulled her in closer to his taut chest, the smell and heat of him sending a wave of euphoria through her.

Lowering back down to her feet, she asked, "You trust me, right?"

"Yes, of course, darling," Will declared smoothly without hesitation. "I've always trusted you." His expression tightened with annoyance as he added dryly, "It's Merrick I don't trust."

Chapter 9

Home Sweet Home

Merrick had not planned to attack when he set out for the cabin, but his hunger and pride had overpowered the real reason behind his detour before heading back to the castle. However, his visit had proven beneficial in more ways than one.

But first, he had to control himself. He had to be patient. Keep his word and stick to his plan. His ego and hunger would have to wait. The time would come for him to have the twins and their magic and keep his word about Karramis. But for now, he had to wait. Wait for his plan to fall into place. Merrick was not going to let an opportunity like this pass him by so easily. He was going to get everything he wanted—even if it meant waiting a bit longer—and still keep his word to those he had made promises to.

~

The castle grounds were blanketed in dark blue shadows as the early dawn hour arrived, the dim glow from the sun peeking over the horizon hidden behind a thick layer of clouds. A chill filled the summer air, but a warmth blew in off the ocean, rolling across the stone mesa and bringing a calm to the area.

Merrick yanked on the large wooden doors, the hinges squeaking as he pulled them open. Darkness loomed back as he stopped just inside, taking in the damp, stale hallway.

He was home.

The air was cold and smelled of dirt, smoke, and old musky greenery. The candles in the sconces on the stone walls were out, and it was unusually quiet. No whistling of the wind. No crackling of a fireplace. No voices. No footsteps. No heartbeats. Nothing. Just complete silence and peace on this side of the castle. His side.

Merrick made his way toward the west wing, leaving the dreary stone hallway and entering a beautifully ornate corridor. Square tiles lined the floor of the wide hallway, white and black polished slabs placed with alternating perfection. Gray stone pillars sat perfectly spaced along the smooth white stone walls, arching at the top into a point. Black iron-and-glass chandeliers hung from the ceiling, untouched for decades. Huge rounded arched windows lined the outside wall with frosted glass and wooden framing. Curtains were pulled open and hung from the ceiling, allowing light to illuminate the hallway. Strolling by medieval armor, beautiful Renaissance artwork, and a statue of a nude woman, Merrick paused at a carved oak door and knocked.

"Just a second," a soft accented female voice called from the other side.

Footsteps strutted closer, the gentle creaking of floorboards sounding in sync as the door opened.

Wearing a full-length black nightdress with slits up to her thighs and a dark purple lace-and-silk robe, Tressa stared wide-eyed at him. "I was wondering when you were going to show up." Her voice was calm despite her surprised expression as she pulled open the door. "Would you like to come in?"

Entering the room, Merrick circled around, admiring the beauty of her flawless mocha skin and long straight silky black hair flowing freely down to the middle of her back.

His light-colored eyes traveled up her body, the voluptuous curvature of her hourglass figure accentuated along the thin material draping over her. His gaze landed on hers, the rich brown of her eyes sparkling from the firelight coming from the candles scattered throughout the room.

Smoothly, he asked as he leaned into her, his breath cascading across her lips, "Why were you not waitin' fer me in my chambers? I'm certain you received word and did not forget I would be returnin' tonight."

"Of course not." Tressa wrapped her robe around herself and concealed her scantily covered body as she arched a quick brow at him before retreating over to the purple wingback chair by her bed. "No, I did not forget. I knew you were returning and that you would be expecting me." There was a familiar cadence to her voice—a relaxed steadiness to it. "And I *was* waiting for you. But it's been hours since the portals opened, and you never showed, so I assumed maybe you decided not to return just yet."

"Well, it seems you were mistaken," Merrick said with an unusually friendly smirk, his tone low as he trailed behind her, his steps barely audible. "I had business to take care of first." Scanning the room with his hands behind his back, he eyed her curiously. "Were ya expectin' company?"

"No," Tressa confessed candidly, shaking her head and leaning back, the folds of her robe opening to expose her cleavage. "Of course not. I was almost asleep when you arrived."

"Hmm. Right."

Grinning, Tressa pointed out with an amused civility to her tone, "You seem to be in a rather good mood."

Matching her expression, he said with mock surprise, "Do I?"

"Yes," she acknowledged, giving him a playful sneering scowl. "It's unsettling."

Merrick let out a humorous scoff, a liveliness entering his features. "My bein' in a pleasant mood disturbs you?"

"Yes, so stop it."

"I cannot fathom why you would say such atrocious things about me, my dear Tressa. I am a delightful person. My mere presence makes people fall to their knees just to worship me."

"Beg for their lives is more like it."

Merrick released a laugh—a guttural, purely joyous laugh. "Why, Tressa, how I've missed your spirited honesty."

Stifling a chuckle, Tressa said, "You look well, Merrick." She slipped a leg out from under her robe and eased it over her knee, the smooth movement elegant and classy. "I take it you had a pleasant holiday?"

"Indeed. In fact, not only was it beneficial in regard to my frivolous and most delectable escapades, but it was also extremely advantageous to my future."

"Well, the months away served you well." Giving him a wry grin, she added, "But it seems your eating habits haven't improved much."

"I beg your pardon," he said with an arched brow and a piercing glare.

She jutted a chin in his direction and circled a finger in the area around her own mouth. "You made a little mess of your last meal."

Merrick wiped his hand across his jaw and chin, peering down and snickering at the blood smeared across it. "Ah, yes, that." He ran his tongue along his hand, eyeing an unfazed Tressa as he swallowed and moaned. "My detour got a tad outta hand."

"And you didn't bother to clean up before coming to see me? How gracious of you."

"Well, Tressa dear," he teased, "I was so eager to see ya that I forgot my manners. I do apologize fer my manky appearance."

Tressa rose to her feet and removed a washcloth from her nightstand drawer. Crossing the room, she grabbed a vase filled with fresh wildflowers and poured some of the water from it, wetting the rag.

"Here." She handed him the washcloth. "Clean yourself up."

Merrick frowned at it, arrogance and humor pulling at his expression. "You want me to wash my face with flower water?"

"It'll make you smell better," she said mockingly with a smile.

"If you insist." Merrick began wiping his face and neck. "So, where is everyone?"

Tressa returned to her chair and crossed her legs, majestic and beautiful. "Well, Niko and Theseus should be nearby."

"I meant where are my men and all the others? It's uncharacteristically quiet 'round here."

Her voice grew tight and sharp. "Well, Merrick, if you'd let me finish."

"My apologies," he said with faux sincerity. "Continue."

"Thank you. So, a lot of those on this side left shortly after you did. Well, most of the vampires did. A few remain, though, or have since returned. But it's been pretty quiet around here lately. At least in the castle."

"And the others?"

"Most of the ones in the caves are still there, hiding out like always. Gastell is in the forest as far as I know. I haven't even seen him since they all returned all those months ago. Haydrin should be back in his room shortly. And I believe Lucas is in his, probably brooding. Plotting. But most likely sulking."

"Lucas has returned already?"

"Yes, he was only gone for two months."

"Why did he return so soon?"

Tressa rolled her eyes and sighed. "I will give you one guess."

Merrick scoffed and tossed the bloody rag in a basket next to Tressa. "What is his fascination with her? If he were a vampire, I could understand it. But other than her blood, there's nothin' particularly special about her."

Tressa let out a breathy sigh, lowering her eyes to the ground and folding her arms.

Merrick slipped his hands into his leather jacket and gave her a judgmental arch of a brow. "Do ya have somethin' to add, Tressa dear? If so, then please, by all means, speak your mind."

"No," Tressa said unconvincingly. "I have nothing to add."

"Hmm. I highly doubt that." Merrick fixed on her dark brown eyes, pausing and analyzing her. "And what exactly is *your* fascination with her?"

Her voice was bitter when she answered, "Absolutely nothing."

Merrick did not remove his gaze as he leaned against one of her bedposts, the casual posture inviting. "You've always been a terrible liar."

"It's just . . ." she continued sternly. "She's a Fire Witch. And you still need fire magic. You need her. She's extremely vital and special, and you need her magic. Having all four elemental powers is the only way you will outsmart the damn prophecy and gain the amount of power you want. Remember? Or did you forget that tiny bit of information? And she's the only one we have found since her mother."

"Ah, yes, fire magic." Merrick scratched his short beard nonchalantly, his voice relaxed. "The remainin' kink in this magical plan. A plan which could've ended long ago if Keya hadn't gone and gotten herself killed in a fire. A tad ironic, if ya ask me." He began strolling around the room, his hands still in his pockets. "You mentioned Haydrin and Lucas, but what about Leif? Has he returned?"

"Not that I'm aware of. I heard he had planned to return tonight as well, but I have not seen or heard from him in months."

"Oh." Merrick faced her, his brow flicking upward in a contemplative arch. "I see. Well, I'm sure if that's what he was plannin', and he's not back yet, he will be here shortly." He made his way toward the door. "I will be retreatin' to my chambers now. It's been yonks since I had a proper bath and an adequate night's rest, so I will be takin' the remainder of the mornin' and afternoon to make up fer that. Then, this evenin', I will meet ya after supper to discuss things further. I expect Lucas and Leif to be in attendance to discuss a few things." He winked at her. "Enjoy the rest of your evenin'. Or should I say mornin'?"

"Merrick?" Tressa strolled over to him and lazily crossed her arms. "What happened when you returned? Whose blood was on your face?"

Merrick grinned superficially, the malevolent expression filled with delight. "Don't worry so much, Tressa."

"Did you kill someone?"

"Not tonight. In fact, I handled myself like the true gentleman I am. You should be quite proud of me."

She unfolded her arms, and they slacked at her sides, the anticipation for him to continue lining her face. "Oh?"

"Aye." He paused, giving her a devious smirk. "I had the pleasure of indulgin' in a wee snack after returnin' home."

Curiosity rose as she stood tall. "Which one?"

"The girl."

"And?"

"And," he breathed, heading for the door and pausing, "they aren't ready. Not quite. But I am pleased to announce a rather brilliant move on my part with the Fire Witch."

"Karramis?" Excitement flashed in her dark eyes.

"Aye."

"Meaning what?"

"Oh, don't worry, you will learn soon enough."

"Why?" She watched him, analyzing the gleam in his eyes. "Why did you go there tonight?"

His gaze locked on her as a slow, callous, and purely arrogant grin graced his handsome and ridiculously charming face. "I simply wanted to assess my property and ascertain the extent of what I will soon be up against. I needed to evaluate the magnitude of their developed abilities."

"So," she said, drawing out the word with an approaching sarcastic response, "you went there to taunt them?"

There was a twist against his lips. "I would never. I was just bein' meticulous with how I would go forth with my plan. Plus, it is rather impolite of me not to properly introduce myself to those I plan to murder. I was merely tryin' to be respectful, my sweet Tressa. I do believe my actions were quite necessary and utterly righteous. Liberatin' even—to both parties. I was very civil. At first."

She crossed her arms, drumming her fingers against her silk-clad biceps. "So, you went there to taunt them."

He gave her a quick smirk as he cocked his head with a shrug of agreement. "Rightly so." Walking under the threshold, he paused outside the door and faced her. "Oh, one more thing. Is the Keep stocked?"

"Yes," Tressa said with a nod. "Lucas and Niko made sure of it."

"Perfect. Well then, I bid you good evenin'." He bent at the waist and bowed, his eyes never leaving hers. "Pleasant dreams."

As Merrick strolled away, Tressa closed the door.

Chapter 10

The east side of the castle lacked the beauty of the west wing. Dark gray stones of various sizes lined the floor and walls of the hallways while smooth gray slabs covered the ceiling and formed a rounded arch along the top. Black-and-silver metal sconces protruded from the walls, each holding a red pillar candle with wax pooling down the sides. Most of the halls lacked windows. Darkness crept beyond the flickering candlelight, the shadows like ghosts dancing along the walls.

One corridor narrowed and twisted, leading to a dreary and dank hallway on the easternmost side of the castle. Moonlight peered through the floor-to-ceiling Gothic-style frames with dirty old glass panes, the glow casting translucent streams of soft white beams along the cold, dusty stones. Large boulder-sized, rectangular carved archways bordered two enormous wooden doors with old bronze handles at the end of the long shadowy passage, the larger of the two thresholds resting at the end of the deserted hallway.

The room beyond the enormous oak door was dark, the moonlight trapped behind the thick red velvet curtains draped along the full expanse of one wall. Fire flickered through another arched doorway, the bright orange glow glinting across the lighter stone walls.

A single set of footsteps advanced on the other side of the door as heels clanked against the stone floor with gentle dexterity.

"You may enter," Merrick called before a knock sounded as the footfalls slowed beyond the slightly ajar door.

Squeaking hinges filled the room as Tressa entered, her deep black hair tucked behind her ears and resting flatly along her back as she swayed forward with grace.

The huge room of crimson, black, and silver was fit for a king. A fireplace was located along one side, and two cathedral-style windows with Gothic arches and crystalline diamond-etched panes sat on either side of it. The hearth reached halfway up to the vaulted ceiling and was framed with a mixture of polished black marble and slate-gray granite, beautifully decorated with swirls carved along the mantel. A large bed with a dark mahogany headboard and draped with a crimson comforter was situated a few feet from the fireplace. Bright red candles flickered throughout the room, fully illuminating it from the darkness as a round, unlit, wood and iron chandelier hung from the ceiling.

Leaning against the dark wooden headboard with bronze studs-lining the black embroidered cushion, Merrick sat, bare chested and covered up, reading. His gaze fixed with careful consideration as he licked his finger and turned the page of the leather-bound book in his hand.

Taken aback as her black skirt glided from the stone floor onto the scarlet rug, Tressa announced with a quirk of her lips, "You're reading."

Not peering up from his book, Merrick replied smoothly, "Am I not permitted to read?"

"Of course you are." Delight brightened her features. "It's just, I haven't seen you read in . . ." She paused. "Actually, come to think of it, I can't even remember the last time I saw you reading."

Merrick's gaze stayed on his book, but she could hear the smile as he spoke. "Aye, it has been a while since I've been able to fully appreciate and savor a thrillin' tale." Gently closing the book, he met her approving gaze. "It would seem your plan to get rid of me worked."

Wearing a violet tunic fitted beneath a black leather corset, Tressa strolled over to him, every sway of her curves making her skirt swish with gentle ease. "There was nothing strategic about it. You obviously needed a break from things to clear your head, and I simply suggested it. There was no selfish planning or anything calculating or beneficial on my part."

"As I've said before, my sweet Tressa, you are a terrible liar."

"Am I early?" she asked, abruptly changing the subject.

Merrick monitored her teasingly, the light blue of his eyes almost gray in the flickering light. "No, you are right on time actually. Did ya notify Lucas?"

"I did."

Merrick laid the book on the table next to the bed. "And what about Leif?"

"Neither Lucas nor I have seen him yet."

Merrick slid his legs out from under the red silk comforter and rose to his feet, completely naked. His lean, powerful figure was taut and pale, every inch of him showing just how formidable he could be. Reaching a black silken robe draped at the foot of his bed, he wrapped it around himself, tying it loosely around his waist. "I'm sure he will be here shortly."

Tressa admired him as a knock came from the main door just outside his bedroom. She blinked and twisted as footsteps moved closer.

Leif appeared in the threshold and leaned against the doorframe with his arms folded, his casual stance matching his smooth, mellow tone. "Apologies for my delay. I was held up."

There was a gleam of amusement in his expression, a teasing taunt Tressa knew all too well, but she ignored it.

"With what?" she asked, facing him fully.

Leif turned his attention to Merrick, his features tightening as irritation laced his response. "It would seem the portals have shifted again, and I ended up in werewolf territory. Now, what the portals are doing there, I have no damn clue. But I had to spend most of the fuckin' night evading the wrath of those ruthless, vicious beasts."

Tressa pressed her lips together, trying to hold back the laughter bubbling in her chest as she said to herself, "Ironic, coming from you."

Leif rotated his blue eyes to her with a challenging glare. "Pardon?"

Tressa shrugged and gave him a quick playful flick of her brow.

Prowling forward, Leif stopped inches away and towered over her, their gazes searing into each other. "No, please. Enlighten us."

Tressa studied him before grinning. "It's nothing. I just find it rather interesting you like to refer to them as ruthless and vicious when you are just as much a beast as they are." She stood, her chest pressing into him. "Maybe even worse."

Merrick sat in a chair next to the fireplace, leaning back and resting his elbows on the armrests as he interlocked his fingers. He angled his head and grinned.

"Yes," Leif drawled, low and sensual, "but unlike them . . ." He forced himself into her, driving their bodies closer together, but she remained unmoving. "Unlike them, I can control every aspect of my ruthless and vicious acts." He let out a low growl, the rumble deep in his chest. "And I have to say, I quite enjoy being bad."

There was no denying it, Leif was attempting to get under her skin. Entice her. Provoke her. Give her a reason to accept his not-so-subtle invitation.

Playing along, she gave him a brief wicked grin. "What's the matter, Leif? Not enough fun while you were away? You really should do something about that before it starts influencing your mood."

"Enough," Merrick said with a bored sigh, rising from the chair and heading toward his bedroom door. "You two are extremely monotonous, not at all as stimulatin' as you once were, so take your outlandish antics someplace else."

"Ha!" Leif blurted with a chuckle, giving Tressa a quick lethal glare as he brushed past her. "It seems you might be forgetting your salacious appetite for easing your own tension, Merrick."

"Oh, I haven't forgotten. In fact, both my appetites were quenched quite a bit while I was away."

"Well, that explains the return of the old Merrick and the incredibly good mood. So, what did you enjoy more of?"

Merrick grinned, malicious and arrogant. "Both. And quite often. First, I, of course, had to quench the pleasures of the beast. Ya know, to help control myself. I didn't want to kill anyone in the middle of anythin' important. That really would've put a damper on things. But then came the fun part—the desires of the man. That raw, biological need. My, how I've missed an endless source of food and women. I almost forgot how much I enjoy the human realm. The women there now are far more vulnerable and less inclined to say no. Not to mention, they are very . . . adventurous."

Tressa placed her hands on her hips. "I thought you didn't approve of easy women."

"I do not enjoy when one is actin' a maggot. And I most certainly do not approve of me bein' the prey of some utterly obnoxious woman. However, I do rather enjoy it when my prey submits when they are hunted."

"Gross. Must we really refer to it in that way? I'm not sure any woman would like being called prey or that they are being hunted. That's not at all arousing."

"You asked," Merrick teased with a sidelong grin.

"Yes, but now I regret it. May we please change the subject to anything else?"

Leif gave her a tauntingly low laugh. "Look who has her panties in a twist. A little lonely while we were all away, Tressa?"

"You know, I do have more self-control than you spineless, sex-addled brutes."

"No, you don't," Merrick and Leif said together, both smirking.

With a bite in her question, she asked, "Could we focus please? We're getting extremely off topic." Looking over at Merrick, she continued, "What the hell happened last night at Karramis's place?"

Merrick's humorous tone faltered, turning casual but serious as he said, "First, I would really like to know what Lucas has been up to this whole time. And since I can hear him comin', I think we should continue this once he is here."

Lucas knocked and entered the room, quickly narrowing his eyebrows as the others gaped at him, still and quiet. "Why the hell is everyone starin' at me like that?"

"Well," Tressa said with a haughty tone, heading over to the table with a chessboard set up at the far corner of the room, "it seems someone else is also wound a little tight these days."

"Piss off, Tressa," Lucas replied with mock irritation as he joined her, moving a white pawn across the board one space.

"What," Leif said to Lucas, matching his faux response, "you're not going to welcome me home? Did you not miss me while I was away? Or did your incessant obsession leave you even more bitter?"

Lucas tossed Leif a sneer over his shoulder. "You're a real dick, ya know that?"

"Why, yes, I—"

"Rhetorical question, mate."

Merrick cleared his throat as a smile tugged on his lips. "Lucas, any updates?"

"Yes, sir," he answered, straight to the point, contemplating his next move as Tressa slid a black pawn two spaces toward him. "It would seem both the children have been residin' within the boundaries of Stoweward and Caerwyn Village. The boy appears to be livin' most of his time in Stoweward, and based on some things I discovered, he's livin' with Pavian."

"Discovered?"

"Yes. Pavian has been trainin' him outside the wards, so I've been able to sense and track both of 'em quite often."

"And?"

He moved again, sliding another pawn two spaces forward. "And from what I can gatha', the boy is really startin' to come into some of his powers. But since I can't get into his head, I can't tell ya what kind of powers he has exactly. Pavian, on the otha' hand, tends to leave his mind wide-open when trainin' him, so I do know the boy has elemental magic. Air to be more precise. I also believe the boy might be able to astral project. And his Guardian magic might be surfacin'. At least Pavian thinks it might be."

"Interestin'," Merrick said as he sat down on a throne-like black leather chair raised on a dais in the back of the stone room. "Anythin' else?"

Lucas blinked in awe as Tressa moved her queen, placing him in checkmate.

Merrick drummed his fingers against the armrest, the two sides of his robe sliding between his legs as he slacked in the chair. "Lucas?"

"Yes," Lucas acknowledged with a bemused glance over at Tressa before rising to his feet, "the boy has also been trainin' with weapons, and he's really gettin' good."

"I do not see that as a threat of any kind," Merrick declared, unimpressed, relaxing even deeper into the chair as Leif came up beside him, standing between Merrick and the decorative partition with a black silk robe thrown over the top. "It's simply a fool's game to think weapons can stop me. Somethin' I'm sure they are fully aware of by now." He waved dismissively. "Anyway, continue."

Lucas strolled over to the foot of the dais. "The girl, on the otha' hand, I know nothin' about. She has remained hidden inside the village this whole time. I believe she is stayin' with Kavana, but I can't confirm. She could be stayin' with Zarrius, though, or someone else. I have only sensed her out a few times, but again, I can't read her mind, so I don't know what kind of powers she has. If she does have 'em, then she neva' uses 'em, as far as I can tell."

"Well, we know she has them," Leif added, "because we saw them, and Haydrin suffered some major burns at the hands of those powers."

"Yes," Lucas agreed with a nod, "she does have fire magic like Karramis, but to what extent, I'm not sure. And otha' than that, I think she might have Drolnogard powers."

A twitch quirked at the corner of Merrick's mouth. "What makes ya think that?"

"The few times I did sense and track her, she was with one or more of the dragons."

"Interestin'." There was a hint of sarcasm in Merrick's voice. "And what about Will?"

Lucas cringed, and his tone tightened. "He has been stayin' at their home with Karramis in Kitra Forest."

"And?"

"And nothin', sir. I can't read Karramis's mind—she has me blocked out still."

"What about Will? Have you not been readin' his mind?"

A low growl rumbled in Lucas's chest, a sound he was unable to control as anger raced across his face, his jaw clenching.

"Oh my, it would seem I've hit a nerve." Merrick glanced over at Leif. "Somethin' I should know?"

Lifting his shoulders, Leif said, "Other than the usual? No clue."

Sighing, Tressa explained, "It would seem Lucas tracked Will and read his thoughts during a rather . . . inopportune moment."

Silence fell before Merrick signaled with his hand for her to continue.

"With Karramis, that is."

Merrick's face flashed with slight amusement. "Really?"

"Yes," Lucas answered, a hostile tone biting the word. "And since then, I refuse to try again. I simply just sense and track 'em to make sure they're still there."

"Is that so?" Leif challenged with a taunting quirk of his brow.

Lucas remained quiet.

Merrick's eyes remained unblinking. "Is that all?"

"Well, not entirely," Lucas admitted, throwing a scowl over at Leif.

"Oh?" Curiosity lined Merrick's simple inquiry.

Lucas hesitated. "Well, I've been trackin' Karramis for months now, sensin' her and followin' her movements, who she's with, and what she's been doin'."

"So," Leif prodded, "you've been stalking her?"

"I haven't been stalkin' her," Lucas corrected with clenched fists. "I've been keepin' an eye on her."

"That's called stalking, Lucas."

With a disgruntled glare at the smirking vampire, Lucas countered, "Do ya have a daily quota of how often ya need to be a complete and utter cunt? Because it sure as fuck seems like it lately."

"Here we go," Tressa mumbled to herself before leaning back in the wooden chair across the room and crossing her arms and legs. "Not this shit again."

Merrick leaned against the other armrest and grinned at her, lowering his voice. "My bet is on Leif throwin' the first punch."

"Really?" Tressa frowned disapprovingly. "Can we please focus here? I'd like to get back to my room at some point this evening."

"Expecting a visitor tonight, Tressa?" Leif asked over Lucas's shoulder with a curious arching brow.

Tressa's face and tone remained composed when she replied, "I'm curious, is your obsession with sex merely a vampire thing or a man thing?"

"Both," Leif and Merrick answered without missing a beat.

Tressa shot her annoyed scowl between them, a lively undertone rising with a smirk. "Do you two think about anything else?"

"No," they said together, both grinning.

"Well," Merrick added, "except eatin', of course."

"You two are disgusting, you know that?" Tressa rolled her eyes and settled her gaze on Lucas, her attempt at not entertaining their childish antics proving harder to fight against as her tone continued to carry an amused cadence. "Do you have anything else to tell us?"

"No," Lucas replied seriously, angling his head in her direction. There was a sadness in his eyes, an emptiness that had only seemed to grow over the last few months. "Not at this time."

"Tell me, Lucas," Merrick said, leaning against his upper legs, "are you happy?" A genuinely sincere question.

Lucas flinched, surprised. "Excuse me?"

"Are you happy?" Merrick repeated, rising to his feet and stepping off the dais as he tugged one side of his robe tighter across his chest.

After a moment, Lucas finally said, "I don't really see how that is relevant."

A cold speculating glare flashed within Merrick's pale blue eyes, void of all emotions. "Just answer the question, Mr. Fraye."

"No," Lucas answered flatly.

"And what would make you happy? Or, should I ask, *who* would make you happy?"

"Ya may ask both, sir."

"Ah, there are those manners again. Right then. So, what and who would make you happy? Though I do believe I already know the answers."

"Then why are ya askin'?" Lucas challenged timidly.

Merrick angled his head and watched Lucas for a moment. "Because I want to hear it from your mouth. I want to see the hate and anger burn in your eyes. I want the pain in your voice to rage. I want that nervous, frightful coward lingerin' just beneath your skin to coil up and die. And I want the assertive, persistent, ruthless, and insufferable Lucas back. The one who would stop at nothin' to get what he wants. The Lucas who arrived on my doorstep willin' to do whatever was necessary to take what he deemed his. The guy who believed the love he possessed was reciprocated but stolen from him. I want that Lucas back. Not this man standin' in front of me. The one who is now afraid of me—the friend who took ya in when no one else wanted you."

Lucas squared his shoulders. "I'm not afraid of ya, Merrick."

"Lies." Merrick gave a cruel chuckle under his breath. "I can see it written all over your face. It has been like that since the minute you saw Camille dead." He began circling around Lucas. "But I am not a monster. I have never once hurt you or left ya unprotected in this castle." He gestured a hand at Tressa and Leif. "We are your family, and we care about you and your happiness. And I want nothin' more than to keep my word to you." With a booming clap, Merrick added with a cheery tone, "And with that beautiful display of emotion, I have some news."

Tressa sat up straight in her chair. "Good news or bad news?"

"Well, it would depend on who ya ask." Merrick continued his casual stroll around the room, his tone and features delighted. "Last night I made a wee visit to some unsuspectin' individuals and can confirm that the boy definitely has some of his powers. But the girl was so terrified of me, all her magic seemed to have evaded her completely. Not even a flicker. Well, maybe something, but not enough to deem her worthy just yet. I have to admit, though, I was a bit disappointed but also a tad exhilarated. I was hopin' to get a gander of her marvelous powers that injured our poor Haydrin, but the fear seepin' from her was so stimulatin'."

"She didn't show any signs of magic?" Leif asked, sitting down on the edge of the dais, leaning back nonchalantly and outstretching his legs.

Merrick shook his head. "Not really."

"But the boy did?"

"Yes. And I do believe, in addition to air powers, he may also have earth magic."

"Really?" Tressa pressed eagerly.

"I got a front row view of Karramis's powers as well."

Tressa rose to her feet. "Her fire magic?"

"Nah," Merrick said, shaking his head. "Her portal actually. I didn't notice any of those fire abilities whilst I was there." He faced Lucas and Leif. "Are ya certain she has 'em? Only you two have seen her use her powers before."

"Yes," Leif answered. "Both she and the girl used them that night a few months ago. But Karramis didn't create it, she only manipulated it."

"She has before, though," Lucas corrected. "At the château afta' she woke up."

"Right," Leif said, drawing out the word. "The night of her infamous escape."

"Shut up," Lucas demanded through his teeth.

With a sharp tone, Merrick continued, "Would you two please shut your beaks? Back to my point, if I may. Well, after a wee debacle with my hunger, not to mention my inner demon decidin' to rear its ugly head, I ended the night by makin' a very interestin' deal with Karramis."

"What kind of deal?" Lucas asked, eager and nervous.

"The exact details I will keep to myself fer now. But I will say this . . ." His gaze focused on Lucas. "By the end of the year, you may just have one thing you've been wantin' fer quite some time. That is, of course, if ya deem to accept it."

"What does that mean exactly?"

"Karramis has offered herself up in exchange fer me allowin' her children more time to prepare their magic."

Tressa narrowed her eyes. "Why would you allow that?"

"It would seem, Tressa dear, that your suggestion to take a break from everythin' really helped clear my mind and allowed me time to strategize and concoct a plan movin' forward. And so, that is what I'm doin'."

"Are you going to share it with us?"

"Nah," Merrick said simply. "You will be filled in when I see fit."

"And why's that?"

Merrick cocked his head, the delight in his gaze flickering. "Because I do not feel inclined to do so at the moment. Do ya have a problem with that?"

"No," she said with a deep sigh.

"Pardon?"

She crossed her arms, but her voice was soft and submissive. "No, Merrick."

Merrick flicked his wrist. "I'm finished with you all. You're dismissed."

Lucas, Leif, and Tressa headed for the door.

"Oh, one more thing," Merrick called after them.

They all rotated and faced him.

Merrick's eyes shifted between Tressa and Leif. "I'm finished with you two. Dismissed." He pointed to Lucas. "You, stay."

Tressa gave Merrick a quick glance before closing the door behind her. Silence filled the room as footsteps retreated down the hallway.

Merrick pointed at the table with the chessboard on it in the corner of the room. "Sit."

Hope gleamed in Lucas's eyes. "Do ya really believe she will give herself ova' to ya?"

"If she truly values her family's lives, then she will." Remaining standing, Merrick towered over Lucas. "But I need to know somethin' first. Somethin' that will help me when the time comes to retrieve my end of the deal."

"I'll help in any way I can."

"Good." Merrick took in Lucas's arrogant and determined expression. "Ah, there's the Lucas I've grown so fond of. Welcome back. Now then, I need to know what happened between you and her in France."

Lucas waited for him to continue, confusion pulling at his brows.

Merrick leaned over and placed his hands on either side of Lucas's chair, the wood creaking as he pressed into the arms and lowered his voice, the deep demand nearly predatory. "I need to know exactly how she escaped at Château Rouge."

Chapter 11

Château Rouge

Eleven months ago
Mid-January

Her time was running out. If Karramis was going to go through with her plan to escape, she would have to do it now. Leif would be back soon, and she could not outmaneuver both of them. And there was no telling if her plan would even work. It had been too long without using her powers willingly, and she was already too weak.

But maybe she did not have to. Maybe she did not have to commit to the extremes of her initial plan, the one where she would end up in pain and danger. The one where she would have to manipulate him into a fit of rage just to force her magic to rise to the surface. Maybe she could convince Lucas, the friend she once deeply cared for, to let her go—using their past and friendship and the love they had once had for each other long ago to keep him distracted while she focused on her powers. She may have been weak, but her abilities had always been powerful—in more control over her than the other way around. Maybe Karramis could simply talk to him and gauge the situation without needing to suffer any additional damage to her already bruised and bloody body.

It was worth a shot.

Her thighs burned as she shifted her weight forward off the wooden table situated on one side of the pristine stone room. The pain along her side throbbed perfectly in sync with her heartbeat, vigorous but steady. She was not sure what hurt more, the dull sting deep within her gut from the blow to her stomach Leif had inflicted or the searing agony of the cauterized stab wound rubbing against the fresh wetness of her bloody nightgown. She halted as her weight pressed into the granite tiles, the soles of her bare feet sticky against the floor. Her knees trembled, and she leaned into the table. She was too weak. Her poor body had not only suffered more damage since waking up, but it had also been immobile for the last eight years. Despite the comatose state being magically induced, it still seemed to have taken a toll on her ability to move normally.

She concentrated on her breathing, the stabbing ache pinching with each slow exhalation as she drove the weakness in her muscles deeper and deeper into submission. Scanning the room, she strategically plotted her exit, just in case her plan did not work, being mindful of her thoughts as she analyzed the best tactic for her escape.

"Why?" Lucas asked, taking another step closer, the smell of him—a mix of bergamot and rich amber—masking the coppery tang filling the air.

Blood. It was her blood smeared along the floor at her feet and across the top of the table. Both old and new, another reminder of the dangerous situation she was in.

Karramis blinked, remembering they were in the middle of a conversation. "Why what?"

"Why should ya be dead?" A genuine curiosity lined his features and tone as his eyes remained engrossed in her deep chocolate gaze.

Karramis reached into her mind, searching for the words she had spoken moments ago. The memory fluttered to life, her part of the conversation echoing silently in her thoughts: *When they sealed the portals, they trapped my powers. When it was supposed to be released from the necklace, it was meant to go back into the island, but it didn't, and I don't know why. And I have no idea how I am alive. I mean, I should be dead right now.*

"Oh," Karramis said, trying desperately not to move as she willed strength into her legs, "because I removed my magic that night."

The wooden shelves in front of her were empty—only candles adorned the mahogany mantelpiece. With the wine cellar to her left and the bookshelf containing old leather-bound classic novels next to the table to her right, it was clear this room had once been used for leisure rather than housing the lifeless body of an undead witch. Twisted metal posts and dark polished wooden steps rose upward to her left, disappearing into the ceiling. A nook sat in the corner of the room on the other side of the stairs, decorated with a leather chaise lounge, a tall bronze lamp, and the small table with Camille's empty bottle of wine. Three narrow horizontal windows rested along the top of the wall above the shelves across the room, the bottom of the panes level with the brown grass outside. Lacking any latches, the windows were useless. But even if they could open, they were too small for Karramis to crawl through.

The room was large, even more so since the center lacked any furniture. Four chairs were stacked together against the wall in between the table and the door to the cellar, an indicator the piece of furniture she had rested on for eight years may have been the focal point of this underground room. But even with the massive area, many of the locations were problematic for opening a portal. No matter where Karramis summoned one of her doorways, Lucas would still be within a short distance of it, allowing him to follow her through. She had to put space between them and give herself sufficient room to create the portal and move through it with plenty of time for it to close behind her. She needed to figure out a way to distract him long enough to accomplish her task and focus.

Lucas sauntered closer with his head cocked, stopping inches from her slackened body as she leaned against the table, his eyes focusing on her wandering gaze. "What are ya thinkin' about, love?"

Karramis whipped her attention over to him. Irritation burned in his eyes as she continued blocking him out. At least one of her strengths remained. Though not magical, it was still comforting to know her weakened state had not rendered her completely useless.

Angering Lucas was the easiest part of the original plan, something she had learned over the years with his tendency to overreact when things did not go his way. However, the consequences following that initial plan would leave her physical state weaker than she already was, thus making her mental strength to control her magic even harder to utilize. Karramis was afraid she would never be able to overpower him or have the strength to fight back if she suffered any more physical damage. She could only endure so much before every part of her would just give up and quit fighting. So, she would stick to her second plan first—keep him talking and treat him like a friend, not her enemy.

Karramis cracked a side grin, and a comical tone lined her words. "I'm thinking about how I ended up living a life that is stuck in a perpetual cycle of horrible tropes."

A moment passed before Lucas laughed, a genuine laugh, remembering her love of books. "How so?"

"Well, let's see . . ." She lifted a finger, counting each item she listed with one hand while the other remained on the table. "Fated destiny, sheltered childhood, dead mother, overbearing father, the *chosen* one . . ." Pausing, she chuckled as her calm tone shifted into a theatrical cadence. "Oh! And rare magic unlike any other, nearly dying but is miraculously saved, a surprise pregnancy, a fake death, sacrificed herself for her loved ones, and now I'm freakin' Sleeping Beauty with a strange resurrection story."

Laughing again, he said with pure hope in his voice, "Maybe you'll get a friends-to-lovers endin'." The words seemed to spew out without his control. "A happy endin' afta' all."

Karramis tensed, and she dropped her gaze to the floor, not wanting him to see the uncomfortable expression on her face as she quickly changed the subject, her voice kind, soft. "What happened to you, Lucas?"

He gave her a quizzical look as contemplation etched in his features. "What do ya mean?"

"What's wrong with you?" Sympathy seeped from her expression, but caution rattled in her gut as the too-sharp question echoed in her head. A poor choice of words. Hurrying to rectify her mistake, she asked carefully, "Why do you hate me so much now?"

"I don't hate ya," Lucas declared sincerely, his cerulean eyes begging for understanding. "I've neva' hated ya, love."

"Then why? Why do all of this?"

His posture relaxed as he placed his hands into the pockets of his pants, the confidence radiating from him mixing with a genuine vulnerability. "Ya told me I could have anythin' I wanted if I truly put my mind to it and if I believed I could have it. And I wanted you. I still want ya. And ya even said I could have ya. Once. Ya even kissed me afta' ya said it."

Memories flashed in Karramis's mind from when she was a little girl. She leaned against the table, her legs weak and shaking beneath her as she pulled that memory to the surface. Her stomach twisted into knots. Lucas had seriously been holding on to her words for all these years, thinking an innocent statement and unabashed first kiss was some kind of binding force making his childhood claim to her an excuse for his actions for all these years.

Karramis blinked up at him, his eyes never faltering as she observed the seriousness filling his gaze. "Lucas . . ." She had to be very careful how she continued. "That was so long ago. We were just kids. I didn't think you were even serious."

He narrowed his eyes as hurt sparked through them. "Well, I was."

"How was I supposed to know that?" A hum of sadness whirred deep inside her gut. A feeling of regret for hurting him—for not believing he would take their innocent actions and hold tight to it for all these years. "I was ten. I never knew you actually wanted to be with me. I thought it was a joke. You know, to help distract me from all the shit I was going through."

"I told ya I loved ya," Lucas said, pulling his hands from his pockets and leaning into her, his arms bracing the sides of the table behind her.

She held back a wince as his body pressed into her, the pain of him shifting her weight more intolerable than his closeness. "Yeah, but years later." There was still kindness in her voice, but it was pinched behind her clenched jaw as she bit back the discomfort. "And by then I didn't see you that way. You told me way past the point of no return. I just didn't see you that way."

"But I neva' stopped lovin' ya."

"Then why did you wait so long to tell me?"

His eyes dropped to her lips, his voice low and deep. "I thought ya knew."

Karramis noticed the shift in his voice, his attention, but she did not react. They were talking, albeit with a bit of tension oozing from him, but they were still talking. Not arguing. Not fighting. But discussing this like civilized people. Like friends even. Well, maybe not entirely like friends, but that was beside the point. He was Lucas, the gleam in his eyes like the friend she had grown up with, just with an uncomfortable yearning lingering behind them.

Wanting to retreat out of his trapped stance, she gently—very gently—and almost playfully eased him back. "Well, you're stupid for thinking that." She smothered the jab of pain shooting along her side and straight into her legs. "You tell me you want to marry me when you're twelve, we share a kiss, and then never speak of it again. Then, after years and years of nothing, you tell me you love me, expecting this spark of love to bloom suddenly, but it doesn't work like that, Lucas. It couldn't happen because you had become my best friend, someone I didn't see romantically. I had already moved on from the idea of something more."

His eyes locked on hers, wide and beaming with realization as he absorbed the honesty clinging to her final words. "Are ya sayin' . . . that ya felt somethin' for me once?"

The question hit her like a ton of bricks, and a twinge of regret rattled in her chest from her stupid, unfiltered honesty, mixing with utter shame and frustration. *Shit.*

This was not something she wanted to discuss—not a topic she had ever wanted to bring up. Especially with him. Because she had felt something for him once. A long time ago. Something she had never told anyone before, aside from Will after the first time Lucas had laid a hand on her. Not even Kavana or her other best friends, Tiffasa and Avery, knew about her feelings.

Karramis had started to see Lucas as something potentially more than just her best friend years before Will had come into the picture. But Lucas had been eighteen and never showed any interest in her—other than the one conversation when they were younger. She had always thought her average and less-than-perfect features and body had deterred him from seeing her as more than a friend, especially since he had a salacious appetite for the opposite sex and never once made a move on her.

"It was a long time ago," Karramis told him, trying to avoid the conversation.

"Tell me," he pleaded kindly.

She took a deep breath before letting it out with a long drawn-out sigh. "Fine. Yes, at one time, for a brief moment, I saw you differently. I wanted there to be something more. But it didn't last long, and I had moved on from it without giving it even a second thought. And you simply became the guy I loved like a brother, yet again. But one who could never be more than that."

"Why?" Lucas asked, a grasp of hope surrounding the question.

This was not the time or place for this right now. She had allowed the conversation to veer way off track. Karramis had to get back to the main reason for this discussion. She needed to find a way out of here, and she was wasting time. But luckily, the second plan was working, and now maybe he would find it in his heart to forgive her and let her leave without any problems and, to her pleading and aching body's hopefulness, without any more pain.

Reaching out a hand, Karramis gently stroked his arm, the dry blood on her hand making her fingers feel rough. "Please, Lucas, let the past stay in the past. We can forgive and forget. Let the years of fighting stop between us. Please just let me go. Let me go home."

Lucas did not move away from her embrace when he asked bitterly, "To him?"

"To my family," she corrected cautiously.

"No," he declared plainly, the word sharp as he slid his arm out from under her hand. "Ya will stay here with me." He grasped her face a little too tightly, and she flinched, startled by his catlike reflexes as his hand cupped her jaw. "I agree, I don't wanna fight anymore. I want us to be together. We can make this work, love." He leaned in as if to kiss her. "I love you."

Karramis let out a derisive snort, a sound she had not meant to make, as she pulled away from him, balancing herself and clutching the table, but his hand remained on her cheek. "And do what?" Irritation bloomed, and her knees buckled, a jolt of pain streaking across her face. "Play house?"

Lucas spotted her discomfort. "Would ya sit down before ya hurt yourself?" He coaxed her backside deeper into the table as he clutched her waist with both hands, the curves of her sides soft under his grasp.

"I don't want to sit. I want to go home."

"Too bad." He lifted her with gentle ease and placed her on the table, his hands remaining on her as he slid her back. "Sit." An unyielding command. "You aren't goin' anywhere." He lowered his head evenly with hers, his gaze fixed and his tone uncomfortably powerful. "If ya would just give me a chance, I can show ya I'm just as good as he is."

The gleam of dominance and determination in his eyes settled in her core. Lucas was not going to let her go, no matter how much she begged. He was dead set on keeping her. Now, whether it was for his own pleasure entirely or for eventually giving her to Merrick, she did not know. Being his friend again and simply asking to leave was no longer an option. He was going to keep her hostage until she either gave in to him or until they could figure out a way to use her portal and return to Kiluemar.

It seemed her first plan was starting to take shape again. She would have to fight instead. And if she was going to do it, she had to do it now, before Leif returned or something else got in her way.

It was now or never.

Karramis was hopeful her two strongest abilities would appear soon after the plan was set in motion, giving her enough power to escape before it was too late. But first she would have to use his love and obsession for her to distract him from her ultimate goal. She had to make him mad enough that he would focus his attention on his anger toward her and not the truth behind why she was playing out these actions. She would have to do the one thing Leif had warned him about—her ability to play off his emotions.

She inhaled, her chest inflating noticeably before she exhaled in a slow release. "Not possible." She swallowed and blinked slowly, preparing herself for what would soon follow after she lowered her inner walls and allowed her thoughts to flow loud and clear. *"He will never be as good as Will."*

Lucas's expression tightened, and his body stiffened as he leaned against her, the weight of him crushing the backs of her legs against the table. The hurried breath coming from his partially opened mouth was warm as it blew her wild strands of unkempt waves. He dug his hips harder and forced her legs apart, pressing himself against the table as she slid back. Gripping the backs of her knees just under the hem of her nightgown, he pulled her to a stop and yanked her forward. He angled his head closer to her face, and she tilted herself away from him.

There was a low rumble in his chest, a savage and ravenous noise. "Are ya tryin' to make me jealous, love?" He gripped her hand as she placed it on his chest, the attempt to shove him away hindered. "Or are ya just tryin' to piss me off?"

Karramis winced as he squeezed her hand. "What's the difference?" She tried to slide away from him, struggling through the pain when he refused to let her go. "Any time I mention Will, you—"

"You will not speak anotha' man's name on your lips again," Lucas growled under his breath as he drew her closer. "So, stop talkin' about that fuckin' bastard."

Unable to control herself, she chuckled softly. "Why? Do you really hate Will that much?"

Lucas gripped her arms and yanked her into his chest, jerking her away from the table.

Squeezing her, he gritted his teeth in her face and said, "Say his name again, and see what happens."

Karramis grimaced and let out a low groan as her body stiffened under his tight grasp. "It's just a name, Lucas." She gave him a mocking snicker as she relaxed her muscles in anticipation for what would come next. "It's not like it can hurt you."

It was working. His anger was coming out in full force. His hands clutched tighter, and she gasped from the pain squeezing her as he gave her a quick nudge and let her go. Flinging back in a staggering sway, she regained her footing as she suppressed the painful moan rising in her throat.

Standing up straight, Karramis gave him a provoking sneer as she readied herself, her muscles loosening for whatever pain would follow as she drew out the next word slowly. "Will."

Lucas pulled back his hand without hesitation, and his fist collided with the left side of her face, a loud yelp erupting from her as the powerful blow sent her stumbling and crashing to the floor with a slapping thud. He yanked her to her feet, lifting her so she stood on her tiptoes. Tears slid from the watery eye resting next to the injured cheek, red and swollen.

Truth and a firm declaration rang in her stifled voice. "You will never be what Will is to me."

A deep growl rumbled from him, wild and fierce, as he let go of her and quickly gripped a handful of her hair, shoving her backward with a powerful thrust. She whirled sideways, and the left side of her face rammed against the coarse stone behind her, her cheekbone scraping against the wall. Hands tugged at her hair, her scalp burning as her head jerk forward and slammed into the stone wall again, her skin ripping open along her temple and cheek. A flash of white sparked behind her closed eyes, the sudden burst of light swallowed by darkness as pain exploded in her head.

She crashed to the floor, her body smacking against the tiles with a fleshy slap as she landed on her stomach. Flecks of white danced across her blurred vision as she drove her eyes open. Her head spun and pounded as her muffled whimpers echoed deep within the voids of her disoriented mind. Her eyes fell shut, her will to hold them open flickering as the room spun. Darkness took over, and the pulse raging within her veins thumped wildly. She could feel each hurried heartbeat in her aching muscles, see it behind her fluttering eyelids, and hear it in her ears. Pain radiated along the left side of her face, burning and throbbing as blood oozed from a deep gash along her temple and cheekbone, dripping onto the floor as she battled against her weak muscles.

Get up. Get up!

Karramis had to get off the floor. She had to get to her feet. She was too vulnerable and exposed down here, and she would never be able to conjure her portal if her hands remained under her body.

Lucas stepped over her, making her flinch from the loudness of his boots echoing in her ears. "No, I'd ratha' ya stay down."

He nudged her in the stomach with his foot and flipped her onto her back. Her low cries rumbled in her throat as he stared down at her. Kneeling beside her, he traced a finger over the gash and the bruise now forming along her face.

She drew in a breath through her teeth and jerked her head away from his hand, the pain and his touch too much to bear. "Don't touch me." It was more strained than she had hoped, the vitality of it lost behind her hoarse tone.

Wiping his finger on her blood-stained nightgown, Lucas straddled her, his thighs squeezing her hips as he pinned her arms down, his body driving her harder against the solid floor.

She clamped her mouth shut and held in a scream as his hand pressed firmly against the wound on her stomach.

He angled his upper body down and rested his lips against her ear. "Make no mistake, love, you will be mine. One way or anotha'. You belong to me. And I will touch ya in any way I see fit."

"Mon dieu," Camille exclaimed in faux shock, glaring over at them from the stairs. "I'm interrupting something, no?"

"Yes, as a matter of fact," Lucas complained as he rose to his feet and straightened his slightly bloody white shirt. "What the hell do ya want, Cami?"

"I heard some disturbing noises down here and wanted to make sure you were all right, mon amour." She made her way over to him, the gleam of amusement sparking in her blue eyes as she glared down at Karramis freshly battered and prone. "Plus, Leif told me to check on you."

"He doesn't trust you," Karramis said with her voice straining in agony.

"No one asked for your opinion," Lucas said, his voice rough and tight, before twisting and ramming his boot into her side.

Karramis cried out with a quick, deep grunt as the air yanked with a jolt from her chest, muffling any sound as she lurched into a fetal position. Vomit rose from her stomach, but she swallowed it down, the lingering acid burning the back of her throat.

Camille snickered as she clapped her hands playfully. "Oh, a show. How delightful."

Lucas lowered to his knees, his voice superior and deep in his throat. "Look what you made me do." He leaned over her, bracing his hands on either side of her head. "I'm not the one to blame for this. You are. I didn't do this. This is all your fault."

He was right. This time, it was her fault. All of it. This was what she wanted. This was exactly what Karramis needed to happen.

"Where's Leif?" Lucas asked randomly, jerking his head over at Camille, still annoyed by her presence.

Karramis did not want Leif to return, not when she could barely handle Lucas at the moment.

"He's still here . . . somewhere." Camille waved her hand dismissively. "He told me he isn't going to stop you from making any more mistakes, and then he left. He didn't seem very happy."

Lucas scoffed. "I don't think Leif even knows how to be happy." Lowering his voice, he added with a roll of his eyes, "Heartless fuckin' cunt."

Karramis angled her head to the side, and her body went lax under Lucas as he kept his attention on Camille. She flicked her gaze between the other two before moving it over to the candles on the shelves. Sliding her hand across the floor very slowly, she concentrated.

Nothing happened. No spark. No smoke. Absolutely nothing.

"Leave now, Cami. I'm fine down here."

"But Haydrin and Gastell are back."

He huffed, his frustration billowing. "And?"

"Haydrin is wondering where you are." Camille crossed her arms and inclined a hip, placing her weight more on one leg. "And Gastell is covered in blood and reeks of death."

"Well, tell Haydrin I'm down here and don't wanna be bothered. And as for Gastell, I would assume he caught himself somethin' to eat."

"Oui. But he smells like *human* death."

"Shit." Lucas lifted a hand from the floor and rubbed his forehead. "Fuck. Okay, let me finish up here, and I'll go deal with him."

Camille smiled down at Karramis, a conniving, wicked grin. "But I want to watch."

"No. Ya need to go back upstairs."

She pouted. "Please?"

Pointing up the stairs, he insisted with a warning glare as he rose to his feet, ushering her away, "Now."

"Humph!" She rotated around and headed up the stairs, stomping up the first few steps before halting. "Fine." Lifting her chin at Karramis, she offered critically, "But you may want to do something about that, no?"

Lucas glanced back and caught sight of Karramis twitching her fingers aimed at the candles. With a quick twist, he closed the short distance between them.

"Knock that shit off," he snapped, driving a steel-toed boot into her side.

A crack sounded, and a deep gasping breath exploded from Karramis as she instinctively clutched her rib cage and rolled into a fetal position. The pain blasted outward from her chest and shot through her, every nerve burning with searing-hot agony. Her muscles seized as a boiling wave of pain sizzled up from her core and coursed through her like a charge of rolling electricity. It wrapped around her, swallowing her—drowning her. Her breath hitched, each inhale more painful than the last. Vomit and bile lodged in her throat, the burn and acidic taste choking her as one of the candles tipped over and rolled from the shelf and the shards of glass from the vase she had broken earlier rattled along the floor.

Lucas and Camille twisted toward the shelf just as the candle collided against the floor and broke in half, each piece rolling to a stop among the rattling remnants of the shattered vase.

"Oh, Lucas," Camille begged enthusiastically, "let me stay." She hugged his arm. "S'il te plaît, mon amour, I can help you. I can siphon her magic. Do whatever you want."

"I don't need any help." He removed his arm from her embrace. "And no one is gonna touch her. Except for me."

"Right." Camille slammed a heeled foot onto the step and rotated around, placing her hands on her hips. "Leif said she has a way of tricking you into believing her lies. It's true, no? She has a way with you. I've seen it for myself over the years. Your love for her clouds your mind." She exhaled, annoyed by her own acknowledgement. "So, I suggest you make sure she keeps her mouth shut and you handle her fast." She made her way up the stairs, whispering to herself, "You clearly can't handle her, since we're still here, even after it's clear her powers are slowly coming back and we can all feel them."

"Lock the damn door, Cami," he called up to her as he strolled back over to Karramis and towered over her. "I don't want any more interruptions."

"What . . ." Karramis could not catch her breath as each attempt squeezed in her chest, her voice low and hoarse. "What are you . . . What are you . . . going to . . . do with me?"

He chuckled, dark and taunting. "Afraid, love?"

Karramis was afraid, but she would never admit it. Not to him or herself. Giving into fear meant she was surrendering, and she was not going to give him that satisfaction. Not again. Never again. She was not going to yield to him. She had spent so many years running and hiding—living in fear every single day. She was not going to do it again. She had to find the inner strength to keep fighting, and not just with her powers. If her training as a Guardian had taught her anything, it was that you can only fight back and win if you are strong enough to handle being hit a few times. If only she had actually trained in hand-to-hand combat growing up. But she had, however, trained almost every day in strengthening her mental abilities, homing in on her mind's innate abilities to control her body and soul. Mind over matter.

Karramis had to push through the pain. She had to because it was the only way she would be able to follow through with her initial plan to escape. And she would. She would escape. She was going to get out of here. One way or another.

Blinking up at him, she accepted what was coming as she drew in a deep breath through her nose, her initial plan to piss him off about to come in full force as she released it slowly through her mouth. "Afraid of you?" There was no fear. No hesitation. Just a purely savage sneer blooming across her face. "No."

Lowering to his knees, he leaned over and gripped her neck and whispered in her ear, "Well, ya should be."

Chapter 12

Point of No Return

Karramis had never regretted her lack of training growing up more than she did in this very moment. With weapons. With hand-to-hand combat. With anything to help her physically right now as her magic wavered in and out, the ebbing of her power weakening under his tight grasp.

Her eyes fluttered, the dim light in the room flickering behind her drooping eyelids. His body shifted forward, and the grip around her neck loosened. Air filled her lungs as she took a breath. She gave in to the heaviness stinging her eyes as a few more deep breaths expanded in her chest, the piercing pain of the potentially broken ribs causing her back to arch.

Karramis forced open her eyes, and her breath stopped as she halted her gasp, the unexpected warmth from his lips pressing harder against hers. The pain vanished as she lowered her back flat against the tiles and stilled, the uncomfortable awareness of him caressing her upper thigh making her skin crawl as her gaze landed on the outside of his lowered eyelids.

She exhaled, and all her pain—the cauterized stab wound, the bruise surely forming along her rib cage, the possibly fractured bones, the deep gash still bleeding along the left side of her face—returned and pierced through her like a million nails pounding deep into her muscles.

His tongue glided across her lips as his knee urged her legs apart, and he eased himself in between her thighs. He bit her, the sharp, unexpected pain relaxing her mouth long enough for him to coax his tongue inside. The hand on her thigh lifted higher under the hem of her nightgown as the other eased behind her neck, lifting her and bringing her closer to him.

With every ounce of strength she had, she lifted her arms and braced them against his broad chest, shoving and pushing them apart.

"What the hell are you doing, Lucas?" she snapped, shocked and disgusted. "Get off me!"

A smug, confident grin was plastered on his face. "I wanted to see what it was like kissin' ya again."

She wiped her mouth, ignoring his weight on top of her and the pain rattling every nerve. "That sure as hell didn't feel like you just wanted to kiss me."

"No worries, love. That's all I was gonna do."

The discomfort from her injuries intensified as her racing pulse pattered deep inside. She fought back the urge to wince as her heartbeat pounded along every nerve and within every muscle. She could not allow her pain to take over again. Surrendering to weakness was not an option. She had to get out of here. And now.

Rethinking her plan quietly in her head again, she mentally agreed with herself to the consequences of her next move.

"Yeah, right." She pushed against his chest again to no avail. "What are you planning to do with me, Lucas? Take me against my will?"

"If I wanted to do that, love, I had plenty of opportunities to do so over the years. Why do ya think you're still in that disgustin' outfit?"

She had not thought about that, now all too aware of how dirty her nightgown was and the sticky blood under the loose material.

"I didn't think you'd appreciate me undressin' ya to clean ya up." A muscle twitched at the corner of his mouth as he leaned back in, his voice low and sensual. "Plus, I'd much ratha' prefer it if you were willin'."

"Not going to happen," she blurted.

"Hmm, we'll just see about that."

"You're sick. You know that?"

Karramis broke their gaze as she eyed the stairs. She had to get him off her. Maybe she could make a run for it.

Lucas cocked his head and assessed her with a calculating glare. "Hmm, what're ya gonna do, love?" He leaned back onto his heels. "Try and run?"

Here goes nothing.

She stared up at him, her eyes set with heated determination. "Yes."

Karramis forced a leg to move, quick and swift as she slid it out from under him, the pain wrapping around her and churning in her stomach as she rammed her bare foot into his chest. Lucas swayed back with a grunt, but a hand flew through the air and grasped her ankle. Her body yanked forward with a harsh jolt as he used her to catch himself. She rolled, her ankle twisting out of his grasp. Urging herself not to give in to the pain, she continued rolling away from him. Her foot slipped on the blood smeared across the tiled floor as she staggered to her feet. She wanted to vomit from the pain ripping through her, but she swallowed it down, the acidic aftertaste making her stomach roil. Her knees buckled as she drove her weight into her legs, the burn in her thighs making her sway. Karramis stumbled again, but she threw her hands out, her palms pressing into the floor as she pushed herself back upright.

A powerful force slammed into her back. Flashes sparked behind her eyelids as the side of her face collided with the granite tiles, the sound of her body smacking against the floor filling her head with echoing vibrations. Lucas's heated body pressed into her back as his heavy breathing forced her disheveled strands to tickle the side of her face.

"Nice try," he breathed arrogantly into her ear. "A very valiant effort there, love." He flipped her onto her back and straddled her, holding her wrists down next to her head. "I was wonderin' when ya were gonna do somethin' stupid."

The collision with the floor sent a sting slicing through the left side of her face, adding to the aching pain along her temple and cheek. She swallowed, and a hot metallic flavor slid down her throat, thick and copious. Blood.

Disappointment and trepidation surged through her as she bucked and fought against his grasp, the tightness of each injury more painful than she cared to admit. But she continued to fight.

"Let me go," she shouted between clenched teeth, her voice strained as blood coated her lips.

A sinister chuckle. "No." There was a gleam of predatory amusement in his eyes as he scanned every inch of her above the waist. "I think I'll just keep ya for myself."

She grunted and lifted a foot, trying to slide it under one of his ankles.

"Now, now, none of that," he said casually, easing to his feet in one swift move and tugging her with him.

"Let. Me. Go!" she repeated in a harsh tone, jerking against his hold at the final word. "I swear, if you don't, I'm going to kill you!"

Lucas released her, a cool scheming calmness washing over his smug expression. "Fine."

Karramis staggered back as he let go of her wrist, confusion and shock on her face and in her voice. "What?"

Lucas glared at her, his eyes burrowing deeper into her as she made sure to keep her inner voice quiet. Concentrating on interpreting his thoughts, she questioned where his mind had disappeared to as his eyes pierced through her and his face became unreadable. Her stomach tightened, the anticipation and worry fluttering and rising in her chest, making her heart hammer under her wounded rib cage. She wanted to wince but was afraid any movement might break their stare. The silence carried on, filling the room with a ghostly bone-chilling presence.

Karramis prepared herself for his next move. He was planning something. She could sense it. Any moment, his usual outburst of emotions would surface—anger, jealousy, resentment. Something.

However, he did not falter from watching her, analyzing her. He was calm, focused, and way too casual with his stance. There was even something off in his eyes, the beautiful blue concealing a looming darkness.

Karramis shifted, the intimidating and uncharacteristic display making her extremely uncomfortable and concerned. What was he about to do to her? The stagnant and charismatic grin on his face expressed confidence and excitement, a plan playing out within his own mind.

Lucas's pupils enlarged as his attention fixated on Karramis.

Growing more anxious as the seconds of quietness and unnerving interaction dragged on, seemingly endless, she jumped at the opportunity to test her magic again. Aware her fire powers were the most unpredictable and not at all reliable tonight, she focused on an ability she had more control over and Lucas was less likely to notice—her telekinesis. She had moved the vase earlier—well, more like she had violently tossed it through the air—but she was still optimistic she could do it again. She just had to figure out a way to do it without drawing attention away from their intense staring contest. Keeping her eyes focused on his, she shifted her mental attention down to her hands as she slowly rotated them, her palms now facing upward.

Telekinesis was one power that could be controlled with only the mind, but Karramis had always used her hands for her powers, channeling them through her palms as a focal point. Many witches could use their whole body as an outlet for their magic, but this was an ability Karramis had never mastered. She had to tread carefully so she did not alert Lucas.

With her eyes concentrating on Lucas's gaze, her peripheral vision caught sight of the only moveable objects she could locate—the two remaining candles on the shelf behind him. She exhaled cautiously, clearing her mind of all outward thoughts of her magic.

"Leave," he said finally with gentle quietness, his tone surprisingly charming.

"What?" she blurted with a sharp and surprised uptick of her voice as she blinked at him with narrowed eyes.

"Ya wanna leave so badly . . . So leave."

It had to be a trick. He was surely testing her.

"Go on then." Lucas jerked his chin over toward the staircase. "You're free to leave."

She hesitated, taking in the distance between him, her, and her exit.

Lucas did not move or speak.

Relief and hope burned inside her, but it was quickly doused by a twinge of warning sounding off in her head. Was he really going to let her go?

She waited, her eyes never faltering from his watchful gaze. Sliding her foot along the floor, she inched it back and then paused midstep. She did it again. Then she took an actual step away from him. She, too, was testing him. He watched her, his intense perusal of her every move as she eased cautiously farther away making her pulse race. Taking a guarded retreat over to the stairs, she inched her way closer, refusing to turn her back to him. Her foot hit the landing of the bottom step. Her hand found the railing, and she leaned into it, every inch of her wanting to scream in agony as she lifted a foot, ascending the first step of the stairwell leading up to the rest of Château Rouge. Then another.

Lucas still did not move a muscle.

Reaching the third step, she paused and drew in a long breath and held it as she gripped the railing. She rotated and bolted, the movement shockingly fast in her weakened state. Her legs burned and quivered as each foot slammed into the wooden steps, the sound echoing off the stone walls.

Pain slammed against her head—a penetrating burst of intense pressure, as if a bag of bricks had crashed into the back of her skull. She lurched forward, tumbling onto the stairs with a thunderous slap, her arms and knees taking most of the damage as something breakable exploded behind her and shards of glass clattered against the floor in the room below.

Footsteps pounded up the steps, the vibration reverberating under Karramis's body as she leaned over the stairs.

"Now, love," Lucas said coolly, "did ya really think I'd let ya go?" He stopped, his boots resting on both sides of her body as he towered over her, his gaze observing her back rising and falling with slow, deep pants. "I didn't spend all those years searchin' for ya and even more sittin' around here waitin' for ya to wake up just to let ya go so easily."

He gripped her hair, and Karramis screamed as he dragged her down the stairs, the ear-splitting cries making her throat burn. Her legs slapped against the steps as she fought to gain her footing and thudded as she reached the bottom landing. Glass sliced into her legs as she was hauled across the broken shards on the floor. Lucas had thrown the empty wine bottle Camille had left on the table by the stairwell at her.

Coming to a stop in the middle of the room, Karramis reached up and grabbed the wrist pulling her hair. "Let go of me!" Her voice was strained, the pure fear evident in each word.

Lucas yanked harder before shoving her back. "No!"

A hand struck the side of her face as she tried to sit up. Her lip split open, and blood trailed down her chin as her head flew sideways. A groan and lingering moan rose from her chest and rattled in her raw throat.

"Why?" he demanded, kicking her. "Why him? What does he have that I don't, eh? We both have blue eyes. We both have accents and magic. We both love ya. What is it about him that draws ya to him and not me?"

"He's . . ." She hesitated, her mind battling over whether or not she should continue with her original plan to escape or keep quiet before he hurt her even more.

Lucas knelt beside her, tucking her messy brown hair behind her ear. There was something intimate about his touch, apologetic almost. "He's what?"

"Well," she noted sternly, "he's not fuckin' crazy for one thing."

Taking in Lucas's malevolent and wild gaze, Karramis braced herself. There was no turning back now.

Lucas shot out an arm and wrapped his fingers around her neck. He squeezed as he lifted her onto her feet, severing her ability to breathe as he strangled her. His eyes went dark, his pupils dilating as anger exploded from him, the evil deep inside taking over.

He stepped back, his hand remaining on her neck as he slammed her back into the shelves, the powerful thrust rattling the candles behind her.

"Lucas," Karramis pleaded with a choking whisper, grasping his wrists with both hands and desperately trying to yank them away.

Karramis tried to fight against her eyes growing heavy as they fluttered erratically, but her body was growing weaker with each trapped breath. Her chest burned, and her lungs convulsed as they urged her to breathe. The pain slowly started to fade from her body as life began to drain with each second, the asphyxiation taking over. Fear soaked into her as the icy chill of death rose from the depths of her soul.

She did not want to die. Not now. Not like this.

Karramis was not going to die.

Magic exploded from her hands as she limply dropped them at her sides, a burst of energy blasting outward and crashing into Lucas as fire ignited behind her, the flames of the candles reaching high above the wicks. Wind swirled, sending the shattered glass of the vase and wine bottle on the floor rattling as mist swirled near the stairs before disappearing.

Lucas was hurled back with a powerful shove, his hand remaining around Karramis's neck as he crashed against the floor with a loud grunt. Landing on top of him, she rolled sideways next to him as he released her. She gasped violently for air as Lucas attempted to grab her, but she slid her leg out from his loose grip. She pulled herself across the floor away from him and hurried to her feet, her weak body and barely full lungs making her quick escape difficult.

Raising her hands, she focused on the nook in the corner, the farthest location in the room from Lucas. The air swirled around as a subtle mist appeared, expanding with each steady rotation, but it vanished.

"Come on!" Karramis rasped through clenched teeth, her voice tight and hoarse. "Dammit!"

She glanced back just as a heavy shove jolted her forward. Her feet flew out from under her, and she landed hard on her hands and knees. Lucas seized her, both hands gripping around her waist as he lifted her and slammed her hard onto her back. Wrestling for her hands, he smacked her. She yelped as her head jerked to the side, a trail of blood spewing from her mouth as her arms dropped to the floor. Sliding her hands against her sides, Lucas pinned them in between her body and his legs as he dropped himself down on top of her, kneeling at her hips. He pressed his weight into her, the sheer mass of him driving her backside hard into the cold tiles.

Karramis screamed, the pain and fear taking over.

Lucas lifted an arm and slapped a hand over her mouth just as loud pounding came from the door at the top of the stairs.

"Lucas!" Camille's muffled voice rang out. "What's going on down there?"

"Go the fuck away!" Lucas called back with a deep annoyed demand. "I got this!"

Karramis bucked, but his weight was too much to fight against. She screamed again, but it was muted behind his hand pressing firmly against her mouth.

"Stop that!" he snapped. "You're only makin' this harder for ya!"

The flames on the candles flickered as her eyes shifted toward them. If she could only get her hands free.

Lucas removed his hand from her mouth and slapped her. "And no more magic!"

Karramis lifted her upper body and spit, only pure adrenaline compelling her actions as red-tinged saliva splattered against his face and blood-stained shirt.

Lucas drew back in disgust. "Fuckin' bitch!" He wiped his face with the back of his hand. "You'll pay for that."

Karramis could no longer feel pain, old or new, as something else formed in her core—a mix of fortifying emotions and blooming power. But she needed a distraction, something to catch him completely off guard so she could use this to her advantage.

"Lucas," she said, her voice and face soft as she controlled her heavy pants, "I'm sorry. I'm sorry for everything."

Something shifted in his demeanor, a familiar flash of the man she had once known.

Placing his weight on his knees, he glared down at her, his eyes monitoring her with both suspicion and admiration.

"I didn't mean to hurt you," she continued. A genuine remark behind a dangerous and utterly stupid plan. "I'm sorry."

His shoulders sagged, his whole body appearing to release the anger and tension as he exhaled.

Karramis kept her eyes locked on his, sadness and remorse blinking up with a pained watery gaze. "I never meant for this to happen between us. You were my best friend, Lucas. I deeply cared for you. So, please . . . forgive me."

Lucas examined the guilt and distress in her beautiful deep brown eyes and the kindness and sincerity in her words. She attempted to smile, but it turned into a grimace behind the discomfort as she shifted beneath his body. He leaned back onto his heels, easing more of his weight off her.

Karramis cautiously slid one hand out from under him, being mindful of his gaze still on her.

Lucas noticed and reached down to take hold of it, grasping her wrist. She did not fight him this time. Her eyes remained on his. No flinching. No faltering. Just two gazes observing, analyzing, testing the situation.

Leaning over her, Lucas lowered her hand to his leg. Surprise shuddered through him when she did not remove it or pull back in disgust.

A moment passed, the anticipation of his next move lingering in the air. Was he going to do it? Was her new plan going to work?

Before she could contemplate another backup plan, Lucas leaned in with a wild need and urged his lips into her, kissing her again, harder and deeper.

But this time Karramis did not fight it. She went rigid under him, the hand on his thigh sliding up and clutching the fabric of his shirt along his side.

A sensual moan vibrated from Lucas as he closed his eyes and pulled her closer to him, cradling the base of her neck before sliding his tongue into her mouth.

Exhaling through her nose, she mimicked his actions as she swallowed the revulsion roiling in her stomach. He had to believe she wanted this. She had to keep him distracted.

Karramis opened her eyes and slid her other hand out from between her side and his leg and draped her wrist over his shoulder, aiming her open palm behind him. She cringed, allowing him to passionately kiss her as another moan rumbled against her lips. She could not see behind him, but she focused, waiting for any signs her portal was opening.

The air in the room went still as another swipe of him invaded her mouth. Then a gentle, cool gust swept through the room, blowing as air forced goose bumps to rise along her arms. Lucas twitched and tried to pull away, releasing from their embrace, but Karramis removed the hand clutching his shirt and slid it up his neck and through his hair, leaning upward farther into his body and mimicking his fiery passion.

This was it, her only chance to get away. There was no room for mistakes. Inhaling, she tilted herself backward, taking Lucas's heated and aroused body with her as they lowered onto the floor. Karramis traced her hands along his neck, keeping her mental connection to the portal behind them. She exhaled and closed her eyes, pulling more of her magic to the surface. It needed to build up if it was going to stay open long enough for her to get away.

Warmth filled her core, spreading rapidly through her veins as she rested a flattened palm against Lucas's chest. With a sudden jerk away from him, she released herself from the kiss and simultaneously discharged the warm, tingling power flowing through her and forced it out of her hand. Lucas vaulted through the air, flying back and colliding with the wall across the room. She held her hand out, an invisible force pressing him against the wall as she struggled to her feet and wiped the taste of him from her mouth. Her body was weak, and her muscles were hard to control as she stumbled, groaning as she fell to her knees. But she forced herself up and hurried toward her portal as her telekinetic powers held him firmly against the wall.

"Karramis!" Lucas yelled, fighting against her magic, the callous expression on his face red with anger. "Ya stupid lyin' bitch! Stop! Don't ya fuckin' dare!"

Stopping short of the magical doorway, Karramis twisted and faced him wholly, one hand aimed at him while the other sat inches from the portal. Her body was hunched over in pain, and her face was bruised, cut, swollen, and covered with blood. But despite the discomfort she was enduring and the shame, regret, and overall brokenness deep within her soul, she had won.

Tears trailed down her face at the realization as a relieved breath shuddered from her. She was going home.

A lingering bit of strength and adrenaline pulsed deep inside her as she said to him, raw but gentle, "Bye, Lucas."

He shoved against her magic. "Ya can't fuckin' hide from me! I'll fuckin' find ya! You're mine!" The shouts echoed through the stone room. "Ya hear me, Karramis? You're fuckin' mine!"

Turning around, Karramis walked into the portal, and her fragile damaged body went limp, surrendering to the pain as the rush of cool misty air consumed her, wrapping around her like a warm blanket as she welcomed the familiar embrace.

Chapter 13

Nightmares

Five months ago
Mid-July

The puncture marks on Rhiannon's neck throbbed as she flopped over on her bed. Her eyes burned from forcing them open, afraid if she closed them, she would see his face and experience the events with Merrick all over again. She turned again, facing James, who was barely visible lying sound asleep in his bed across the room.

Her eyelids grew even heavier, the weight so powerful she no longer had control over the fight to stay awake. The burning intensified as she watched the dots on the digital clock across from her blink, counting along with each flash.

One second.

Two.

Three.

Erasing the dryness coating her eyes, she blinked, and a tear slid down her cheek. Each flicker of her eyelids brought more darkness as she drifted further into unconsciousness.

Four seconds.

Five.

Her body sagged deeper into the mattress, the cool caress of the thin blanket easing her into a state of slow, shallow breaths and a steady heartbeat. Her vision blurred, and the red glow from the clock blinked behind a thin line of awareness before everything faded into a dark oblivion.

Deep crimson dripped through the shadows of her mind, coating all the inner walls with blood. A metallic tinge filled her senses, causing her lethargic sleep-laced body to tense. Phantom growls snarled within the walls of her thoughts, and her head twitched violently away from the sound. Sharp, jagged teeth flashed within the darkness as the air in her lungs froze. She could not breathe. Her back arched, and a whimper rose from deep within her chest as something dark and empty stalked closer. The shadow stretched out a hand, the icy chill of its touch reaching and taking hold, but it was not her who it held.

"Rhiannon," a quiet voice said from far away as two hands gently shook her shoulders.

She bolted awake and scurried into a sitting position, evading the hands touching her. Panting and covered in sweat, Rhiannon focused her gaze as she scanned the room.

"It's okay," the familiar voice went on from a few feet away, the person it came from leaning against the bed.

A haze coated her vision, and she was unable to see anything but a faint dark silhouette in front of her.

"It's okay," the voice repeated. "It's me."

Through the hammering of her pulse in her ears, Rhiannon recognized the voice.

"James?" she breathed.

"Yeah." The bed bounced as he stood up. "Watch your eyes."

The lamp on the nightstand next to the bed clicked on, and Rhiannon winced and blinked her eyes closed.

"Sorry." James sat back down on the edge of her bed. "Are you okay?"

"I'm fine," Rhiannon said emotionlessly, still trying to catch her breath.

Shifting her stinging dry eyes over to the digital clock sitting on her nightstand, she sighed in defeat. She had only been asleep forty minutes.

"You keep saying that," James said, unconvinced, cutting her a worried gaze, "but I don't believe you."

"I'm fine," she repeated with a slight bite of annoyance in her tone. "I'm just tired."

James observed her bloodshot eyes. "Were you having a nightmare?"

"No."

She did not want to admit Merrick affected her—another fear rattling her to the core. Another weakness.

Raising his arm, James reached a hand for her, but she jerked away.

"I'm sorry," he blurted, alarm and regret beaming in his brown eyes.

"It's fine." Her eyes blinked with guilt. "I . . . I just don't want to be touched right now."

Despite the three times she had scrubbed herself in the shower earlier, she could still feel his touch on her. The sensation of his hands stroking her skin, her body. His mouth on her neck. The warmth from him, but the chill skittering up her back as he held her. His hot, blood-coated breath on her ear.

He nodded in understanding. "Do you want to talk about it?"

"No."

"But it might—"

"No," she insisted, broken and distant. "I don't want to talk about it."

Rhiannon did not want help, and she definitely did not want to talk. She needed time to process everything first. Alone. Play back all the mistakes she had made. Figure out why she had been unable to react. Analyze why her magic had failed her completely this time. Find the reason why she was always the one getting hurt. Understand what she could have done to not disappoint her family. But more importantly, she just wanted to sleep right now. She did not want to think or feel. Rhiannon wanted to fade into nothing so she did not have to experience anything, even if for a short time.

Calmly, he asked, "But why?"

"I just don't."

"But you need to. If not with me, then with someone— anyone."

"I don't need to because I'm—"

"Fine?" His tone was sharp and skeptical. "Who are you trying to convince, Rhiannon? Me or yourself?"

Throwing the blankets back, she pushed off the bed, nearly shoving him to the floor. "I'm fine." She stormed over to the closed door. "I just want to be left alone."

"Fine," he replied in a huff. Rising to his feet and trailing behind her, he added, "But I know you're not okay. I can feel it."

She rotated around, her face annoyed but her voice low. "Stay out of my damn head."

James matched her demeanor and tone. "I don't have to read your mind to know something isn't right with you. Plus, I can't anyway."

"What do you mean?"

"I stopped hearing you earlier. Even when I tried, I couldn't find you. I tried so hard to comfort you, to tell you I was there and that you weren't alone. But I couldn't get to you. It was like I lost the connection somehow. My mind was void of you completely. I can still feel your emotions, though. Feel what you're feeling right now. So, just talk to me."

Rhiannon stared at him, pondering what to say next.

"Please." James cautiously took a step closer, kindness and concern exuding from him. "Talk to me. I can help you."

Swallowing the lump rising in her throat and ignoring the burn in her chest, she announced hollowly, "Like I said, I'm fine."

The harshness of her words and dishonest declaration wrapped around her heart like a fist and squeezed. She turned and reached for the handle of the door, pulling it open. Her footsteps pounded down the hall as she headed for the front of the cabin.

"Rhiannon," James called, adamant but kind as he trailed behind her.

Shuffling came from his parents' room as he stopped a few feet from his sister, her hand resting on the handle of the front door. She did not face him.

"Rhiannon?"

"What?" she answered, her voice tight with emotion.

"Where are you going?"

"I need some fresh air."

Will and Karramis exited their bedroom and stopped a few feet behind James, who kept his distance from his sister, giving her space. His parents watched, analyzing the situation and allowing their children to talk.

Rhiannon flung the front door open.

"Hey," James said with a hint of defeat in his gentle voice, closing the distance between them. "I'm sorry. I'm sorry you were hurt again and that I couldn't stop it. That I couldn't save you again. But please, please don't shut me out. Tell me . . . Tell me what I can do."

"Nothing," she confessed solemnly.

"Please, let me help you."

"I don't want any help, James. I just want you to leave me alone." And with that, she exited through the threshold, closing the door behind her.

James turned to his parents with misty eyes. "What do I do now?"

"You give her time," Will said, shifting his sympathetic gaze to Karramis. "You just give her time. And when she's ready, you'll be there for her."

~

Rhiannon had walked around the outskirts of the forest lining the cabin for hours before she had decided to return, but she still did not want to go inside. Not yet. The walls inside consumed her, swallowed her as they closed in around her. There were too many things driving the fear and failure she felt to the surface, sleep being one of them. Inside she would want to close her eyes and allow her mind to fall into a deep state of nothing. But it would not last. The nightmares would eventually return.

The morning sun had finally reached over the top of the trees to the east, and the sky was filled with drifting clouds in various shades of gray. The heat of summer was returning as the sun glided higher into the sky, but a cool breeze blew across the field, minimizing the unbearable temperatures from the previous days.

Rhiannon was still dressed in an oversized nightgown as she sat down on the steps of the porch, scanning the area as Mother Nature greeted her. The wind smelled of jasmine, sea salt, and juniper, with a hint of sweet berries, most likely from the lush garden around the side of the cabin. Birds called out in the distance—the subtle songs of blue jays and robins, a screeching of a hawk, and the cawing of seagulls.

The front door clicked opened, and Rhiannon twisted and watched as her mother exited with two ceramic mugs in her hands.

"Good morning," Karramis said, handing Rhiannon a steaming cup of hot chocolate.

Rhiannon slid two fingers through the handle and cupped the mug. "Thank you. I don't think it's cold enough for hot chocolate, but thank you."

Karramis sat down beside her and took a sip of her coffee. "It's less about keeping you warm and more about making you feel better."

Rhiannon kept her eyes forward. "Sorry, but I don't think hot chocolate is going to fix my problems this time, Mom."

"How about," Karramis started, pulling a folded napkin from her pajama shorts, "your favorite cookies?"

Rhiannon unfolded the napkin and sniffed the warm fresh-baked cookies. "When did you have time to make toffee snickerdoodles?"

"When you were out walking."

Rhiannon took a bite and moaned in indulgence. "I forgot how much I love your homemade cookies."

"I missed making them for you." Karramis smiled. "And James."

Rhiannon grinned as she took another bite. "Do you still sing and dance like a complete weirdo when you're in the kitchen?"

"Of course. At least when we were at the manor I had a radio, but here I'm stuck listening to the same music your dad brought with him over and over again. There are only so many times I can listen to the same songs before I go insane. I'd kill for some new music. Okay, maybe not kill, but some new music would be nice."

They both sat quietly as Rhiannon finished her cookie and eyed the hawk overhead as it circled around again.

"Mom," Rhiannon said softly. "Are . . . Do you think . . ."

Karramis caught the worry in her daughter's voice as she spotted her watching the hawk with deep concentration. "I'm sure they're okay."

Rhiannon sagged her shoulders as her stomach twisted with a nervous wringing sensation. She picked up the cup of hot chocolate and gripped it tightly, her watchful gaze tracking the unfamiliar hawk.

"I wish we knew for sure. What if Merrick—"

"He didn't," Karramis said with unwavering conviction.

"How can you be so sure?"

"There's a history there that allows both of them some protection. At least for the time being."

Curiosity bloomed in Rhiannon's chest. "Meaning?"

"It's a long story. Both are. And I'd rather talk about you right now."

Rhiannon faced forward, apprehension stiffening her muscles. "I'm fine."

Karramis arched a brow and tilted her head. "Right." Her voice was dubious and sarcastic. "That sounds familiar."

Rhiannon rotated her head, her eyes catching the glint of sunshine in her mother's deep brown irises. "What does that mean?"

"That's what I kept saying over and over after I returned a few months ago." Karramis gave her a half smile as she took another sip of coffee. "I was trying to convince myself by saying it repeatedly, but . . ."

"But what?"

"Your dad didn't believe me."

"Why?"

"Because he knows me better than I know myself most days. Well, that and because I had horrible nightmares. Still do some nights."

Rhiannon blinked a few times before asking, her voice low, "Really?"

"Yeah. The nightmares are all too consuming sometimes. I can't sleep because of it. I'm too scared to close my eyes some nights. I live everything all over again. I can feel everything. Every injury, every emotion, the overwhelming sensation that I'm about to die. I see the rage and raw hatred aimed at me. I can taste my blood again, the disgust rising in my stomach from his touch, the taste of him in my mouth. Even certain sounds still haunt me."

"Why didn't you tell us any of this?"

"Because it made me feel weak, like I couldn't control myself enough to fight it by myself. And because most people who suffer a trauma prefer to weather that storm alone. But your dad knew the truth, and he refused to give up on me. He helped me. Not just from the physical and mental parts of it, but the emotional too. He knew I wasn't okay, so he let me know he was there and that when I was ready, I didn't have to deal with it alone. And when that storm was too much, the nightmares, the dark days, all the defeat and regret of not fighting harder until it was almost too late, he was there to battle it out with me. So, let someone be that for you. Talk to me. James. Anyone. But don't do it alone. Even though you are battling the storm, it doesn't mean you can't ask for an umbrella."

Karramis reached over and rubbed Rhiannon's back before standing up and heading for the door.

"You know," Karramis said as she paused, "it's not about what happened to you but rather how you handle it. Trauma happens to everyone, but it's how one carries it that makes all the difference. If you don't want it to make you seem weak, then don't give it that power."

Rhiannon pivoted, a hint of hope flashing across her face. "How do I do that?"

"Instead of allowing it to slow you down as it drags behind you, pick it up and carry it. Only then will it make you stronger."

"But what if I can't? What if I'm never ready?"

"You will be," Karramis said, confidence etched in her features. "When you least expect it, you will be. And you will be stronger because of it."

Rhiannon was skeptical of her mother's words, the hope and faith behind them. Those things were not something she was worthy of. She was afraid she would never overcome the immense trepidation taking root even deeper in her mind, body, and soul.

"How can you be so sure?"

Squatting beside Rhiannon, Karramis held her hand and declared wholeheartedly, "Because you're my daughter. And when we get knocked down, we always stand back up. It may not be right away, but we do eventually stand. The hardest part is finding that strength to do it."

Unsure what to say, Rhiannon turned away and leaned against the railing.

Karramis kissed the back of her head and headed back toward the door.

Strength. That was the problem. Rhiannon was not strong enough. She was the weak link. Even Merrick had seen it, sensed it. It was something she had feared after the first attack, and after last night, it had planted deep inside her, taking even more strength from her—robbing her of the control over her own body and mind.

It was not anyone else's fault for what had happened to her. It was hers. She was the one who had failed. She had not only disappointed her magic, her family, and destiny, but she had failed herself.

"Mom?" Rhiannon said softly, not turning around.

Karramis stopped under the doorframe. "Yeah?"

"Do you still carry it? The things that make you unable to sleep at night?"

"Yes." A simple reply. "Every single day."

Chapter 14

Drifting in and out of consciousness as the afternoon sun beamed sporadically through the thick clouds, Rhiannon welcomed any rest her body would surrender to, but it never lasted long. Behind every moment of deep sleep linked to her unwavering fatigue were more horrible memories, phantom pains, and abhorrent thoughts, and it drove her to bolt awake as she remained sitting on the stairs outside.

"Rhiannon?" James said softly behind her as the front door clicked shut.

Keeping her gaze forward, she leaned back into the railing, her eyes fluttering as the sun breached from behind a fast-moving cloud. "I still don't want to talk about it." The declaration was quiet and laced with weariness.

"I know." Understanding and sadness coated his words. "I just brought you something to eat. I figured you might be hungry." He set a plate filled with cheese, crackers, and mixed fruit on the porch next to her. "Mind if I sit?"

"No, it's fine," she said quietly, eyeing the plate. "Thanks, but I'm not really hungry."

James sat down on the opposite side of the stairs and leaned against the other railing. His shoulders sagged as apprehension flooded his face.

He shifted nervously and rotated to face the trees, leaning forward and resting his forearms against his bent legs. "Why won't you talk to me?"

Rhiannon blinked but kept her eyes focused in front of her. "I just don't want to."

James turned his pleading eyes to her. "But why? Are you mad at me?"

"No," Rhiannon announced, surprised by his question, finally meeting his gaze. "Why would I be mad at you?"

James lifted his shoulders and shook his head. "I don't know, maybe because you refuse to talk to me."

Rhiannon was unsure how to respond. She wanted desperately to talk about it, especially with him, her best friend, but she could not find the words to express what she was feeling.

"Please," James stated, his voice hopeful and insistent, "let me help you. I want to help you." He waited, but she did not react. "What are you thinking? Give me something. If you're not mad, then what are you?"

A lump rose in her throat, and she quickly swallowed it as she drove away the burn in her eyes, denying her emotions the ability to surface. "I'm not thinking about anything."

James could feel the roller coaster of emotions flowing through Rhiannon. However, her mind was blank—or maybe not blank, but rather distant, as if she were deeper into the dark voids of her mind than he could understand.

"Liar," he said, no condescension in the declaration, only a soft-spoken truth.

Rhiannon heaved a sigh before rising to her feet.

"Hey." James gently grabbed her wrist and pulled her to a stop, their eyes locking. "When you need me, I'm here."

Dipping her chin in a single nod, she slid from his hold and retreated down the stairs. "I know."

Rhiannon rounded the corner just as a familiar golden eagle came into view over the trees to the west. Without a hint of reluctance, she ran toward it.

James twisted around and bolted from the stairs as he heard her hurried footfalls rustling through the grass and followed her.

The outstretched wings elongated as feathers disappeared into skin, the light ivory contrasting against the darker quills. A dark blue shirt appeared along the bird's body as it lengthened into a tall, lean, athletic torso, and khaki pants emerged with human legs as white shoes sprouted just below the hem. A mouth, nose, and forehead shifted into place, taking over the avian features in the blink of an eye. Combed strawberry-blond hair rose along the top of the head as it morphed into the size of a human skull. Emerald-green eyes went from large rounded sockets to a beautiful almond shape, the color seeming brighter as Aidan shifted wholly into human.

"Aidan!" Rhiannon called in relief as she crashed into his chest, throwing her arms around him.

Aidan grunted as the jolt of her hug sent him stumbling back a step. "I'm all right, piuthar bheag." He wrapped his arms around her. "I'm okay."

She peeled herself away from the embrace, worry pinching her face. "Uncle Pavian?"

Squeezing her shoulders, he observed the dark circles under her eyes and the exhaustion sinking into her features. "He's okay."

Rhiannon let out a deep sigh of reprieve, the concern lifting a weight from her shoulders. "I was so worried."

"I know. And I'm sorry it took me so long to come back, but somethin' came up."

Unease settled back into her. "Is everything okay?"

Aidan hesitated for a moment as James neared. "I feel I should wait for the others before discussin' this with you." His eyes blinked up at James. "I'm glad to see you both are all right." He ran a finger over the puncture marks on Rhiannon's neck, and his body stiffened, his tone straining with anger. "I never should've left you."

"If you would've stayed," Rhiannon said, brushing his hand away and covering her injuries, "he would've killed you. Plus, it's healing, so it's fine." A helpless gleam darkened in her eyes as her unconvincing expression lifted to Aidan. "Really, it's fine. I'm fine."

Aidan furrowed his brow but kept his opinions to himself. "Where are yer parents?" He glanced between the twins. "I need to let them know they will be expectin' company shortly."

"Who?" James asked.

"Yer aunt, uncle, grandfather, and Sterling Andralae."

"Who's that?"

Aidan motioned toward the cabin as he started walking. "I will fill you in on what I can, but first we need to get yer parents."

James hurried ahead. "I'll go get them."

Strolling over to the cabin, Aidan asked Rhiannon, "Are you sure ye're all right?"

"Yes," she replied.

Aidan eyed her, unconvinced by the flatness in her tone and her refusing to meet his gaze. "Do you want to talk about it?"

"No."

"All right. But just know you aren't alone. Even in the darkest moment, the slightest bit of light can bring you home."

Rhiannon kept her eyes on the ground as they reached the front of the cabin. "Thanks, Aidan."

He gave her a gentle nudge with his elbow. "Anytime, piuthar bheag."

Karramis stepped onto the porch first and smiled as she took in Aidan. "I'm so glad you're okay." She descended the steps and gave him a hug.

Will leaned against the pillar along the threshold of the porch, lazily folding his arms over his chest. "Run into any trouble last night?"

"No," Aidan said as he withdrew from Karramis's embrace, "I flew ahead to make sure Pavian wasn't goin' to encounter anythin' that wasn't supposed to be on this side."

"That was smart," Rhiannon admitted with a quizzical arch of her brow.

Aidan gave her a mocking grin. "Thanks. I have my moments."

"Sorry, I didn't—I just meant—"

"No worries, lass. I'm only givin' you a hard time." He let out a soft chuckle. "I know what you meant."

"So," Karramis said, "what's going on, Aidan? James said you had some news."

"Something bad happened, didn't it?" James asked, resting his back against the railing along the stairs.

"To be honest with you," Aidan admitted, "I'm not quite sure. All I know is Zarrius received some news early this mornin', soon after Pavian and I returned to the village, and summoned him and Kavana right away. They're all headed here now to discuss it with you. I was simply asked by Zarrius to notify you of their arrival."

Aidan was not part of Zarrius's guard, nor was he a Guardian, but his official demeanor and formal declaration made Rhiannon even more anxious. Fear tightened around her stomach, constricting and writhing as nausea traveled up into her esophagus, the burn matching the ache pounding against her ribs. Wrapping her fingers inward, she drove her nails into her sweaty palms as she focused on her uneven breaths. She had to control herself. Her emotions were not going to take over. She would not cry. She refused to shed another tear.

"When will they be here?" Will asked, coming up beside Karramis, his arm brushing hers as he reached out his pinky and caressed her hand.

"Shortly. Within a few minutes actually. I only shifted at the outskirts of Kitra Forest, and they were travelin' fast."

James glanced over at the forest to the west as the others appeared. "Perfect timing."

Zarrius emerged first, flanked by Pavian. Both were riding solid black horses. Kavana followed behind on a chestnut horse with a white blaze and socks. Appearing last were two other horses, both gray with black spots. One was without a rider, most likely Aidan's, and the other had a younger woman mounted atop. All five horses galloped closer with effortless speed and pure grace.

Zarrius's winged horse, Galahad, came to a stop first. The creature's silky black wings were pressed tightly against his body, and he stood nearly half a foot taller than the other black horse, who halted behind him, carrying Pavian. He was riding Shadow, James's horse. Kavana, riding in on Rhiannon's horse, Cinnamon, reached out and pulled on the reins of the horse with no rider, and they both settled behind Pavian and Zarrius. Tugging on the mane of the last horse, a young woman with dark brown hair and warm skin dismounted and ushered the animal over to a patch of lush grass along the side of the cabin.

Rhiannon skimmed her eyes over the young woman. Curves and flawless light tanned skin accentuated the beauty of the vivacious lady, her eyes a shade darker than her mother's and brother's rich brown. She wore a flowing long dark blue dress but no shoes. Dark tresses so brown they were almost black were pulled back into a loose braid as her curly tendrils lined her round face. There was something about her that made Rhiannon let out an even breath. There was a calm radiating from the woman. Serenity. Warmth. Like she was the bringer of peace.

"Everyone," Zarrius said, sliding off Galahad, "I'd like you to meet Sterling Andralae."

Karramis's eyes shot to him. "Andralae? As in Marie Andralae? The seer?"

The sense of calm and peace drained from Rhiannon, as did the blood from her face. "Seer?"

She met her grandfather's stern but soft expression, a hint of worry lining his bluish-gray eyes. Her body went stiff, and her limbs became heavy. She had only been around her grandfather a handful of moments since arriving back in Kiluemar, and each time he was always kind and cordial, but there was still a strong presence surrounding him that made Rhiannon nervous. He was confident, tough, and wise, always appearing bored and yet alert at all times. Power, strength, and dominance radiated from him. Even though she had never seen the strictness and controlling nature her mother and aunt talked about, she could sense it from him. He was not someone anyone would want to cross. But despite everything, his light silvery-blue eyes glimmered with an undeniable sheen of comfort and hope—something she had learned over time from her father and Aidan was a way to ease her panic and worries.

Zarrius's eyes locked on Rhiannon, the lines around his weathered mouth deepening as he turned between Karramis and Rhiannon. "Yes, Sterling is a seer."

Rhiannon glanced over at her mother and saw the tension in her shoulders ease a bit as her chest rose with a heavy sigh. Her grandfather's ability to lesson negative emotional responses apparently worked on her mother as well.

Karramis reached out a hand. "Pleasure to meet you, Sterling."

The seer strolled forward and slipped her fingers into Karramis's palm. "The pleasure is all mine. My mother told me and my sister all about you. How you are the vision of the great prophecy." Her hand dropped to her side, and her eyes turned to James and Rhiannon. "Or at least part of it."

Grief lined Karramis's features. "I'm sorry to hear about your mother's passing. Marie was a wonderful woman."

"She is deeply missed." Her words were taut. "But she refused to be a pawn. My sister and I would do the same if it came to that."

Still sitting on the steps, James asked, "What do you mean?"

Sterling faced him, sadness and anger glistening in her eyes. "My mother was almost captured by Merrick seven years ago. He wanted her magic, but she fought him. And when she tried to kill him, he murdered her instead. Right in front of me and my sister. I was only fifteen at the time, and my sister was twelve."

"I'm sorry," James replied, regretting his question.

"Thank you. It cannot be undone, so I do not dwell on it."

"Sorry to ask this," Rhiannon chimed in, "but do you have powers like your mother? What about your sister?"

"Cecilia hasn't shown any signs of possessing our mother's gift, and I hadn't either. That is, until two nights ago."

Karramis squared her shoulders and gave a look of understanding to her father and siblings. "Another verse?"

All three of them nodded, but Zarrius answered, "Yes. Sterling had a vision in her dreams and was compelled to write it down."

"Why are we just hearing about it now?" Rhiannon asked as a nervousness pooled in her lower stomach.

"Because," Kavana answered, composed and unnervingly firm, "seers don't know the acts they are performing right away. Some don't even know they've seen, or in the case of this prophecy, heard anything. If someone isn't around or the magic in them doesn't force them to write it down, some visions or words are lost."

"I only woke this morning," Sterling admitted softly, "having lost a whole day. And when I saw the writing, I went straight to Zarrius."

"Seers are usually only supposed to see visions, hence their name," Pavian said. "They don't speak of what the future brings. Those gifts were given to oracles, but they have been extinct for centuries. And when seers or oracles experienced their powers, it was sometimes linked to strange events or periods of lost time."

James's brows pinched into a questioning frown. "But if the seers here are seeing and speaking the possible future, wouldn't that mean they are both?"

Zarrius nodded. "Technically, yes."

"I do believe we are getting off track here," Karramis interrupted, facing Sterling. "Is what you saw and heard part of the previous prophecy?"

"I believe so."

Fear and panic returned to Rhiannon in a wave of warmth, filling her veins with surging heat as her heart sank against her stomach, the nausea bubbling deep in her gut.

"I wrote it down for you," Sterling continued, reaching into a pocket of her dress and handing Karramis a folded piece of paper.

Will rested his hand on the small of Karramis's back, peering over her shoulder as she stared for a moment, her eyes fixed on the paper with an anxious expression.

"What does it say, Mom?" James asked, stepping over to his parents.

Rhiannon could not move. It was as if her feet were made of concrete and her bones were leaden. She felt as if she would crash to the ground at any moment. Her heart pounded in her chest, the rapid thumping echoing within the chaotic thoughts bouncing around in her head. She forced a quick shake, trying to alleviate some of the noise so she could hear her mother speak as she fought against every ounce of her wanting to hide and never come out.

Karramis's chest heaved as she read the words, her voice strained from worry.

The shadow of darkness will soon emerge,
when hidden powers unite and surge
The darkest magic once foretold,
will reap within an evil so old
Two as one bound together,
a rare event will be the tether
Five among the purest soul,
a power invoked and given control
Death will knock at the fated door,
within the circle will stand the four
A life taken and never to return,
for all magic within must burn
Black and white will cover the land,
and all will fall with this final stand
Created magic will be the cost,
left with none and soon be lost

"What does all of it mean?" Rhiannon asked, her eyes darting between everyone. "Does it mean we're going to die?"

"No," Karramis said reassuringly.

"It sure as hell sounds like it." Rhiannon's words were loud and shrill. "Why can't magic just give us a damn clear picture of what the hell we're supposed to do? Why all this cryptic crap? Why the damn mind games?"

"Rhiannon," Kavana and Karramis said, advancing over to comfort her.

"No!" Rhiannon stepped back, evading them. "Don't touch me."

"I'm so sorry," Sterling offered wholeheartedly. "I didn't mean to cause you so much pain."

"I don't blame you," Rhiannon declared, her words harsh and tense, anger burning across her face. "No, I don't blame anyone." She stumbled back. "But I . . . I can't do this! I can't." Distress settled on her face as she turned to her brother. "James, you can't—I don't want you to . . ." She hesitated, not wanting to say the words. Exhaling, she admitted, "I don't want to die."

"Rhiannon," Karramis said as she gripped her daughter's shoulders, "listen to me. You are *not* going to die. Do you hear me? I will not let your life end because of this damn prophecy. We are going to fight and win. You are going to survive." She tilted a head to James. "Both of you are going to survive. I've always believed that. And I will do everything in my power to make sure I am right."

Will walked up behind Karramis and eased his arm around her back, resting a hand on her hip. "And you know how your mum loves being right." He chuckled under his breath as the tension relaxed on his wife's face, and she gave him an annoyed yet playful sneer. "What? You do."

Karramis took the twins' hands in hers as her brown eyes bounced back and forth with a comforting gaze. "Life is a war." Her voice was sincere and encouraging. "Every single day is a battle. A never-ending fight to survive. And you can either go through it swinging a sword or waving a white flag. The choice is up to you. But remember this—the outcome of whatever choice you make will depend on what you do once the true enemy shows up."

"Who's the true enemy?" James asked, confused.

"You are."

Rhiannon narrowed her eyes, her face and tone devoid of all emotions. "We're the enemy?"

"Yes." Karramis brushed a strand of Rhiannon's hair behind her ear and ran her other hand down James's arm. "Because you are the voice in your head telling you it's not possible. You're the emotions controlling your actions. You're the eyes that see the mistakes and flaws. You're the judge, jury, and executioner of your own life. *You* are your own worst enemy."

"And until you learn how to win the battle with yourself," Zarrius said softly as he stepped forward, "you'll never win the war." He raised a hand to Karramis's back and leaned in. "It's nice to know some of the things I taught you stuck. I always figured it went in one ear and out the other."

"No," Karramis said, glancing over at him, "I was listening. I was always listening. I just didn't want to hear it at the time.

But your words have always stayed with me, Dad. And they always will.”

Rhiannon was lost in a trance—her mind somewhere else completely, focused on nothing yet consumed by everything. Words rambled around in her head—prophecy verses and encouraging yet difficult-to-comprehend promises and declarations. Everything ran rampant in her mind. She had no control, no time to process and rationalize every little detail. It was consuming, pulling her into a dark place where she felt nothing. Wanted and needed nothing. Was nothing.

Rhiannon broke away from her mother’s hold and stormed off.

“Rhiannon?” James called, rushing after her.

Karramis and Kavana gripped either side of his arms.

He shot them both an annoyed scowl. “What are you doing?”

“Let her go, Son,” Will begged earnestly.

“Why?” James asked, concern and hopelessness taking over his features. “She needs me.”

“Yes,” Aidan said, stepping in front of him and cutting off his advancement toward her, “she does. But until she figures that out on her own, you need to let her go.”

“Why?” he repeated.

Karramis released him. “Because if she doesn’t admit it to herself first, she’ll never admit it to you.”

“Just give her time,” Kavana offered, soft and comforting. “She’ll come around. She’s strong-willed, but even she needs time to process things.”

"Kind of like your mum," Will added.

"I know it's hard to let her go," Pavian said, grasping James's shoulder. "To allow her to figure things out herself. But if she's anything like your mom and aunt, if you push her, she's only going to push back."

Aidan and Will nodded in agreement.

"The women in this family are stubborn," Pavian continued, "but they are also resilient, true fighters, and some of the strongest, most determined women I've ever known. And before you know it, she'll be back in your face telling you off and showing you just how powerful she is."

"And . . ." James sighed. "What if she doesn't? What if what happened yesterday and learning about this other verse brings her on the verge of jumping over the edge?" He watched as Rhiannon headed toward the trees to the east. "What if she doesn't come back from this? What if she's lost for good?"

"Do you really think that will happen?" Karramis asked.

"No." There was no thought, no hesitation. "No, I don't."

Chapter 15

The Wait

Leaning against the railing, James watched the grazing horses and the trees where Rhiannon had disappeared hours ago.

"What're you still doing out here?" Karramis asked as she closed the door behind her.

James heaved a heavy sigh. "Waiting for Rhiannon."

"No sign of her yet?"

"No."

"You know she's going to be okay, right? She just needs time to process everything."

"It's all my fault." Regret filled his tone.

Her expression was tight as she lowered her brows. "What is?"

"What happened to her. It's all my fault."

"No." Karramis leaned over next to him, her arms braced against the railing. "No, James, what happened was not your fault."

James dropped his gaze. "Yeah, it was. If I hadn't pushed Merrick's buttons, if I hadn't told him I wasn't scared of him, then maybe she wouldn't have gotten hurt."

"Listen." Karramis grabbed his chin and angled his head toward her. "No one could've predicted what happened last night. Maybe if you had kept quiet things might've ended differently. Maybe not. Maybe Merrick was just looking for an excuse to assert fear and dominance. Merrick's an alpha male—a vicious, self-absorbed, evil, and extremely smart alpha male. He takes pleasure in people cowering before him. But you didn't. You stood up to him. In a way, you challenged him. And he took that as a threat, so he acted accordingly."

"Yeah, and Rhiannon was the one who got hurt in the process."

"Yes." Karramis sighed, dropping her hand. "She did. And no one can take that back. No one can fix the mistakes that were made. We can only learn from them. But maybe it will help her."

"How?"

"Sometimes trauma or strong emotions can trigger that switch inside a person. That switch that tells you to fight back or surrender. And your sister is a fighter. She's a survivor. I know she is. She just doesn't know it herself yet. I can see it—I can feel it—deep inside me because . . . well, because I was her."

"You mean with running all those years? From Lucas?"

"Yes. Among other things." Karramis gave him a sidelong grin. "Rhiannon is very much like me in many ways. She wears her heart on her sleeve, and she allows her emotions to cloud her judgement and actions. She worries about things she can't control. And the worst of it is she's afraid. But not just from obvious things. She's afraid of making a mistake. Failing. She's afraid of messing up and someone else getting hurt because of it. Losing someone. Fear is the most powerful emotion next to pride and love. Those three things are what drive us all. But instead of using her fear for power, she's allowing it to control her."

"But how do we fix that? How can we help her fight the urge to surrender to fear?"

"We can't. We don't have that kind of power over her. Only she can decide to take control. She is the one who has to decide she wants to fight."

"Do you think she will?" James asked incredulously.

Karramis smiled at him. "I have no doubt about it."

"But how can you be so sure?"

"Because, like I said before, she is like me in many ways. I have faith in her, and you should too. Never underestimate her."

"I do have faith in her." Sincerity and hope clung to his words. "I do. I believe she can do it."

"Then the next time you get the chance, make sure you tell her that. She looks up to you, James. In her eyes, you're her hero, so make sure she knows you aren't giving up on her. Then maybe she'll have the courage to be her own hero one day."

Karramis patted his arm and pushed herself upright. "Pavian wants to talk to you, but I wanted to check on you first."

"Is everything okay?"

"Yeah, but I'll let him be the one to fill you in."

Karramis headed for the door.

"Hey, Mom," James said softly, peering over his shoulder, "what's going to happen when Merrick comes back?"

Karramis paused with her hand on the doorknob and blew out a shaky breath. "You will prove to him that you two aren't going down without a fight."

"And will you be there with us?"

She smiled again. "Of course."

The agreement his mother had made with Merrick had remained in his thoughts since last night, the worry of what she might have agreed to setting his nerves on high alert.

Concerned, James asked, holding her gaze, "What deal did you make with Merrick?"

"Nothing I can't handle," Karramis admitted with a grin.

Her response had not answered his question.

"Does Dad know what it is?"

"Yes."

Good. At least someone knew what she was planning, even if it was not him. And his father would never allow her to willingly walk into danger, at least not without a clear escape plan in place. Maybe it was not as bad as James thought it would be.

"Is he okay with it?" he asked, trying to gauge the severity of her deal with Merrick.

"No." Karramis forced a chuckle. "But he trusts that I know what I'm doing."

James had never doubted his mother's strength or determination, but then again, she had never battled against

Merrick. Even her abilities, though rare and stronger than others, were no match for Merrick's stolen magic.

"And do you?" There was reluctance in the question, an uncertainty in wanting to hear the answer. "Know what you're doing, that is?"

Karramis arched a brow, amused by the question. "I'd like to think so."

James peered into her eyes, both sets of rich brown staring at each other. "You're not going to surrender, right?"

Karramis remained quiet as she stepped back over to him and kissed his forehead. "Never."

"You're going to fight?"

Her face beamed with reassurance. "Of course."

"Promise?"

"I promise."

James smiled. "Good. I'm going to hold you to that."

A click sounded at the door, and Pavian stepped out, greeting James with a tight squeeze of the shoulder.

James patted his arm. "How are you doing? I mean, after last night."

A small smirk twitched along one corner of Pavian's mouth. "Shouldn't I be the one asking you that instead?"

"I'm perfectly fine."

"Really?" Pavian studied him. "I find that hard to believe."

The front door opened wider, and Zarrius and Sterling stepped onto the porch, followed by Kavana, Aidan, and Will.

James watched everyone make their way down the stairs. "What's going on?"

Zarrius gave a quick high-pitched whistle before facing James. "We must get Sterling back to the village before nightfall. Then, tomorrow morning Pavian will escort her back to Stoweward before he leaves."

James shot a puzzled gaze over at his uncle. "Leave? Where are you going?"

"That's what I wanted to discuss with you," Pavian said. "I'm going to be gone for a little while."

"Why?"

"Because . . ." A somber expression took over Pavian's features, but his voice remained steady. "After Merrick's comment last night, I believe something may have happened at MUSE."

"Do you think he did something?"

"I'm not sure, but I have to go check it out. I have to make sure everyone is okay."

"When will you be back?"

"In a few weeks. I'll only be gone until the next full moon."

Zarrius mounted Galahad. "Son, Sterling and I will go on ahead. Say your goodbyes and meet up with us shortly."

Pavian nodded. "Yes, sir. I'll be right behind you."

"Be careful, Dad," Kavana said, holding the reins of Sterling's horse as Karramis helped the seer onto the animal's back.

James angled his head in his aunt's direction. "Are you staying?"

"For a bit," she answered. "If you don't mind me and Aidan crashing here."

"Not at all." James smiled over at Aidan. "It'll be a slumber party."

"Sounds fun," Aidan added. "As long as you don't snore."

"No promises." James swiveled back over to Kavana. "But why? Not that I don't enjoy all the company, but why are you deciding to stay?"

Kavana gently patted the side of Sterling's horse and glanced up at her. "Take care, Sterling. Be safe."

"I will," the seer said with a curt nod. "And again, I'm sorry for any stress I might've caused."

"No," Karramis stated, "it is not your fault. Thank you for coming out here and giving us the message." Her eyes met her father's. "Be careful. I will be in the village later this week to discuss this further, Dad."

"I look forward to seeing you again," Zarrius said, winking and nudging Galahad forward.

Everyone watched as the two horses headed away from the cabin.

To no one in particular, James asked, "Why doesn't Galahad just fly them back?"

"Father has never been a fan of flying," Pavian answered.

James huffed out a low laugh. "Then why does he have a winged horse?"

"Because," Will responded with a boyish grin, "they're cool."

Laughter broke out among the group.

"Anyway," Kavana said, clearing her throat, "to answer your other question, James, Aidan and I are staying to make sure Rhiannon is okay. After what Aidan and your parents told me, I want to make sure she's okay. She needs support right now, and we're all going to be here for her."

James ran his fingers through his messy dark brown hair. "And what if she doesn't want it?"

Kavana folded her arms over her chest as a look of encouragement filled her face. "Trust me, she does. Rhiannon just needs a moment to clear her head. And once that's done, she'll break down. Then afterward, she'll pull herself together and analyze it from a different perspective. The only problem is, she sometimes forgets to do the breaking down part and just tries to go straight to being her normal self again—rationalizing a situation before letting go of whatever she was holding in. However, like me"—Kavana pointed at Karramis—"and her mother, she needs the breaking down part to happen or she'll never really be able to move on."

"Yeah," Karramis agreed, "that release of emotion, that acknowledgement of internal defeat, is like a weight being lifted off our shoulders. Or like a wave washing away all the negativity. It's a healing process for us, whereas for guys, or at least most of the guys I know personally, they wash their emotions away with alcohol or by other means. Yes, they sometimes retreat into their mind and break down too, but most of the time they choose to hide those pent-up feelings with drinking or some form of aggression."

"Or sex," Kavana added bluntly. "One of my favorite tactics too, I might add."

Karramis gave her a criticizing scowl. "Or that." She focused on James. "But I don't recommend that option until you are at least twenty-five."

Pavian, Aidan, and Will choked on a laugh.

Karramis turned her scowl to them. "Could we focus here?"

"Sorry," Pavian said, stifling his laugh. "Continue."

"Anyway, as I was saying . . . Shit, what was I saying?"

James chuckled. "Something about what guys do with pent-up feelings."

"You know, darling," Will acknowledged sweetly, "men do use other means to handle their emotions too, right? Most just hide it."

"Yes, I do know that," Karramis replied, "I was just speaking from a woman's perspective." She faced James again. "But yes, we all deal with our emotions differently, so you just have to give Rhiannon time to figure it out on her own. Then, when she's ready, she'll let us know. We just have to be patient and let her know we are here when she needs us."

"Well," James said, "I've already done that last part."

"Then all you have to do now is wait."

Kavana wrapped her arms around James's shoulders. "But we can all wait together. At least for a day or two. I'm not sleeping on the floor longer than that."

James slid a worried expression over to Pavian. "Wait, does Raina know you're leaving?"

"No," Pavian said, shaking his head. "I will tell her tomorrow. After I drop off Sterling, I'll head home. But then I'll have to leave the following morning. That's what I wanted to talk to you about. I was wondering if you would stay with her and Liam while I'm away. I'm not entirely comfortable leaving her while she's still in the early stages of her pregnancy. She's often exhausted or sick still, and Liam can be a handful some days."

"Of course. I'll head back when Aunt K and Aidan head home." James peered over at his dad. "Can I use Callie to get home? Shadow takes way too long."

"Absolutely. You may use her whenever you like. But remember, you also have the dragons as well."

"Right." James gave a low laugh. "I forgot about them."

"How's that going, by the way?" Pavian asked James.

"Much better actually. I can communicate with them as well as Rhiannon now, just not from as far away as she can. Oh! Speaking of Raina, do you think she's well enough to teach me more about astral projection while you're away?"

"I'm sure she'd love that."

"Great." A moment passed before James cleared his throat, aiming his eyes toward the ground. "May I ask a question? Something has been bothering me since last night."

"Sure," Karramis answered, not sure who he was directing the question toward.

A look of confusion gleamed in James's eyes as he lifted his head. "How did he do it?"

"Who?" Pavian asked, equally confused. "And do what?"

"How was Merrick able to hurt her like that?"

Karramis narrowed her eyes. "What do you mean?"

"Uncle Pavian told me Merrick can only eat when he's in his true demonic form. But last night he didn't completely shift to bite her or drink her blood."

Pavian sighed, his demeanor shifting to an authoritative role. "That's because he only drank her blood in his vampire form. But when Merrick wants to eat, he has to transform."

"Because of the second curse?"

"Yes. When the thirst takes over, the bloodlust, he becomes a vampire. But when his true hunger comes into play, he turns into something entirely different. Thirst drives one, and hunger controls the other."

Directing his next question at his mother and uncle, James asked, "Have you seen him before? I mean, in his true demonic form?"

Karramis shook her head. "No. None of us have. Well, your grandfather has—once. And up until last night, I'd only ever met him one other time."

James hesitated, afraid the answer to his next question would make his actions last night even more painful. "Was he going to kill her last night, or . . . or was he planning to do something else to her? Physically, I mean."

"No," Karramis stated with genuine reassurance, sensing the meaning behind his carefully worded question.

James's features were soft, but his eyes were filled with a lingering worry. "How can you be so sure?" He swallowed. "He seemed to be enjoying himself a little too much. I wanted to kill him for touching her like that."

"Merrick wouldn't have killed her because he is determined to get her powers," Pavian said. "It's one of the things he desperately wants. He believes your and Rhiannon's magic will break his curse or, if nothing else, allow him to control it."

"And to answer your other question," Karramis cut in, "as far as we know, Merrick doesn't mix pleasures. Rhiannon was simply a snack. A taunt to show his power. Yes, he got . . . satisfaction from what he was doing, but it's not the same as other carnal pleasures. The pleasures of the beast are not the pleasures of the man."

James pondered another thought. "How much magic does he actually have now?"

Karramis lifted a shoulder. "I don't know. But I know it's a lot. And after witnessing some of them last night, I can tell you he definitely has elemental witch powers and telekinesis for sure. But he has to have a lot more, and I mean a lot, to affect the portals in such a way. Just coming back through sent the realm into a frenzy, even if only for a moment."

James gave a quick glance over his shoulder, eyeing the tree line behind him. "How was he able to do what he did to us? I mean, with that choking thing he did."

Pavian clicked his tongue, driving the spotted gray horse's attention. "Aidan, do you mind if I take your horse back? I'll leave Shadow and Cinnamon here with you to take back when you are ready."

"It's fine with me. I'll most likely fly back anyway and scout ahead for any possible dangers." Aidan eyed Kavana. "I don't want anyone else to get hurt."

Kavana arched a brow, a hint of playful annoyance in her tone. "You do know I'm very capable of defending myself, right?"

Aidan wrapped an arm around her waist. "Yes, I'm very aware, but that doesn't mean I can't be chivalrous and protective."

"My hero," Kavana said mockingly, leaning into him and gently nudging his ribs. "Don't lie. You just hate riding a horse."

"True." Aidan tossed James a teasing grin. "They really start to hurt my arse after a while."

James snickered as Pavian jumped smoothly onto the horse.

"I have to go catch up with the others," Pavian said, tugging the reins so the horse faced west. "I need to get to the village and get some things in order before I leave."

"Are you going by yourself?" James asked.

"No. I will be taking Tenarick and Quinian with me."

"Do you think something bad happened?"

Pavian lowered his eyes. "Yes. I hope I'm wrong, but Merrick wouldn't have made a comment like that if something hadn't happened."

"Maybe it's a trap."

"That's not exactly Merrick's style."

Karramis placed a hand on his leg. "Please be careful. You have a wife and son who need you and a child who needs to meet their father when they arrive in this world."

"I know." Pavian rested a hand on top of hers. "I'll be okay. Don't worry so much, Kare. It'll give you wrinkles and gray hair." He glanced over at his other sister. "Just like Kavana."

"Hey!" Kavana lifted her hands to her hips. "I do *not* have wrinkles. And I've only found four gray hairs lately, but I pulled them all out."

"Still counts," Pavian teased before urging the horse into a steady trot.

"Asshole!" Kavana called after him, flipping him off.

"Love you too!" Pavian yelled over his shoulder.

"You two have a strange relationship," James pointed out with narrowed eyes.

"And you and Rhiannon don't?" Kavana questioned, tone smooth and playful.

"She doesn't call me an asshole."

"Just wait," she added with a laugh. "She will soon enough."

James glanced behind him again. "Should we go find her?"

"If she's not back before sunset," Will said, "Aidan and I will go searching for her."

"Okay." James plopped down on the steps again. "So, is anyone going to answer my question?"

Kavana climbed up the stairs. "I think I'm going to go in and start dinner. I'm starving."

"Need help?" Aidan asked, following behind her.

"Sure, as long as you actually help and don't hover over me and eat everything in sight."

"I can't promise anythin', but I will definitely try to control my grazin' habits."

Aidan and Kavana both entered the cabin, the door closing behind them.

Karramis and Will took up a seat near James on the steps.

"It was an elemental magic that did what he did," Karramis finally answered.

James drew his brows together. "Meaning?"

"I'm not sure entirely, but it was either air or water magic. Based on what I was feeling, though, I bet I know which one. I think Merrick used air magic to remove the oxygen from our lungs."

James blinked in disbelief. "Air Witches can do that?"

"Yes," Karramis said with a nod. "They have to be exceptionally powerful, though, because that is an advanced ability. Only extremely skilled witches can do it."

"Could I possibly do it too one day?"

"Yeah."

"Good." His tone was savage and raw. "Because I'm going to use it on that fucking bastard." His gaze shot to his mother, his voice apologetic. "Sorry, Mom."

Will clamped his mouth shut, but a chuckle still escaped him.

Karramis rolled her eyes at her husband. "It seems you're learning bad habits from your father. But it's fine, James. After last night, I think that one was deserving."

"Me?" Will questioned comically, drawing out the word. "Your mouth is far more vulgar than mine. You make grown men blush with your mouth."

Karramis drew up a brow and gave him a wicked smirk. "What an odd choice of words."

"Gross," James stated, scrunching his nose.

Will smiled as he leaned over and kissed Karramis. "I'm going to head inside and help with preparations. I'm utterly famished, and those two will destroy the kitchen if you leave them unattended for too long."

"Hey, Dad," James said, rotating to face him by the door, "when will you go look for her?"

"I'll head out after I eat. I promise. I'll find her and make sure she's safe."

An approving smile appeared on James's face. "Thanks."

Karramis squeezed her son's leg before rising and following behind Will. She paused at the door and watched James as he stared at the forest to the east.

Her voice was soft as she told him, "She isn't struggling with what happened to her. Not really. Those are simply details that will fade over time. What she is struggling with is herself. She's fighting with herself because she didn't do more to stop it, didn't fight harder."

James tilted his head. "It sounds like you speak from personal experience."

"I do."

"And what pulled you out of it?"

"Time. But mostly, it was your dad. He helped me find my way back. He reached into the darkness and pulled me out. He didn't give up on me."

James twisted back around and peered over at the forest. "Then I will do the same for her. I won't give up on her. I'll pull her out and show her she isn't alone."

Even though he had lost the mental connection with her, he could still sense her emotions, every ache flowing deep inside her. And one way or another, he was going to drive those to the surface and help her face each one. Together.

Chapter 16

Into the Darkness

The pain was consuming, an invisible ache clutching tightly around the vital organ giving the body life. An agony so powerful it held each part of the mortal vessel with acute phantom asphyxiation. The stomach twisted into gut-wrenching knots as an acidic wave of guilt rose into the throat, stopping short behind a thump of unfathomable emotions. Limbs ached as regret burrowed into the bones. Anger rippled through each muscle. Hatred coursed through the veins. Shame took root deep within the mind. And yet the heart was where it all joined, combined into one massive catalyst of overwhelming pain. Pain, which was only physical in the deepest sense but still held control over the mental and emotional facets of the vessel.

Rhiannon wanted to feel all those things again. The same things she had felt after Haydrin had attacked her all those months ago. Sense every emotion again, even if they overwhelmed her. Sense anything to remind herself each breath she forced in and out of her was for a reason. She wanted to feel something to prove to herself she was still alive. But she felt nothing. She was empty. Covered in a cloud of darkness. She was so tired, both her body and mind lost behind a veil of numbness and exhaustion. All she wanted to do was sleep. Sleep away the hollowness sweeping through her and consuming her very soul.

The blades of lush grass poked against the exposed skin under her sandals and tickled her ankles as Rhiannon made her way through Kitra Forest. A mix of pine, elm, and oak surrounded her, their dense canopies blocking most of the light from above. Only tiny slivers of rays beamed down, streaking along the grass, uprooted branches, boulders, and moss-covered ground with a kaleidoscope of luminous hues of white, yellow, and orange. Jasmine and fresh earthen aromas—a perfect blend of dirt, grass, and assorted foliage—permeated the clean salty air. The unusual summer heat was unnoticeable within the protection of the forest as the cool breeze from the coast blew through the branches, creating a calm hum among the undulating awnings of the trees.

Uncertain where she wanted to go, Rhiannon trudged forward, making her way closer to the opening near Sunrise Mesa. She did not want to go home. She wanted to be alone, and the cabin was not the place for her right now. There was too much attention on her. Too many people asking questions. Too many unknowns causing her lack of emotions to dredge up involuntary conclusions about herself. She just wanted silence. She did not want help, nor did she want to talk. Rhiannon just wanted to disappear for a moment. Allow all the chaotic ramblings in her head to slow into one cohesive thought—a rational and constructive thought—and not the traitorous impression that was taking root deeper inside her mind. The thought that, despite the prophecy, she was unworthy of her magic. That she was helpless, hopeless, and a burden to those around her.

Leaving the forest, Rhiannon stopped among the shadows under the trees. *"Oakley?"* Her inner voice was choked behind emotions she was unable to pinpoint. *"Raeth?"*

She closed her eyes and drew in a long breath through her nose before releasing it slowly. The lump in her throat eased, and the burning sensation forming behind her eyelids subsided.

"Please," she said, the sound of her own voice distant, even within her mind. *"Please, someone come for me."*

Rhiannon lowered to her knees and leaned against her heels, tucking the skirt of her long sundress and her hands between her thighs. She hung her head and squeezed her eyes closed.

I will not cry. I refuse to cry.

Flapping echoed across the stony plateau, and Rhiannon jerked her head up, eyeing two dragons flying in a circle a few yards outside the mouth of Emrys Cave. With their small stout bodies and earthy tones, she recognized them as Earth Dragons, but she was unsure which ones.

"Raeth?" she called out telepathically. *"Oakley, is that you?"* They did not respond.

Another dragon emerged from the cave and took flight, but all remained unaware of her presence.

"Terramina?"

Ignara crested the top of Maevis Mountains, pulled back her wings tightly against her body, and nose-dived before flinging open her wings and gliding effortlessly a few feet from the ground. Harkin followed behind her, chasing her as he soared downward, his plunge quicker, faster, and far more harrowing as he flipped over before outstretching his wings and sailing upside down over the stones.

The five dragons coasted through the sky with grace and flawless control, each dip, tuck, and flip showing no signs of hesitation or error. Raeth, Oakley, and Terramina, with their leaf-shaped wings and rough bodies of dark green and various shades of brown, soared through the sky like the drifting of leaves in the fall, circling closer to the ground. Black and red glided higher above as the two Fire Dragons cast huge shadows along the sun-covered rocks and dirt.

Rhiannon stood and stepped away from the forest floor and onto the rough uneven stones. The rocks under her sandals clattered, and all five dragons arched their wings and halted in midair, the stiffening of their bodies evident as they angled their heads in her direction. They monitored her every step, observing the unexpected presence of someone in their territory before recognizing her and soaring over in her direction.

A whoosh of air flowed across Rhiannon as flapping circled around overhead. Lifting her gaze, she exhaled a sigh, and relief filled her chest, the warmth blossoming through the icy ache of defeat that was slowly spreading.

Raeth landed first, cocking his head as something sad flashed in his eyes. He nudged his snout into her stomach, the soft, kind gesture laced with a pleading glare.

Staring at him with a confused expression, she gave him a forced smile, one filled with sorrow. "I'm okay."

Oakley and Terramina followed behind him, the three Earth Dragons advancing closer. The creatures were similar in appearance, but subtle differences allowed others to distinguish them. Raeth's and Oakley's almond-shaped eyes had flecks of golden honey scattered among their rich amber irises. A mix of brown, gray, and dark green colored their long round bodies, giving the illusion of large rocks covered in mud and moss, but Raeth was grayer along his back and face. The horns on their heads and faces were the color of dark storm clouds, but Oakley had part of his right horn missing at the tip. A profound curve rested along his mouth, making it appear as if he were always smiling. Terramina was slightly larger than the other two and had moss-green eyes, a deep scar slicing through the left side of her face and eye, and long-healed wounds through both wings and against one of her back legs. She lacked the gray hues along her body, the rich browns and dark green making her appear even more muddy and decorated in moss.

Rhiannon glanced up as the shadows overhead continued to circle the ground beyond the trees. Harkin flew higher, angling his head in all directions as if keeping a watchful eye on the surroundings. Ash and black scales covered most of his body, while dark crimson decorated his underbelly. Bright red and scarlet gleamed below him as Ignara swooped gracefully through the sky. Her black wings outstretched as she coasted overhead, each elegant flap sending a wave of warm salty air down to the ground.

"What are you all up to?" Rhiannon asked, her external voice sounding loud in her head.

A figure caught Rhiannon's attention, and she pulled her eyes away from the dragons, her gaze lifting toward the sky over the mountain peaks to the north.

Phosmeratae tore through the clouds with effortless beauty, his bright white feathers glistening under the sunlight as clouds in the distance rolled closer to the island.

Gratitude pinched Rhiannon's throat as the burning sensation returned to her eyes, her attention moving between the three Earth Dragons. "Did you call him?"

Phosmeratae landed behind the three Earth Dragons with a ground-shaking rumble, and Rhiannon craned her neck back and peered up at him. The lizard-like features on the creature's scaly face and the feathers were a deep contrast to the rich greens of the trees he towered over behind Rhiannon. The golden-yellow of his eyes seemed to glow against his white feathers and scales. His wings folded inward and pressed against his massive body like a bird as the four-legged dragon sat back against his haunches.

Rhiannon focused on the dragons, their silence within her mind echoing with a piercing, thunderous cry. Closing her eyes, she pulled herself inward, reaching for the adamant darkness blocked deep inside her thoughts. The voices were distant as she clung to them, reaching harder toward them. She wanted to take hold. She needed to not allow them to fall deeper into the darkness.

Breathing in a shuddering inhale, she opened her watery eyes, the relief showing in her faint smile.

"Please," she pleaded in her mind to them, *"take me away."*

"Welcome back," Oakley said, moving toward her and lowering himself to the ground. *"Where would you like to go?"*

Rhiannon climbed onto the dragon's back and leaned over, wrapping her arms around his wide neck and hugging him. *"Somewhere safe."*

Raeth, Terramina, and Phosmeratae stretched out their wings. With a strong push, they took to the sky, joining Harkin and Ignara before they all shifted and headed toward the coastline to the east.

Oakley rose to his feet and trotted after them, expanding his wings and flapping them with slow, steady beats. *"You are with us now, so we will keep you safe."*

"We will protect you," Raeth added, swooping upward with a strong flap of his wings, soaring into an aerial flip before gliding over to Rhiannon and Oakley and flanking them.

Terramina mirrored Raeth, hovering a few feet behind Oakley's other side as Ignara and Harkin drifted closer to the ground below Rhiannon and the Earth Dragon. Phosmeratae slowed and rose higher a few hundred feet, casting shadows as he flew overhead, the beating of his wings sending a rush of air down onto the dragons and Rhiannon.

A warm sense of calm filled her stomach and radiated through her body as tension lifted from her shoulders. They were surrounding her. The dragons were not only encircling her to protect her, but to show her no one and nothing was going to get to her without getting through them first. For the first time in months, Rhiannon truly felt safe.

As the cliffs along Sunrise Mesa came into view, Rhiannon watched as the two Fire Dragons parted and plunged downward over the edge of the land, diving toward the water below. Oakley reached the steep overhang of rocky terrain and coasted down, narrowly missing the gentle waves lapping over the sandy white shore. Rhiannon held on tight as she leaned over the side of Oakley, the dragon lowering to allow her hand to break through the surface of the water. His wings flapped and brushed against the waves, sending a spray of cool salty mist into the sky. The spray cascaded down and sent an energizing jolt of freshness along Rhiannon's bare arms and legs. Terramina and Raeth swooped in front of Oakley, weaving and twisting as they glided above the water, tilting occasionally to slice the tips of their wings through the surface. A rush of air crashed into Rhiannon as Phosmeratae propelled himself into the sky, the coolness of the water and breeze sending a tantalizing surge of excitement along her nerves. The Air Dragon climbed higher before disappearing into the clouds, joined by Harkin and Ignara.

Oakley rose higher as he tilted sideways, turning around and heading back to the shore.

Faint voices filled Rhiannon's head as a familiar thrill rose in the center of her chest, warming and spreading to her stomach and tingling deep in her core. A sensation of undeniable awareness and a powerful pull tugged at her soul and called to her like a beacon in the night. Magic. She focused on the voices, the soft, distant declarations of a bonded magic. A connection linked to friendship, trust, loyalty, admiration, and protection.

Dragons.

Rhiannon was sensing the Water Dragons deep within the ocean below. Streaks of blue appeared just below the surface as rippling waves flowed against the current.

"They can feel you," Terramina said as she flew alongside Oakley. *"Sense you calling them."*

"I didn't even know I was calling them," Rhiannon admitted, twisting back to watch the waves move unevenly behind her as the Water Dragons stayed below the surface.

"Your call is not always the words you speak," Oakley added, the youthful tone of his voice deep and husky. *"Sometimes it is simply a feeling that takes over us. Almost like your subconscious is calling us instead of you."*

Oakley descended and landed on the sandy coast of East Shores, and Terramina and Raeth followed behind him.

"I can't control it." Rhiannon swung her leg over the dragon and held the skirt of her dress as she slid off his back. *"I don't*

even know I'm doing it most of the time. I guess that's why you and Raeth came for me when I was in Full Moon Forest before."

Rhiannon's gaze moved from Oakley to Raeth, both dragons giving her a single nod of confirmation as she fought back a yawn trying to break free from her.

"Would you like us to take you home?" Terramina asked kindly as she watched Rhiannon force down her tiredness.

"No!" Rhiannon blurted out loud, the sharpness in her tone surprising to both her and the dragons. Apprehension filled her words, and the dragons sensed a strange mix of feelings pulsing below the surface as she continued internally, *"Sorry. It's just . . . I'm not ready to go home yet."*

Raeth nudged her in the side and angled his body around her, lying down at her feet. *"Then we will stay here until you are ready."*

The corner of her mouth lifted as she sat down and leaned back against the curve of Raeth's front leg and the tip of his folded wing. Oakley came forward and formed a semicircle next to Raeth, lowering himself near Rhiannon's curled legs.

Rhiannon lifted her hands and folded them under her cheek as the steady breathing of Raeth drove her eyes closed.

"Rest," Terramina pleaded softly.

And without a second thought, Rhiannon drifted further into a welcomed slumber as Raeth unfolded his wing and wrapped it around her, not only shielding her from the sun but reminding her she was safe.

A tightness clutched around her lungs and squeezed every shallow breath from her as her closed eyes fluttered. Her chest ached, and an icy hollowness filled her stomach. Her skin was clammy and hot, but chills shivered up her spine. Flashes surged through her, the images in her dreams flickering like a raging thunderstorm and streaking across the backdrop of her mind. Her heart hammered with a thunderous rumble, and a booming aftershock rattled deep inside her and jolted her body into convulsive twitches. Her cries faded behind a solid wall of adamant strength and burned her eyes, the trapped tears falling as silvery raindrops in her subconscious instead. The shimmering droplets glowed within the puddles slowly rising higher and higher, pooling and causing a pain to burn behind her eyelids.

"Rhiannon!" a deep voice called, distant and muffled.

Her eyes fluttered open.

Dusk had arrived, the sky painted in dark blue clouds as the softer hues of sunset lined the horizon below the storm rumbling overhead. Rain battered against something nearby as Rhiannon blinked, trying to adjust to the dimness surrounding her. She reached up a hand and brushed her fingers against something smooth and thin. A wing. Raeth's wing. She was lying under the Earth Dragon's carefully arched wing. Lightning flashed and lit up the world outside the membranous flesh as the waves nearby crashed against the shore.

"Rhiannon," the voice said again, softer and closer as shadows moved among another flash of lightning.

"Daddy?" Rhiannon whispered, confused after recognizing her father's voice through the grogginess clouding her mind. Her voice was childlike and soft, and it took every bit of strength to keep her eyes open.

Will crouched under the wings shielding Rhiannon from the rain. Not just Raeth's, but Oakley's and Harkin's as well. They had created a canopy over her as she slept, braving the storm so she could rest.

He brushed the back of his wet hand across her face, the innocence in her features reminding him of the brief time he had been given with her when she was a little girl.

"I'm here," he said quietly, lifting her into his arms. "I've got you."

Water dripped from his drenched hair as he pressed her into his chest, and she shivered from the coldness seeping from his wet clothes.

The two Earth Dragons and Harkin shifted and stood, keeping their wings outstretched over Will and Rhiannon.

The rain directly outside the arched wings had stopped abruptly but continued to fall heavily in the distance. Carrying Rhiannon out from under the protective covering, Will glanced upward, spotting Phosmeratae towering overhead, his massive outstretched wingspan blocking any rain from dropping onto them.

The overwhelming exhaustion continued to control Rhiannon, and she drifted in and out of consciousness as her father mounted Terramina.

Will situated himself on the dragon's back and lowered Rhiannon down, angling her against his chest and gripping her tighter.

Terramina and Phosmeratae jumped into the sky at the same time, working together and continuing to shield Will and Rhiannon from the rain.

Rhiannon forced her eyes open as the ascent into the air drove Will to tense beneath her and his thighs to tighten around the dragon.

"I don't . . ." Her ability to talk was lost behind the tiredness seeping into her muscles. "I don't want to go home."

"All right," Will said, understanding she was not ready to face what she was feeling just yet. "I'll take you somewhere else safe."

Echoes surrounded her as Will carried her into the mouth of Emrys Cave. Wet soil and musk wafted past her nose as the rain outside magnified within the cavern. Thunder exploded overhead and sent a rattling vibration along the smooth onyx stone. Icy blasts caressed her skin as they stepped deeper into the cave, but warmth soon met her as she was lowered onto a bed. A rush of exotic wildflowers and sea salt filled her senses, the smells of her mother sending comfort to every part of her. Rolling over, she welcomed another wave of familiar scents— the nettle bushes along the outskirts of Caerwyn Village, a subtle whiff of suede and cedar, and the gentle touches of lavender and jasmine in full bloom. Her father.

Will pulled a thick blanket over her. "Get some sleep. I'll be right back."

She settled into the warmth and relaxed her body, allowing herself to sink deeper into the mattress.

"Dad?" Rhiannon whispered, barely able to keep her eyes open.

Will glanced over at her as he turned on the oil lamp hanging from the low and narrow archway at the entrance to the makeshift room. "Yeah?"

"Stay. Please."

Moving quietly over to the corner of the room, Will grabbed a blanket draped over a rocking chair and made his way back over to her. He sat down on the floor next to the bed and covered himself up as he leaned his head against the mattress.

Rhiannon slid a hand across the bed and placed it on top of her father's still-wet shoulder. "Just until I fall asleep."

Will rested his hand over hers and squeezed just as she closed her eyes and drifted off to sleep. "I'll stay as long as you need me."

Chapter 17

Reaching Out

Thunder clapped as a bolt of lightning lit up the sky. Rain pounded against the rooftop, the downpour sending large droplets of water splashing upward from the soggy ground. A clean earthy musk filled the humid air as the scent of mud and grass flowed within each steady gust of wind.

A winged shadow coasted downward as another flash of lightning magnified the bright green eyes of the bird gliding to the ground.

"Where is she?" James asked Aidan as he shifted back into his human form.

Aidan's strawberry-blond hair was darker as it rested flat against his head. Water dripped in puddles from his plaid button-down shirt and dark khaki pants, and his saturated shoes squeaked as he ascended the steps onto the porch.

Shaking his head wildly, Aidan wrung the hem of his soaked shirt. "Where are yer mother and aunt?"

James pointed behind him with his thumb. "Inside." Panic filled his voice. "Why? Did something happen to Rhiannon?"

"No," Aidan said abruptly, trying to erase the tightness pulling at James's features. "Nah, she's fine, lad. No worries."

James glanced in the direction Aidan had come from, his eyes squinting to see past the heavy rain. "Where's my dad?"

"He's with her."

"And where is she?"

"May I go inside and change first?" Aidan shivered. "Parts of me are a wee bit numb at the moment, and I'd very much like to feel them again." He placed a hand on James's shoulder. "I promise, she's all right, though."

James gave a single nod. "Okay."

Opening the door, Aidan kicked off his shoes outside the threshold. Wet footprints and droplets of water trailed behind him as he entered.

Kavana peered up from the book she was reading. "Did you find her?"

"Yes." Aidan stopped short of the rug in the center of the room and began unbuttoning his wet shirt. "She's with Will."

"And where's he?" Karramis asked as she entered the living room from the hallway with wet hair and wearing an oversized shirt, the hem resting midthigh.

Kavana eyed her sister, a grin of amusement lifting one corner of her mouth. "You *are* wearing something underneath that, right? I mean"—she pointed at Aidan—"you do know you have company."

"No," Karramis said sarcastically, a playful smile tugging at her lips, "I'm completely naked under this." She winked at

Aidan as he peeled off his shirt, her voice now sultry. "Hey there, you."

Aidan smiled at Karramis, matching her teasing tone. "Hey to you too."

Kavana closed the book and rolled her eyes. "You two are extremely weird."

Aidan and Karramis laughed as Kavana rose to her feet.

"Yes," Karramis said, easing out of the laugh and lifting the hem of her shirt, revealing a pair of shorts. "Of course I'm wearing something under it. I don't make a habit out of running around with nothing on. I mean, not unless Will—"

"Please, Mom, for the love of all things holy," James interrupted, disgust lining his face, "do *not* finish that sentence. I don't need to know what you and Dad do when we are not around."

Karramis grinned at him. "Who said you aren't around?"

"Eww! Mom!"

Karramis and Aidan laughed again, Kavana joining in as she headed over to the chair next to the couch. Lifting a backpack leaning against it, she pulled a few pieces of clothing from the bag.

"Here," Kavana said, handing Aidan the clothes. "Go take a shower and get warmed up." She jerked the clothing away from Aidan just as he reached for them. "But she's okay, right?"

Aidan nodded. "Yes, of course. If she weren't, I would've told you all right away."

"I know. It's just . . ." Kavana's gaze moved from James to Karramis and back to Aidan. "We've been worried about her."

"She's all right, my love. She just wasn't ready to come back yet."

Aidan pulled her against his chest, and she let out a shrill squeak as the cold wetness from him seeped through her clothes. He kissed her, and the tension in her body relaxed as she leaned into him, pressing her lips to his.

~

"What do you mean she didn't want to come back yet?" James asked as Aidan sat down on the chair, his new clothes dry but his hair still wet from showering.

James had been impatiently waiting as he sat between his mother and aunt on the couch, both lost within the pages of their books.

"Where was she?" James added. "Where is she now?"

Aidan rubbed the stubble on his chin. "We found her right after the storm started. Well, Terramina actually found Will and brought him to Rhiannon. I followed to make sure she was all right. But I guess she had fallen asleep on the East Shores. She didn't want to return home, so Will took her to the cave and stayed with her. He asked me to come tell you, so you wouldn't worry."

James leaned forward against his legs, his voice low and rough. "But why didn't she want to come home?"

"I'm not really sure, lad. I didn't speak with her."

James dipped his head, the sadness in his voice mirroring his expression. "I think she's mad at me."

Karramis narrowed her eyes and twisted to him. "Why would you think that?"

James ran a hand through his hair. "Because I didn't save her." He blew out a heavy sigh. "I'm supposed to protect her. I always told her I would keep her safe. And after the first attack here, I made myself a promise to keep my word. And I failed her. I failed myself."

"James," Karramis said, taking his hand, "you didn't fail yourself. And you sure as hell didn't fail her. No one knew the full strength of Merrick's abilities. None of us were able to stop him."

"You did."

"I only slowed him down. I only played with his emotions and distracted him."

"Yeah, but you still stopped him. You still got her away from him. All I did was piss him off, which only led to him hurting her even more. I caused her pain. And I only made it worse because I couldn't keep my dang mouth shut. I wasn't able to rectify my mistakes and help her."

Kavana mirrored his body language, the softness in her voice equal to his mother's. "She doesn't blame you, James."

"You don't know that. She doesn't even want to come home. She's avoiding me. In more ways than one."

"How do you mean?" Aidan asked.

James did not answer for a moment. "Right before the attack, I lost the connection with her. I couldn't hear her voice anymore. I could feel her, though. I felt every emotion during the attack, but her voice disappeared completely. I tried to reach her, but I couldn't. I think she shoved me out."

Karramis narrowed her eyes at Kavana before turning her gaze to James. "When exactly did you notice the connection sever?"

"Right after Merrick started using his powers on us. I couldn't connect with her completely anymore. I thought maybe it was because her mind was blank, but once Merrick started hurting her, I tried again, and that time it felt like I had run into a solid wall. I felt this blockade slamming into me, pushing me further and further out of her mind."

"Hmm," Karramis and Kavana said under their breaths.

"What?" James asked. "What does *hmm* mean?"

Kavana's blue eyes focused on him. "But you can still sense her? I mean, her emotions."

James nodded. "Sort of."

"What do you mean by that?"

"After the attack last night, I could feel something was off about her, but I couldn't pinpoint it. It was like she was empty. Like all her emotions had shut down."

"And you . . ." Kavana creased her brows. "You said you felt as if there were a wall inside her mind?"

Curiosity took over his features. "Yeah. Why?"

"Because," Karramis continued, "I think when your Guardian magic surfaced, both of your minds were flooded with the mental power needed to bind to the realm, and it created an instinctive protective shield. That might be why you are having a hard time connecting with her, because some mental powers can be stronger sometimes and interrupt or interfere with the others."

James glared at her, waiting for her to continue.

"You and Rhiannon are connected mentally, and not as regular telepaths, but with your own unique magic. And that magic somehow blocks out other telepathic abilities. That part I'm sure of because Lucas can't hear either of you."

"And?" James drawled.

"I'm getting to that." Karramis shifted and angled herself to face him fully. "Do you remember when I told you mental strength outweighs actual physical strength?"

"Yeah."

"Well, as mental powers get stronger, the ability to shield oneself from other invasive mental abilities is easier to control, but some who are very strong with their powers can do it without knowing. For example, I'm also able to block out Lucas. I learned how to do it as a teen. My friend Avery—a telepath— taught me how to do it. I simply had to allow my mental abilities to grow and take root within my mind, creating this protective barrier and shielding my inner thoughts. I had to link my emotions and magic together and build up that wall within my mind. Now, sometimes that wall gets a crack in it, or I allow it to come down a bit, but it's still there. Both consciously and subconsciously. Sometimes when my emotions are heightened or something causes me to get overwhelmed, I have to work harder to keep it up, but it's easy enough to do."

"Guardians can also do this," Kavana added. "It's present in us as soon as our powers come in, but we can't keep it up all the time, though. Not like your mom can."

"Why?" James asked.

"We're not sure. But your mom's magic and abilities are very unique. Guardians are powerful, but not like her. We have a strong mental connection to the realm with our magic, whereas hers is more innate and primitive. She doesn't need the realm's magic to pull from. But with me and the other Guardians, this allows us to tap into that magic and pull strength from the island and place it into us. It allows us to be faster and stronger and even heal from minor injuries quicker. It also heightens our senses. Well, our hearing at least."

"So, like a vampire almost?"

"In a way, yes," Kavana continued. "Maybe not as extreme, and it only works for a short amount of time, but it does give us more of an advantage. But lately, we haven't been able to do it at all."

James faced his mother. "But this doesn't work for you, the Guardian abilities? I mean, you didn't show any signs of that when Lucas and the others attacked. And you didn't heal afterward. You also mentioned before that you can't teleport between the portals."

"Well, none of us can," Kavana pointed out. "At least not anymore."

"Yeah," James went on, his gaze moving back to his mother, "but you never could, right?"

Karramis shook her head as a crease formed between her eyes. "No. I've never had true Guardian abilities beyond the connection to the portals. And even then, it was never as strong as it should've been. The only portal I have true control over is my own. But even that can be challenging sometimes."

James leaned back, his attention still wholly on his mother. "What do you mean?"

"I can conjure a portal on command—that's easy enough. But I have to focus on the area in front of me as if I'm literally opening a doorway. I have to open my mind up and fracture the existence between time and space. The hard part comes next. Once the portal is open, I have to focus on where I want to go. If I step in blindly, I could end up who knows where. My portal is linked to me and vice versa once opened. We are connected, but the doorway only works if I can focus on keeping it open and controlling it as I go through it. The mental strength I need for my portal has always been easy to control, but only when I practice. My ability to master my mental capacity has always been my strongest power. That's never been the issue with me. It's fighting against the physical pain and exhaustion that rises from me stretching past my mental limits that prevents me from advancing my powers. It takes a lot to manipulate magic in a way you aren't used to controlling."

"So . . ." James paused a moment. "So, you think maybe Rhiannon didn't shut me out on purpose?"

"Maybe, but I don't know for sure. You and Rhiannon could be opposite from everyone else. Maybe her magic and emotions kicked in and made it so she's able to do it without trying—allowed her to put up that wall to protect herself."

Rubbing the crease between his eyes, James asked, "Do you think Merrick caused that to happen?"

Karramis shrugged. "Possibly. Her physical magic may not have shown up last night, at least nothing we could see, but it's possible her mental abilities snapped into place. Maybe Rhiannon is opposite from the others. Maybe she is able to do it without trying. You two can already block out Lucas subconsciously somehow. Not to mention you're supposed to have magic unlike any other, so it's possible you both might have to work to lower your shield instead of keeping it up."

Silence filled the room as the adults watched James, his expression etched with a question.

"Mom," James said a few moments later, his tone soft and hesitant. "I've been meaning to ask you something, but it never really seemed like the right time to bring it up. But since we're talking about your magic, I need to know something that has been bothering me for some time now."

Karramis gave him a quizzical look. "What is it?"

"When you did the spell that night, the night we all thought you died, why didn't you come with us? And what did you mean about waiting for a waning night and the part about your heart?"

Karramis took a deep breath, the memories of that night sparking a hint of unease in her eyes. "I knew my magic would be weak, and I wasn't sure if I would be strong enough to summon my portal, keep it open, and send all of us through, so I chose to send you and Rhiannon instead. Honestly, I wasn't even sure I would be able to do that. I needed the spell to send you back while I held open the doorway. I needed the spell to be the connection between me and the portal, so you both would end up where I needed you to go. I chose to focus all my strength on getting you two home instead."

Karramis paused before continuing, "I also didn't want anyone using my magic against me, something I was sure Lucas would figure out how to do, so I decided to remove it altogether."

"You can do that?" James asked. "I mean, anyone can remove their magic at will?"

"Yes," Karramis and Kavana answered together, both nodding.

"But," Karramis went on, "it only works for a short amount of time. To make sure it isn't returned, the person either has to die or find a way to keep the connection blocked."

James narrowed his eyes. "Like sealing the portals?"

"Yes," his aunt said.

"Or, in my case," Karramis added, "I placed my magic into the necklace. The necklace had powerful stones that would help bind the magic and protect it until it was released. Then, with the spell and necklace, the magic would stay trapped until your dad had enough time to get you both out of Kiluemar and seal the portals. Then, once the waning night arrived, long after the full moon had come and gone, my magic would be released from the necklace and returned to the island."

"But . . . why did you want your heart to slow? Why did you want to die?"

Karramis sighed as she closed her eyes in a slow blink. "I didn't want to die, James. I desperately wanted to go back with you both. But I always thought I was meant to die for you and your sister. And I thought that time had come. I didn't want my portal or my powers to be the reason you two were caught, so I removed my magic. All of it. But the dragons' blood, that powerful magic inside me, is what kept me alive all these years, constantly keeping the hole in my heart from killing me. I wanted the spell to keep me alive long enough to make sure I could hold open the portal. Once I threw the necklace in after you both, I had mere seconds to close it before my heart would give out."

Aidan shifted in the chair and crossed an ankle over his knee. "Did you ever figure out how you survived? Why you were stuck in that magical coma all those years?"

"No," Karramis answered, shaking her head. "And I don't know if I ever will. I tried researching it and even asking Tenarick and some of the other older creatures, but no one has ever heard of something like that happening before. It's just another unexplainable thing about me, I guess. Magic is definitely a fickle thing, if you ask me."

"Why . . ." James started to ask but quickly drew back.

"What?" Kavana asked, tilting her head toward him.

"How are we supposed to stop him?" James finally said. "Merrick, I mean. He's just too strong."

"We practice." Karramis clasped her fingers around his chin. "We all get stronger, faster, and more mentally and physically powerful. We fight back. We figure out how to outsmart and overpower him."

"But what if it isn't enough?"

"Then we'll cross that bridge when we get to it."

"How can you be so positive about all this?"

Karramis smiled at him, dropping her hand into her lap. "Because I believe you and Rhiannon can stop him. I don't think the path you are on is meant to end here. Destiny might've put you on this journey without a map to guide you, but if you truly open your eyes, you'll see the direction you are supposed to take is right in front of you. You just have to be willing to open your eyes and take that first step forward. Because if you don't, you will be lost forever."

James considered before asking, "Do you really think Rhiannon's magic only put up a wall to protect her mental powers?"

"I'm not really sure," Karramis said. "That's something she will have to tell us. But I think her mental abilities and all her emotions from last night created a wall inside her mind to protect her. Something drove her magical instincts to shield her from whatever was taking root in her mind. The stronger your mental abilities are, the thicker the wall can be. And that is also why I believe she can do this. We just have to give her more time to figure everything out about herself and her magic. She's smart. She'll figure it out soon enough."

James kissed his mother's cheek. "Thanks, Mom. I'll give her more time, but if she doesn't come around soon, I'm going to have to show her just how stupid she is being."

Kavana laughed. "I wouldn't say it like that, though. She might just smack you."

"Good," James said with a grin, standing up. "At least I would know she's back to her old self again." Stopping at the entrance to the hall, he paused and faced them. "I'm going to try and get some sleep."

"Good night," the three adults said to him as he disappeared down the hallway.

~

James stared into the darkness as he lay in bed, his thoughts drifting deeper into his mind as he focused on his sister.

"Rhiannon," he called, his inner voice pleading and soft as he closed his eyes tighter.

Reaching out an invisible tether, he searched for her.

"Please let me in."

The words echoed, bouncing off the emptiness filling the darkness. He concentrated harder. A tug jerked in the center of his chest, and his body grew warm and weightless.

"If you're out there . . . and you, too, are lying awake, just know that I'm here when you need me. All you have to do is reach out and I'll be there to take your hand."

Chapter 18

Destined Choices

A tightness surged through her chest, the suffocating grip accompanied with a wave of intense warmth, both curling around her lungs. A silent gasp of air burst from Rhiannon as her eyes shot open. Clutching the fabric of the blanket, she wildly searched the unfamiliar room. A rush of memories filled her mind—flying with the dragons, the gentle rippling of the ocean waves zooming by below her, falling asleep on the beach, her father lifting her in his arms, the cave.

"Dad?" she whispered, searching the room.

She leaned over the edge of the bed and spotted Will sleeping on the floor, curled up with his arm under his head. Not wanting to wake him, she eased off the opposite side of the bed, bringing the blanket with her. She was still dressed in the clothes and shoes from the day before. At least she thought so since she was unsure what day it was.

Rhiannon made her way around the foot of the bed as she took in the room.

A tiny flame in an oil lamp hanging nearby filled the small area, the soft luminescent orange glow flickering throughout the almost barren living space. Smooth jagged stone acted as walls, the dark sides colored with obsidian and rich charcoal. The uneven stone arched upward and faded deep within the shadows, the enclosed cave appearing as if it lacked a ceiling. Water trickled and dripped nearby, echoing off the walls and filling the silence with a soothing serenade. The fresh salty richness of the ocean filled the clean air as familiar scents rested in the stillness, the aromas of her parents and the earthiness of the dragons. A makeshift bed rested in the center of the area, a wooden platform supporting a mattress with a single sheet tucked under the corners with various blankets and multiple pillows scattered across the top. A thin off-white sheet hung across a taut rope in the far corner of the room while another oil lamp was placed within a recess along the wall not far from what Rhiannon could only determine was a temporary dressing area. An old rocking chair and small end table sat a few feet from the foot of the bed, and a large chest lay next to them, housing what appeared to be various sizes of books.

Pulling the blanket off her shoulders, Rhiannon covered her father and quietly made her way out of the cavern. Exiting, she slipped as she stepped down from the slight edge leaving the area. The onyx stone beneath her was slick and smooth, the flat pathway leading into a narrow corridor. Darkness swallowed her as she continued through the cavernous hallway, retreating farther away from the light of the oil lamp in the stone threshold. After a few feet, Rhiannon exited into a large open cave, a place she recognized as the area where she had first met Raeth and

Oakley only a few months ago. The walls were a mix of the same black and dark gray as the cavern room, but the ceiling was hundreds of feet in the air and held beautiful stalactites of rich brown. The sounds of water echoed louder, both trickling along the walls and dripping in the distance. A rush of salt and stale earthy aromas filled the cool air and sent a wave of goose bumps trailing up her bare arms and legs. Shades of light blue lined the floor near the cave entrance to her right, allowing Rhiannon to conclude it was no longer dark outside. To the left, darkness concealed the rest of the open area as the ground inclined and disappeared farther into the cave.

Stepping into the light, Rhiannon noticed the blue hues of either dusk or dawn filling the area outside. Three large figures rested at the mouth of the cave as she continued forward, the slick smooth stone ground changing to small pebbles and dirt beneath her feet.

Raeth, Oakley, and Terramina raised their heads as the clattering of rocks rattled off the interior walls. The two smaller dragons were curled together within the mouth of the cave while Terramina lay a few feet outside, the light overhead illuminating more of her coiled body.

"What are you all doing out here?" Rhiannon asked, her voice dry and hoarse. "Why aren't you sleeping inside?"

"Your father asked us to keep watch," Terramina said, her tone making Rhiannon hear a sense of pride radiating from the dragon.

"Oh," Rhiannon thought, her words not directed at any dragon in particular. *"Where are the others?"*

"Phosmeratae returned to the mountain," Raeth said, nudging Rhiannon in the side with his nose, urging her to pet him. *"And Will asked Ignara and Harkin to keep an eye on the cabin for the night. They should be returning shortly."*

Rhiannon peered outside as she stroked Raeth along his neck. *"So, it's morning then?"*

"It is." Terramina headed over to the others. *"It has only been a short time since your father brought you here. Were you able to rest?"*

Rhiannon gave a half shrug. *"A little."*

"Would you like one of us to take you home? Maybe you will be more comfort—"

"No, it's okay," Rhiannon said softly, pausing for a moment. "But can one of you take me somewhere else please?"

Raeth lifted himself to his feet. *"Where would you like to go?"*

"I will go too," Oakley said, standing up next to him.

Rhiannon lifted the corner of her mouth in a weak smile before shifting her attention over to Terramina. *"Would you please stay here so if my dad wakes up before I get back, you can tell him I'm okay and went out for a bit?"*

Terramina gave a slow nod. *"Of course."*

Raeth lowered down, and Rhiannon climbed onto the dragon's back, readjusting herself as he returned to all fours.

Turning around, the dragon exited the cave, Oakley following closely behind.

Rhiannon peered over her shoulder, her inner thoughts aimed at Terramina. *"Thank you . . . for everything."*

A softness filled the dragon's voice. *"You are very welcome."*

~

Rhiannon stood on the edge of a cliff, her toes mere inches from the ledge angling in a sharp drop-off and descending to the crashing waves below. Eyes closed, she cradled herself, her arms crossed in a tight hold over her ribs as she rubbed her chilled skin.

A swift cool breeze blew in off the ocean and coasted up along the walls of the cliff as dark pewter clouds hovered overhead. Waves sounded all around, a mix of ebbing and splashing joining the harsh collision against the bluffs. A freshness filled the salty air as it danced among the lush oak canopies and thick elm branches nearby, emitting a rich blend of grass, jasmine, and earthy undertones across the cliff. The warmth of the sun was lost behind the ominous clouds, the sky appearing thick with rain and lingering fury. Long blades of thick grass blew in rolling waves and brushed along Rhiannon's ankles and feet, the sensation unnoticed as she held still and stayed quiet.

Her eyes remained closed as she focused on the sounds surrounding her and the steady rhythm of her measured breaths. Her chest rose, inhaling deeply through her nose, fighting the sting of salty air tingling against her senses. Holding it, she focused, pulling her thoughts inward and allowing them to rip free from inside her heart, her soul, and her living essence.

One. Two.

A coolness loomed in her nerves, an unyielding mass of frozen nothingness seeping into her veins.

Three. Four.

An emptiness radiated deep within her core, the hollowness reaching out and taking over her body.

Five. Six.

A tightness pulsed under her ribs, the urge to claw out the ache gnawing at her taut muscles.

Seven. Eight.

A burn in her chest rippled outward, catching in her throat and lingering in her stomach.

Nine. Ten

Opening her eyes, Rhiannon exhaled through her mouth, long and ragged. Her gaze lowered as she leaned forward, her toes resting over the edge of the cliff.

Nothing.

No fear. No shock. No hesitation. No feeling whatsoever.

Only the lingering invisible marks of a broken mind and damaged soul remained.

She was empty. Alone. Lost.

"Rhiannon," a familiar voice said in her mind.

"Yeah?" she replied without turning around, Raeth's presence behind her making her take a step away from the ledge.

Rhiannon's connection to the dragons was stronger than that of any other Drolnogard before her, even her father. Her magic linked her to them somehow. All Drolnogards could hear what the dragon's spoke within their minds, but only when they were actually speaking. However, dragons did not have thoughts, no inner monologue. They would only speak internally when they had something to say. But Rhiannon was connected to them on a deeper level. She could send her emotions outward to them, allow them to sense what she was feeling, and depending on how strong they were, her emotions would call out to them like a beacon or distress call. The more powerful her emotions were, the farther they would travel.

Raeth took a step closer. *"I apologize for interrupting."*

"It's okay," Rhiannon said, her voice muffled within the breeze as she continued to stare out over the cliffs, her arms still crossed over her body. "Did you need something?"

Rustling came from behind, and the Earth Dragon sat down beside her, angling his head in her direction. *"Is everything all right?"*

Rhiannon glanced over at him and dropped her arms as she placed a hand on the side of the dragon's neck. Oakley came up on her other side, the tip of his wing brushing softly against her back.

Peering over at Oakley, Rhiannon gave him a gentle smile. *"I'm all right. Or I will be."* She blew out another long breath. *"I just . . . I just need time."*

"For what?" Raeth asked.

"Maybe we should get going," Rhiannon said aloud with an exasperated sigh.

Oakley twisted and glanced behind him. *"But your father is on his way here with Terramina."*

"Oh," Rhiannon whispered as she turned around, spotting the Earth Dragon descending toward the ground.

Rhiannon walked over to her father and Terramina. "What are you doing out here?"

"Looking for you," Will said with a kind smile as he slid off the dragon.

"I'm sorry I left like that, but I had Terramina stay behind to tell you where I'd gone."

"Yes, I know." Will headed over to the boulders lying a few feet away. "Did you sleep well?"

Rhiannon followed him, rubbing the chill returning to her arms. "Yeah."

Will lifted a brow at her.

"No, not really. I mean, I got some, but . . . but I guess some is better than none."

Will lowered himself to the ground and leaned against a large boulder, jutting his chin over to the area next to him. "Join me?"

Rhiannon sat down beside him. "We were just about to head back."

Will scanned the cliffs and ocean before him. "Did you know this is my favorite place on the island?"

Following his gaze, Rhiannon answered plainly, "Yeah, Mom told us."

Will angled his head, their eyes meeting. "Is that why you came here?"

"Raeth and Oakley brought me here. I asked them to take me somewhere so I could think, so they brought me here."

Both shifted their eyes back toward the cliff. Only the whispers of the wind and sounds of the waves filled the air for a long moment.

Rhiannon leaned her head back and closed her eyes as she rubbed her neck.

"That's healing nicely," Will said, watching her run her fingers over the scabs along her skin.

"Yeah." Rhiannon opened her eyes, her gaze locked in front of her as her head remained against the boulder. "I guess that's one good thing about being able to heal."

Will's brow pinched with uncertainty as he glanced at her. "Is that what's keeping you up? The fact you were hurt again?"

"No, it's not that." Rhiannon shook her head as she lowered her gaze to her lap.

"Then what is it? Talk to me."

Rhiannon fiddled with her nails as she thought about her next words. "It wasn't the pain. That didn't even really last that long. And honestly . . ." She took in a deep breath. "It wasn't even the attack really. Well, it was the attack a little bit, but not entirely.

I mean, at some point I kind of blacked out—mentally retreated someplace else. I no longer felt anything. I was just . . . frozen."

"That's understandable. That was quite traumatic, Rhiannon."

"Yeah . . ." Her gaze shot to him, her voice tight and low in her throat. "But I froze. I'm not supposed to freeze."

"You were in shock," Will said, placing a hand on her outstretched leg.

"No." Her voice was rough. "No, I wasn't. I wasn't in shock. I don't even think I was afraid. No, I was weak. Plain and simple."

"You were not weak," Will said sympathetically, taking her hand into his. "You're not weak."

"Yes, I am. Even Merrick knows it."

Will flinched at her words. "What do you mean?"

"He said he could feel my magic and how I was weak."

"Merrick is a bloody bastard who's completely off his rocker. He's just trying to get in your head."

"Well, if that's the case, it freakin' worked."

"You aren't weak, Rhiannon," Will stated firmly. "You've proven that many times. You simply need more training, more control over your powers and emotions."

"I've been trying, though."

Will gave her an incredulous glare. "When?"

"Research is still training. I'm learning about magic and how it works."

"But you aren't connecting with it. You aren't making it a part of you. You aren't learning how to control it. It's not easy controlling magic. It's not like snapping your fingers or waving a wand. It takes focus and complete domination and manipulation over every inch of yourself. You have to pull yourself inward and feel the magic coursing through you, joining as one entity within your very core. When you and magic finally connect, it's like you can feel every layer of skin, every bone, every fiber of your muscles and tendons. You can feel each organ working separately and together, the oxygen in your lungs, your heart pumping the warm blood through your veins. That essence inside you becomes one with you."

Rhiannon stared at him, dumbfounded by the vivid details. "That's . . . a bit intense."

"Yes," Will agreed with a nod, a seriousness in his voice. "It's very intense."

"But I don't feel that with the Drolnogard magic."

"Some magic comes easier than others, while others are harder to master. Drolnogard magic is all mental, while elemental magic is both mental and physical. You have to master and control both aspects of that kind of magic to bring it forth."

Rhiannon moved a strand of hair from her face and tucked it behind her ear. "But what if I never figure this all out? What if I'm not meant to stop him? What if I'm only supposed to die so James's full powers can activate, and he's the one to stop all this?"

Twisting to face her, Will placed a finger under her chin and urged her gaze over to his. "Is that what you think?" His voice was kind, but his expression was sad. "That you're only meant to die?"

An uneasiness lined her features. "I mean, why shouldn't I think that? James is clearly more powerful, not to mention I'm the one who's always getting hurt. *I'm* the weak one." Lowering her eyes back down, she whispered, "Maybe my destiny, the only reason I'm here, is to die so it triggers his full potential."

"No." Will shook his head and dropped his hand. "Destiny is simply the journey, not the final destination."

"I don't understand," Rhiannon said softly, meeting his gaze.

"Destiny is the path leading you towards something, but free will is the compass guiding you along the way. Destiny is not the final outcome—it is merely a journey some are forced to take. The choices made will dictate where those who accept it end up." Will held her hand. "You're facing this challenge right now. You walk on your path of destiny as we speak. And make no mistake, there will be obstacles. Trial and error, wrong and right, twists and turns. You might even get lost a time or two, but those things will lead you in many different directions until, ultimately, you reach the end of the path. And where your journey ends will depend on you and the decisions you make." He smiled. "Your life and this destiny are the path you were forced to take, but the choices along the way will lead you to where you choose to be in the end. You get to decide which way you want to go on your journey, Rhiannon. No one else has that kind of power over you."

Her eyes burned as she blinked at her father. "But I thought destiny was how things are supposed to be, not what could happen."

"If your destiny were meant to get you from one point to another in a straight line, then I'm quite certain magic never would've given you the powers you have and the powers yet to surface, nor would a prophecy have predicted you."

"Yeah, but what if I was only created for one reason—to die?"

Will paused, the harsh yet simple question shocking him.

Swallowing down the tightness in his throat, he asked simply, "Doesn't everyone's journey in life end with death?"

"Well, yeah . . . I—I guess so. I mean, we all have to die. Even immortals die eventually. But . . . but what if destiny placed one on a very specific path where no matter which way they go, they are destined to die once they reach the end of the road? What if their journey ends on the edge of a cliff?"

"No one truly knows when they will die. Even magic and destiny can't determine that."

"But what if my destiny says otherwise? What if my only path—my fate—is to die a premature death? Then isn't it impossible and pointless to fight it?"

"No." Will shook his head. "Nothing is impossible. It's only impossible if you believe it to be. And pointless? Nothing in life is pointless as long as you never give up and keep going. As long as you live each day as if it were your last, it is not pointless. You've got to believe there is more to your story. You've got to have hope and faith that your destiny isn't etched in stone but rather drawn in the sand."

Rhiannon paused, pondering his words.

A long moment passed before Rhiannon said, refusing to meet his eyes, "Dad?"

Will turned his head toward her, taking note of her faltering gaze. "Yeah?"

"What if . . ." She exhaled. "What if I never become as brave as James? What if I never figure out how to control my fear, and I'm always the weak one?"

"Again, you aren't weak, Rhiannon. And as for being brave and controlling your fear, fear and bravery are both superficial and interchangeable feelings."

She lifted her eyes to face him. "How so?"

"Both shape us into who we are and who we end up being. They both change how we react and the choices we make. But experiencing fear doesn't make you weak, and being brave doesn't make you strong. However, feeling both makes you real and normal—makes you human. One usually comes with the other. You just have to find the balance between the two, for one will surely get you killed while the other might just save your life."

"Which one is which, though?"

"Now *that* is the real question. And I, unfortunately, cannot give you the answer."

Rhiannon knitted her brows. "Why not?"

A gentle smile appeared across his lips. "Because you're the only one who can answer that question for yourself. Because, in the end, that is another choice only you can make."

"But what if I fail?"

"Oh, you most certainly will fail," he acknowledged, plain and simple. Taking in her puzzled and deflated expression, he added reassuringly, "You have to fail because failure is part of life. If you don't fail, it means you never tried. And those who never try have never truly lived."

Thunder rolled through the clouds as a bolt of lightning stretched across the sky over the ocean.

Rising to his feet, Will held out a hand. "I think we should get going before we get caught in this storm."

Rhiannon placed her hand in his and lifted to her feet. "Can I stay in the cave a bit longer?"

Will replied approvingly, "Of course. You may stay there as long as you wish. Do you want me to stay with you?"

Rhiannon shook her head. "No."

"You sure?"

"Yeah, I'm sure. I have the dragons to keep me company."

Will pulled her into a hug. "All right. I'll bring you some clothes and something to eat later."

"Thanks." Her hands lifted slightly as she lazily embraced him. "And some of the books by my bed."

Retreating, he grinned down at her. "Sure. Anything else?"

"Yeah, actually." Rhiannon paused. "I have a question."

"What is it?"

"Where am I supposed to go to the bathroom?"

Will let out a deep laugh. "I'll show you."

"Thanks, Dad," Rhiannon said with a quick smirk as they headed over to the dragons, "because I really have to go."

Chapter 19

Lesson Learned

A grunt exploded as Karramis heaved over in pain, the punch to her gut driving a blast of air from her mouth. She clutched her stomach and leaned into her leg, her chest rising and falling in rapid irregular bursts.

Will advanced, wanting to evaluate her, but halted. "Come on, darling." Encouragement bellowed from him, rough and tight. "Breathe through it. Push it away." He lifted his arms and placed his fists next to his face as he shuffled closer to her, reading another tactical attack. "Come on. Again. Your opponent won't pause for you to take a rest."

"Jeez," James said under his breath, wringing his hands nervously as he watched from the front steps of the porch. "He's being too rough on her."

Kavana sat next to him, calmly observing the training session. "She's fine. Your mom has suffered far worse than a blow to the stomach."

"Is he actually hitting her?" The concern rumbled through him, his words rough behind an uneasiness.

"Of course," Kavana said, baffled by the ridiculous question. "How else are you supposed to learn to fight?"

Recovering, Karramis swung a fist through the air, throwing her body into the punch as she twisted her hips. Will blocked it with a slap to the side of her arm. She countered and pivoted on the other leg, twisting her hips and throwing another punch, connecting with the side of Will's arm, her aim too low. She lifted a leg and kicked out, her attempt to connect with Will's stomach blocked with a thud against the side of her ankle. Swinging an arm, Will hooked a fist through the air. She pulled back, the side of her face narrowly missing the connection of his powerful punch.

"Pay attention to my body," Will said, his voice ragged as he shuffled back a step with his fists slack in front of his chest. "Predict my next move."

Will swung again, and Karramis ducked as she aimed a strike for his stomach, landing the punch against his side.

Arching sideways, Will grunted but quickly pulled himself upright. "Good." Strained discomfort filled the proud approval. "Again."

Her other fist whipped through the air, but he sidestepped, and she stumbled as the force of her weight pushed her forward. Regaining her balance, she rotated, but Will hurtled toward her and rammed a shoulder into her side. Her feet flew out from under her as she propelled down. She landed hard as her back slammed against the ground.

"Don't let your guard down," he panted, his voice never faltering from that powerful yet encouraging command as he circled her.

Gasping, she fought against the pain ripping the air from her lungs as she scanned the area for her opponent, her eyes always searching and trying to never stray from her attacker. Spotting Will, she rolled away as his bare foot nearly rammed into her side. She rolled again, but he was faster. His other foot slammed down onto her stomach as she came to a stop. Her body lurched inward on itself as she clutched her abdomen, and a breathless gasp erupted from her.

"Get up," Will said, the firmness in his tone powerful and authoritative despite the look of pure regret and remorse on his face. "Your defenses are down as soon as you hit the ground."

She took a deep breath and swung a leg out, swiping it along the ground. "Not necessarily."

Her shin connected with the back of Will's ankle, and his body flung back, his feet flying out from beneath him. He threw his hands out and rotated midair, catching himself before the full weight of his body collided with the ground. Karramis hurried to her feet, but Will kicked out, and the blow smacked into the side of her thigh. She tumbled and rolled onto her stomach. Sliding her legs under her body, she pushed herself up. Two powerful hands gripped her waist and flung her sideways through the air. She landed hard on her back and let out a labored pant, the air escaping her lungs sounding guttural and pained. Will pressed a foot into her chest and towered over her as he balled his hand into a fist. She tugged sideways, but her attempt to roll away was blocked as he stepped on either side of her and plunged himself down onto her body. The weight of him drove her hips hard against the ground. She curled her hands into fists and swung, but he grasped her wrists and squeezed, causing her fingers to weaken as he propelled her arms down beside her head. She thrashed and bucked beneath him.

"Come on, fight back," Will demanded through heavy breaths. "React, don't think. Pass the mount."

Karramis squirmed beneath him as he squeezed his thighs tighter against her hips. Her face pinched with pain, and her body went lax as beads of sweat trailed down her face from her drenched hair.

Leaning over with a cheeky grin, Will kissed her. "Don't do it." The softness in his voice and the unexpected embrace made her stiffen beneath him. "Don't give up now, darling. I promise to make it up to you. But only if you can best me."

Karramis narrowed her eyes and arched a teasing brow. Locking an ankle over his, she lifted her hips upward with a powerful thrust. Will rolled sideways, taking her with him between his legs. Mounted on top, she tore a wrist from his grip and rammed an elbow into his thigh once, twice, three times before her arm slid between her body and his leg. She hooked it around his muscular thigh and swung his leg over her head, rolling him away from her. Using the momentum of the rotation, Karramis hurried onto his back and curved an arm around his neck, placing him in a choke hold.

Leaning into him, she smiled and placed her mouth against his ear. "I win." There was nothing but genuine amusement and playful haughtiness in her statement as she kissed his cheek and released him. "I look forward to my reward."

Still on the ground, Will rotated onto his back and gripped her upper thighs as she straddled him, a boyish grin playing on his lips. "I bet you are."

She gave him a teasing flick of her brow and kissed him, the soft moans rumbling inside their heaving chests. Covered in sweat, Karramis and Will panted heavily as their lips pressed harder together. He drifted his hands along her legs and over her hips, trailing slowly up to her waist.

"Uhm," James said, averting his gaze, "did they forget we're out here?"

Kavana grinned. "It would seem so."

James covered her eyes. "Don't watch them, you weirdo."

"I'm pretty sure they can hear us."

"We can," Will admitted, smiling against Karramis's lips.

Chuckling, Karramis sat back as he gripped either side of her waist. He gently squeezed and urged her back down, but she flinched in pain as she sucked in a breath.

"Sorry," Will said sharply, the guilt present in his voice and on his face.

Karramis pinched her eyes together as she breathed through the sudden rush of pain. "It's fine." She stifled a groan, the rumble catching in her throat. "I'm just a bit sore."

"Let me take a look."

Her expression tightened as she stood up. "Really, I'm fine."

Gripping the hem of her sweat-drenched tank top, Will repeated firmly, refusing to brush the subject aside, "Let me take a look." He eyed her when she did not lift her arm from her side, the seriousness and concern in his gaze unyielding. "Please?"

Karramis exhaled and raised an arm. "Okay, fine, if it'll make you feel better."

"It really would."

Will lifted her shirt and exposed the lower section of her stomach below her rib cage. Smooth white lines stretched across her soft skin, the signs of motherhood and imperfect beauty resting against her average hourglass waist. A newly formed scar lay near her ribs—one of the constant reminders forever etched onto her skin of why she now trained to defend herself.

Having refused to practice hand-to-hand combat growing up, Karramis always believed her Guardian abilities were not up to par with her other magic, so she often relied on her powers to protect her. However, after she nearly died because her magic was faulty, Will had convinced her she needed to learn how to fight. He believed Karramis needed to know how to protect herself, and she agreed. She would never allow another person to lay a hand on her again without taking them down with her.

Karramis sucked in a breath through her teeth and squeezed her eyes together as Will ran his fingers along a bruise forming just below her scar.

"Sorry," Will said, drawing his fingers away from her stomach.

"It's not that bad," Karramis said reassuringly. "Nothing I can't handle."

Footsteps rustled against the grass, and Karramis and Will turned to find James jogging over.

"Are you okay, Mom?" James shifted his eyes to her stomach and spotted the black and blue hues deepening along her skin. His gaze widened. "Holy shit!" His shocked expression shifted to his father. "You really do hit each other."

Coming up behind him, Kavana said confidently with a verifying shrug, "I told you."

Will narrowed his eyes. "How else would I properly prepare her for a fight?"

"Uh, I don't know," James declared a bit too sharply, baffled. "But maybe you should've pulled your punches a bit."

"I'm fine," Karramis said, tugging her shirt down. "If I don't learn how to take an injury, I might end up in another dangerous situation. Part of learning to defend yourself is training your body to take a hit and not allowing the pain and panic to take over and slow you down."

Uncertainty lined James's features. "Isn't the point of training to learn how *not* to get hit?"

"That is the ultimate goal," Will said. "But if you think you're too good not to get hit, then you're extremely foolish. Even the most experienced fighters can make mistakes and suffer a hit sometimes."

"Do you think you can handle getting hit, James?" Kavana asked with a smugness to the question. "It seems Pavian has been skipping some very vital training lessons with you."

Pivoting around, James faced her. "He's trained me to fight."

"In hand-to-hand combat?"

"Yes. He's just never actually hit me before. At least not on purpose. But I think I can take a hit."

A gleam of excitement flickered in her gaze. "Want to test out your theory?"

"Seriously?" James asked, scoffing as he arched a brow. "You want me to fight you?"

She crossed her arms at the derision in his tone. "Scared?"

James glanced down at her, pondering the question. Roughly six feet tall and a good eight inches taller than his aunt, he felt the size difference between them would give him an advantage. And with his weapon training, his arms were far more muscular now, and his shoulders were broader, while her petite frame was less than half his size.

"I don't want to hurt you, Aunt K." There was a sincerity that lingered in his cocky tone. "It seems a bit unfair to me."

Karramis choked on a laugh. "Careful, James, Kavana is an exceptional fighter. And she's been training since she was about eight years old."

"Yeah," James stated, a hint of mockery seeping from his words, "but she's . . ."

"I'm what?" Kavana asked as he trailed off. "A woman?"

"No!" James eyed his mother and aunt with an apologetic expression. "No, it has nothing to do with that. I mean, I just witnessed you"—his gaze stopped on his mother—"holding your own. I would never think that just because you're a woman you can't defend yourself. It's just . . ."

"Yes?" Kavana drawled, the harshness in her tone matching her sharp features.

"It's just . . ." He hesitated. "You're so dainty and fragile. And I just can't see you as a fighter. A dagger-throwing ninja? Maybe. Skilled archer? Sure. A stalking-through-the-darkness and kill-you-in-your-sleep assassin? Definitely, no doubt. But a quick, fierce, murder-you-with-my-bare-hands kind of fighter? No, not at all."

The expression on Kavana's face tightened into a sinister stare, her eyes gleaming with a challenge.

"Uh-oh," Will said with a grin, grabbing Karramis's hand and retreating away a few feet, "now you've done it."

James widened his eyes as he took a step away from his aunt. "I didn't mean to offend—"

"Block!" Kavana demanded harshly as she swung a fist through the air.

James's arms flew up and guarded his face as Kavana's hit landed with a thwack against his forearm. His eyes shot to her as he scanned her body, trying to determine her next move.

"Again!" Kavana moved in the blink of an eye, her hips pivoting as her punch collided with his stomach.

A grunt erupted from him as a jolt of pain surged across his abdomen, a burst of burning agony rippling deep within his midsection. Drawing in a wheezing breath, he hopped from side to side, shaking off the discomfort. He curled his hands into fists and readied his stance. His heart pounded as his chest heaved in uneven waves, a rush of adrenaline settling into his taut muscles.

James hurtled a fist at her, but Kavana dipped down and swiped her foot across the ground, kicking his feet out from under him. He landed with a thud on his back as a gasping moan rumbled from his body. Swinging his feet around, he launched to his feet and whipped his fists through the air. He twisted and flung his weight into a punch.

"Not bad," Kavana said, evading his strike.

A jab came at her, and she ducked. James kicked out, but she rotated away, throwing out her leg and ramming her foot into his back. James stumbled, his hands pressing into the ground as he regained his footing. He twisted, the sweat lining his hairline trickling down his face.

Damn, she's fast.

Winded, he panted, the burn in his chest traveling up his throat. "Okay, I might've underestimated you."

"That was your first mistake, lad," Aidan called out from the porch, leaning against the pillar with his arms casually folded across his chest and a grin plastered on his face.

James rotated toward the cabin and spotted his parents now next to Aidan, watching intently as if unfazed by the fact their son was getting his ass kicked.

James lurched forward as a knee slammed into his stomach.

"Fuck!" James groaned, the pain ripping through him like an electric shock.

James was inexperienced when it came to hand-to-hand training, opting for sword fighting and archery as his preferred methods of defense. However, the little fighting he did have was enough to remind him that his first mistake just now was looking away. Eye contact was a must when fighting. Always know where your opponent is at all times, and never look away.

"Another important lesson," Kavana said, shuffling back. "Ignore distractions."

Kavana was skilled, fast, and smart. And she clearly was not going to go easy on him. So, if she wanted to fight, he was going to give her a fight.

"Yeah," James said, catching his breath. "I know."

James charged forward, and Kavana crouched into a squat and braced for impact. Crashing into her shoulder, James was launched up, his body flipping upside down as he flew over her. He slammed against the ground, and a loud grunt burst out of him.

"Ow," he said, drawing out the word with a ragged breath.

He struggled to his feet, lifting his arms lazily in a fighting stance. Kavana grinned as she hooked a fist through the air, but James slapped it away. She twisted at the hip, driving a punch into the side of his arm, and he groaned but did not stumble. Kavana kicked a leg out in front of her, but he blocked. She turned, kicking out another leg, this one making contact with his thigh.

"I give up!" James yelled as he staggered, sidestepping and leaning over, placing his hands on his thighs. "I give up." He panted as his aunt lowered her fists with a wide victorious grin on her face. "Holy hell!"

"Still think I'm dainty and fragile?" Kavana asked with her hands on her hips, winded as satisfaction twisted at her lips.

"Yes." James panted. "But you can definitely kick my ass, that's for sure. You're a freaking badass, Aunt K. Where the hell did you learn how to fight like that?"

"Tenarick and a few of the other elves taught me over the years. They're all about speed and agility."

"Wow," James breathed respectfully, "that was nothing like the training I've had so far."

"Pavian and most of the other guys here," Aidan said from the porch, "includin' me, mostly train to fight with weapons. We're taught the structure of each weapon first, then about speed, stance, and precision, all while gettin' stronger so we can handle the weapons. And finally, when we find one we're more comfortable with or more connected with, we train with and master that weapon."

"Most females prefer to train in archery or hand-to-hand combat," Kavana added. "I've always preferred fighting with my hands. It allowed me to always know where my weapon was because it was attached to my body."

James rubbed the soreness radiating along his stomach. "I never even got a hit in."

Kavana smirked. "Nope."

Karramis leaned against the railing. "A skilled fighter can always recognize a move before it's acted upon by reading the body of their opponent."

James headed over to the porch. "I tried that, but she was too dang fast."

Kavana followed beside him. "But I've been training since I was very young."

"But you never trained as a kid?" James asked his mother as he reached the bottom of the stairs.

"No, I never trained to fight when I was younger because I was always getting hurt. I was beyond clumsy and ended up with broken bones, severe concussions, black eyes. You name it, and it probably happened to me. Once I even ended up in the infirmary with a huge open wound from a sword along my upper thigh, and I was only carrying it."

"Holy—that's insane."

Karramis nodded. "Yeah. So, after that, your grandfather prohibited me from training anymore. I was only allowed to stick to practicing my magic."

"But you are training now?"

"Well, I'm not thirteen anymore."

"And after what happened . . ." Will's voice was tight with anger as he stood behind Karramis, his hand sliding into hers. "I wanted to make sure she could protect herself if her magic ever failed again. I refuse to have her reliant on her powers when she can simply learn to fight instead." He kissed her cheek. "She will never be in a situation like that again if I have any say."

Karramis faced Will and slid her fingers through the belt loops of his jeans, pulling him into her. "I should've listened to you all those years ago when you wanted me to train. I never really thought I would need it since I had my magic to protect me. But . . ." She removed her fingers and trailed them up his arms, stopping at his neck before pressing her lips to his. "I was wrong."

Aidan let out a scoff, the simple sound filled with shock as he slapped his leg. "Well, fuck me sideways and call me a faerie. Did I hear that right? Did Karramis just admit she was wrong? Quick, someone write down the date so we can keep it for the records."

"Shut up," Karramis snapped, her tone playfully tight with annoyance as she rolled her eyes at him.

Laughing, Kavana added, "Damn, too bad Pavian wasn't here to witness this. He might've fallen over from shock."

James pinched his lips together, holding back a laugh.

"Both of you need to shut up," Karramis announced, angling a not-so-intimidating scowl over her shoulder at her sister. "You make it sound like I've never admitted I was wrong before."

James arched a brow. "Have you?"

Karramis shot him a look only a mother could give, one that brought pure terror and regret to the child.

"I'll shut up now," James said under his breath.

Kavana and James made their way up the stairs, both stifling laughs.

Stopping, James turned to Aidan, curiosity sweeping across his face. "Wait, are faeries real?"

Aidan chuckled. "No. Not in the sense people see them today."

"What do you mean?"

"Faeries are real, but not the little humanoid pixie-like creatures with wings. That was simply made up as part of a joke to see how much those in the non-magical realm would believe. But we do use the word faerie as an umbrella term for all magically born creatures with elemental magic: elves, dryads, nymphs, those kinds of creatures."

James fanned his shirt, the heat of the afternoon becoming unbearable again as he made his way inside. "Hey, Dad, do you know when Rhiannon will be ready to come back?" He sat down on the couch as the others trailed behind him. "It's been four days already. I really need to head back to Stoweward. I told Uncle Pavian I'd help Raina."

Will exhaled as he sat down between his son and Karramis. "I'm not sure, Son. But I check on her every day to make sure she's all right and has clean clothes and enough food."

A somberness filled James's voice. "How is she?"

"She's . . . tired."

"Does she need anythin'?" Aidan asked as he reclined in the chair next to them.

Will shook his head, lifting an arm so Karramis could lean into him. "She hasn't asked for anything else other than what I've already brought her. And I showed her where she can wash up and bathe."

Kavana sighed, sadness now on her face as she exited the kitchen with a glass of water in her hand, heading over and sitting on Aidan's lap. "I went yesterday to check on her, but the dragons didn't seem inclined to let me in." Her eyes settled on Will. "Has she talked to you about it yet?"

"A little."

"Is it smart leaving her alone?" James shifted his worried gaze between the others. "I mean, aren't any of you afraid she's out there all by herself with who knows what?"

"No," Will answered as he idly traced his fingers along Karramis's arm. "She's safer there with the dragons than we are here."

"But shouldn't someone be out there with her? Why are we leaving her alone? Why can't we just go get her and make her listen to us?"

"We've all tried," Karramis said, a hand now resting on the top of Will's thigh as she leaned into his chest. "We've all tried talking to her—tried being there for her. But she's asked all of us to give her space. We have to respect that, at least for a bit longer. We aren't going to leave her to deal with this alone. We just need to give her a moment to get out of her head first. You can't help someone who isn't ready for it."

Aidan caressed Kavana's arm, mirroring the actions of his best friend. "I even went out there with your dad to see if maybe she'd talk to me, but she politely asked me to leave her alone. And she's always been very open with me."

"I promise, James, we will help her," Karramis vowed softly. "We all will. We just need to give her a little more time first."

"How much time, though?" James slapped his legs and rose to his feet, a tightness pinching his voice and features. "A day? A week? A month?"

Reaching out a hand as she leaned forward, Kavana rested it on James's arm and gently pulled him to a stop. "She's just not ready."

"But why?" James asked, sliding from her loose grip and pacing the room. "She's never shied away from talking about what is bothering her before. Why now? Why this time? She was attacked before—"

"Yes," Karramis agreed, "but she disappeared after that time as well."

"It's true." Kavana nodded. "Even though she was living with us, she still hid out in the library most of the time. She buried herself in there, trying to distract herself from what had happened. That's what she's doing now. Your sister has to analyze things in ways we don't understand sometimes, but it's how she has always been."

"No." James shook his head as he folded his arms over his chest. "It's not the same this time. There's something different. She's different. It's like she's lost or something. It's like she wants to reach out, but something is holding her back. I can feel it. Deep down she wants help—I can sense it. I just don't know how to make her see it."

Karramis strolled over and placed her hand on his shoulder. "It's not your job to always save her, James."

Defeat pooled in his eyes. "Yes it is, Mom. I'm supposed to save her, and she's supposed to save me. We've always been there for each other. Even when we were apart all those years, I knew something was missing. I somehow sensed her. And I can sense that she's hurting right now, and I can't do anything to stop that pain from consuming her. She needs me, and I need her. How do I help her? Tell me, how do I show her I'm here and she isn't alone if she doesn't let me in? Please tell me how to fix this."

Karramis cupped his jaw and ran her thumb along his cheek. "I can't answer those questions for you. But I think—no, I know, without a doubt, you already know how to answer them yourself. You know her better than she knows herself. So, reach deep down inside and figure it out. Then, once you do, find a way to respect her but also push back. Show her you aren't going to give up on her."

Considering, he smiled before taking hold of his mother's face and kissing her forehead with a quick peck. "I think I know what might help me. Or should I say who?"

Chapter 20

A Clever Plan

Inside Emrys Cave was quiet. Only the soft sounds of water in the distance filled the stone chamber. A coolness lingered in the air, crisp and stagnant, as a subtle glow of a flickering flame danced along the walls, the soft orange streaks illuminating the room.

Rhiannon leaned into the pillows propped up against the stone wall as she inclined along the bed. Blankets draped over her legs and were tucked in along her hips. Multiple books lay scattered while some rested open and facedown. Papers, old and weathered, were spread out on top of the rumpled sheet and blankets next to a leather-bound notebook.

Approaching footsteps filled the silence as a shadowy figure entered the room.

"Hey," Ryan said casually, emerging from the shadows of the dark corridor and entering the cavernous room.

Surprised and a bit confused, Rhiannon asked, "What are you doing here?"

Being the source of humorous conversations, helpful research, comfortable companionship, and the occasional adventurous outing, Ryan Hillvec was a close friend to Rhiannon. The nineteen-year-old had met her while she was staying with her aunt in Caerwyn Village. Soon after she had arrived, Rhiannon had buried herself in the various books and archives in the library, which was managed by her step grandmother, Randolyn. The young man had discovered her asleep one morning after arriving in the library, a frequent occurrence of hers. A friendship had blossomed over the months and had grown even stronger after he had revealed a few weeks ago that he was a werewolf. Werewolves had been the cause of her fears after being attacked by one soon after returning to Kiluemar, and he had been helping her learn to control her emotions linking to the uncertainties she was feeling, while also teaching her more about the creatures, their curse, and how he was not like the others due to his other magical abilities.

"Saying hi," Ryan answered, standing in the obsidian-and-charcoal-colored threshold as he folded his arms over his chest, the light from the lantern overhead casting a flickering shadow on the stone wall as he leaned against it. "So . . . hi."

"Did James send you?" There was a tightness of annoyance in her tone.

"Well, hello to you too," he replied, the mockery in his voice matching his teasing expression. "Aren't we a big ball of sunshine today."

Ryan reminded her so much of James with his tapered dark brown hair and eyes the color of milk chocolate. He was an inch or two shorter than her brother but was just as lean and muscular and had the body of a fighter—training being a must for all non-magical residents on the island. However, Ryan had a sharper jawline, a rounded chin, and a slightly deeper complexion, more of a warm beige than fair.

Rhiannon sat up straight and asked again, "Did James send you?"

"He did," Ryan said warily before pausing, preparing himself for the question he was about to ask. "So, how are you doing?"

"Fine," she lied.

"Hmm." He let out a soft chuckle. "Right, he said you'd say that."

"Well, I am."

He watched her for a moment, those once lively, welcoming blue eyes filled with an unwavering distance. "Want to talk about it?"

"There's nothing to talk about."

"All right then." He pushed himself off the archway and lowered his arms as one hand moved to clutch the strap of a bag draped over his shoulder. "Mind if I stick around for a bit?"

Rhiannon shrugged. "If you want to."

"I do." His serious, pensive demeanor relaxed as he stepped farther into the room.

Ryan stopped beside the bed and removed the strap of the leather satchel draped across his chest and placed it at the foot of the mattress, the only clear spot left.

"So," he said, drawing out the word as he eyed the array of books and papers scattered along the bed, "read anything good lately?"

The teasing in his lively, deep English tone caused her to narrow her eyes at him as she scoffed, flinging off the blankets. "Very funny."

Ryan laughed under his breath, but it stopped abruptly.

She walked around the foot of the bed, halting as she spotted Ryan staring at her with a perplexed look on his face.

"What are you looking at?" she asked with a sharp tone, confused by his perusal.

His gaze stayed on her body. "You . . . You're wearing sweatpants."

Understanding his words but even more confused by his statement, she asked, "What?"

"Sweatpants," he repeated, pointing at her dark gray pants.

"I heard you the first time." Her brows drew together as she shook her head with a quick dumbfounded jerk. "So?"

"So? I've never seen you in anything other than a dress before." His eyes lifted to her messy ponytail. "And I've never seen you with your hair up before."

They stared at each other for a moment.

Curiosity bloomed in Rhiannon's chest as an indistinguishable expression entered his features. "Why is that so weird?"

"It's not weird, it's just . . . different. You seem so natural. So relaxed . . . and real."

"Uh . . . thanks?"

Ryan shook his head, pulling himself from her gaze. "Anyway."

Rhiannon shrugged and continued over to him. "So, why are you here?"

"James sent me."

"I know that much." She rolled her eyes. "Jeez, he doesn't know when to give up, does he?"

"Meaning?"

"I asked him to leave me alone—said that I needed more time."

"It's been a week, Rhiannon. He's just worried about you. He hasn't seen you since you last told him to leave you alone. He just wanted to make sure you were all right."

She drew her eyes away from him and pointed down at the overstuffed bag now lying on the bed. "What's all this?"

"Well, yesterday," Ryan said, grabbing the bag, "your brother came and asked me to drop by and see if you were all right and to bring you a few things. He said you've already asked almost everyone else to leave you alone, so he asked if I would help. He told me that, technically, we wouldn't be going against your wishes this way."

"Clever," Rhiannon said flatly. "So, does that mean you'll leave me alone if I ask you to go away?"

He considered. "Are you going to?"

Rhiannon stared at him for a moment before lowering her gaze to the bag. "What's in the bag?"

"Oh, uhm . . ." Ryan lifted the flap and pulled a large aged tome from the bag. "This one is actually from me."

"Wow!" She took the book from him, joy returning to her eyes as she ran her fingers gingerly across the dark crimson cracked leather cover. "Where did you get this?"

"Randolyn found it in the stuff from the attic of the old worship hall. I thought you might enjoy being the first one to look at it. I only opened it to see the dates. It's a collection of records from over three centuries ago. There are a few more like this at the library now." Angling his head down so he could meet her gaze, he said softly, "When you're ready, of course."

"Thanks," she said, sincere and gentle.

Ryan smiled and continued rummaging through the bag. "James sent over a notebook for you, just in case your other one was full. A dagger. Some snacks. And a bag of something—I'm not sure what exactly. Oh, and a torch."

Her eyes narrowed. "A torch?"

"Yeah." He pulled an item from the bag and clicked it on, shining the bright light in her face.

She slapped at his hand and averted the beam away from her as she blinked the spots from her eyes. "Now that I'm completely blind, I no longer have use for the flashlight." Placing the book on the bed, she pulled an item from the bag. "Why did he send a dagger?" She unsheathed it, the nearly ten-inch blade sliding out with ease. "It's not—"

"Whoa!" Ryan twisted away as the blade came inches from his arm. "Careful with that thing." He grabbed her wrist and inclined the tip of the blade away from him, carefully taking the leather-bound handle of the dagger. "You're going to take an eye out with this thing."

"No I'm not," she said with a scoff, rolling her eyes.

He slid the blade into the sheath. "Do you even know how to use one of these?"

"Uh, yeah. You stab with the pointy end."

There was a tightness in her expression, but Ryan could sense a hint of teasing in her tone. "Technically, yes. But also no." He placed the weapon under the pillow and glanced over at her. "It's there if you need it."

"Thanks."

Ryan stared at her, the emptiness in her voice making his tone kind and concerned. "How are you doing?"

"Fine," she answered as if it was a reflex, the annoyance now on her face and matching her tone.

"Liar."

The sharpness linked to the word sent a jolt of irritation through her. "I don't appreciate being called a liar, Ryan."

"Well, then stop lying."

"I'm not."

"Liar."

"Stop it!"

Ryan hesitated, the need to get an answer out of her evident on his face. "What are you feeling, Rhiannon? Say it. Say it out loud. Stop bottling it up. Talk about it. It's the only way you're going to move past it and start healing."

Rhiannon folded her arms tightly over her chest. "I think it's time for you to leave now."

"No," he said, the irritation in his voice matching hers. "I'm not leaving until you admit you aren't fine—until you admit something. Stop holding it in or it will only consume you."

Her gaze burned into him, a challenge. But Ryan did not falter.

Slapping her legs as she dropped her arms, she advanced closer, her chest nearly touching his. "Fine! You really want to know how I'm feeling?"

"Yes," he answered, soft and genuine.

"Do you really want to get into my mind"—she tapped a finger against the side of her head—"and see all the emotions trapped deep inside?"

"Yes."

She scoffed, frustration filling her tone. "I'm freakin' confused! That's what I'm feeling, Ryan." She started to pace, her voice lowering as she rambled on. "I feel like I'm so damn lost that I'll never find my way out. I'm so tired, but I can't sleep. I want to be left alone, but I don't want to be lonely. I'm empty, and yet I feel like I'm about to explode with every emotion bubbling up inside of me. I'm numb, but I still feel everything. I'm too anxious to try, but not trying makes me anxious."

He took a step toward her but halted.

"It's like I'm here," she continued, her struts becoming more chaotic as a tightness strangled her words, "but I'm not, like I'm on the outside looking in. I'm falling, sinking deeper and deeper into this darkness, but I'm too tired and scared to swim to the surface. But it's right there, right in front of me. I can see the light, but each time I reach out it gets farther and farther away." A shuddering breath rattled through her, deep in her chest, as she inhaled before exhaling and driving away the emotions wanting to escape. "I feel everything, yet I feel nothing. And I'm stuck in this darkness with something, but I don't know what it is. I can't hear it. I can't see it. I can't see anything. But I know it's there—watching me. Taunting me. Stalking me. I want to run. I want to fight. I want to do something. Anything! But I can't. I can't control myself long enough to do anything."

Sadness and worry took over Ryan as his friend unleashed herself in front of him, letting go of all she had bottled up for a week now, maybe even longer.

Gripping her head through her hair, Rhiannon crouched down, her voice muffled as her chin pressed into her chest. "Dammit! And my mind won't shut the hell up." She slid her fingers from her hair and clasped the sides of her neck as she lifted her head up at Ryan. "How can I feel so many contradicting things at the same time? It's like I'm losing a battle with myself as I fall deeper and deeper into nothing." Her body sagged to the floor, her backside pressing against the cold stones as she curled her legs inward and hugged her knees. "I'm lost, Ryan. I've lost my way, and I'm afraid I'll never find my way back."

Strutting over, he knelt beside her, the need to physically comfort her—to grab her hand or grasp her shoulder—itching inside him, the same way his parents would have comforted him, but he resisted, opting to sit next to her instead. "It's all right to get lost sometimes, because then you have the chance to find a new path. A better one."

Rhiannon leaned over and eased into him, the side of her cheek resting against the outside of his upper arm. He cautiously lifted an arm, and when she did not move away, he pulled her into his side, wrapping his arm around her shoulders. He held tight as she remained still.

A warmth pooled in Rhiannon's body as a comforting tightness rose in her chest, a mix of sadness and calm. But defeat quickly took over at the realization of him next to her—consoling her, holding her, touching her—sliced through every nerve. Every part of her wanted this embrace, this warm and familiar reminder she was not alone. But as the tightness squeezed harder and the lump in her throat rose higher, the feeling of an emotional breakdown traveled up from her core, and tears formed in her eyes.

"Let me go," she demanded, pressing into his chest.

The determination in her voice did not match the acceptance of his embrace, the admiration for his relentless and unwavering friendship. Rhiannon wanted this. Needed it. But she would not allow him to see her vulnerable. She would not show him she was weak.

Ryan released his hold on her and pulled back in a hurry. "I'm sorry." Pure remorse laced his words as his apologetic gaze landed on her watery eyes.

She fought back the tears. "You need to go."

Her eyes burned as she pushed the sadness out of her body and replaced it with rage. They were not going to fall. She was not going to cry.

"Rhiannon." He hurried to his feet. "Please—"

"Leave!"

Advancing over to the bed, he pleaded, "Rhiannon, please let me help you. I know what—"

Rhiannon shoved him, the forced rage in her rough voice not matching the sadness on her face. "I don't want your help. I don't want anyone's help."

He planted his feet firmly on the ground. "I'm not leaving you—"

"Leave," Rhiannon demanded, her voice firm and powerful.

"No."

An insistent scowl flashed across her face as she lurched forward, her palms slamming into his chest as she shoved him. "Get out!"

The loud command echoed off the cave walls as Ryan lost his footing and landed hard against the ground, the heavy thud of his backside slapping the cold stone mimicking his deep grunt.

Rhiannon clasped her hands over her mouth, the instant regret settling in her chest and churning in her stomach. "Oh my gosh, Ryan . . ." Her voice was muffled through her fingers. "I'm so—"

"Do you need anything else?" he asked softly, hurt and shock filling his sullen features as he stood and dusted himself off before walking toward the stone archway.

"I . . . I'm . . ." Shaking her head, she whispered, "No."

Stepping down out of the room, he paused and stared at her. The pain of her actions was unbearable as another apology lingered on the edge of her lips, but the words were lodged in her throat.

Finally, he asked, ever so gently, "Do you mind if I come back and check on you again?"

Rhiannon considered, but her mind quickly wandered to another thought as her gaze narrowed. "Wait, you can't leave. The dragons." She stepped forward. "I should walk—"

"It's fine." He held up his hand, preventing her from walking closer. "Your brother brought me on Callie. He's waiting outside for me."

"Oh," she said quietly to herself.

She had never thought to wonder how Ryan had gotten here, let alone into the cave with the dragons standing guard. It had never crossed her mind that, despite this being his idea, James was right outside.

Taking a tentative step forward, she added, her voice remorseful and her features pinched with guilt. "Ryan, I'm so s—"

"I should go."

"Okay," she whispered as she dropped her gaze.

"So . . ." Ryan slid his hands into his pockets. "May I come check on you again?"

Rhiannon hesitated, her expression indecisive as she met his hopeful stare. "You know, you really don't have to do that."

"I know I don't have to, but I want to."

"Fine," Rhiannon said after a moment, not rude but rather a simple response, "if you want."

"I do."

"Just not right away," she added tightly. "Please. I'm just not ready for company right now."

"Well, since you said please." He gave her a half grin. "How long would you like me to wait?"

"Give me another week. Or two."

"I'll check with your dad after a week and see what he thinks and go from there. Is that all right?"

She nodded.

He gave her a gentle smile as he stepped into the darkness of the narrow corridor. "Oh, I almost forgot." Appearing back in the dim light, he added, "James asked me to make sure you got the tiny bag he sent over for you." He gave her a quick smirk and low wave. "See you soon."

Rhiannon did not say anything as she watched him leave.

Sitting on the bed, she poured out the remaining contents of the satchel. A thick black notebook and an array of snacks tumbled out. She gasped in delight. Bags of homemade cookies, nuts, dried fruit, pieces of chocolate, and freshly made popcorn spilled out across the bed. She snatched up one of the bags without hesitation and removed a chocolate chip cookie, taking an unnecessarily large bite.

A soft moan rose as she closed her eyes. Rhiannon absolutely loved cookies.

Retrieving another as she swallowed the last bite, she halted, her gaze snagging on a small leather bag under the food. Her eyes widened with surprise, and a dull tightness clutched her chest, twisting and warming before dropping in a sudden rush into her stomach.

The dark brown pouch with thick black string laced through bronze-colored grommets looked very familiar. She returned the cookie to the bag and lifted the leather pouch. It was heavier than she had expected. She shook the bag, and clanking rattled inside it. The tightness in her stomach eased and filled with a warm tingling sensation. The tension that had been lingering in her shoulders lifted. Tears burned the backs of her eyes as she exhaled, driving away the emotions threatening to escape. This was her brother's bag, something she had not seen in years. It was the gift she had made him when she was six—a gift given for their birthday.

She opened the bag and emptied the contents into her hand. Three tiny rocks and a folded-up piece of paper came out. The rocks were similar in size and shape, nothing special about them. But she remembered why he had kept them. These were the three rocks he had carried in his pocket when they had returned home from the river the day she had saved him from drowning. The day her magic had first arrived and the day Lucas had sensed her magic. Returning the rocks to the bag, she unfolded the paper and read the note.

Even though I wasn't supposed to remember you, I could still somehow sense you were missing. This bag and these rocks were the only things I made sure to bring with me from my old life, the life I was forced to live without you. But I've always felt you, Rhiannon. I've always known you were out there. You are my sister, my best friend, and my other half. We are forever joined. And when you need me to blow away the dark clouds hovering over you, let me know. Or if you still need more time to ride out the storm, I can just be the shelter to protect you from it. But either way, when you're ready, you know where to find me. - James

Chapter 21

Rhiannon sat in the rocking chair in the corner of the room, reading a book with her legs curled in on herself. A single oil lamp rested on the small table next to her, the chamber nearly dark outside the steady glow. Wrapped in a blanket, she eased a leg out from the thick material and pressed the ball of her foot gently into the floor. Creaks filled the dimly lit area as she rocked back and forth with unwavering rhythm.

"Watch your step," she called out, keeping her eyes on the book and turning the page.

"Ouch!" Ryan's voice echoed, his shadowy figure stumbling as he entered the cave.

A light chuckle rose from Rhiannon. "I told you to watch your step."

Ryan huffed as he moved out of the darkness and into the light next to her. "And exactly how do you reckon I watch my step when it's pitch-black in here?"

Lowering her book, she peered up at him with a quick side grin. "I can see just fine."

"Yeah, where there's light," he said lightheartedly as he observed her kind and playful tone. He turned the dial on the lamp and illuminated more of the room. "Much better."

"Ugh," Rhiannon complained with faux exasperation, her book retreating with her under the blanket. "Too bright."

Ryan snickered and dimmed the light a bit. "Are you a vampire now or something, sunshine?"

Rhiannon popped her head out from under the blanket and aimed a scowl at him. "Sunshine?"

"What, you don't like it?"

"No."

"Fine." He strolled over and plopped down on the foot of the bed, a gleam of mischief in his dark brown eyes. "Then how about dollface?" He cringed. "Ugh, no, far too delicate and meek for you. Ooh, how about firecracker? No, that's a tad cumbersome. What about darling? Yeah, no, definitely not. That's far too intimate."

She glared at him. "Do you always carry on conversations with yourself like this?"

Tossing her a roguish grin, he said with absolute arrogance, "Of course. I find myself to be marvelous company."

"You think mighty highly of yourself. Anyway, how about just calling me Rhiannon?"

"Too impersonal."

"But that's my name."

He shook his head disapprovingly. "Nope, we need a name that's special. Unique." Clapping his hands together in a single slap, he rose to his feet, casually strolling over to her. "Oh! I know! Sparky."

Rhiannon scowled at him, the arch of her brow creasing her forehead. "Sparky?" An insinuating insult in the question. "Like a dog?"

"No, of course not," he declared sharply, a bit embarrassed. "Like the spark of a flame. You know, since you have fire magic."

"It still sounds like a dog's name," she admitted, a trace of wittiness in her tone. "Might be more fitting for you."

"Ooh!" he exclaimed, laughing. "Why, Rhiannon, did you just make a joke?"

A twitch tugged on her lips as she fought the urge to smile. "Maybe."

"That was rather cheeky of you." He sat back down on the bed. "Anyway, so no sparky?"

"Definitely not sparky," she said flatly.

"Right." He smiled, his gaze observing the life flickering back in her blue eyes. "Okay then, how about angel? That seems fitting for a Guardian."

She narrowed her eyes, her gaze burning into him. But despite her stern expression, a wave of calm and comfort washed over her. Up until now, she had not realized just how much she had missed him—his sense of humor, his playfulness, his friendship, the sense of ease and peace he brought to her, just like James always did.

"Ah, man! Really?" he asked, a hint of teasing mixing with the seriousness on his face. "But I really liked that one. Plus, it's so fitting. I mean, you *are* a Guardian. It's perfect for you."

"No."

"Fine, but forget about being sunshine since you just rained on my parade."

Rhiannon lazily tossed her book at him. "Oh, hush!"

Ryan jerked sideways, narrowly missing the book as it collided against the wall and toppled onto the bed. "Hey! That almost hit me."

"Yeah, well," Rhiannon said with a bright genuine smile, "that was kind of the point."

Ryan returned the gesture, his eyes filling with satisfaction. "There it is."

Her expression dropped, and confusion settled in. "There what is?"

"Your smile."

Rhiannon stayed quiet as she rose from the rocking chair, taking the blanket with her. She grabbed hold of the lamp and headed over to the side of the bed she usually slept on and placed the light source on another small table. Ryan watched intently, his features tight with perplexity and intrigue as she made her way over to him. She stood there in front of him, unmoving as she eyed him in the dim glow, the silence and uncertainty making the room thick with anticipation.

She leaned over and wrapped her arms around his neck, hugging him as the blanket consumed them. "Thank you."

"For what?" he asked, surprised, lifting his arms and hugging her back, his embrace warm but hesitant.

She leaned away. "For being such a weirdo and making me laugh."

"Well, I quite enjoy the making you laugh part. It is a rather nice laugh. But I'm not so sure I enjoy being called a weirdo." He gave her a friendly smirk. "However, if it makes you appreciate my wittiness, I'll take it."

Rhiannon wrapped the blanket around her midsection, holding the ends in place under her arms. Leaning over the bed, she collected the various papers and books and placed them in a pile.

Ryan twisted around and began helping her. Grabbing an open notebook, he flipped lazily through some of the pages. Sloppy writing and strange doodles littered the pieces of paper. Notes about creatures and magic lined the pages. Words of spells and the prophecy were scattered throughout, the writings accompanied by questions, random drawings, and a disarray of illegible sentences.

"Are you secretly a serial killer?" Ryan asked, trying to decipher the notebook.

"What?" Rhiannon asked. She lifted her gaze from the bed and stopped on the notebook in Ryan's hands. "Oh. Yeah, I tend to write faster than my brain can keep up with sometimes. Hey, at least I can read it."

"I'm glad someone can." He stopped on a page, the words snagging his attention. "What's this?"

Rhiannon angled herself closer and glanced at where he was pointing. The page was covered in various Roman numerals, random numbers, and a sequence of four digits circled multiple times, along with the second verse of the prophecy.

"Oh, that is the research I did on the Roman numerals that were found on the paper my mom was given. Remember? The one Marie gave her before James and I were born."

Ryan gave a silent nod as he examined her notes. "You figured it out." The statement was soft and filled with awe.

Rhiannon shrugged dismissively. "That part wasn't that hard really."

"So," Ryan started as he lowered the notebook onto the pile of other things, "what happened in 1747?"

"Now, that's the part I don't know. I haven't figured it out yet." She placed the pile of books and papers on the floor and wrapped herself in the blanket, strolling over to her side of the bed. "Nothing I've found so far"—she dropped down onto the mattress—"mentions anything significant happening that year."

Ryan sat down on the other side of the bed across from her, twisting to view her wholly but keeping a good amount of space still open between them. "Did you find anything else?"

Rhiannon shook her head, folding the blanket tighter across her body, her sweats alone unable to keep her warm. "Not really." She held back a yawn. "Nothing tangible."

A moment passed in silence as Ryan fingered through a few more pages.

"Ryan," she said, his name soft and uneven on her lips.

His eyes met hers, noticing the sadness in her gaze. "What's the matter?"

"I . . ." Her voice cracked. "I'm sorry for pushing you the other day. I didn't mean to do it. I was just . . ."

"Angry?" he guessed.

She gave a slow nod and dropped her gaze. "Among other things. But yes, I was angry. Not at you, though. I promise." Deep blue eyes met the brown ones staring back. "I know you were only trying to help. I was . . . I don't know what I was really."

"It's all right." One corner of his mouth lifted as he tossed the notebook onto the foot of the bed. "I forgave you the second after it happened."

"Why, though?" she asked, disbelief narrowing her eyes.

"First off, because I knew you didn't mean to do it. Second . . . Well, because it meant you felt something again. You reacted. That you truly weren't completely empty. Granted, I wish you would've unleashed it on someone else, because you are a lot stronger than you appear." He chuckled as she flashed him a sidelong glare. "But if it meant seeing a sliver of hope from you, I'd gladly take it."

Rhiannon watched him for a moment. "Why are you so nice to me?"

Ryan stared at her, baffled by the randomness of her question. "Why wouldn't I be? I'm your friend." He arched a brow. "We are friends, aren't we?"

"Of course. It's just . . . Never mind."

"No. What were you going to say?"

She hesitated. "I've never had a friend before. I mean, other than James and Aunt K. It's . . . It's nice, you know? Having someone else."

"I agree." He smiled, and a moment passed before he turned his attention to a new stack of books in the far corner of the room near the rocking chair. "So, what are those?"

Rhiannon pivoted, angling her head before facing him again. "Books." An unwavering sarcastic reply.

"That much I gathered, smartass. I meant, what kind of books? More archives?"

"No," she said, grinning. "Fiction. My dad brought them last week for me. They were a gift from Aunt K for my birthday. She didn't want me to get bored, so she sent them over for me."

"That was nice of her."

"Yeah, I thought so. She knows books help me feel a little less lonely and help me escape."

"Really?"

"Yeah. Reading has always been my friend. And yes, I know that sounds strange, but it's true. I never feel completely alone when I have a good book in my hand."

"And did you? Feel alone?"

"Well, when you live isolated from the outside world, you tend to get a little lonely sometimes."

"And . . . are you lonely now?"

Silence filled the stone room as Rhiannon dropped her gaze, the pain and sadness lingering in her eyes.

"So," Ryan said with a deep exhale, quickly changing the subject, "what's this one about?" He leaned over and took hold of the hardback book she had tossed at him earlier, the one she had left at the foot of the bed. "It looks like you're almost done with it."

"It's a fantasy about magic and faeries."

He gave a playful scoff as he flipped through the pages. "You know faeries aren't real, right?"

"Not in the technical sense, but yes, I did know that."

He glanced up at her and chuckled. "You actually sound a tad disappointed by that."

"I kinda am."

"Why?"

She sighed, giving him an exaggerated dreamy smile as she rested a cheek on her hand and pressed an elbow into her thigh. "Because I'd love to be swept away and taken to a magical world."

An incredulous look focused on her. "Uh, you do know you live on a magical island, right?"

"Yeah, but we don't have eternal fall or handsome warriors with wings."

"Wings? Really? I never figured you'd be a wings kinda girl."

"And what kind of girl do you think I am exactly?" Both intrigue and challenge laced her words.

Lifting his hands in surrender, he shot down the question. "Uh-uh, nope. Not going to do it. I'm not going to answer that.

That sounds like a complete and utter setup. That right there is dangerous territory, mate."

Rhiannon drew back in disgust.

"Eww," Ryan snapped, hearing the potential nickname for the first time. "Nope, I don't like that one at all."

"Good," she admitted. "Neither do I."

Scanning the room as if searching for a new topic, Ryan propped up the pillow next to hers and leaned against the dark stone wall.

His features softened, shifting to a comforting kindness as he asked, "How are you feeling today? Are you ready to talk about what happened yet?"

Mirroring his actions, she hesitated as she drew the blankets higher over her body, the chilled stone at her back making her even colder in the dank cavern.

"If you're not—"

"No, I am . . . It's just . . ." She inhaled slowly through her nose before letting it out even slower through her mouth. "I . . . I'm scared, Ryan. And I don't just mean I'm scared of being attacked again or all the other dangers around here. I mean, I'm terrified of messing up. Of not being good enough. I'm afraid I will make a mistake and cost people their lives. I'm afraid I was chosen by mistake."

Ryan lifted a hand but drew up short as he twisted to face her fully. "I'm sure James is afraid of all that as well."

"No," she said, shaking her head. "I don't think James has ever experienced being scared. At least not like me. He's so fearless and brave. Always has been."

"I'm positive he has. We all have. I mean, only idiots, liars, and sociopaths claim they don't fear."

Rhiannon snorted, the light chuckle catching in her throat. "Well, I could definitely classify James as one of those."

Ryan laughed. "Let me guess, idiot?"

"Yeah," she answered, trying to hold in her amusement, "he's done some pretty idiotic things in his life. And I should know because I'm usually the one stuck in the middle of those foolish and reckless antics."

"I've met him, so I can only imagine." He watched her for a moment. "Rhiannon?"

"Yeah?"

"Why won't you talk to him?" he asked gently. "Why did you shut him and everyone else out?"

Rhiannon lowered her lashes, her eyes focusing on the space between them. "At first it was because I didn't even know what to say." She exhaled, lifting her gaze back to him. "And honestly, I wasn't even sure what I was feeling. It was as if I was completely disconnected from myself and my emotions. It was like my ability to feel anything was completely severed. I felt nothing. I was literally empty inside."

"You didn't feel anything at all?"

Rhiannon shook her head. "Not at first. But then I started feeling again, and I was in no way prepared for all of it at once."

"The fear?"

"Actually, I was prepared for that this time. But no, it was a bunch of other things. Embarrassment. Disappointment. Shame. Sadness even."

Confusion pulled at his features. "What would make you feel all those things?"

She paused before answering. "Embarrassment because I didn't ask for help afterward. Instead, I ran away. I hid. I just thought I could figure it all out on my own, you know? I felt disappointed in myself for allowing my emotions to take control and render me useless yet again. Ashamed because I'm not strong enough. And for believing the prophecy might be wrong about me. I feel like I'm not worthy enough to be part of all this. Like it's some mistake. But not James. No, he was destined for this, I'm sure. He has embraced it since day one and flourished."

"But do you?" A firm, genuine question. "Do you want all of this? This world? The magic? The life you are being forced to live?"

"I do . . . I do want this. I mean, I love the idea of having magic. But . . . I don't know. I want to be brave and powerful. I want to stop whatever is coming. I'm just . . . I don't know. Ask me again once I start figuring this all out. What about you?" She blinked as shock settled on his features by the shift of attention, her question one he had never been asked before. "Do you like having magic?"

There was a distance in his eyes—a helpless, tormented sadness looming deep inside him. "Honestly, I don't really know either. It's different for me, though. I've only ever used my abilities to fight the dark magic from taking control over me. I've never really had the chance to do anything extraordinary or meaningful with my magic. Anything good."

"If you could, though, would you give it all up?"

"Yes," Ryan said simply without hesitation. "If sacrificing all my magic meant I could live a normal life—and maybe leave here, go to university, fall in love, get married, and one day have children who would never have to suffer the pain my mum and I do—then yeah. Yeah, I would. I'd give it all up."

"Really? Without a single doubt?"

"Yeah. I'd much rather have no magic than live forever trying to cage the monster inside of me."

"Or," she said, drawing out the word casually and playfully, the tension and hurt in his eyes filling her stomach with unyielding sadness, "maybe you could just learn how to control the monster instead. Use it to your advantage."

Ryan shook his head. "It doesn't quite work that way."

"Why not? I mean, you never know unless you try."

"But," he said, returning to the original topic, "you don't want this?"

"No, I do. I do want this. Really. I—I love my magic. It's just . . . I'm afraid I'm going to fail. I'm afraid I'm going to make a mistake and someone is going to die. That he will die because of me. Because of my weaknesses." A shuddering breath blew from her lips. "I can't lose him, Ryan. I just can't."

He slid down the bed and propped his head up, his elbow digging into the mattress. "You're the one always getting hurt, but you're worried about him?"

"Yes. Because I felt him dying."

Ryan sat up, the shock plastered in his widened gaze. "You what?"

"The whole time Merrick was hurting him and my family, I felt James's pain slipping away as he was dying right before me. It was like every part of me was being stripped into shreds of nothingness. Like my soul was being broken and forcefully ripped from my body. I couldn't take it, and my mind shattered. Every emotion hit me at once, and a wave of energy blasted through me, and then I faded into darkness. I completely blacked out. I couldn't feel or react, and if I did, I had no control over it. I disappeared into a place where nothing and no one could hurt me. I'm not even sure where that was exactly, but I was no longer in control of myself. And in that moment, I was okay with it. I was okay with being the one who took his pain, his suffering. But when I returned from where I had taken myself, all that hit me in one fell swoop. That wave of energy washed over me, giving me every emotion back at once, along with the images of what had happened and the feeling of Merrick all over me. It was like being hit with every emotion, pain, and bad thing that ever happened to me all at once. And when it sank in and settled deep inside me, I felt nothing. Absolutely nothing. It was like all the levels of grief flooded me and then drained away. I was empty of everything."

Silence lingered between them as Ryan gave her a look of understanding. There was kindness in his eyes and a softness to his features.

An unexpected chuckle escaped her. "I guess that's one way to control my emotions. Just shut them off completely."

"No," Ryan said, "that's not controlling them, Rhiannon. That's losing them. And that's not the same thing. You need your emotions to fully embrace who you are. Without them, you lose your humanity, and then you're no better than the enemy. If you don't feel every part of life, are you really alive? You need to feel everything, the good and bad, to truly live."

"But I . . . I don't think I can do this." She let go of the blanket, and the edges slid down her arms. "I feel like I'm in this deep hole, and no matter how hard I try, I can't get out, and the walls are slowly caving in on me." She lowered her voice. "I'm in too deep, and I just can't seem to get out. I can't do it."

Ryan reached out but stopped. "Rhiannon?"

She lifted her head, the sadness and defeat deep in her eyes.

"Rhiannon, you do realize you're only sixteen, right?"

"Uhm, yes. I'm well aware of my age."

Chuckling at her sarcastic retort, he said, "Damn, maybe smartass should be your nickname. But anyway"—the seriousness returned to his tone—"you've spent a good portion of your life completely cut off from the rest of the world. You've never really been given the chance to experience life. I don't think you give yourself nearly enough credit. You've handled everything thrown at you far better than most people your age.

Even now, you're handling the trauma you've faced much better than most probably would. You were attacked—twice now, I might add—not to mention you're carrying the weight of the world on your shoulders right now. Literally. Or the weight of *this* world at least. You were thrown into a world you are expected to save with magic you have no control over. Yet. And you're surrounded by so many unknowns and what-ifs. And still, you're fighting."

She released a breath. "Hiding is more like it."

"No." His hand inched closer along the bed, stopping just before reaching her bent knee. "Fighting. You are fighting to push past the trauma you suffered. The fears. You're trying to balance everything, all while trying to figure out who you are and what you are. You could've walked away. You could've said this wasn't something you wanted. And yet here you are, still trying. I think that says a lot about you."

Closing her eyes, she lowered her head. "But what if I can't do it?"

Ryan pushed past the reluctance and curled a finger under her chin and gently lifted her head. His gaze locked with hers as she opened her eyes. "You can. And you will. I know it. James knows it. Your parents know it. Your whole family knows it. We all believe you can do this. Hell, even magic thinks you can do it. You were literally born for this. And I don't believe you are a quitter." He lowered his hand and leaned back away from her. "Don't be afraid of the path you are on. You were placed on it for a reason. Instead, use everything you're feeling as an accelerant. And when you're ready, strike a match and light that shit on fire. Make an explosion that rattles the whole damn world."

A warmth filled her chest as her eyes held an intense look of admiration and gratitude. Her heart pounded, and flutters filled her stomach as a sense of hope returned to her body. Her gaze fixed on him as a burning sensation lined the backs of her eyes, and a tightness rose in her throat. His words echoed in her head and radiated through her body. It was as if those words had sent a shock to her system, bringing her back to life. She believed him. Rhiannon truly believed Ryan and the others knew she could do this. But it was her own negativity pulling her into a state of defeat. It was her own thoughts that drove her into a place of unworthiness and emptiness.

"You know," Ryan stated, his voice low and deep as he sensed a shift in her demeanor, a feeling he was unable to pinpoint, "it's okay, right?"

Rhiannon blinked twice before clearing her throat. "What is?"

"Everything you're feeling and all the things you aren't. And it doesn't make you any less or any more normal. It simply makes you human. We all handle things in our own way. There's no wrong or right way to deal with trauma or mental health. As long as it works for you, then it's the right way. But you just have to remember one thing."

Rhiannon arched a curious brow. "What?"

"That you aren't alone. So, don't think you have to fight this battle by yourself. An army of ten is far stronger than a lone soldier."

Rhiannon let out a low chuckle.

"Are you laughing at me?" Ryan asked, tossing her an amused grin.

"Not at all," she admitted, pressing her lips together.

"Liar."

Annoyance flickered across her face. "What did I tell you about calling me a liar?"

"Then stop lying," Ryan said with a humorous lilt.

She tossed him a teasing sneer. "I wasn't. I was laughing *with* you, not at you. It's just you weren't laughing, yet." She playfully nudged him. "You're just a little late to the game, Hillvec."

"Well, then tell me what you were laughing about, and maybe I'll join you."

A long, drawn-out yawn escaped from her mouth as she lifted a hand and covered her lips. "It's just . . ." She shook her head. "Never mind."

Ryan scowled at her for a moment, a glint of wonder filling his gaze. "If you say so."

She yawned again. "I do."

"Are you getting tired?" He glanced at his watch. "It's not really that late."

"A little." She blinked slowly, fighting the tiredness tugging at her eyes as she laid down. "I haven't been sleeping very well, so it hits me at odd times."

"I'd say so," Ryan said, rising from the bed. "It's only four in the afternoon." He unfolded another blanket resting on the foot of the bed and draped it over her, tucking it in at her shoulders. "I should get going and let you rest." He headed for the archway but paused, turning to face her. "Do you want me to come back again in a few days?"

Rhiannon did not answer, her eyes now closed.

"I'll be back to check on you soon," he whispered, heading into the stone hallway.

"Ryan," Rhiannon called out quietly.

He returned, stepping up and pausing in the archway. "Yeah?"

She did not open her eyes, and her voice remained soft and low. "Will you stay with me a bit longer? Just until I fall asleep."

Surprised, he asked, "Are you sure?"

"Mm-hmm." Her eyes remained shut. "Yeah."

Ryan headed over to the bed. "Of course." He adjusted her blanket again before grabbing her book and sitting down on the floor.

"Ryan?"

He leaned against the bed and opened the book. "Hmm?"

Rhiannon reached out a hand as if searching for him, her eyes fluttering open. "I don't want to be alone anymore."

Taking hold of her hand, he said softly, "You never were."

Chapter 22

Fractures and Shadows

Warmth wrapped around Rhiannon as she sensed him next to her, both the blankets and presence filling her with comfort. She turned over under the covers, the thick material weighed down on one side. The dim light from the oil lamp still lit the room as she peered up at the figure leaning against the pillows through the haziness clouding her vision. She blinked repeatedly, trying to clear the sleepiness from her eyes. Her gaze drifted upward and settled on a familiar face.

Leaning against the wall next to her, James quietly read a book, the brown in his eyes a rich golden color in the flickering light.

She drew in a ragged breath, and it snagged in her throat as a sudden pressure seized her ability to breathe.

"Hey, Sis," he said softly, tilting his head and smiling down at her.

Her stomach twisted as the hollowness in her core filled with a surge of emotions, bubbling up and spilling out in a wave of overwhelming intensity. A gut-wrenching pain squeezed in her chest as each breath trembled over the lump rising up her throat.

"I . . . I felt you dying," was all she said as tears broke free and slid down her face with uncontrollable sobs.

"Hey," James whispered, lowering the book in a rush and sliding over to her, lifting her into his arms and cradling her. "Hey, it's okay." He rubbed her back as her chest rose and fell, the heavy shuddering breaths rumbling against his chest. "Shh, it's okay. I got you. I'm here. I'm right here. I didn't leave you."

James held Rhiannon as she cried in his arms. Her stifled emotions finally freed themselves as she gave in to them, allowing her brother to see it all. The vulnerability, the anguish, the pain and hurt. Everything. All the emotions she had been trying to fight against—trying to hide—since the attack. She released them as heavy sobs filled the stone room. Warm tears trailed down her flushed cheeks as each shuddering whimper rumbled deep in her chest. All the agony, mental and physical wounds, and every feeling she had were set free. A complete escape of everything she was holding back. It was real and raw, untamed and uncontrolled, but more importantly, it was liberating, energizing, and freeing.

Rhiannon did not want to be caged anymore. She no longer wanted to be lost and trapped deep within the all-consuming darkness filling her mind. She wanted to be free again.

Shuddering as she inhaled, Rhiannon lifted her tear-filled gaze from her brother's chest and met his eyes. "I'm so sorry."

Confusion creased his forehead, but a gentleness filled his eyes. "What do you have to be sorry for?"

She wiped her cheeks with the back of her hand. "For pushing you away. For lying to you."

"About what?"

"I . . . I'm not fine. I'm not okay."

"I know."

The words were so simple, but the care and compassion behind them made her blink as another round of tears slipped from her eyes. "I don't know how to be okay anymore."

Gently gripping her shoulders, James eased her up into a sitting position, his voice firm but understanding. "It's okay not to be okay. But you will be . . . One day, you will be. And I'll do anything I can to help you get there. If you let me." He lowered his arms and grabbed hold of her hands. "You are not alone. We will get through this. I promise. Together."

"But . . ." She inhaled, the shuddering sound faltering behind a sniffle. "I almost lost you. He almost killed you because of me."

"No, he didn't," he said firmly, the tightness in the statement not directed at her as regret and irritation washed over his sympathetic expression. "No, Rhiannon . . . He almost killed me because of *me*. Not you, but me. And it almost got Mom and Dad killed too. Because I couldn't keep my damn mouth shut. But you . . ." The softness returned to his voice, his eyes. "You saved me—all of us. I know you may not see it that way, but it's true. You did. But I . . . I was the one who almost got us killed—got *you* hurt. And I'm sorry. I'm so sorry for that, Rhiannon. I'm sorry I caused you pain and couldn't save you because of my mistake. You had every right to shut me out—to push me away. I get why you did it."

She stared at him, the realization of his words forcing the sadness to rise back to the surface. "Y-you think I'm mad at you? That I pushed you out and ran away because I'm angry with you?"

"Well, I . . . I mean, yeah. And I don't blame you."

"No," she said reassuringly, kind and soft, "no, that's not why."

He blinked at her, the bewilderment churning in his eyes. "Then why?"

"Because . . ." She took a deep breath and exhaled, driving away the memory. "Because I could feel it. All of it."

"Feel what?"

"Death." She closed her eyes and shuddered. "I could feel death starting to take you. And in that moment, it was the worst pain I had ever suffered through. But . . . But it wasn't physical pain. And right then and there, I didn't want to feel it anymore— I didn't want to feel that pain when it happened. So, I pulled back from it. And when Merrick had me, I thought he was going to kill me, so I broke our connection completely. I . . . I didn't want you—I was trying to stop . . ."

"Me from feeling the pain of not only losing you," James finished for her, the words coming freely and openly, "but from me actually feeling your soul leave your body as well." He smiled at her as a feeling of complete wholeness returned to his mind, body, and soul. "How'd you do that?"

She shrugged, brushing off the amazing ability she had mastered. "Apparently, I'm much stronger mentally than I am physically."

James let out a playful snort as he gently punched her arm. "I could've told you that."

"Hey," she snapped with faux annoyance before punching him back on the arm.

"Ow!" Rubbing his bicep aggressively, he chuckled. "That hurt. Where the hell did you learn to hit like that?"

"Aunt K," she stated proudly.

"Oh, well, that explains a lot."

A moment passed as they laughed.

Finally, Rhiannon said, "James?"

"Yeah?"

"I'm ready to go home now."

~

Three months ago
Mid-September

Rhiannon sat on the porch in her nightgown as the darkness slowly faded behind the hues of dawn. Deep teals and sky blues stretched across the eastern sky below the darker shades of night as burnt orange erupted from the horizon. A calmness filled the crisp air as a cool breeze blew evenly with the soft scents of dew-kissed grass, rich amber, fresh rain, and an earthy musk mixing together. Closing her eyes, Rhiannon drew in a long, deep breath, taking it all in, for the early morning temperature and aromas were the first signs of the soon-to-be changing season.

A click sounded from the front door, and Rhiannon twisted around just as Karramis strolled out, wearing a matching set of pale pink shorts and a sleeveless night shirt and holding a blanket.

"Did I wake you up?" Rhiannon asked, pivoting back around.

Karramis flapped the blanket open in front of her, fanning it out and sitting down. "No." She draped the blanket over her and Rhiannon's bare legs. "Not at all."

Eyeing her with a stern gaze, Rhiannon asked, "Really?"

"Okay, fine, you did wake me up."

"I'm sorry."

"It's not your fault. I'm an extremely light sleeper."

"I'm still sorry."

Karramis glided her arm under her daughter's and leaned into her. "Couldn't sleep?"

Rhiannon tilted her head and rested it against her mother's shoulder. "I slept fine. It's just, something woke me up."

"Do you know what it was?"

"I thought I heard someone calling me, but I think it was just my imagination. I've been hearing it for a few days now. More since I got back, but once I focus on it, it disappears."

Karramis looked over at her. "Is it James?"

"No," Rhiannon said positively, shaking her head, "it's a female voice. And it's muffled, like it's really far away."

"Hmm, it might be another ability. Maybe your telepathy is getting stronger and you are hearing other voices."

"Maybe. I don't know."

A moment passed as Karramis and Rhiannon stared out in front of them.

"Mom?" Rhiannon said, dropping her gaze to her fingers as she picked her cuticles.

Karramis reached over and placed a hand over her daughter's fidgeting fingers. "Yeah?"

"How did you do it?"

"What do you mean?"

Rhiannon lifted her head, her soft eyes stopping on her mother. "How did you survive the aftermath of everything that had happened to you? How did you come back from all of that and be able to control your powers again? To feel normal again."

Awareness and understanding bloomed in Karramis. "Still having nightmares?"

Rhiannon nodded, her voice tight and low. "How did you do it? How did everything not break you and drive you into a dark place?"

"It did." Karramis's tone was sincere and pragmatic. "The first half of my life, I didn't know anything about the prophecy beyond what I learned in school. I didn't know it was about me. Then when I did learn about it, I thought . . . I thought it was a joke. That there had to be some mistake. There was no way I was the savior who would save magic. The idea scared me. It even made me angry, to be honest. And this all happened around the same time I met your dad. And that alone made even more emotions flutter to the surface."

Rhiannon smiled. "Was it love at first sight?"

Karramis grinned and shook her head. "Not exactly." She sighed. "Love is a very strong word. It isn't just a feeling—it's a surrendering of one's self. A vulnerability. It's this overwhelming sense of fullness taking control of you, like every part of you is finally together, complete. And you can't do anything about it. It's a tiny crevice opening up inside of you that allows light to shine through, and over time, that crack gets bigger and bigger until that light grows brighter and brighter. Love is something that consumes you. It's not something you feel."

Rhiannon propped her arm on her leg and rested her cheek against her loose-fisted hand.

"No," Karramis continued with a smile as she spotted the dreamy gaze beaming in her daughter's eyes, "it's something that literally becomes a part of you. It's a string of emotions that wraps around your heart, and some of those emotions are stronger than others. But it's not until they all level out that you can truly feel what real love is, beyond the physical attraction and desires. And true love isn't just any love—it's so much more than that. It's loving someone and being *in* love with that person. It takes over not only your heart, but your mind and soul. So no, it wasn't love at first sight, but rather an instant attraction. But I *was* drawn to him, a force that pulled and pulled, tugging me toward him. There was this instant connection. Everything inside me refused to let him go. I did, however, fall fairly quickly for him. But . . . I didn't love him. Not at first. In fact, I wouldn't allow myself to admit it to myself, even after I knew I did."

"Why?"

"Because I was scared. I've lived most of my life in fear. And I felt that meeting him was a mistake because as much as I wanted him, I didn't think he wanted me." Karramis gave a faint smile. "But he eventually proved me wrong. But even then, I was still scared. And when I left with you and your brother, when I agreed to run away, it was the hardest thing I ever had to do because I was leaving him behind. But I did it anyway because I was so afraid. I was so terrified they'd find me, find us, and take you two away. So, I disappeared, and not just physically, but mentally as well. I stopped using my magic. I stopped living. I simply existed to protect you and your brother. I was only surviving. And that took me into a dark place. I tried so hard to fight it, tried to make sure I was happy for you both, but it was hard."

Rhiannon held her mother's hand.

"But everything that happened after they found us was the breaking point for me," Karramis went on, welcoming the touch. "When Lucas and the others came that night, I was beyond terrified. But even though my fear consumed me, I wouldn't let them take you both. I wouldn't let them win. So, I fought back. Something snapped in me that day. Was I scared? Absolutely. And there were a few times when that fear wanted to take over again, and it did. But I never allowed it to stick around for long.

I refused to give in to it. And the same thing happened when I woke up again. I knew I couldn't rely on my magic, but I still fought. I couldn't give in to the fear again. I was tired of being a coward. I was not going to be a victim. I was not going to be used or die on their terms."

Gently squeezing her mother's hand, Rhiannon lifted her blue eyes to hers. "How can I find that kind of strength in myself?" A softness settled in her words. "How can I be in control when I'm not even sure what I'm trying to control?"

Karramis rotated to fully face Rhiannon, both her hands now clutching her daughter's. "That is up to you." Her eyes were gentle and matched her tone. "Once you've survived being broken down or left among the darkness, you learn to ignore the fractures and shadows that would've once defeated you. You learn you're not so easily swayed by the bad things that once ruled your very existence. You just have to be willing to pull yourself together and find the light first." She cradled Rhiannon's cheek. "You need to be willing to fight for yourself, fight to survive. No one can truly break you or pull you into the darkness without your permission. You are in control. You. No one else."

A tear slid down Rhiannon's cheek. "I don't think I can do it by myself."

Karramis leaned over and kissed her forehead. "No one said you have to. You aren't alone. And you never will be. But this is something only you can fix. Only you can control what you are feeling inside, Rhiannon. Don't wait for someone else to save you. Be the hero in your own story and do it yourself. Use those broken pieces and forge them into something new, something that is unbreakable."

Chapter 23

Magical Bonds

James burst through the door the next day, frantic and sweating. "Mom? Dad?" He slammed the door as he raced inside. "Rhiannon?"

"What happened?" Karramis and Will shouted, rushing from their bedroom.

"What's wrong?" Rhiannon said a second later, catching up to her parents as they all exited the hallway.

"Is Raina okay?" Karramis asked.

His chest burned as he took a few shallow breaths. "Yes." He leaned over and rested his hands against his slightly bent knees. "Raina is fine."

"Then what is it?" Will asked in a hurry. "Is someone hurt?"

"I'm not sure," James admitted, still trying to catch his breath.

"What the bloody hell does that mean? And where's Callie?"

"Outside." James's features pinched with concern. "Uncle Pavian didn't show up, and neither did Tenarick or Quinian."

"What?" Karramis said as a flash of panic skimmed across her face. "What do you mean? He was supposed to return last night. They all were."

"I know that. But when Raina woke me up this morning, she said he never came home. I told her he was probably just with Grandpa—telling him everything he found. But before I even left for the village to find out, both Grandpa and Viktor showed up." His somber eyes stopped on his mother's. "He never came home last night."

Shock and disbelief settled in Rhiannon's taut expression. "What do we do? Should we worry?" Her eyes widened. "What if Merrick got him?"

Shaking his head, James reassured her, "No, he couldn't have. He's been here the whole time. In fact, Viktor was monitoring the forbidden side all night, and there was no disturbance. Plus, I didn't feel anything."

Karramis glanced over her shoulder at Rhiannon. "That would explain why you didn't feel anything last night either."

"So," Rhiannon said, "what's the plan? What do we do?"

Sitting down on the couch, James shifted his attention between his parents and sister. "Aunt K and Aidan are going out to look for them. Aunt K thinks maybe they got caught up at the school, or maybe the portals in the non-magical realm moved around like the ones here keep doing."

Rhiannon let out a relieved breath. "Yeah, she's probably right. Maybe they weren't done at the school or lost track of the portals." She sat down beside her brother and glanced up at her parents. "It's possible, right?"

"Yes," Will answered, his hand idly stroking Karramis's back, "it's definitely possible."

James suddenly perked up, tilting his head slightly as Rhiannon narrowed her eyes and zoned out.

Silence filled the room.

Will paused his hand on Karramis's back and arched a brow at her. "What's happening?"

Karramis shrugged and gave a questioning frown. "No idea."

"Shh," James said, tapping his ear. "I'm listening."

Whispering, Karramis asked, "To what?"

"Shh!" Rhiannon added loudly, waving a hand frantically.

James twisted sharply in her direction. "You hear it too, don't you?'

"I'm not sure what I'm hearing. I think . . . I think it's a woman's voice."

"No." James moved his head slowly side to side in disagreement. "No, it's definitely a guy's voice." He paused, straining to hear better. "At least I think it's a guy. It's too far away and . . ."

"Distorted," the twins said together.

Karramis cocked her head, her puzzled expression focusing on her children. "Did you two just—"

"Yes," Rhiannon said with a smile, glancing over at James. "I guess we forgot to tell you, but we can hear each other again."

She paused and narrowed her eyes, listening. "But . . . But I can hear someone else inside my head like I told you before."

Karramis rubbed the scar along the side of her face. "Is it your telepathic powers?"

"I—I don't know."

Karramis's eyes widened, and a grin twisted on her lips. "Hang on." She grabbed the twins' wrists and pulled them toward the front door. "Come with me."

"Where are we going?" Rhiannon asked.

"Outside. I think I know what you're hearing. Or rather who you're hearing."

Karramis pulled them onto the porch and dropped their arms as she searched the sky, blocking the sun with her hand.

"What are you looking for?" Will asked, coming up behind her and following her search of the sky.

Karramis grinned as she pulled her shoulders back. "I knew it." She pointed toward the trees in the distance, her finger aiming at two birds circling a few hundred feet away. "It's your Messengers."

"Really?" James placed a hand over his eyes to block out the bright rays as he searched the sky. "It's about time. I thought I heard mine months ago."

"That is a bit longer than usual," Karramis said.

"How long does it usually take?" Rhiannon asked, stepping down the stairs and monitoring the birds.

"Well, Pavian got Edrick about a week after receiving his powers, but Kavana and Meadow had to wait a lot longer for Robin and Starla. I think almost two, maybe even three weeks."

Rhiannon tossed a look over her shoulder. "What about you?"

"I don't have a Messenger."

"Why?"

"I'm not sure. I just never received one."

"So, why are they just flying around over there?" James asked. "And do we get to choose which one is ours?"

"No," Karramis said, "they've already chosen you. That's why you can hear them. And they are flying around because you haven't called them yet. They've probably been searching for you, just waiting for you to connect with them. Messengers choose you, but you have to call them to accept the bond. Once you do, you will be able to hear each other better."

"How do we do it?" Rhiannon observed the birds circling around in the distance, each sweep bringing them closer to the ground. "How do we call them?"

"Well, your aunts and uncle just focused on the voice and started talking back to it, urging it to come closer."

James joined Rhiannon in the grass and stood quietly, focusing on the voice in his head.

The two figures flew over the tall canopies, swooping down as they cleared the forest, coasting a few feet above the ground.

Two large birds arched upward into the sky as they flew within a couple yards of the twins and circled overhead.

A mix of light brown and tan with a softer shade of tawny speckled the underside of one bird. With wings stretched out and expanded the length of almost four feet, the great horned owl was a magnificently graceful creature as it swooped under the roof and landed on the porch.

The other bird, with a dark brown body and feathers reaching from its neck and along its face, soared with a wingspan of over six feet before perching on the cap of the railing at the edge of the stairs. The bald eagle froze as it eyed James, the fixed stare not threatening but friendly.

James stepped over to the eagle and ran his hand down the sleek feathers along the bird's back as Rhiannon ascended the stairs and sat down next to the owl.

Karramis slid her hand down Will's muscular arm, gliding her hand into his and interlocking their fingers as she glanced between the twins. "So, what're you going to name them?"

"Athena!" Rhiannon said excitedly without hesitation.

"How did I know you were going to say that?" James asked rhetorically.

"Hmm, I wonder," his sister teased.

"What about you, James?" Will asked, leaning into Karramis, his hand gently squeezing hers. "What will you name yours?'

"You don't have to come up with a name right now." Karramis rested her cheek on Will's muscular bicep. "You can think about it first."

"Zeus," James answered with a smile.

Surprise sparked across Rhiannon's grinning face. "Zeus? You want to name him Zeus?"

"Yeah, it's fitting."

"How so?"

"I mean, Grandpa has Hermes, and you have Athena now, so why not name him after the god of all gods? Plus, Zeus is the god of the sky, and I control air, and he's represented by an eagle, so that just seems even more perfect to me."

"God of the sky?" Rhiannon furrowed her brow. "An eagle? How did you know that?"

"Everyone knows that," he said with a shrug. "It's common knowledge."

Rhiannon's gaze fixed on him even more. "Oh, really?"

He scowled and rolled his eyes. "Okay, fine. If you must know, I read it on the back of a cereal box. But hey! At least I read it, right?"

Rhiannon chuckled under her breath as she stroked Athena.

Grinning, Karramis urged Will forward with her as she headed for the door. "I think we'll leave you both to get acquainted with your Messengers."

Will playfully stepped into her, wrapping his arms around her and pulling her into his chest as they entered the house and closed the door behind them.

James stared at Rhiannon as she caressed the fully alert owl. He focused on her, seeking the slightest possibility of hearing her thoughts.

"Can you hear me?" James asked her through their telepathic bond.

"Yes," she answered out loud, "of course I can hear you."

"Good, just checking." Stroking Zeus, James watched her, a somberness playing at his features. "I missed you, you know. When you were in the cave."

Rhiannon blinked slowly as she lifted her gaze. "I know. But I'm glad it happened the way it did."

Confusion struck him. "Why?"

"Because I needed to process everything by myself. I needed to figure out what I was feeling on my own before I could allow someone else to help me. You can't always fix me, James. You can't always be the one saving me."

"Why not?" he asked, coming up and sitting beside her on the porch.

"It's not your job to do so. You are my brother. You're not supposed to be the knight always saving the damsel."

James held back a grin as he eyed a watchful Zeus scanning the area. "But you're so good at being the damsel."

She smirked and playfully punched his arm. "Shut up!"

"Ow!" James rubbed his bicep. "Could you not bruise me please?"

"Oh, hush," she teased. "I barely tapped you."

James scoffed. "Tapped me? That was downright abusive."

"Stop making fun of me."

"I'm not," he said with a sharp tone. "That really hurt."

"Oh." Remorse filled her tone. "Sorry. I didn't think—"

"Gotcha!" James laughed as he jumped to his feet. "I totally got you there."

Rhiannon bolted to her feet and curled her hand into a fist, punching him in the same area. "Jerk!"

"Ow!" James clutched his arm. "Holy hell, Rhiannon! That really freakin' hurt this time." He considered for a moment. "Did Aunt K teach you to fight or just how to throw a punch?"

Her brow flicked up. "Is there a difference?"

"Uh, yeah! A big difference."

"How so?"

James angled a foot back and lifted his fists near the sides of his face. "Come on." He waved his hands, urging her to advance toward him. "Hit me again."

Rhiannon flinched. "What? No."

"Yes, come on. Hit me again."

"You're crazy. I'm not going to hit you."

The corners of his mouth rose as teasing entered his tone. "That's right, you're not because this time I'm ready."

"Are you trying to taunt me?" she asked, folding her arms over her chest.

"Is it working?"

She rolled her eyes. "No." Her arms dropped to her sides as irritation fluttered to life. "Dammit, yes."

Rhiannon planted her feet slightly wider than shoulder width apart and angled her body so her left side was closer to her brother. Lifting her arms, she placed them near her face as she curled her fingers into fists before twisting at the hips. She threw her body into the punch, slicing her arm forward through the air. James sidestepped, and she tumbled forward. Hurrying upright, she rotated around, facing James fully as she rested her feet closer together. She lifted her hands into the ready position.

James lowered his fists. "Well, there's my answer."

Rhiannon relaxed her arms. "What do you mean?"

Closing the narrow distance between them, James shoved both hands into Rhiannon's shoulders. She stumbled back and fell with a heavy thud on her backside.

"Ow!" she snapped. "What the hell did you do that for?"

"Because you didn't maintain your stance."

She pushed to her feet, dusting off her hands and the skirt of her dress. "Yes, I did."

"No, you didn't," James pointed out sternly. "If you had maintained your stance, I wouldn't have been able to push you over like that."

Rhiannon scoffed, placing her hands on her hips. "Okay, fine, I didn't maintain my stance. So what?"

"So what?" Frustration saturated his tone. "So what? You know once you are down, you are more vulnerable, right? You're more in danger of losing the fight."

"Why? Aren't there ways of getting out of it once you're on the ground?"

"There are," he said with conviction, "but do you know any of them?"

She thought for a moment. "Well, no. But you can teach me."

James arched a brow. "To fight?"

"Yeah," she said without a hint of mockery, only eagerness. "Teach me whatever you can. How to control magic. How to fight with it. How to use my hands as a weapon. Teach me how to use the dagger you gave me. And how—"

"Wait," James interrupted, his surprised gaze flinching back. "I didn't give you a dagger. I don't even know how to use one."

"But Ryan said . . ." She trailed off, pondering the idea as to why he had lied to her.

Understanding, James said, "I guess he thought you'd feel safer with it."

"Yeah . . . I guess so."

James sat down on the steps. "Anyway, are you sure you want me teaching you?"

"Yeah—yes." She joined him, tucking the hem of her skirt under her legs. "I trust you. And you've proven time and time again that you will do whatever you can to protect me." She paused. "Plus, I don't want anyone else to know."

"Why?"

"Because . . . Well, because I want to show them I can do this without them seeing me struggle. They all have so much faith in me, and I just need to find that kind of faith as well. I know this won't be easy for me, and I know I will probably fail more than once. But I know I can do this. At least I think I can. I just have to get out of my own head. So . . . will you help me?"

"Of course."

Smiling, Rhiannon flung herself sideways and hugged him.

"But on one condition," he said, wrapping his arms around her.

"Yeah, of course." She withdrew from the embrace. "Anything."

James grinned. "Okay, maybe two conditions."

Rhiannon scowled, the regret from agreeing quickly rising. "What?"

"First, you have to do what I say, whenever I say it. I can't do this if you aren't going to take my advice and trust me completely."

"That's fair. Just don't get me seriously hurt or killed. Oh! And don't be a jerk. Or overly bossy. Treat me like I'm your student, not your sister." She playfully nudged him with her elbow. "I mean, don't forget, I may not have magic as strong as yours, but I do know where you sleep."

"Right. I'll keep that in mind."

"Anyway, what else?"

Folding his arms, he smirked. "You're not going to like this one."

"Why?" Rhiannon copied his body language but glared at him suspiciously. "What is it?"

James paused before answering with a smug twist of his mouth. "You have to wear pants."

Chapter 24

Borrowed Gift

One month ago
Mid-November

The sky was painted with a flawless blend of blues. Dark indigo housed the remaining stars of the night as the rich navy flowed into royal blue, cascading down among the vivid cerulean. Dew covered the ground like a blanket as the crisp morning air smelled of autumn. Yellow and orange leaves rested sporadically among the foliage as fog rolled through the quiet roads.

Fall had arrived in Kiluemar, a lot colder than expected.

Constructed soon after the residents of the island had taken refuge here, Caerwyn Village consisted of various sixteenth-century Western European buildings covering many acres of land inside the boundaries. Single- and two-story homes with small gardens lined the outer area, while the once-bustling structures of the bakery, butcher shop, blacksmith, multiple churches and taverns, a schoolhouse, and assorted other merchant shops filled the center. Over the years, many of the buildings had fallen into disarray due to abandonment as

- 358 -

residents of the village deserted their homes, either choosing to live in the newly built upgraded town of Stoweward, which was approximately five miles to the north, or deciding to leave the island altogether after the dangers became evident. However, several homes and a few buildings still radiated the pristine, stunning, and quaint beauty of sixteenth-century architecture.

The library was a new feature of the island, having only been recently turned into one by Randolyn Natomna Ward, Zarrius Ward's third wife, a few years ago. Located in the central part of the village and nestled quietly among two abandoned stone buildings, the library was much different from its neighbors. Stone walls covered in white plaster with wooden beams rising vertically decorated the exterior. Two wide three-pane bay windows lined the walls on either side of the solid wooden door, while long narrow casements blended perfectly into the siding on the second floor. A large brick fireplace jutted out on one side of the building, and the chimney stretched above the rooftop. Having first been used as a brothel, and centuries later as an inn, the new library was one of the three largest buildings on the island.

Exiting the library, Rhiannon drove away the quietness of dawn as she closed the door with a bang, the sight of a familiar face through the thick fog snagging her attention and startling her.

"Holy hell, Ryan!" she snapped, her hand flying to her chest as she jumped. "Are you trying to scare the crap outta me?"

He strutted closer with his hands in the pocket of the dark gray hoodie he wore, the smooth casualness of his stride like a cat stalking through the night. The hood covered his brown hair, but there was a vivid kindness and breathtaking comfort radiating in his dark eyes from behind the shadows as the low-hanging material draped over his face.

"Sorry," Ryan admitted with a low chuckle, the grin he flashed her beaming across his face, "but it isn't like I said boo or something."

"No," she clarified, the word filled with a humorous but firm retort, "but just appearing behind someone without a sound, and through the fog nonetheless, isn't exactly *not* trying to scare them either."

"Right. But admit it, even if I'd called your name first, I still would've scared you."

"Yeah." She paused, releasing a snicker. "You're probably right."

Ryan lowered his hood as his breath clouded in front of his face. "What are you doing here anyway? I thought you were still back home."

"No." Rhiannon zipped up her jacket and headed down the road, looking over her shoulder to make sure he was following. "I came back a few days ago to get some more research done. I'm not sleeping well again, so I figured I could make better use of my time."

"Oh," Ryan said as he strolled beside her, sliding his hands back into the front pocket of his hoodie. "Well, I haven't seen you in weeks. I've missed having you around here. So, what's new?"

Rhiannon flexed her fingers, trying to drive away the cold biting at them. "Well, I'm still having issues controlling my magic. I mean, I'm getting better with some of it, but I'm still not good enough. And I'm really struggling with my fire magic. It's like the few times it surfaced was a fluke or something." Pulling on her sleeves, she gripped the material and plunged her covered hands into her pockets. "And . . . Aunt K and the others didn't return last month. I'm starting to worry."

"Well, maybe they'll come on the next full moon in a few days." A softness entered Ryan's features. "Is there anything I can help with?"

"No," Rhiannon said, the unease in her voice matching her downward gaze. "I'm not sure what you could help with, but thanks."

"Anytime. But . . . uhm, are you at least getting your emotions under control?"

"No," Rhiannon answered regretfully, her stare remaining on the ground in front of her. "That's the annoying part. I just can't seem to get past being afraid all the time. Even when there's no real reason for it, something is always putting me on high alert, as if I'm waiting for something bad to happen."

They strolled down the dirt road as the fog slowly started to lift, showing more of the buildings lining the pathway. The sun appeared along the horizon and peeked out from the trees surrounding the village.

Rhiannon folded her arms over her chest and shivered as a cold breeze brushed across her, her knee-length dress and thin jacket doing nothing to help fight the chilly autumn morning.

"You'll get there," Ryan said encouragingly with a side grin as he came to a stop and removed his hoodie. "I have faith you will figure it out eventually."

Rhiannon halted and twisted around, perplexed as she observed his actions. "What are you doing?"

A dark blue long-sleeve shirt remained against his lean athletic torso. "Here." He offered Rhiannon the hoodie. "Before you freeze."

Rhiannon shook her head and lifted her hands. "No, it's okay. You need it."

"No, it's all right. You need it more than I do. Plus, it's not that cold to me."

"Are you sure?"

"Yes."

"Thanks," she said gently as she grabbed it and eased the oversized hoodie over her head.

He was right. The body heat lingering made the soft, thick material unbelievably warm, and it wrapped around her. Her body sagged into it, relaxing and welcoming the embrace. The scent that remained was even more warm and inviting, sending a wave of calm over her, reminding her of a crackling fireplace and rich musky vanilla with a hint of lush oak and jasmine. The scents were familiar, both reminding her of the library and the beach, two of her favorite places on the island.

Rhiannon blinked and lifted her gaze, clearing her throat and returning to their previous conversation as she strolled back down the dirt path. "I just hope it's sooner rather than later."

Ryan monitored her as a strange expression floated across her face but quickly disappeared. "So . . ." He followed suit and trailed beside her. "Where are you heading now?"

"Home really quick. I have to get some pants."

Rays of light streaked along the ground and illuminated the dirt with a bright yellow as they rounded a corner, the adjacent path opening up on either side.

Stepping into the full glow of the sun and out of the shadows of the buildings, Ryan said, "Then I'm assuming you're meeting James later today."

She continued forward, the warmth of the sun lining her face as she peered over at him. "How'd you know about that?"

"I saw him not too long ago when he came to see Zarrius, and he told me he had been helping you train."

"So much for not telling anyone," she said, slightly irritated.

"I don't think he meant to say anything, if that makes you feel any better. I had asked how you were, and he kind of let it slip when he mentioned seeing you later that day." He paused, giving her a sidelong grin. "How pissed does he get when you show up like that?"

She lifted an eyebrow, confusion and intrigue painted on her face. "Like what?"

"With trousers on but still wearing a dress."

"Hey," she said with a breathy chuckle, smiling, "his condition was I had to wear pants. He never said anything about not being allowed to wear a dress." Her voice was laced with sarcasm and a humorous undertone. "It's not my fault he wasn't clear enough."

A low laugh rumbled through him. "So, where are you heading exactly? Where is home right now?"

"Back to Aunt K's. I'm going to try and get a quick nap before meeting James over at the area under Ember Cliffs."

"The grotto?"

"Yeah, that's where we've been training lately."

Ryan narrowed his eyes. "Why there?"

"Because it's quiet—secluded. There are fewer prying eyes and distractions. I'm not very good at fighting yet, so I don't like people watching me. Plus, I can practice my water powers there."

"That makes sense."

Rhiannon glanced back down the path and then over at him, halting and aiming her pointed thumb over her shoulder. "Hey, didn't you have something to do back there?"

He stopped, turning slightly to face her. "No—shoot, I mean, yeah. I told Randolyn I'd clean out one of the rooms upstairs before she came in this afternoon. More documents were found, and she wants to keep all of them in the library for safekeeping."

"What kind of documents?" Rhiannon asked curiously, her eyes bright with interest.

"I'm not sure, but I'll let you know."

"Thanks."

"Of course."

Rhiannon continued her leisurely stroll toward Kavana and Aidan's place. "Hey, can I ask you something?"

His brows creased at the hesitation and tightness in her voice. "Should I be worried?'

"No, why would you think that?"

"You got all serious and . . . timid."

"Right." Rhiannon shifted her blue eyes up and met his, her pace never faltering. "Well, I was just wondering why you gave me that dagger. James told me he didn't send it, so you must've."

"I did." A gentleness seeped into his voice and features. "I gave it to you because I thought it might help you feel safe. Even if it remained sheathed, I thought it might act as a safeguard for you, like it had done for me when I was younger."

Stunned, Rhiannon asked, "It's yours? Your personal dagger?"

"It is. Well, it was. But now it's yours."

Rhiannon stopped as they came to the front door of the house. "Thank you . . ." She bent over and unzipped her calf-length black boots, unbuckling the strap that held the sheathed dagger around her lower leg. "But I can't keep it."

"Why not?" he asked, refusing to take it from her.

"Well, first of all, it's yours—"

"No, it's yours," he insisted. "I gave it to you."

"And second," she continued sharply, the appreciation still present on her face and in her tone, "I still have no clue how to use it. James doesn't know how to use daggers."

Ryan placed his hands in the pockets of his black jeans, ignoring the weapon still held out to him. "I could teach you."

She flicked up a brow as she widened her gaze, consideration streaking across her face. Learning to use the dagger might come in handy, but Rhiannon already struggled with the other weapons James had tried to teach her, causing her to only focus on hand-to-hand fighting.

"No," Rhiannon said a moment later, "it's okay." She took hold of his wrist and pulled a hand from his pocket, flipping it over and placing the dagger, strap and all, in his open palm. "I think this should stay with you." She opened the door and paused in the doorframe. "Thank you, though." Her eyes locked with his. "For letting me borrow it."

"You're welcome," Ryan replied with a sincere softness. Turning to leave, he paused and glanced over his shoulder. "See you later?"

She smiled. "Oh, you know it. I want to see those documents."

Returning the gesture, he waved as he continued forward.

"Hey, Ryan," she called out, taking a step after him.

"Yeah?" he said, facing her and strolling backward as he kept his steady pace.

"How about this weekend? I'll bring hot chocolate, and we can catch up. Go through those documents together."

"Absolutely, just let me know when." A corner of his mouth lifted. "I'll bring bagels."

Rhiannon cocked her head and grinned. "Make it chocolate chip muffins and we've got a deal."

"I believe I can arrange that."

"Good."

"See you then, angel," he said, immediately frowning and shaking his head with disapproval in unison with her. "Yeah, no. That one really doesn't sound right either."

"No, definitely not," Rhiannon agreed with a low chuckle before entering the house and closing the door behind her.

Chapter 25

James dismounted Callie outside the entrance to the grotto on the southern banks of Cavern Beach. Removing his socks and shoes, he dug his feet into the sand, the coolness matching the crisp chill in the air. Stroking the winged horse's neck, he watched the waves lapping across the shoreline, their quiet splashes the only sounds filling the harbor.

Glancing down at his watch, James said to Callie, "We're a bit early, so I'll just hang out with you, if you don't mind."

A low snort came from the winged horse as she gently nudged James in the side.

Moments later, a shadow soared across the beach, causing James to jerk his head upward.

Raeth circled around overhead, swooping through the air over Half Moon Harbor and gliding through the sky gracefully. His leaf-shaped wings stretched out in full glory as they flapped, sending the creature higher before he tucked them back and took a nosedive. Landing hard, the Earth Dragon sent a wave of sand flying up around him.

"Where is she?" James asked, concern rising in him with the fact Rhiannon was not with the dragon.

Jutting his head in the direction of the entrance to the grotto, Raeth answered, *"Right there."*

"Hey!" Rhiannon called, exiting an enormous fissure along the side of the cliffs and running toward them.

Heading toward her with a hurried stride, he asked, "What're you doing here already?" He peered down at his watch again. "We weren't supposed to meet for another twenty minutes."

"I got here early to practice. Raeth told me you'd arrived already, so I came out to let you know I was here."

"Early?" James slowed as she jogged to a stop, his socks tucked in the shoes hanging from his hand. "How long have you been here?"

Rhiannon rotated her bare feet in the sand, heading back toward the cliffs as her brother strolled beside her. "About an hour."

"Any luck today?"

"Kind of. I'm able to manipulate it better, but I'm still having a hard time maintaining it."

"We'll focus on that today then—do the same thing we did last time."

Rhiannon blew out a breath. "Okay."

The sand cooled even more beneath their feet as they stepped into the shadows, entering under the huge archway slicing through the side of the cliff and stepping into a domed cavern.

Sand carpeted the ground leading under the jagged fissure, the twelve-foot-wide notch rising over a hundred feet tall along the rock formation below Ember Cliffs. A sandy white shore covered one side of the cathedral-style stone temple, making a half-moon shape, while the other side was flooded with calm crystal clear cerulean-and-teal water. The interior walls were painted in rich shades of tan and copper with thick layers of alternating rock spanning the entire room. Sunlight filled the cave as it beamed in overhead from a large opening along the ceiling, bouncing off the water and creating a breathtakingly magical fortress.

"Ready?" James asked, jumping right into training as he tossed his socks and shoes aside.

"I think so," Rhiannon replied, a hint of uncertainty lingering in her tone.

"Come on," James said with enthusiasm, "you're getting so much better. You even said so yourself, so give yourself some credit."

"Right." Rhiannon sighed, trying to erase the anxiousness rising in her stomach, but to no avail. "If you say so."

"I do. And I'm the oldest, so you have to listen to me." He nudged her arm. "So, what exactly were you working on earlier?"

"I was trying to focus more on my water magic. Like I mentioned before, I can manipulate it, but I can't seem to maintain it. I also can't do much with it once I start urging it to move. So, maintaining and controlling are the parts I'm having trouble with."

"Did you ever ask Aunt Meadow for help?"

Meadow was their mother's younger sister, and she shared the same magical abilities as her niece. Meadow was not only a Guardian, but she was also a Water Witch. Having been trained in controlling her ability since she was eleven, Meadow was the best person to get advice from regarding this aquatic power.

"Yeah," Rhiannon answered. "She gave me some advice on how to become"—her voice was laced with mockery—"one with the water, whatever the heck that means."

"Well, maybe you can talk to her more about that later. Anyway . . ." James stepped aside and glided his arm through the air, presenting the still water. "Shall we begin?"

Raising her arms, Rhiannon opened her hands as she focused on the water. The cool, damp air caressed her palms, sending an energizing tingling racing up her arms. Her fingers tensed as she spread them apart.

The water rippled.

Heat filled her chest as the comforting warmth traveled up and down her body, activating every nerve. She relaxed her fingers, and her hands grew weightless. A stream of water rose from the surface, swirling in a slow-moving dance as it flowed upward. More water joined in as the shoreline retreated. The whirlpool floated higher, reaching upward as it ascended toward the opening in the cavern ceiling.

It swirled, reaching five feet.

Ten feet.

Fifteen.

"Come on," James said to himself, clutching his hands in excitement as the sounds of rushing water filled the cave. "You can do it. Keep going."

Twenty feet.

Water flowed together, becoming wider and thicker as it stretched higher into the sky above the cavern lake. Fish flopped on the wet sand as more shoreline came into view, the tides pulling away with a gravity-defying surge.

Thirty feet.

Moving away, James retreated to the back wall of the cave. "Good. Higher." His words only audible to himself.

Forty feet.

Rhiannon's arms trembled as she continued to lift the swirling whirlpool upward with one hand and drive the remaining water out with the other. She groaned as her body grew weak, the dancing tower of water stilling. She fought against her muscles seizing in pain, a burning sensation rising like acid in her veins. Drawing strength from the water, she pulled the energy from the element and tried joining as one with it.

"I can't," Rhiannon called out over the raging water, struggling to keep hold of the powerful force trying to pull itself back down.

"Yes, you can!" James insisted loudly a few yards behind her as he stood next to a narrow crevice along the cavern wall.

The water spun in a wild vortex, a spinning rush of waves fighting to reenter the lake below. A surge of power filled Rhiannon as she fought to control the element, an energizing recharge driving her to push herself harder.

Fifty feet.

Water pulled farther away from the shore as the cave filled with the deafening echoes of undulating waves.

"James," Rhiannon yelled over the noise, "do it!"

"Are you sure?" he bellowed, hesitation lining the question.

"Yes! Do it now!"

James lifted his arms as he whipped toward the fissure jutting down along the stone wall, the darkened entrance to another cave. He focused on the air deep inside the crevice—cool, thick, and clean, the element clinging to his senses. His muscles tightened, strengthening as each breath pulled in more power. Wind swirled around him, sweeping across his skin and sending a charge of energy through his body. He called to the air, forcing it to collect in a central location within the stone chamber. Every gas, particle, chemical, and vapor pulled together, condensing into a storm waiting to be set free.

Eerie screams echoed from the entrance nestled in the shadows, the howls traveling through the hidden cavern with lightning speed as James released the energy he had created. Vibrations reverberated off the stones as the storm raged closer. Dodging aside, he twisted around as his back slammed against the stone, the burst of powerful wind narrowly missing him. The gale-force air erupted from the slick stone walls and rattled the pebbles lining the entrance, shooting out and blasting a wave of sand outward with an explosive boom, the airy screams echoing with a thunderous roar. James kept his hands raised as he drove the wind forward across the sand and into his sister.

Rhiannon jumped as the outburst slammed into her with a startling jolt, forcing her to collapse to her knees. Pain burned through her as she held strong to the tower of flowing water. Agony seared through her, intensifying as she maintained control of her powers. Her muscles quivered, the weakness taking over as emotions rose inside her.

Doubt. Fear. Defeat.

"Don't give in!" James shouted encouragingly, dropping his hands and stepping toward her. "Use it! Fight it!"

"I can't!" Rhiannon yelled.

The pain was too much, too hard to control. She could not fight the anguish, the hopelessness.

"Yes, you can!" Pure hope gleamed in his eyes, his voice. "Get out of your head. Take control!"

Rhiannon rose to her feet, her hands shaking more than her knees. Slowly backing away from the shoreline, she made her way closer to James, following the warm presence he was radiating. Tears streamed down her face as heated pressure clamped down in her chest, tightening and squeezing with an unyielding ferocity.

"Don't do it," James pleaded, gentle but stern. He stood behind her and leaned into her ear. "Don't give up."

Rhiannon lowered her lashes, the tears pooling in her eyes and falling as she dropped her shaky hands.

James widened his eyes in a rush as he clasped his sister's shoulders, quickly twisting both of them around and shielding her as the whirlpool came crashing down, the water splashing with a loud slap before sending a wave rushing toward them.

The small tidal wave sent James and Rhiannon sliding across the sand, and they came to a stop a few feet from the narrow cavern entrance.

"You almost had it," James said proudly, completely soaked.

Rhiannon sighed, wringing the water from her dress as she stood up. "It still wasn't good enough."

"But did you see what you did there? That was amazing! Give yourself—"

"I want to do it again," she interrupted sharply, irritation tight in her voice as she walked back over to the water.

"Okay," James said, the sympathy attempting to counter her emotional response as he followed behind her. "We can try again, but what about your fire magic? Did you want to try that first? Maybe switch it up?"

She sighed. "Yeah, sure. I guess."

"I'm glad I didn't bring matches." James pulled a lighter from his wet pocket. "Do you want to try controlling it, or maybe see if you can conjure it this time?"

Examining her palm and balling it into a fist, Rhiannon replied with disappointment in her voice, "Let's try controlling it first."

Rhiannon had conjured her fire magic twice now—once while being attacked by Haydrin, and again when she had found out Ryan was also a werewolf. Both times she had been afraid, triggering a defensive reaction, but each time she had not had control over it. The night of the attack, she had needed James's help, his strength and determination flowing through her and allowing the flames to release from her body. When Ryan had told her he was a werewolf, her fear had mixed with anger and resentment, driving both her water and fire magic to the surface. But again, she had not been the one controlling it. It was almost as if, both times, the powers were controlling themselves, only flowing through her and using her as an anchor. Now, after months of practice, she was still unable to summon her fire magic.

~

Rhiannon collapsed on the ground, exhausted. She rubbed her cool, clammy hands, brushing her fingers over her palms as she gazed down.

"I'm never going to get this," she said, defeated. "I can't do it."

"Come on, get up," James said firmly, clicking the lighter and igniting the flame. "Let's try again."

"James, I've been at this for over an hour now." Rhiannon glanced up at him. "I'm tired. I'm hungry. And I just want to go home and go to sleep."

"Come on, Rhiannon." He reached out a hand. "You're *so* close! You're getting stronger. I know it. I can feel it. Can't you?"

"No." She wiped the sweat from her brow. "I'm too weak. I can't do this. It's not working. My magic just isn't working right. I'm broken."

"You're not broken," he said softly as he squatted in front of her.

"Yes." She inhaled a ragged breath, meeting his gaze. "Yes, I am."

"No, you're not, so stop saying that." The persistence was adamant, direct and steady, almost commanding. "You just need to stop beating yourself up so much and try a bit harder."

Scoffing, she argued, the harshness rough behind the tightness in her throat, "I *am* trying. I'm trying really, really hard. But . . ." She sighed, her shoulders sagging. "Never mind."

"No, say it."

A moment passed before she exhaled and unleashed everything she had been holding back now for months. "It's just too much. I can't handle it all. I mean, my life went from nearly graduating high school early to 'Hey, Rhiannon, guess what? Magic is real and alive. And there is this magical island that's been hidden from the outside world for centuries now. Oh, yeah! And you're a witch. But not a normal witch. No, not at all. Nope, you're a rather powerful witch who was created to kill this bad guy who wants you dead, and he will stop at nothing to accomplish this, including killing your entire family. But don't worry, your dormant powers are supposed to help you and help save the entire magical community and magic itself. Oh, and guess what else? You have a twin brother, your parents are alive, and your best friend is a freakin' werewolf.' "

James blinked and waited for her to continue, allowing everything she had kept bottled up to finally come free.

"And I still can't completely get past what happened." Her eyes burned as she fought back the tears. "It's always in the back of my mind, haunting me. Bad things just keep happening to me. I'm scared. I'm scared all the time. And I'm so tired, I just want to sleep. But when I'm awake, I'm anxious every time I leave the house, even in the village. I—I can't fight it." Defeat settled in her pained expression. "It's no use. I can't do it. I can't fight it. I just don't know how to control my fear."

"Okay, fine then," James said simply with no condescension as he leaned his arms against his crouched legs. "Fine, so you are broken."

Rhiannon chuckled at his brazen honesty. "See, I told you."

His brown eyes burned with determination, hope, and pride as he stood up. "Yes, you are broken, but you are not shattered." He reached out his hand. "Now, get up, put yourself together, and show the world just how badass you can be. Show everyone else they have something to fear."

She hesitated, peering up into the serious and sympathetic eyes of her brother before grabbing his hand. "What's the difference between being broken and shattered? Isn't that the same thing?"

"No," James said, pulling her to her feet. "A broken glass can still hold water, while a shattered one lies in pieces among the puddle. Every time you try, every time you choose not to give up, you are refilling the glass. And eventually, the water will overflow. And when that happens, it will no longer appear as if it is leaking. So yes, you are broken, but even the broken can be fixed in one way or another."

Rhiannon glared at him, narrowing her eyes. "Did you read that on the back of a cereal box too?"

"No," James said teasingly with flawless arrogance, "a fortune cookie."

Rhiannon's eyes drooped into a contemplative scowl. "Seriously?"

James breathed a chuckle. "No."

"Oh."

The seriousness returned to his face. "Look, once you figure out your strengths—your purpose beyond just your magic—it will be the glue that puts you back together. You have to believe in yourself, Rhiannon. Like I do. I believe, without a doubt, you can do this. You are stronger than you know. You just overthink sometimes. You focus on the past and future too much. But you need to focus on the right now." He wrapped his arm around her shoulders. "I promise we'll figure this out. It might not be today, but we will figure it out. You can't give up now, not when you're so close. I mean, you have some pretty amazing powers."

"Seriously, is there some sort of club I'm unaware of or something, where you and Ryan get together and brainstorm motivational speeches to make me feel better?"

Flinching back in surprise, James said with a grin, "No, why?"

"Never mind," she answered with a sigh.

"Okay then," James continued, still confused. "Let's figure this out together. Let me help you. But you have to be willing to trust me."

"I do trust you." There was no doubt in her words. "I mean, why wouldn't I? I've trusted you with all of this. And I trust you with my life."

A smile streaked across his face. "Great, I'm glad to hear that." He paused, pondering a thought. "Because I think I may have figured out a way to help you jump-start your magic."

"And . . ." Rhiannon asked reluctantly, drawing out the word, "that would be?"

James remained silent, mulling over the idea in his head. Rhiannon focused on him, but his thoughts were distorted inside her mind.

"Let's try this again," James finally said, "but with a different approach."

She raised a skeptical brow. "And what does that mean exactly?"

James flashed her a devious grin, a playful expression entering his features.

"What are you thinking?" she asked dubiously, glaring at him.

James relaxed his face as he scooped up his wet socks and shoes, heading for the cavern entrance.

"James," Rhiannon called, annoyed by his lack of response, and stepping after him, "what are you doing?"

Exiting the grotto, he shielded his eyes as the sun sat closer to the horizon. "Looking for Raeth and Callie."

"Why?"

"We need to go find someone." He smiled at her. "Hey, when's the next full moon?"

"Uhm, in two days." Rhiannon folded her arms. "Why?"

"I have an idea."

"Clearly. But would you care to share it with me?"

His rich brown eyes filled with delight as his cheeks grew flush, rising with his cunning grin. He rubbed his dimpled chin before tapping it.

"Uh-oh," Rhiannon said, dropping her arms. "You have that I-have-a-stupid-idea look on your face."

Chuckling, he asked, "So, I know you trust Ryan . . ." He paused. "But just how much do you trust him?"

"Why?"

"Because . . . I think I figured out a way for you to fully embrace your fears. Maybe Mom is right. Maybe you need to fully break before you can rebuild yourself into a new person. Maybe the darkness is where you need to go, but this time with a little help. I think you need to reconnect to your emotions again. Open your mind up to everything—fears and all."

"And how do you suppose we do that? And what does Ryan have to do with it?"

The corners of his mouth rose in a devilish grin. "I think it's time he lets the werewolf come out to play."

Chapter 26

Words of Wisdom

Ryan Hillvec was not a typical werewolf. He was able to control a part of his transformation by tapping into his Celestial Witch magic, forcing the curse into submission. But his ability to do this came with consequences.

The first werewolf had been cursed centuries ago when a Celestial Witch killed the man his wife was having an affair with and tricked her into consuming her lover's blood as punishment for her infidelity. But the spell was tainted by dark magic. As it flowed inside the woman's body, the magic seeped into her unborn child—the lover's child. The dark magic fused itself deep into the baby's blood and cursed the unborn child, thus creating the first werewolf. Now, everyone who carried the cursed bloodline, linked to the magic of the full moon, would live a life plagued with an uncontrollable transformation, a change only brought forth when the one carrying the blood lost their virginity, the act of procreation being the trigger for the curse.

But soon after Rhiannon had learned Ryan was a creature she feared, she had also been informed he was not like the others.

His curse was different. He could control his transformation because he was like the witch who had cursed them, a witch given powers linked to the full moon or a celestial event. His magic allowed him control over his werewolf curse. However, those abilities were the cost he had to pay for stopping the curse from taking control.

Ryan could halt his change, but only at the expense of his powers. Most Celestial Witches only had magical abilities when the moon was in the night sky or when a cosmic event occurred. The closer the celestial event was to Earth, the more powerful the witch would become. All Celestial Witches had abilities even when the moon was not full, but they were weaker. If a witch wanted to access the full strength of their abilities, they would have to cease all use and recharge themselves in between full moons or celestial events. The longer a witch went without using their magic, the stronger they would be the next time they called forth their powers.

However, Ryan rarely used his magic for anything other than halting his werewolf side from coming out. Every full moon, he would use his powers to fight against the curse trying to take control. He would suffer an agonizing battle each month as he summoned every bit of his celestial power to stop the dark magic from bursting through. Sometimes he would allow the monster to come out, choosing to suffer a different kind of agony as he kept watch over his mother, the carrier of the cursed bloodline. But when he did this, he would still use his magic to retain who he was, a self-awareness allowing him control. On occasion,

Ryan would crave the full use of his celestial magic outside of stopping his curse, so he would complete the change and give in wholly to his werewolf side.

~

Rhiannon leaned back against her hands as the cool sand rested between her fingers. Eyes closed, she pressed back harder and splayed her fingers deeper into the sand, the smooth graininess a welcome sensation.

"Hey," Ryan's voice said behind her as the sand muffled his footsteps. "Relishing the beautiful autumn evening?"

Eyes still closed, she buried her toes, wiggling them as the chilled shoreline tickled her feet. "Just trying to enjoy some peace and quiet before tonight."

Ryan seated himself beside her just as an enormous cloud blocked out the sun. Glancing up, he widened his gaze. It was not a cloud.

Five figures, all varying shapes and sizes, soared overhead from the cliffs to the east. Dragons.

Deeply contrasted against the white above them, two Fire Dragons careened flawlessly with outstretched wings. Harkin and Ignara. Black and red glided with ease and grace underneath the massive Air Dragon, Phosmeratae, as he sent a rush of wind down with a single smooth flapping motion of his feathered wings. His beautiful snow-colored body eased in and out of the clouds of similar color, each slice making the sky swirl around him. Raeth and Terramina weaved between the two Fire Dragons, evading each thrust of the other creature's black membranous wings as the smaller dragons soared down along the water, their feet grazing the surface of the gentle waves within the harbor.

"We have company," Ryan said nervously, eyeing the creatures overhead as he bent his knees and slid his bare feet into the sand.

"I know. They told me you were here." Rhiannon opened her eyes and tilted her head over in his direction. "Are you still scared of them?" A curious yet teasing question.

"No," he lied, "of course not."

Skeptical, she lifted a brow and grinned.

"All right, fine. Yes, they still scare me." His gaze shot back to the dragons. "I don't think they like me very much."

She watched as the creatures coasted over the water of Half Moon Harbor, the steadiness of the calm waves lapping along the shore almost hypnotizing. "Trust me, if they didn't like you, you'd know. They're just very protective of Drolnogards, so they tend to be extra cautious when it comes to those around us."

Ryan leaned forward and rested his outstretched arms over his knees as he monitored the flawless maneuvering of the dragons. "Do they act that way with your mum or your aunt and uncle?"

"They have more of an understanding with my aunt and uncle. The dragons know they are Guardians, and they are meant to protect the island, so the dragons let them do their job. But for the most part, everyone, even my family, leaves the dragons alone, and vice versa. Now, my mom is different. She is a special case with them. She carries their blood inside her, so they don't feel she is a danger to them. They can sense it somehow, and they will protect her as much as they would protect us. But she can't communicate with them, so it makes her a bit uneasy sometimes when one of us isn't around."

"I can totally relate," Ryan admitted with a slight nod.

Silence fell over them as Rhiannon stared out in front of her, lost in thought as the dragons retreated away from the harbor, gliding farther out over the endless sea.

The vibrant cerulean water along the shore was calm, ebbing and flowing in slow, steady waves, barely making any sound as it washed over the ivory sand. Shaped like a waxing crescent moon, Cavern Beach wrapped around the harbor, starting at Ember Cliffs and curving around before joining the southern tip of the West Shores. Cliffs jutted hundreds of feet upward from the beach all around, while various caverns lay within them, some hidden and some not. The largest one opened a couple hundred feet behind where Rhiannon and Ryan sat, just beneath the gorge carving into the cliffs on the northwestern side of Dryad Forest and more than a mile from the entrance to the grotto to the south.

Eyes still locked on the harbor, Rhiannon asked, "Do you think it will happen today?"

Ryan angled his gaze over at her, his eyes narrowed. "What?"

"The dancing waters."

A few months ago, Ryan had convinced Rhiannon to leave the confines of Caerwyn Village and explore more of the island. Cavern Beach was one of his favorite spots in Kiluemar, so he had brought her here. And while here, he had mentioned how, when he was younger, he would venture out near the harbor to watch the Water Dragons and mermaids swim together during a full moon. Eventually, the magic of the moon and the island would join them, illuminating the mermaids' tails with bright, vibrant colors and making the whole harbor glow below the surface.

"No," Ryan said, a sadness entering his tone.

Disappointed, she asked, "Why not?"

"I'm not sure. I had forgotten how much I enjoyed seeing it after telling you about it, so I came back on the next full moon, but nothing happened."

"I wonder why they stopped."

"Maybe they figured there wasn't any point with most of the people here gone or hiding out. Or maybe the magic of the island stopped showing up."

"Do . . . Do the merfolk know what is happening around here?"

His brow lifted. "Merfolk?"

"Yeah," she said flatly, giving him a dumbfounded scowl. "Are there only females?"

"No," he answered with a shake of his head, "there are males as well. Havelock and Troy are the only males left. And then you have Cordelia, Kalonni, Nayda, and Cora."

"Wait a minute." Rhiannon twisted toward him, her knees inches from him. "You know them on a first-name basis?"

"They only have first names," Ryan teased.

She went on as if she had not heard him. "But you know them personally?"

"Yeah, of course. I've lived here my whole life, so I've ventured out many times to explore. I've been all over the island. I know quite a few magical creatures." He nudged her arm. "I'll take and introduce you to them."

Rhiannon dragged her fingers through the sand. "When was the last time you saw the merfolk?"

He thought for a moment. "It's been quite a few years, come to think of it."

Glancing over at the sun inching closer to the horizon, she watched the dragons far in the distance as she drew in a deep breath, letting it out in a heavy sigh.

"What's wrong?" Ryan asked, leaning forward to see her face better.

"It'll be dark soon." She glanced down at the watch on his wrist. "How long before the full moon rises?"

"This time of year," he stated, not checking the time, "the sun will set completely in roughly an hour, give or take. Then we have less than an hour before the moon starts to rise. Once it hits the horizon, I will start to shift."

Rhiannon folded her arms as a nervousness blossomed in her chest. She shivered, the trepidation mixed with the cool breeze blowing off the water sending chills up her spine. She closed her eyes and focused on her breathing.

In through her nose, out through her mouth.

One. Two.

Slow and steady. Deep and controlled.

Three. Four.

Her eyes shot open as Ryan's warm body eased closer and his upper thigh grazed against her bent knee.

Blue eyes met his as she took in his sympathetic, concerned stare.

"I'm okay," she said. "Promise. I'm just nervous."

"You're not scared?"

"A little."

"A little?"

"Okay, a lot." She inhaled a shuddering breath. "But I can do this."

"If it helps, I'm scared too," Ryan offered in a tone she had never heard before. It was rough and bleak. "I haven't turned in a long time."

"Why?" she asked, genuinely interested.

Ryan twisted and aimed his gaze over at the harbor. "Because it's painful. And when I choose to change, I don't usually allow myself to use my magic to control the monster I become. I allow it to take over." He peeked over and observed the confusion lingering on her face. "If I allow my werewolf side to take full control, then I have access to my witch magic again, at least for a month. But I also have the traits of a werewolf in human form."

"The strength and healing abilities?"

"Yes."

"What . . ." She paused, unsure how to ask the question. "What does it feel like? To transform into one."

"Well," he started with a deep exhale, "it's nothing like a shapeshifter. It's not a smooth transition by any means. It's extremely painful. Bones break and reform, expanding and thickening as the skeleton transforms and grows. The skin shreds apart as muscles rip through and form a new layer of thick flesh. Fur sprouts, and each hair is like a tiny papercut slicing along the skin. Features contort and twist as a new face forms. What I become is larger and more muscular. Gums tear apart as teeth sharpen and grow, the raw taste of blood already on our tongues. I become an animal—a pure, raging monster."

"Okay, you can stop now," she said sharply, scrunching her face as if she could feel what he was describing for herself.

Ryan gave her a half smile, the seriousness of his tone fracturing. "Hey, you asked."

"Yes, and now I deeply regret it. So . . ." Another question sprouted in her head, but this one lingered on the tip of her tongue. "Uhm . . ."

Cocking his head, Ryan flicked up a brow. "Curious mind wants to know?"

She nodded.

"Just ask then. I have nothing to hide."

"How . . . How do you handle that kind of pain? And how did you survive it the first time? I mean, you . . . you were so young.

I can't even imagine suffering that kind of pain when I was that age."

Rhiannon had also learned something else about him soon after discovering he was a werewolf. Being a witch may have been a blessing when it came to controlling the monster inside of him, but it had also been yet another curse forced upon him. He, again, was not like other werewolves because his curse was not triggered in the usual manner, but rather it had arrived shortly after his celestial magic had fully surfaced—when he was only twelve.

"My dad helped me through it," he said as a somberness seeped into his features. "And I almost killed him in the process. And completely destroyed the house trying to get to him. But he was prepared, having dealt with my mum's transformation a few times."

A curious brow rose as she asked, "Did he use his powers?"

"He did. Celestial magic can control werewolves to a certain degree. That's how I'm able to control the transformation or have some conscious awareness when I'm the monster. But it takes almost all of my stored-up powers to do so."

"Then why . . ." The thought faltered, the uncertainty behind the question making her nerves rattled. "Why do this for me? Why is this so important to you that you're willing to risk going through that kind of pain for me?"

"Because deep down I still scare you," he acknowledged wholeheartedly, his kind eyes meeting hers. "And I don't want you to be afraid of me anymore. And because all of this terrifies you—the path you are on, the unknowns, the dangers, the future. It all hinders your full potential. And learning to master all your emotions will help you master your powers."

"But why?" A raw, honest question. "Why help me face my fears by going through all that?"

"Well, because I'm your friend and I want to help. And because I know what it's like to be lost in the darkness, searching for a way out."

A moment passed before she asked, "And have you? Found your way out?"

"No." His gaze dropped as he rubbed his palm along his pants. "No, but I did learn how to see in the dark." Brown eyes lifted again, meeting the deep blue watching him. "Magic is part of us, just like the blood in our veins and the heart beating in our chest. But unlike those things, we can control it, like breathing. It's not meant to weaken us, but rather to make us stronger. We are human, though, and being human means we have emotions. I mean, it's called humanity for a reason. But we can take those emotions and use them to fuel our magic. So use it. Use those emotions, Rhiannon, and let them ignite inside you. Don't be afraid of them. Let them burn to the surface and explode. You can't fear the storm if you control the weather."

She blinked at him, a sense of awe washing over her. "How old are you again?"

Grinning, he said proudly, "I'm wise beyond my years, but I turned twenty last month."

She nudged him. "That was a rhetorical ques—wait! Last month? Why didn't I know about this?"

He shrugged. "Probably the same reason I didn't know yours before. We never asked each other."

"Right." She paused as another question popped into her mind—a question she had been curious about for a while now. "So, if . . . if your curse arrived when you were twelve, then when . . . when did you . . . ?"

Embarrassment rushed through her body and mixed with a strange sense of curiosity. Ryan was her friend, and he had always been open and honest with her. But the question she wanted to ask might be pushing her over a line she was not allowed to cross, an invisible line of personal and private things not shared between friends—especially friends of the opposite sex. What was considered inappropriate? Would it be offensive in a way? She did not know.

But she was curious. She had been isolated her whole life, only living vicariously through books. She had never kissed anyone before, and honestly, she had never been in a situation where she wanted to, had never felt that kind of passion, love, or even lust before. She was not even sure if she wanted to feel that with everything else going on with her and her life. But even James questioned what life would be like for him outside of magic and this world—maybe not out loud, but he did wonder about things any normal teenager would think about. College. Love. A career. The future. And there was a genuine interest boiling up inside Rhiannon too—how to live as a normal sixteen-year-old. Just a normal teenage girl.

But Rhiannon did not know how to do that. She was not even sure what was normal, let alone how to act normal. Ryan was her friend, plain and simple. And yes, he was a guy, but the fact of the matter was he was still a friend. A friend who had experienced something she never had and maybe never would. The curiosity she had looming in her was simply that, the need to fill her inquiring mind with details she had no real knowledge of. Life.

"Are you broken?" Ryan asked after a moment of silence, staring at her with an arched brow as he waved a hand over her face.

Surprise pulled her from her trance. "What?"

"You stopped midsentence and got all flushed."

Her cheeks became warmer as heat spread across her face. "Oh, sorry." Movement caught her attention in her peripheral vision. "I was just—" She shifted her gaze. "Mom?" The sight of her mother sent a trickle of panic through her as she rose to her feet, dusting the sand from her hands and dress.

"Hey," Ryan said as he rushed to his feet, the need to hear the question she was about to ask burning inside him.

"We'll finish this later." Pointing at the sunset, she added, "It's almost time to start preparing."

Brushing the sand from his backside, he lowered his voice, the color of his cheeks deepening. "I haven't."

Confusion struck her. "Haven't what?"

"Done that. It."

She stared at him, her eyebrow angled upward as she cocked her head, the most confused look plastered across her face.

He groaned and rolled his eyes, both embarrassment and a playfulness entering his features. "You're really going to make me say it, aren't you?" Pausing, he waited, but she continued to gawk at him. "Fine." He lowered his voice even more as Karramis continued toward them. "I haven't . . . been with anyone that way before."

"Oh?" The dumbfounded gaze remained on her face for a moment before realization sank in and her eyes widened. "Oh!" Surprise raced through her. "How the heck did you know I was going to ask that?"

"It was written all over your face," he answered quietly as he eyed Karramis.

Stunned, she asked, "Wait, really?" When he nodded, she matched his tone and leaned into him. "How come you never said anything before?"

"It's not like I go around broadcasting it everywhere I go, not to mention living with a curse kind of deters someone from wanting to expose themselves that way to someone. It's a part of me I'm not willing to share with just anyone."

A moment passed as she took in his words. "I'm sorry."

"For what? You have nothing to be sorry for. It's not like it's your fault."

"I know, it's just . . . I don't know. I'm just sorry you have to deal with it."

Ryan gave her a quick smile. "Well, thank you. I appreciate you saying that."

Karramis came to a stop beside them and gave her daughter a side hug. "What are you two talking about?"

"Nothing," Rhiannon said, caught off guard by the question. "H-how did you get here?"

Her mother raised her hands and wiggled her fingers. "Portal. Remember?"

"Oh, right. That's not what I meant to ask."

Karramis arched a brow. "Well, what did you mean to ask then?"

She cleared her throat. "I meant to say, in the nicest way possible, I might add, what are you doing here?"

"James told me what you all were planning to do tonight." Karramis glanced around. "Where is he, by the way? He should be here by now. He left about twenty minutes before I did."

Rhiannon held her mother's gaze and lifted a finger up toward the sky to her left. "He's coming."

Seconds later, Oakley shot over the steep cliffs, the Earth Dragon coasting overhead against the sky as the setting sun dipped farther toward the horizon.

Eyes wide, Ryan gave Rhiannon a small grin. "I have to admit, that is rather impressive."

"Thanks," Rhiannon said modestly, shifting her gaze over to him before returning it to the dragon, who swooped down closer to her and the others.

"Hey," James called with a wave, jumping from Oakley as the dragon hovered a few feet above the ground. He ran over to them. "Sorry I'm late. I had to pick up something first." He removed the backpack draped over his shoulders and tossed it to Rhiannon. "Here."

"Ow," she said with a grunt as the bag slammed into her stomach. Her eyes lifted to her brother. "What's this?"

"Open it," James said, trying not to laugh.

Squatting, Rhiannon unzipped the backpack and peeked inside, rummaging through the contents.

A frustrated sigh escaped her as she scowled up at James. "Seriously?"

"What?" he asked coolly behind the loose fist over his mouth, attempting to hide his smile.

"You're a jerk, you know that?"

Karramis furrowed her brow as she leaned over, taking note of the random clothing in the bag. "What is it?"

Rhiannon yanked out a pair of jeans, a blue long-sleeve shirt, a thin dark gray jacket, socks, and light gray sneakers.

She angled her head, the intense stare stopping on her brother. "What do you have against dresses?"

"Nothing," he replied casually as he lifted a shoulder. "It's going to be cold tonight. Plus, you really don't want to get that pretty dress of yours all dirty, do you?"

Rhiannon shoved the items back into the bag. "You know, James, a girl is just as capable of kicking someone's ass in a dress as she is in freaking pants."

"Oh, I don't doubt that, but I would still rather you wear those"—he pointed to the backpack—"so you don't freeze to death tonight." He lifted the zipper of his jacket higher as a teasing tone entered his voice. "You should be thanking me, not calling me a jerk."

"Fine. Thank you." Nothing but sarcasm laced her words as she leaned over and snatched the jacket from the backpack and put it on. "There. Happy?"

"Extremely." James shifted his attention to his mother. "Hey, what are you doing here? I just saw you."

"You're just now realizing I'm here?"

"Well, no, I noticed you were here before—I'm not completely oblivious. It's just, I'm surprised you're here." He narrowed his eyes. "So, why are you?"

Rhiannon relaxed her tight features. "You're here to stop us, aren't you?"

"No," Karramis said, shaking her head.

Rhiannon questioned critically, "Really? You're not? I thought for sure you wouldn't approve of this idea."

"I wouldn't say I necessarily agree with it, but I know why you're doing it. And I have to respect your decision to try and find a way to overcome the obstacles holding you back. I, more than anyone, can understand why you are doing this. But I am here to talk to you first." She faced James. "Both of you."

Ryan twisted, angling his body in the direction of the water. "Then I'll give you three some privacy."

"No, Ryan, it's okay." Karramis reached out a hand and gently grabbed his wrist. "Maybe what I'm about to say will help you one day. So, please . . . stay."

The corner of his mouth twitched upward. "Of course, ma'am."

"You may call me Karramis. I think you've proven you are more than just an acquaintance to this family."

Ryan smiled with a single nod.

"Now then . . ." Karramis took a deep breath and blinked between the three of them before exhaling. "As your mother and friend"—she tossed Ryan a quick smirk—"I feel it's my duty to pass off some words of wisdom. Something that took me a long time to figure out."

"What's that?" James asked, sliding his hands into the pockets of his jacket as the cold air started to nip at the back of his neck.

"Well, over the past few months, you both have come into your own in many ways, and not just with your magic. You have grown into two amazing individuals. I couldn't have asked for two better kids to call my children. But I know you're both still struggling with things, mostly you." She stopped her gaze on Rhiannon, cradling her daughter's face as her voice became soft. "But it's okay. Everything doesn't have to fall into place all at once. Everything happens for a reason."

Karramis trailed one hand down Rhiannon's arm and clasped her hand over her daughter's, and using the other removed James's hand from his pocket and held it.

"I know," Karramis continued, "with every fiber of my being that you two can do this. And I don't just mean tonight. You're fighters. You're strong, resilient, stubborn, and brave."

"I don't feel brave," Rhiannon whispered as she lowered her head.

Karramis squeezed her hand. "But you are. You are, Rhiannon. Being here tonight proves it. You aren't giving up. And that in itself is a form of bravery."

"But how can I be brave if I . . . I don't know. I don't even know what I feel anymore."

"It's okay to be scared, you know."

"But I'm not. I mean, not in the same way I was before. At least, I don't think I am." Rhiannon sighed. "I don't know. It's hard to explain. I . . . I'm not afraid of the event about to take place, but more of failing."

"You know, I'm scared too," James said, turning his head to face his sister.

Shock rushed through her at the lack of hesitation in his declaration. "You are?"

"Yeah, of course. I mean, I may not show it, or even feel it as strongly as you do, but I'm very scared. I'm scared of a lot of things—of losing you, or any of those I love. I'm afraid of failing or letting people down. I'm afraid of dying."

"But you act so . . . so fearless all the time. You've never once hesitated or acted scared. You just . . . react."

"Yes, exactly," Karramis said, soft but energetic. "And that's what you're trying to learn how to do yourself. To allow your adrenaline to take over and your natural instincts to kick into gear. To not hesitate. To not think, but simply react. And to use those instincts as a reflex. Being brave doesn't mean you aren't afraid, and being afraid doesn't mean you aren't brave. It just means one is simply stronger than the other in each situation. But they both live inside us, driving us to make the choices we make. Do I go left or right? Do I stay or flee? Should I, or shouldn't I? Life is nothing but choices. Good and bad. Stupid or smart. Do I stand up and fight, or do I cower on my knees? But you need to be the one to make those choices, to decide which one is going to control you—fear or bravery. That choice is up to you and only you. Do you run, or do you fight?" She drew out a deep breath. "Bravery and fear can be of equal measure. You just have to learn how to find the balance."

A moment passed as Rhiannon stared at her mother, James, and Ryan with an arched brow as a sense of wonder and amusement bloomed across her face. "Seriously, is there some secret motivational group that meets up once a month or something, and I've just missed the memo?"

"No." Karramis let out a low chuckle, confused by the question. "What would make you think that?"

"You and Dad"—she pointed over at James and Ryan—"and these two are always saying these deep and encouraging words of wisdom, and it just makes me wonder where you're all getting it from."

"I'm a very wise person," James said, grinning as he tugged on the collar of his jacket.

"I don't know about a group, but I have my dad to thank for that," Ryan admitted as he glanced over his shoulder at the sunless sky.

Rhiannon followed his gaze, the tone of her voice tight as she faced her mother. "You should go. It's almost time."

"Okay." Karramis hugged James. "Be careful please."

"I will," he said, squeezing her.

She stepped forward and grasped Ryan's face. "Thank you for doing this. For helping her. But please, you be careful as well."

Ryan gave her a curt nod. "I will."

"Come with me really quick," Karramis said to Rhiannon as she turned them around and headed away from the guys.

"What's wrong?" Rhiannon asked nervously.

"Oh, nothing." She waited to continue as they took a few more steps away. Pulling something from her jeans, she added, "Here."

Rhiannon held out her hand as her mother placed a small metal tube in her palm.

It was roughly four inches long and slightly thicker than a pen. A button appeared on one end of the steel device, while the other housed a tiny hole.

Rhiannon tilted the hand-held device toward her mother. "What's this?"

"It's a tranquilizer." Karramis took the device. "It's potent enough to take down a werewolf. Just press this side"—she placed the edge with the small hole flush along her arm—"hard against the body, then press the button. It doesn't matter where you stick it, as long as it's there long enough to release the sedative." She handed it back. "Three seconds tops."

Rhiannon took the device and put it in her jacket pocket. "Do you . . ." She swallowed. "Do you think I'll need this?"

A faint smile tugged on Karramis's lips. "It's better to have it and not need it than need it and not have it."

"Thanks."

"Of course. It's a mother's job to protect her children. But it's also a mother's job to make sure her children can handle themselves. I will always fight for you, until my last breath, but you also need to be able to protect yourself. And I need to know you can do this without me—that you no longer need me and can take care of yourself."

"But," Rhiannon said, the word sounding tight in her throat, "I'll always need you, Mom."

"No, you won't. You may want me to never leave you, but you won't need me."

"Isn't that the same thing?"

"No, sweetie," Karramis said. "When a child needs their mother, it means they can't survive on their own. But you, Rhiannon, don't need me. Not anymore. Because I know, if it came to it, you could survive without me. You are independent, resilient, strong, and a fighter, and you are my child." She kissed her daughter's forehead. "Now then, be careful."

"Thanks, Mom," was all she said as she watched her mother stroll away, lifting her hands and disappearing into her swirling misty portal as it shrank behind her. "All righty then." Her words were tight as she released them with a heavy sigh. She rotated her bare feet through the sand and headed back toward the shoreline. "Let's get this over with."

Chapter 27

Friend or Foe

Various shades of blue and pink trailed along the horizon as stars sparkled overhead within the navy sky. Darkness surrounded the harbor, the light of dusk dwindling rapidly.

"Where's Ryan?" Rhiannon asked, stopping next to her brother.

Shifting his gaze from the beach to the hidden caverns to his right, he pointed. "He's heading inside already."

Not wanting anyone around when he shifted, Ryan was a tiny figure in the dimming light as he strolled away from them toward the larger cavern on the beach. It was not only because he refused to allow the others to see the painful process of transforming, but he also wanted to remove his clothes, because if not naked, he would rip through them and have nothing to wear when journeying back home later.

Rhiannon searched the sky, spotting the slight shadows of the dragons still flying over the water in the distance. *"You should all go home now."*

The dragons arched upward and around, their bodies dipping and soaring over to them, all six sending back overlapping responses to James and Rhiannon.

Phosmeratae, Ignara, and Harkin circled overhead as the three Earth Dragons landed behind the twins. James and Rhiannon rotated and headed over to them, their silhouettes barely noticeable in the deepening darkness.

"You want us to leave?" Raeth asked, concerned.

"Yes, please," Rhiannon answered, her inner voice reaching all the dragons and James. *"I can't have you here tonight."*

"Are you sure?" Terramina's voice matched Raeth's worried tone.

"Yes, I'm sure." Rhiannon nodded. *"Thank you."*

Movement shifted through the shadows as a rush of air crashed into James and Rhiannon, the dragons all taking flight.

James faced her. "You might want to make sure they—"

"Oh, right!" Rhiannon blurted, cutting him off as her mind took over. *"Hey, if you all happen to feel anything later coming from me—"*

"Or me," James added.

"Right, or him, please stay away. We will be okay. I promise. Just keep your distance. Okay?"

Various voices sounded in the twins' minds as the six dragons responded in reluctant agreement.

Moments later, James and Rhiannon sat on the beach, both watching the darkness move in front of them as the waves washed over the sand a few feet away.

Silence settled between them as the minutes ticked on, and they both mentally prepared themselves for what would soon come.

A deep, harsh scream exploded from the cave, the most gut-wrenching human cry they had ever heard echoing off the stone walls of the cavern and amplifying as it rang out across the open harbor.

James and Rhiannon shot their gazes over at it, and James gripped his sister's arm through the darkness as she nearly bolted to her feet.

"I hate that we're making him do this," Rhiannon confessed, the anguish in her voice evident as she bounced her legs, the anxious twitch making James even more nervous.

"I know," James said, low and gruff. "But he wanted to help."

"I know that, but it doesn't make it any easier for me to accept. I'm the reason he's in pain right now." She squeezed his hand as she fought back the urge to cry, the sounds of Ryan's screams getting louder. "What will you do? I mean, the plan is for him to attack me, right?"

"Right," he said tentatively, a strange hitch catching in the word. He cleared his throat. "I will just watch and make sure you're safe."

Another scream echoed from the cave, the sound traveling like an out-of-control freight train. A snarl mixed with a deep growl resonated across the harbor and sent chills racing up Rhiannon's spine, and James instinctively clutched her hand tighter as the noise crashed into them.

Rhiannon pinched her eyes together as a warm tear slid down her cool cheek. Ryan was suffering, and she could not help him. She could not take his pain away. He was now bearing the agony of transforming for her selfish needs—to help her face her fears. The anguish of what he was going through made her sick to her stomach.

Silence returned as darkness enveloped them.

Half Moon Harbor was on the southwest side of Kiluemar, and the cliffs obstructed all signs of the celestial wonder making its appearance. But a faint glow lit up the sky as the air grew colder, calmer. Gentle waves glided across the sand, the sound of water sloshing the only thing surrounding them within the shadows.

Rhiannon held her brother's hand tighter before pulling it away and hiding both hands in her pockets. James had been right—it was very cold tonight. But she would never admit it to him. However, it was not only the weather causing the unease as shivers traveled up her spine, a tightness squeezing in her lower abdomen and goose bumps rushing over her skin.

A loud, deep, monstrous growl burst from the cave, no longer human in any way. Roaring followed, the harsh animalistic call consuming the night. Then another, a howl echoing quieter, this one much farther away and seeming to answer the first.

Rhiannon rushed to her feet as panic swept through her. "What the heck was that?"

James matched her actions as he gripped her arm, his tone riddled with uncertainty. "I'd rather not find out." Ease entered his words. "Maybe it was Ryan just . . . just taking back control."

Howling came again in the distance, deep and louder. It was not coming from the beach. And it was getting closer.

Taking a step back, James peered out through the darkness. "I have a really bad feeling about this." He swallowed. "I don't think we thought this through all the way."

"Really?" she replied critically. "Now you're having doubts. A little late, don't you think?" She grabbed for his arm as they moved away from the cliffs. "Oh, and this was all your idea, I might add. All you. There was no *we* in this freakin' fantastic idea."

"No, but you did agree to it."

"Yeah, and I really need to stop doing that." Rhiannon tensed as a growl rumbled somewhere through the shadows. "James?" Her voice was low and casual. "I take it back."

"Take what back?"

"When I said I wasn't scared. I lied. I lied big time. Because I am most definitely scared now."

A distant howl came again, and Rhiannon jumped.

"Shit!" James slapped his hand over the one clinging to his arm. "It's too damn dark. I can't see anything. Why the hell didn't we bring any flashlights?"

"You did," Rhiannon corrected, stepping away from him.

"No, I didn't," he said, sure of himself.

"Yes, you did," she argued. "There was one at the bottom of the backpack."

James twisted and searched through the darkness, frantically kicking for the bag. "Aunt K must've put it in there."

Scoffing, Rhiannon followed his lead as she glided her feet through the sand. "It figures it would be Aunt K who gave you the jeans for me."

"Really?" he complained, searching in the opposite direction as a low growl echoed across the harbor, the sound unnerving as it came from all directions. "You're going to bring this up now? I don't think this is the right time for this."

"Well, if I'm about to die, I think this is the perfect time to tell you how much I hate jeans. And if I would've died in them, I would've come back as a ghost and totally haunted you."

"Good to know. Now, can we please find the damn backpack?"

"You know what?" she snapped, a playfulness to her words.

"No," he said mockingly, sensing the tightness in her teasing tone. "What?"

"This was a stupid idea." The statement was clipped with frantic irritation as she continued searching.

"Probably."

Rhiannon's foot collided with something. "Ah-ha!" Quickly unzipping the bag, she tossed the clothing out as she blindly thrust her hand into the backpack. "Got it!"

James rushed over to the rustling coming from her direction and crashed into her, gripping her arms to stable them both. "Turn it on!"

"I can't, you're holding on to my arms!"

James released her. "Oh, sorry."

Rhiannon clicked on the flashlight, and a blinding beam of light shot out from it, illuminating the area around them and most of the sky directly above.

"Holy hell!" James shouted, ramming his eyelids closed and jerking his head back. "Is this a flashlight or a damn spotlight?"

Terror shot through Rhiannon, seizing her muscles and sending her pulse into a frenzy. She stilled. Eyes wide, she clutched the flashlight. Her hands trembled as a hum of awareness settled in her chest and a strange sensation tickled along her spine.

"What's wrong?" James asked softly as he angled the flashlight in her hand sideways and aimed the bright beam away from them.

Her voice fell to a whisper. "It's too quiet." She swallowed. "And I'm pretty sure we're being watched."

James listened, and the feeling of eyes on him slithered through his nerves. Taking the flashlight, he grabbed Rhiannon's wrist and pulled her behind him. He took a few steps, urging her back with him. The beam of light slid upward as he lifted the flashlight and completely illuminated a wolflike figure prowling forward.

It was huge and dark, the coloring barely visible in the shadows so far away. It stalked closer, the silhouette's calculated movements slow and silent as it prowled in a hunched position. The creature opened its mouth, the light catching the shimmering of drool dripping from its sharp snarling teeth as it prowled closer on all fours.

James stepped back, taking Rhiannon with him.

The creature was more wolflike than Haydrin and much larger than any wolf either of them had ever seen or heard of. The front limbs appeared slightly longer than the hind legs, and sharp oversized black claws reflected in the light, each paw gliding with unnatural stealth across the sand. Deep amber eyes reflected back, their rich color luminescent and intense, staring with unyielding aim. It was on the hunt.

Rhiannon lifted to her tiptoes and peered over her brother's shoulder. "Is that Ryan?"

James did not move. "I think so."

The amber in the eyes suddenly disappeared behind a bright silver glow, the specks radiating like the full moon glistening along the surface of the water.

"Uh, is that supposed to happen?" James asked, taking a few steps back.

Retreating away with him, Rhiannon shrugged, her voice tight with tension. "I—I have no idea."

The werewolf halted and lowered down to his haunches. Low guttural whimpers escaped him as he dropped to his stomach and rubbed a large clawed paw across his head. A long high-pitched whine echoed through him as his head twitched side to side. He chuffed and yipped as he rose on all fours, shaking his head wildly as he backed away.

"What's wrong with him?" Rhiannon whispered.

"I don't know."

She tapped weakly against his back as her attention pulled to the cliffs overlooking the harbor. "Uh, James." There was a casual calmness in her voice, one filled with a smooth panic. "We have a problem."

He angled his head back toward her but kept his eyes on Ryan. "What?"

Reaching around him, she gripped his wrist and jerked the bright beam upward a few hundred feet over to the dark silhouettes standing along the cliff, their outlines lit up from behind by the moonlight ascending farther into the sky.

"We have company," Rhiannon muttered, still calm but alert.

The light settled on two other large canine creatures standing along the edge of the cliff. One was dark gray, nearly black in the distance, and hunched over in an unnatural way, as if the weight of its upper body tipped it over. There was a familiarity to him that sent a pulse of fear surging through Rhiannon's veins. She drew in a low breath as realization sank in. It was Haydrin. But his eyes were all wrong. Similar to Ryan's, they glowed a bright silvery white.

Standing next to him was a solid black creature. It was similar to Ryan in the sense it was more wolf than Haydrin, but this one was larger than Ryan, its size nearly matching the raw power and strength of Haydrin, even from so far away. This one's eyes were also glowing like the moonlight, brighter and harsher than the others, almost as if the light radiated from deep inside the creature and not just from its eyes. A flicker of color shone through the darkness, the silvery glow faltering and shifting to a bright glowing red.

Haydrin snarled and lifted to his hind legs, letting out a long echoing howl.

Rhiannon froze, the chill shooting down her spine slicing through her nerves as fear settled deep in her bones. She recognized the one with red eyes as well, and the surge of nausea rumbling in her stomach exploded, launching through her midsection in a wave of prickling terror. It was Raamko, the large black wolf from her astral projection.

The two creatures watched intently as the twins peered up at them, all four staring at one another. A growl snarled from Haydrin as he eyed them before tossing back his head again and howling.

"Seriously," James said under his breath, afraid they would attack if they heard him, "how the heck did they know we were out here?"

Rhiannon had not even heard the question.

James thought for a moment before he gritted his teeth and declared, "Probably that lunatic Lucas."

Gripping her brother's arm, she stepped back with him, the movement slow and steady. "James?"

Raamko lowered its head as it took a step closer to the edge of the cliff, its eyes shifting back to a moonlit gaze.

Snarling zoomed across the sand, and James whipped the flashlight toward it. Ryan had continued stalking them, and he was only a few yards away now, eyes glowing even brighter.

"Yeah?" James whispered, continuing to move back with her, each step deliberate and calculated.

Rhiannon's voice was low and tight. "I change my mind."

"About what?"

Jerking the light back up to the cliffs, James stopped the beam on Haydrin and Raamko before tossing it back at Ryan.

She swallowed. "I don't want to do this anymore."

"Kind of late now, don't you think?"

A moment passed as the two continued to slowly back away.

"So . . ." Rhiannon said, halting as James came to a stop. "Any words of wisdom right now?"

"Yeah . . ." He began slowly toeing off his shoes. "Run."

<h1 style="text-align:center">Chapter 28</h1>

Fight or Flight

James pivoted, his sock-clad feet sinking into the sand as he clutched Rhiannon's wrist. Hurrying forward, he tugged on her, but her rigid body refused to move.

"Nope," James announced in a steady but demanding tone, "no time for that." He yanked her arm, and the bright glow from the flashlight reflected off her blinking gaze as she shifted her eyes over to him. "Nice of you to join me. Let's go!"

He tugged again, and this time she followed, both racing toward the cliffs slightly off to the side of where Haydrin and Raamko watched them from high above.

"Where are we going?" Rhiannon shouted through her heavy panting.

"We need to get to the portal!"

Snarls echoed all around as Haydrin and Raamko continued to peer down within the dense stretch of trees of Dryad Forest, the gentle lapping of waves the only other sound around them. The tall pines behind them towered above as lush trees curved around, thinning out the closer they got to Grotto Bridge. A few hundred yards away, directly below where the creatures watched, lay a swirling watery vortex along the beach, the bright beam of the flashlight reflecting off it. The portal.

"We'll never make it!" Rhiannon shot a look over at Ryan and noticed the bright white eyes still staring at them, now much closer as he continued forward, his advancement slow but determined.

"Don't look!" James shouted as he continued to grasp her arm.

Panting, she ran faster, trying to keep up as she urged her legs to push through the burn. Her feet sank into the sand as the loose soil kicked up behind her.

A rush of fear rose in her chest and squeezed her lower stomach. "Too late!"

Two booming howls erupted, one above them and the other off to the side. Bright silvery moonlit eyes glowed directly to their left as Ryan charged after them, unfazed by the sandy shore as his quick effortless stride closed the distance with each pounding thrust of his muscular legs. Another set of glowing gray eyes shimmered in the distance, the two bright orbs descending downward from the cliff in one swift movement. Haydrin flew through the air before landing with an audible thud against the beach. The extreme plunge hundreds of feet did not seem to have fazed him as he raced forward. Radiant silver eyes bounced erratically behind another set, both growing larger in the darkness as Haydrin trailed behind Ryan.

Rhiannon halted, forcing her brother to a stop. "They're coming!"

"Yeah, I'm aware!" James breathed heavily, the panic lined with raw humor as he eyed the two creatures barreling toward them. "Shit!" He twisted around in one smooth movement and launched forward, taking Rhiannon with him. "This way!"

The moonlight had reached more of the land overlooking the beach and slowly erased the darkness from the bay.

Rhiannon searched, her gaze chaotic as she glided it along the edge of the cliffs, being mindful of her pace next to her brother as the red glow of Raamko's eyes pulled her attention. The creature was still watching them from overhead.

A snarling bark and drawn-out growl echoed behind them. Haydrin and Ryan were closing in.

"Where are we going?" Rhiannon exclaimed, her words uneven and breathy.

Pain radiated along James's thighs as each racing step hurried them over to the shoreline. "We need to get to the water."

"And do what?" she demanded. "Go for a swim?"

"No, smartass." He panted. "I'm hoping werewolves don't like water."

Pain burned up her legs as her thigh muscles constricted. "We'll never make it!"

"Not with that kind of attitude!"

James slid to a stop, his feet burying deep in the sand as he yanked Rhiannon in front of him and pointed. "Go!"

"No!" Her hands were trembling. "I can't!"

James cupped her face, the grip firm as he gave her a pleading stare. "Look at me." Heavy breaths blew from his mouth. "Yes, you can. You are in control."

A spark flickered in her behind the fear—a tiny light of determination, love, even a bit of bravery shimmering to life and growing deep inside of her.

Nausea boiled in Rhiannon's stomach as growls and snarls came closer. "What about you?"

James whirled around and flung out his hands, a rush of air rippling from his forearms and bursting out from his palms just as Haydrin plowed into it a few yards away.

Heat swelled in her chest, the burning ache of trepidation mixing with the heavy breaths rushing from her body in uneven bursts, but shock and awe came out with a long exhale. "How?"

Magic rushed past the snarling werewolf as it fought against the invisible wall of air, the sand blowing with an uncomfortable fierceness around the ferocious beast.

"Just go!" James angled a palm over to Ryan and lifted the charging creature back through the air, the movement quick and effortless as the werewolf soared backward on a phantom breeze. "I'll be right behind you!"

Ryan yelped as he landed, but he rose to all fours quickly and charged again. James barely had time to notice as Ryan crashed into the wall, both sets of glowing white eyes narrowed into predatory slits.

James yelled, the power inside him faltering, "I could really use a damn weapon right about now!"

"And do what with it?" Rhiannon asked from behind him, the teasing tone laced with pure terror. "Piss them off even more?"

His magic surged, the heat of it like a charge deep within his bones, the intensity growing as he fought to maintain it. He pulled in a long breath, the smell of the cool salty breeze flowing into his lungs. He could feel it, feel the air, every particle, every bit of magic linked to the natural element. He drew in another breath—this one longer, deeper. Absorbing every ounce of it and fusing it to his blood and bones, every part of him. The heat grew, the power inside him charging as he became the air, the magic.

Everything around them changed—shifted, slowed, and morphed into something ancient and undiluted.

The ground around them began to rumble, the slow, unsteady shaking vibrating beneath their feet.

Rhiannon's eyes widened as she stepped back, her gaze watching the ground as if searching for the source of the disturbance. "James, we need to go. Now!"

Reaching out, she clutched her brother's upper arm just as an outward blast exploded from James's hands. The powerful rush of air tore across the surface of the ground, sending the sand and magic barreling toward the two werewolves like a wave before slamming into them. Ryan and Haydrin were pushed back, soaring upward and into the sky like weightless rag dolls.

"Holy shit, it worked," James announced with shocked arrogance.

The werewolves slammed into the sand with a thud in the distance, their yelping cries booming as they scurried to their feet.

"Oh, fuck!" James twisted around, the movement swift and smooth. "Time to go!" He gripped Rhiannon's wrist and yanked. "Run!"

An overwhelming sense of dread started to coil around her insides, squeezing and wringing all hope from her body as they continued racing toward the water. Maybe if she could get to the water, she could use her magic to help them too—use her water magic to pull Haydrin and Ryan into the ocean so they could get to the portal. So, she pushed her legs harder, faster, each sinking slam of her foot into the sand never hindering her drive to help her brother, to save him.

"Run!" James yelled again, tugging on her arm.

"I am!"

An intense warning shot through the twins like an electric current. It raced up their spines, the icy shock forcing goose bumps to erupt along their skin. Realization bloomed in their cores as the sense of both creatures right behind them took over.

Rhiannon lurched forward as her hand slipped from James's grip, and a scream exploded from her as the sudden and unexpected force whipped James around. He stumbled and crashed onto his back, a deep grunt bursting from him as the flashlight flew from his hand, landing out of reach with the beam shining out toward the water. Without faltering, James shot to his feet, shaking and clearing the disoriented sensation settling in his head. Another scream echoed, this time louder, drawn out, and accompanied with a deep rumbling growl.

Sharp, jagged teeth clamped down on Rhiannon's forearm as she shielded her face. Pain shot through her, the long canines ripping through her jacket and puncturing her flesh. Warmth quickly filled the inside of her sleeve as blood seeped through the shredded material and oozed out from underneath the snarling jaw refusing to let her go. She gritted her teeth and yelled, the throaty roar rising deep within her chest. Haydrin's dark pewter head jerked as his lips curled up, and blood dripped from his teeth and lined his black gums. His eyes reflected the luminescent silvery hue as the beam from the flashlight shone upon them and erased the dark features along one side of his face.

James launched himself toward them. "Rhiannon!"

Power swelled inside him, rising from the center of his chest and stretching outward in a wave of intense energy. A surge of warmth filled his veins as his blood heated, the magic inside shooting to the surface again. Within seconds, James's core vibrated as his power consumed him with ease and precision. The wind began to swirl, the powerful whirls of air driving his clothes against his body and forcing his tapered dark brown hair to blow wildly across his forehead as the sand at his feet churned upward around him. Rippling currents of energy prickled along his skin as he tossed his arms in the air, aiming the controlled magic at the creature tearing into Rhiannon's flesh and pressing her body flush against the shoreline.

The power shot from him in an eruption of airy energy, the release emanating an explosive boom as he drove it into the beast. Wind crashed into the side of Haydrin, and he lurched sideways. Rhiannon let out a shrieking wail as his teeth dragged along her arm, slashing open her sleeve and digging deeper into her flesh. Blood gushed from the tight jaw still clamping down on her as red splattered across her face.

"Shit!" James cried out, horror and regret racing through him.

James propelled himself in the direction of the werewolf, but a rush of air and streak of dark shadows zoomed past him. He halted, his feet digging into the sand as Ryan hurtled into the side of Haydrin. Sharp teeth fastened tightly around the gray beast's scruff as Ryan's dark brown body continued the momentum and rolled onto his back. A yip sounded from Haydrin, followed by a deep growl as the beast unhinged his jaw, releasing Rhiannon. The two werewolves rolled out of the glow of the flashlight, their dark silhouettes coming to a stop as the sounds of water splashing filled the area.

James ran to Rhiannon. "Are you okay?" His voice was shaky, tight, and raspy as he slid to his knees beside her. Ripping the sleeve of her jacket along one of the tattered seams, he wrapped the material tightly around her exposed wounds. "Rhiannon?"

She winced as the pressure squeezed against the throbbing pain radiating up and down her arm and deep inside her flesh. The muscles burned as her hurried pulse gushed blood from the lacerations sliced down to the bone. Shock took root in her nerves, the agony hidden behind a frozen gaze and blank mind.

A distant voice called her name. It was James. She focused on it, following it from the darkness slowly consuming her.

"Rhiannon," James repeated softly, shaking her.

She blinked, her attention focusing on the two werewolves now fighting among the lapping waves. Snarls, growls, and barking yelps rang out as the moonlight eased closer to the shore. One set of silvery eyes glowed as Haydrin's gray coloring appeared within the dim light. Snapping his jaw, he snarled and chuffed before rising to his hind legs and swiping a clawed paw through the air. Ryan dropped to his stomach and rolled, lifting back to all fours in one swift movement. His gaze shot to Rhiannon. His eyes were a rich amber color again. The moment of distraction cost him as Haydrin pounced and slashed his sharp claws across Ryan's dark brown back. A pained yelp barked from him as he stumbled to the side.

"Rhiannon," James said again.

A hollowness churned in her stomach as the urge to help seized her. Ryan had saved her. Concern pooled and settled deep in her chest as her breath caught, the burn coating her throat. Pressure wrapped around her core, forcing an unsteady shudder from her mouth as unease shivered up her spine. She had to help him.

James shook her again. "Snap out of it, Rhiannon!"

The sudden jolt startled her, and she snapped out of her stupor. "We have to help him!"

Rhiannon slid her arm from her brother's tight hold and took over putting pressure on her wound. She winced at the shift in contact along her forearm as she rose to her feet. Scanning the ridge of the cliffs, she spotted Raamko. The black wolf was still standing along the overhang of the bluffs, its now-glowing white eyes focused on the events unfolding below. Rhiannon faced Ryan and Haydrin, but the two werewolves had halted and were once again stalking toward them, both sets of eyes glowing silvery white.

"Shit," James said under his breath. "What the hell is wrong with them?"

James took a step toward the flashlight, but Ryan snarled as his glowing gaze focused on him. The dark brown werewolf lunged forward with a single step, and the twins stumbled back. Rhiannon fell to the ground, but James caught himself. Reaching for his sister, he halted as Ryan snapped at his hand. The werewolf stalked forward in a slow circle, urging James away from Rhiannon.

Ryan slowly turned his head to Rhiannon as both werewolves circled around her, getting closer with each passing movement.

The beam from the flashlight glided across the sand as James watched the steady advancement in horror. It was a slow taunt—a predator circling its prey. His eyes widened in alarm and shock, and he froze, all bravery seeping out of his body. Both Haydrin and Ryan had stopped and were now towering behind Rhiannon, their massive jaws mere inches from the side of her face.

A low growl filled Rhiannon's ears as hot iron-scented breath blasted the back of her head. The sound of a tongue gliding over a salivating mouth came from beside her. Something landed on her shoulder as she held her injured arm to her stomach. Drool. One of the werewolves had drooled on her. A hard snout brushed the side of her head as strands of her hair blew in hard, uneven gusts. One of them was sniffing her. Shallow and hurried breaths burned her chest. She was afraid to move. Afraid to breathe. Closing her eyes, she drew in a shuddering inhale.

James blinked as he fixed on his sister and the werewolves. He had to think of something. He had to help her. But the last time he had used magic, he had gotten her hurt.

Haydrin was much larger than Ryan and had a more humanoid body. His front legs were similar to muscular arms, but they were unnaturally long and covered in fur. Massive palms with furry elongated fingers acted as paws with sharp claws. Pointed ears rested on his oversized head, both missing a chunk along the opposite sides. His massive snout, longer than Ryan's and twice as large, snarled and revealed jagged, uneven teeth. His canines along the top and bottom of his mouth were longer than the bridge of Rhiannon's nose as he rested his snout against the side of her head. A puff came from Ryan, the sound causing Rhiannon to stiffen. The dark brown werewolf's head angled downward over her head, his chin almost touching her shoulder. He was smaller than Haydrin but larger than a wolf. In fact, he appeared more wolflike in the body and face than the werewolf standing next to him, except for the similar front legs and paws. Shaking his head, Ryan backed up, his eyes blinking amber before flicking back to the moon-white glow.

"Ryan?" James said in a low voice, stepping forward.

Haydrin snapped and snarled, the action sending a wave of terror racing through a startled Rhiannon.

A splash came from the water as a warm tingling sensation vibrated through James. A feeling he was very familiar with.

"Do you feel that?" James asked Rhiannon, his inner voice calm and hopeful.

Rhiannon remained completely still on the ground.

James had to get the werewolves away from her. He had to distract them. If he could only get them away from her, then he could use his magic to fight them. So, without thinking, he ran.

A snarl and bark came from behind him. Glancing over his shoulder, he spotted both Ryan and Haydrin racing after him. He smiled as the magic inside him rose to the surface in one fell swoop. He slid to a stop, his feet digging into the sand. Raising both hands, he sent a burst of air toward them, the thunderous wind zooming across the beach as sand followed in its powerful wave. The magic crashed into the two werewolves and sent them flying backward, less than a few feet from where Rhiannon had risen to her feet.

Rhiannon yelped as she staggered back, the sudden shock of the two creatures scurrying to their feet startling her.

"Seriously, James?" she snapped, a slight teasing in her voice. "Could you please not send them back my way?"

"Sorry," he said with a shrug, "you can hit me for that later. If we survive." Signaling for her to come where he stood, he demanded, "Come on!"

Hesitation did not linger as she bolted, reaching him as the werewolves raced behind her. The twins lurched sideways, both sensing the other's plan as they headed in the same direction. Heading north along the beach, James and Rhiannon zigzagged over the sand as the werewolves raced after them. Ryan dashed to the right and headed straight for James as Haydrin launched through the air, narrowly missing Rhiannon as she weaved.

The water in the bay rippled, the sound distinct even behind the pounding footfalls of the two monstrous creatures.

Ryan hurtled forward, his hind legs jumping with a powerful thrust as he landed on top of James. A pained grunt echoed from him as Rhiannon was taken down a few feet away, her screams resonating through the bay.

A claw sliced through the air as Ryan slashed downward, and James let out a muffled cry as his back burned with fiery pain. Heat pooled along his shirt as the cool breeze brushed over the new wound along his back. He fought, but it was no use. Ryan was too heavy. He screamed again as another searing pain swiped across his back, his bloody skin even more exposed to the crisp air. Calling forth his magic, James twisted his arm back along his side and pointed his palm upward, the quick movement sending a ripping pain through his frayed skin and muscles. He gritted his teeth and groaned as a rush of air blasted from his hand. Ryan lurched, his hind legs burrowing into the sand as the werewolf fought against the powerful shove. The creature drove another slash across James's back, and a scream echoed out.

Rhiannon landed against the ground and rolled, sand flying up all around her. Coming to a stop, she sank into the soft shore. Her attention zoomed to the werewolf as he leapt, but Rhiannon rolled away. Claws ripped through her jacket as Haydrin's paw landed beside her upper arm. The sudden sting of pain radiated through her as it began to throb, her hurried heartbeat pumping the blood from the new wound. She rolled again and hurried to her feet, eyeing the werewolf as she slowly backed away. Haydrin lowered his head and snarled, the bright silver-white eyes focusing on her.

Another gust erupted from James as the air around him churned. Swirling wind grew stronger as he fought through the pain burning along his back. He slid his hands under his body and pushed as the air magic crashed into Ryan, but the werewolf remained towering over his prone body. Heat radiated through James's veins, deepening as it filled his body. A surge of power rumbled deep inside, rising to the surface with an earth-shattering thrum. He dug his palms into the sand and pushed himself up, the ground under his hands rumbling and coming alive.

Reaching into her jacket pocket, Rhiannon pulled the tranquilizer out as the werewolf prowled forward. The ground rippled around her, the gentle quake vibrating beneath her feet. The moonlight shone down on the bay and illuminated everything as it glistened off the unnatural waves. Blood seeped from the newly ripped material along her arm and coated the side of her jacket and the skirt of her dress as she steadied her trembling hand. Pain surged through her nerves as the two injuries she had suffered continued to flow through her, the one along her arm dulling with each passing moment.

Haydrin crept closer, and Rhiannon shot a glance over at James as the ground rumbled, her attention skimming past Ryan hovering over her brother, the idea formulating in her mind coming to fruition.

"James!" She propelled herself in his direction, disregarding the dangers now chasing after her. "This is a really stupid idea." Her tone was regretful and loud as the footfalls pounded behind her. "Crap! This is a really bad idea!"

The ground rumbled as the shaking intensified under James's hands, the sand rippling in strange wavelike motions. Heated energy billowed deep inside him, clawing and ripping itself out from the depths of his core. A hum of power rang in his ears, and he screamed as the magic burned through him, the invigorating sensation a blast to his senses.

As the wave of rippling sand crashed into her, Rhiannon stumbled to her knees. She rolled just as Haydrin landed in a wide stance over her, all four of his paws pressing into the sand as he urged his legs into the sides of her body, holding her in place. She flinched as the werewolf snapped at her face, his glowing white eyes bright as he cocked his head. Distant voices echoed in her head, the muffled words telling her to take cover. Her eyes widened as she focused on Haydrin, his mouth hanging open as his sharp teeth inched closer to her neck. A strange sensation rolled through her as the ground below her delivered a tingling energy through her body, filling her insides with a strange but familiar heat as it wrapped around her.

James. She could feel him—his emotions, his power.

Ryan fell sideways as the shaking intensified. Rolling onto his side, James raised an arm and forced the air swirling around him outward. The creature whimpered as he landed hard on his back, but Ryan hurried on all fours. James tried getting to his feet as the ground continued to shake. Pain took over and seized his muscles, and his knees buckled. He fell back down, hunching over on his hands and knees. The rumbling slowed as the searing agony coursed along his back. James's breathing became ragged as the heavy pants burned his lungs.

Rich amber eyes stared out at James as the werewolf moved closer, his advancement slow and controlled. Hanging his head low, the creature let out a quiet whine. His eyes blinked into the bright silvery moonlit gleam again, and he halted, his lip curling up into a snarl. Ryan shook his head and ran a paw over his ear, rubbing vigorously. The amber in his eyes returned.

The quaking ground slowed as Rhiannon remained still. She did not want to move. Any sudden movement would cause Haydrin to immediately attack. She needed time. Time to summon her water powers. She focused on the hum of magic coming from the ocean, pulling it into her within seconds. She may not have had the ability to control her fire magic, but her water abilities were strong enough to help her in this moment.

Adjusting the tranquilizer in her hand, she wrapped her fingers around the metal tube.

"James," she called out in her mind, *"if you can, run to me."*

James glanced over his shoulder before leaning back onto his heels. *"I'll try."*

Pushing himself up, James hunched over and rested his hands on his upper thighs. He took a few deep breaths as he attempted to push through the pain. His gaze lifted and stopped on Ryan, whose eyes had returned to the unnatural bright white glow again.

"Son of a bitch," James grumbled as he twisted and raced in his sister's direction.

The movement shot a piercing sting along the slash marks across his back, and he hissed through his teeth as the pain took control of his muscles. His body went rigid as he slowed, arching his back at the agony slicing through his tattered flesh.

Rhiannon took a deep breath and held it as she rammed the tranquilizer against Haydrin's muscled humanoid side, but before she could push the button, the werewolf rose up on his hind legs. Her arms shot up in instinct to shield her face, and she dropped the metal tube. As the werewolf's front paws plunged down toward her, a gust of wind barreled into the massive creature, sending him flying backward through the air.

Rhiannon twisted and spotted her brother, his arm raised and his hand outstretched. "Thanks!"

"Anytime," he said, pain rippling across his face as he continued to stumble in her direction.

Rushing to her feet, she hurried after him.

The sound of sloshing water echoed as the waves receded away from the shore.

Haydrin had returned to his feet and charged as Ryan closed in behind James.

Rhiannon slowed before colliding into James, both grunting and moaning as the impact ignited the pain along their wounds. Quickly wrapping her arms around her brother, she pulled them both to the ground and tucked his head into her chest, shielding him.

"What are you doing?" he demanded, his voice muffled as he winced.

"Just brace yourself."

"For what?"

"For impact."

Just then, a tidal wave surged in from the bay, the rushing water drowning out all other noises. The ocean rose hundreds of feet into the air and rushed across the sand. James jerked his head from Rhiannon just as a dark blue shadow filled the area in front of them and flowed closer as the full moon gleamed on the waves headed in their direction.

Panic stabbed in James's lower stomach, and his breath caught in his throat. "What the hell?"

Rhiannon gripped her brother's arm as the giant wave rushed forward, the cool mist coming from the swell reaching the twins' exposed skin. Tossing up her other hand, she aimed a palm out at the massive powerful surge. An explosive sound echoed as waves shot out around, curving as the water flowed past them. James gawked, dumbfounded as Rhiannon held back the water directly in front of them, shielding them from the powerful wave. Yelps sounded as the water took over the beach, both Haydrin and Ryan falling victim to the tidal wave consuming the bay.

As fast as the water had come in, it receded back out to sea.

Rhiannon stood and pulled her brother with her as both stared out at the calm waters of the bay.

"How the hell did you do that?" James asked, stunned and still gaping at his sister in amazement.

She gave a modest shrug. "I just controlled the water and pushed it away from us."

"But . . ." He paused, his eyes shifting back to the water. "How did you create a wave like that?"

Rhiannon grinned over at him. "I didn't." She pointed at the bay. "They did."

Through the glow of the full moon, six shadowy figures with long necks and spiky frills rose from the surface in the distance before diving back into the water.

Water Dragons.

"I knew it," James said. "I knew I had sensed them." He gripped Rhiannon's shoulder. "I guess we owe them a huge thanks for saving us."

"Are you okay?" Rhiannon asked, twisting and spinning him around to examine his back.

His shirt and jacket were ripped to shreds, barely hanging on at the shoulders and along the sides, blood coating every inch of both fabrics.

"I'm okay," he said, wincing as she lifted the clothes.

The flesh was ripped open in multiple deep gashes, the long slices clean and precise. Each slash splayed open, exposing gruesome dark sinew below. Blood covered his skin, the mix of crimson and sand spreading across his mutilated back.

"How are you standing right now?" she questioned.

"I guess the same way you were after being attacked."

Rhiannon let go of the two shredded materials in her hand and spun around, awareness sinking in. "Where is he?"

The area was dark, and the flashlight was nowhere to be found, the light likely broken with the impact of the wave.

"Where is he?" Rhiannon asked again, panic filling her words as she searched the dim glow of the moonlight for Ryan. "Where did they go?" Her gaze shifted to the cliffs, but Raamko was gone. Dread and fear pulled at her midsection, but no longer from the dangers. "Ryan! Where is Ryan? We have to find him and make sure he's okay."

Rhiannon ran toward the cliffs, and James followed behind her, the pain in his back settling to a dull ache as the blood dried along his clammy skin.

A large shadowy figure lay motionless in the sand, and Rhiannon sprinted toward it but halted as the lighter hues of the creature's fur came into view.

Haydrin.

"Is he dead?" James asked, lifting his chin and peering over at the werewolf to see if he was breathing as he came to a stop next to his sister.

Cautiously, Rhiannon moved closer.

She jerked back as the werewolf took in a deep breath. "He's definitely still alive."

Pulling something from his pocket, James squatted beside Haydrin's unconscious body before jamming it into the muscle along his hind leg.

Rhiannon shifted forward. "What did you do?"

"I sedated him."

"Where did you get a tranquilizer?" she asked, realizing the one she had was lost.

James stood up. "Aunt K gave it to me before I left her place."

Muffled groaning echoed through the darkness—human, not animal.

Rhiannon frantically searched the area. "Ryan?"

A long, drawn-out moan followed.

"Ryan!" she called, squinting as she ran and trailed along the base of the cliffs. "Ryan!"

James searched in the opposite direction. "Ryan?" Shadowy movement a few feet away pulled his attention. "Over here!"

Rhiannon ran over to him and noticed James removing his jacket, draping it over Ryan's naked body resting flush against the base of the cliff, his face angled away from them.

"Oh my gosh," she whispered, lowering to her knees. She placed her hands along his shoulders, eyeing the gashes along his body, given to him by Haydrin, as she gently rolled him over, the jacket shifting along his hips. "Ryan?"

James readjusted the tattered clothing draped across Ryan's midsection. "He's alive. And he doesn't appear to have any broken bones."

"Ryan," she said again, resting a hand on his cheek. "Can you open your eyes?"

Moaning, Ryan fluttered his eyelids open, the rich brown meeting Rhiannon's worried gaze.

She smiled down at him. "Hi."

"Hey," he rasped with a low groan.

"How are you feeling?"

"Like I was slammed into a wall by a powerful tidal wave."

"You were," she said, chuckling as she gently gripped his bicep. "Can you sit up?"

He groaned, pushing his hands into the sand. "I think so."

"Here," James offered, leaning over, "let me help you."

Ryan accepted his hand but flinched and pulled in a hissing breath through his teeth.

"Sorry," James said, helping him stand.

"It's all right," Ryan stated quietly, his tone pained and strained as he clutched the jacket draping around his midsection. "It's all right. I'll heal eventually." His eyes went wide and shot to Rhiannon, regret and disbelief lining his tight features. "Rhiannon, I'm so sorry." Panic and remorse lined his words. "I'm so, so sorry. I don't know what happened." He shifted his gaze between her and James. "It was like I had no control over myself. I kept blinking in and out of awareness."

"Has that ever happened before?" Rhiannon asked, narrowing her gaze.

Ryan shook his head. "No."

"Do . . . Do you happen to know what color eyes you have as a werewolf?"

"Yeah, my dad said they're a dark honey color, like my mum's."

"Well, they were that at first, but then they turned to this strange silvery-white color and started glowing."

"Haydrin's too," James added. "And his eyes weren't like that when he attacked before."

"Raamko's were also like that," Rhiannon added.

Bewilderment creased Ryan's brows. "I've never heard of anything like that happening before." He took a step but halted as he pressed his lips together, the cool breeze brushing across all his exposed skin.

Rhiannon noticed the apprehension. "What's wrong?"

Embarrassed, Ryan admitted, "Uh, I'm extremely naked under this thing, and it's not doing much to keep me completely covered up. Plus, it reeks of blood."

Rhiannon started removing her jacket. "I can't do much about the blood, but here. It's still torn, but mine's in better shape."

"Thanks." He stared at her, his lips still pressed thin.

"What?" Her tone was casual and confused.

Circling his finger around, Ryan insisted, "Turn around."

Rhiannon groaned and rolled her eyes. "It's not like I can see anything." She lowered her voice. "Or even want to."

"Well, just in case," Ryan said with a quick twitch tugging on his lips. "I mean, you are a curious one."

"Eww." Turning around, Rhiannon folded her arms. "Whatever."

A deep exhale came from where Haydrin rested, and the three of them shot their gazes over at him, but the werewolf was still unconscious.

James faced his sister. "So much for Merrick's deal with Mom."

"What do you mean?"

"Haydrin attacked you tonight. He could've killed you."

Rhiannon kept her eyes on the werewolf. "But he didn't. And I think that was on purpose. It was almost as if he had control, like there was some recognition of his actions. There was a hesitation there. I mean, yes, he hurt me, but it wasn't like before when I knew he wanted to kill me."

James knitted his brows. "What do you mean?"

"I don't think he wanted to kill me tonight. At least I didn't sense that was his ultimate goal this time around."

"Then what was his goal?" Ryan asked, coming up from behind her.

Dropping her arms to her sides, she drew in a deep breath before letting it out. "I'm not sure. But whatever it is, I'm sure it isn't going to end well."

A moment passed before Ryan nudged her arm, his bare skin still cool and damp. "Hey, by the way, you handled yourself well tonight. You should be quite proud of yourself, blaze."

"No," she answered flatly, not even glancing over at him.

"What?" he quipped with a low chuckle. "You don't like that one either?"

Rolling her eyes, she headed over toward the portal. "I don't need a nickname."

"Oh! Come on!" Ryan trailed behind her, gripping the jacket wrapped around him. "I like that one."

Coming up beside her, James added teasingly, "I like it too. It's a good one."

Silence fell as Rhiannon considered.

"Fine," she finally said with a huff, "at least it's better than sparky."

As the three of them turned to head toward the cave, the waters just beyond the opening of the bay glowed, the bright lights glimmering with luminous colors all dancing together.

Chapter 29

The present
Mid-December

Rhiannon was curled up and fast asleep in an oversized chair tucked within the alcove of a large room on the second floor of the library. Books lay open on the floor, and stacks scattered throughout next to piles of paper, notebooks, and loose old pieces of records dating back centuries. Coals burned in the huge stone fireplace in the corner, the heat extinguishing the approaching winter air seeping in from the gaps in the windows, the soft crackling and high-pitched whistle filling the otherwise quiet room. Having spent months helping to organize the boxes of books and documents located throughout the island, and continuing her own research, Rhiannon had spent almost every day and night here.

The attack at the beach last month had created an unyielding sense of unease building up inside Rhiannon and yet an even more powerful need striking a chord inside her, this adamant determination to find out more about herself and the magic she had been given. She had to master her abilities and discover the reason behind the symbol of the prophecy. There had to be a reason for it. But what?

Creaking sounded through the room, and Rhiannon jerked her head up, eyeing the dimly lit room through blurred vision.

"It's only me," Ryan said softly as he stepped under the threshold and into the room, holding a long beautifully wrapped gift.

Sleep lined her raspy tone. "What are you doing here?" She glanced around, noticing the dark sky outside the window. "What time is it?"

"Almost midnight." Placing the gift on the floor next to the chair, he strolled across the room and leaned against the wall, tucking his hands into his dark gray hoodie. "Have you been here all day again?"

She sat up and rubbed the remaining sleep from her eyes. "Yeah."

His eyes met hers, the crease between his brow taut as he took in the dread on her face. "No word on her yet?"

"No. And Aidan has been out searching for her with the others. Grandpa and my parents thought it would be safer if James and I stayed within the protective boundaries. And I didn't want to be at the house alone, so I figured I'd make myself useful here."

"What about Pavian?"

"He was supposed to return last night, but I haven't seen him."

Rhiannon grew silent as the events of the last month unfolded again, the shock and fear of what had happened in the non-magical realm rising from the pit of her stomach as an icy chill shot up her back.

Pavian had returned during the last full moon with Kavana and Aidan, but their return had been filled with horrible news. When Pavian, Tenarick, and Quinian had arrived at MUSE five months ago, the school had suffered not only significant fire damage, but a loss so great that Pavian had ordered the remaining structure to be demolished as he and the other two traveled the world, notifying families of the horror left in the wake of a vicious attack.

After making sure his sister and Aidan had returned home safely, Pavian had returned to Stoweward, ensuring Raina and Liam were all right after his extended stay. However, he had to return to the non-magical realm a week later to finalize the report with the local and government authorities—something only a tactful, influential, and intelligent person could handle. And with Pavian being just those things and the next in line to take role of head Guardian, he was sent back by Zarrius.

And two nights ago, Kavana had gone missing, having never returned home after working late with Zarrius on guard duties.

Bile crept up Rhiannon's throat, and she swallowed, forcing it down as she pointed at the gift on the floor. "What's that?"

The corners of Ryan's lips turned up as he accepted her need to change the subject. "It's a present." He picked it up. "For you."

Rhiannon sat up straight and flashed a wide smile. "Really?" She took the long, narrow gift as he handed it to her, placing it on her lap. "You got me a gift?"

"Of course. Christmas is in a few days, and I figured you would be home with your parents, so I wanted to make sure you got this before you left."

"Thank you." Grinning up at him, she asked, "May I open it now?"

"Yes."

Excitement rolled through her as she pulled the bright blue bow from the top and ripped apart the silver paper. It was a dark polished box with bronze hinges and a clasp.

She opened it, and her eyes widened, her gaze twisting up toward Ryan. "I can't accept this. I told you—"

"I know what you said," he interrupted, pulling the dagger from the velvet-lined box, "but this one isn't mine."

She flashed him a scowl.

"I swear," he admitted with a chuckle. "I had this one made just like mine, but this one is yours."

"Really?" Surprise and gratitude warmed her chest as he nodded. "Thank you."

Carefully grasping the blade, Ryan lowered the handle down to her. "But"—he jerked it upward, just out of her reach—"you have to learn how to use it before you can wear it. Deal?"

A hint of annoyance glinted across her face but quickly faded. "Deal."

Ryan headed over to the fireplace, stepping over the mess spread chaotically across the floor. "Is James in Stoweward?"

Rhiannon placed the dagger back in the box and snapped it closed. "Yeah. He went back after Aunt K went missing. He wanted to make sure Raina and Liam were okay and to wait for Uncle Pavian to return."

"That must be hard on him—trying to help them whilst everything else is going on."

"I think he enjoys it, taking care of them. It helps keep him busy and distracted. But I know he worries about Raina. The stress isn't good for the baby, and Alfina and Nina keep having to make house calls. But James has been keeping her distracted as well with her teaching him astral projection."

Placing a log in the fireplace, Ryan peered over his shoulder. "Is he any good?"

"He is, actually. I mean, he's got the dreaming astral projection part down, but he's hoping to master the being awake and doing it part."

"What's that? Dreaming astral projection."

"When you have to be asleep to do it."

"Right. I guess that was kind of self-explanatory."

"Yeah," she said with a low laugh, "kinda."

Ryan headed back and squatted over an open notebook with Rhiannon's handwriting. "Any luck?"

"No. I still can't figure out what the symbol means. There's nothing referencing it in any of the old books or the new documents we found. The only thing I've been able to find is all the drawings Mikel Dorrasa did. And there are hundreds of them that he did throughout the years.”

Flipping through the notebook, he paused and ran a finger over one of the pages. “It looks like you might’ve figured out some of the prophecy, though.”

Rhiannon lifted from the chair. “Not really.” She sat down on the floor next to him, adjusting the hem of her skirt to cover the black skin-tight pants along her chilled legs. “It’s all guesses really.”

Ryan glided his finger over the first line. “The shadow of darkness will soon emerge, when hidden powers unite and surge. Well, that’s easy. We all know that’s Merrick.”

“And I think the next line is too. I mean, he had dark magic in him, and the prophecy predicted him, right?”

“Right. And he is very old.” He glanced up at her. “Right?”

She nodded, reaching for another notebook. “Yes.” She fingered through the pages. “He’s almost seven hundred years old.” Stopping on a certain page, she added, “According to the records we have when he first arrived here, he was born in 1332 in Ireland.”

“Wow, that is old.” Ryan glanced back at the notebook in his own hands. “And I’m assuming this next part is about you and James.”

“Yeah, and the event must be when we try to stop Merrick. But I can’t figure out the rest.” She sighed. “I had Aidan and Randolyn trying to help me, but they couldn’t figure it out either. And my parents are certain the rest hasn’t unfolded yet for us to decipher. But . . ." She trailed off, her voice becoming soft and sullen. "I'm pretty sure the rest means some of us, including me and James, are going to die before this is all over."

Silence fell between them as both flipped through a few more pages.

Ryan's attention halted on one of the pages. "What's this all about?"

Rhiannon leaned over and observed where his finger had landed. "It's a section about Aidan and Nina."

"Why?"

"I have notes on everyone."

A puzzled expression lined his features. "Really?"

"Yeah."

"Why?'

Her eyes rose to his. "I'm very thorough."

"Do you have notes on me?"

"I do. But it's not like I found a hidden diary somewhere with all your deep, dark secrets in it."

He flinched with a carefree shrug. "You already know all my deep, dark secrets."

"Okay," she said with a curious grin, "then why do you seem so nervous?"

"I'm not, it's just weird and kind of creepy knowing someone has a bunch of notes on me."

"And your parents," she added menacingly with a hint of humor in her voice. She smirked, her voice returning to normal.

"But it's only the stuff from the documents after they first got here and after you were born."

"Right." His gaze moved back to the book. "Hey, I didn't know Nina can shift into a falcon. I thought her animal was a fox."

"She can do both."

His eyes shot up as he cocked his head. "Seriously? She consumed the essence of another life into her?"

"No. Both Aidan's and Nina's parents were shapeshifters, so their magic is extremely potent."

"Why do we all not know about this?"

"I wasn't even supposed to know about it, but I had found old medical records and it had listed a Reade child as having the ability to shift into a falcon. I thought maybe Aidan and Nina had a sibling or something. But when I asked him about it, he told me the truth."

"Why hide it?"

"Because Aidan and Nina both agreed when they were younger to never talk about her powers because it would make her a target. But Nina was born with the ability to shift into two animals—one of land, like her dad, and one of air, like her mom. Aidan can only shift into a golden eagle, but his magic is very powerful, and it allows him to shift completely—clothes and all. It's something many people have seen him do before. But Nina can't do that. And to protect herself, she never shifts into her other animal. Aidan prefers it to appear as if he is the more powerful shifter—making him a potential target instead of her."

"So, their mum was a . . . ?"

"An owl. And their dad was a stag."

"What happened to them?"

"I'm not sure about their mom, but their dad died when Nina was a baby. He was killed during one of his shifts."

"Oh, wow."

Rhiannon yawned and covered her mouth. "Yeah."

Ryan closed the notebook and placed it on the pile of books behind him and rose to his feet. "Come on." He offered his hand. "Let's go."

Accepting his help, she rose to her feet, her brows pinched in confusion. "Go where?"

"I'm taking you home. You need to get some sleep."

Rhiannon opened her mouth, but he cut her off.

"Some real sleep. In a bed."

"I don't want to go back there. No one's home." Her gaze dropped to the floor as she swallowed. "I don't want . . ."

"How about I stay there until you get some rest? I can just hang out on the sofa or something." He picked up a book and waved it at her. "I can catch up on my reading. Would that be all right?"

"You don't have to—"

"I know," he interrupted, soft and kind.

She stared at him before breathing out a soft chuckle. "Okay. Thanks."

Heading for the stairs, he said, "You're welcome."

Rhiannon grabbed the box with the dagger, and she and Ryan started down the creaking old stairs and headed outside as a familiar female voice filled her mind.

Rhiannon halted and listened.

"What's wrong?" Ryan asked beside her, the one-sided conversation shadowing the light in her eyes.

"Something's going on." Her voice was distant and hollow.

Athena soared through the darkness over the top of the library, the great horned owl screeching and squawking with bone-chilling distress.

Ryan eyed both Rhiannon and her Messenger. "What's she saying?"

"It's my mom," she whispered as the color drained from her face. Lifting the lid, she pulled out the dagger and dropped the box as she bolted down the path. "We need to find my grandpa!"

Racing after her, Ryan shouted, "Why? What's wrong with your mum?"

"Because . . ." she said through heavy breaths. "Merrick is at the cabin." Horror poured from her eyes as she slowed and peered over at him. "He's come to claim her."

Chapter 30

The Deal

Five months ago
Mid-July

The wall of water closed behind Rhiannon, and Merrick stalked around Karramis, the warmth of him seeping into her as he leaned over, his lips caressing her ear. "What could you possibly offer me that I'm not inclined to simply seize myself?"

A moment passed, and then she answered, her demeanor and cadence unyielding and poised. Fearless. "Me."

There was a twitch of intrigue. "Well, it does seem you are a rather popular topic of conversation among a few people I regularly acquaint myself with, so I wouldn't be completely opposed to simply takin' you instead. For now."

"Fine," she said without hesitation.

"Fine? Well, that's a tad disappointin'. I figured you'd put up more of a fight, especially as a Guardian. Shame. That would've been rather entertainin'."

"I will go with you," she continued, "on one condition."

Merrick scoffed. "You are in no position to be makin' negotiations."

"No, I'm not. But I hear you're in the market for my magic, so I'm willing to bargain. Plus, you're a prideful and honorable man, right?"

"Aye, I'd fancy myself as such."

"Well, then let me propose a deal with you. A trade. Me for them. But I get to instate the terms."

"You know," Merrick said dryly, "only the strong survive."

Karramis narrowed her eyes, her voice flat by the random statement. "Was there a point to that remark?"

The smoothness of his advancement was swift and keen—a predator waiting for the right moment to strike.

He watched intently and pulled the scent of her into him with deep inhales, smelling her, analyzing her. "It would seem that enchantin', luscious mouth of yours is huntin' fer the monster." He leaned down, his nose nearly brushing against hers as his feral, captivating stare remained unblinking. "You might want to be careful, though, because once the beast comes out, ya might not be so eager to meet it." He cocked his head when she did not yield, not even a flicker of fear showing on her face. "I find it quite extraordinary how you've managed to survive all these years. It would appear you have a bit of luck on your side. I will say this, you are certainly a persistent and audacious woman, but it would also seem you are incredibly resilient as well." He eyed her, the intrigue and pleasure burning deeper in his gaze. "I would very much love to discover what exactly flows within those veins of yours."

"So, you do want me then? My magic?"

Delight sparked in his eyes, and he lifted a brow, flashing her an inviting smirk. "Well now, those are two entirely different questions with two very different answers."

Karramis gritted her teeth, but the question came out calm. "Do you want my magic or not?"

His enticing grin remained as the thrill disappeared from his eyes. "I shall not divulge those things, nor will I disclose what I have arranged for you. I will, however, admit that you are coveted by many."

"Then you'll make the deal." Not a question, but rather a no-nonsense statement.

"I did not agree to that. I will simply hear ya out first and make a decision then."

"All right, that sounds reasonable enough," she said candidly. "Then the deal is you will take me instead of them. And I will go willingly. I promise I will not struggle when you come for me. I will not fight."

"How noble of you. A parent sacrificin' their life fer their child. A life fer a life. But ya do know I will still come fer 'em? I will steal their magic and kill 'em, even after you are long gone. I shall not agree to any form of mercy after our deal is made. Nor will any modifications be offered."

"And that's where my conditions come into play."

Merrick arched a brow and interlocked his fingers behind his back. "Go on."

"Give them two years," she continued, steady and composed, not a hint of trepidation in her voice. "Two years to learn their magic and train. Let them have the chance to fight back in a fair, equally matched fight."

He considered, arrogance beaming in his captivating gaze. "They will never be equally matched to me."

"If that's true, then you have nothing to worry about. But let the years of waiting be worth it. Let them challenge you. And if they lose, you will know you did it fair and square and not by taking down two helpless, defenseless children. Allow the fear behind the prophecy to come to a head. They are supposed to stop you, right? They're supposed to be the ones to take you down and save magic. But wouldn't it be more satisfying . . . and alluring if you beat them when they were at their strongest? When the true battle of the prophecy came to a final stand."

Merrick thought for a moment, his gaze fixed on her as he considered.

"Two years," Karramis said again. "You've already waited centuries. What's another two years to you?"

"Indeed." His tone was smooth and casual. "And I will agree to this deal on two conditions."

"Anything."

"Anything?" Amusement sparked in his eyes as a wicked grin twitched along his lips. "Now, you really shouldn't agree to such things unless you are truly willin' to give anythin' in return."

A muscle tightened along her jaw. "What is it you want from me, Merrick?"

"Well, that is neither here nor there. But anyway, as per the terms of our agreement, I simply require that I be the one to decide when the trade shall occur. And . . ." He drew out the word. "I will allow your children more time, but only until their next birthday."

"No," Karramis said tightly, taking a step toward him, "that's not what—"

"Those," he said, his voice sharp and deep, "are *my* conditions."

The water continued to rise around them, Merrick's magical wall seeming effortless.

"Agreed," she finally said with a shaky breath. "One year. But . . . when will you come for me?"

"Since I am bein' rather generous right now, I will not take what is rightfully mine and agreed upon until the night after the final full moon of the year." He gave her a deceptive smirk, quick and wicked, and Karramis took note of the strange expression. "Allow for farewells and all."

Karramis squared her shoulders. "It's a deal then, my life for theirs. I will go with you willingly, and you will give them one year of protection."

He bowed his head, a slow single nod. "You have my word. They will be spared with a trade, life for life. One year. They have until the full moon after their next birthday to live without fear of capture or death."

Five months. Karramis would only have five months to plan and prepare for him to come for her. But when he did, she would be ready.

"All right then," she finally said.

And with that, the wall around them dropped, sucking back into the grass around them.

Chapter 31

A Price is Paid

The present
Mid-December

The nighttime air was cold and crisp, the lingering scent of snow filling the air. Winter in Kiluemar was approaching, a season the island had never fully witnessed before within the protective magical barrier.

Clouds hovered overhead, their thick dark shadows sliding smoothly across the sky. The full moon shone behind them, casting streaks of luminescent silvery-white beams of light along the darkness around the cabin, shades of navy, indigo, and charcoal painted beyond the illumination along the porch.

But through the stillness of the night, the shadows of midnight crept closer.

He was coming.

Tonight, Merrick would arrive to claim what was his.

And this time, Karramis would be ready for him. She had prepared for this—contemplating every possible outcome and worst-case scenario. Or so she thought.

But the night came and went, and Merrick never arrived. That is, until the next evening when he came to claim his part of the deal—life for life. And when he finally showed up, he left with both Karramis and Will.

～

Wind swirled through the air as mist danced with the wintery breeze, forming a portal twenty feet within a dense set of dead trees before discharging Karramis with a less-than-graceful exit. Hitting various trees, she plummeted down, snapping the branches clean off before slamming hard against the ground, dispelling all the air from her lungs. Her body remained still as her mind drifted unwillingly into darkness. Everything around her and inside her consciousness faded slowly into oblivion, getting lost deep within a void of silence and nothingness.

The black shadows blanketed her, pulling her deeper into an emptiness where pain, fear, and defeat refused to dwell. But she did not welcome the wholeness and peace of the darkness or the vacant coldness driving her further into its grasp.

Air filled her lungs, an overwhelming surge of strength pulling her from the darkness. She gasped and flung open her eyes. Panting, she drew in more air as the pain settled back into her body. Her face stung, burning as the cold wind seared into her cheek like hot iron. The two sets of puncture wounds on her neck and along her wrist throbbed with her thundering heartbeat as more blood trailed from the open wounds. But it was the mind-numbing ache radiating from her stomach halting her ability to breathe. The pulsing injury sliced into her with every inhale and exhale, forcing her to sense every damaged inch of skin, every sliver of impaired muscle, damaged nerves, and puncture of internal flesh.

She focused on her breathing as her body trembled, the pain and coldness taking over every part of her. Her head spun, and a haziness clouded her vision.

White. Everything around her was covered in white.

More oxygen filled her lungs as each breath surged through her with a painful jolt, but she had to keep breathing. She had to fight the agony taking over her. But her stomach hurt—the burning and sharpness were too much. She wanted to vomit, but she swallowed it down. Her body grew weaker with each passing minute. She had to get up. She had to fight. But she could not move. Her mental strength could not combat the surrendering of her body.

Blood escaped her midsection with each heartbeat—her insides run through without a hint of hesitation or regret—and tainted the newly fallen snow under her with bright red.

Karramis lifted her head, but the sheer mass was hard to fight. The heaviness pulled at her neck, the muscles straining against her efforts and choking her. Her vision pulsated with her heartbeat as her eyes struggled to take in where she had landed.

Trees. Dead trees. Harsh, mangled trees stretching their monstrous branches toward the sky. Fresh undisturbed snow stretched out before her and clung to the ominous forest. A coldness lingered in the air, producing a unique scent brought on only by the freezing temperatures of winter, but it was riddled with death. Even the trees stood in absolute silence as the wind remained still, both seemingly awaiting the dangers she would face soon enough.

She was in Shadow Forest.

Karramis had managed to escape just outside the walls of Casteya Castle, her magic only taking her as far as her damaged body and drained mind would allow. But it was not enough. She was going to die out here.

Giving in to the realization she would not survive much longer, she allowed her eyes to close as she surrendered and passed out again.

~

Will tore through the sky atop Callie as she flew over Maevis Mountains, slicing through the thick dark clouds with ease. The winged horse's flapping matched Will's heartbeat as it pounded in his chest. The pain in his body and face faded, veiled behind the sheer adrenaline coursing through him. Moisture lingered, the cold air turning brittle as the gentle kisses of winter sent goose bumps rising along his skin beneath his long-sleeve shirt and jeans.

Soaring over the tower next to the castle, Will was unsure of his next step. His mind could not come up with a sensible plan. All logic and strategy escaped him. Only pure love and determination fueled his actions. He had to save her. Somehow. Even if it meant dying in the process. She had rescued him, and now it was his turn to return the favor.

Urging Callie to land just before the archway leading into the tower, Will jumped off and landed quietly on his feet. Refusing to draw attention to himself, Will stalked through the snow in utter silence, a perfect mix of stealth and control.

Will stopped. Reaching over his head, he unsheathed the short sword strapped to his back and listened.

Nothing.

There was pure silence engulfing him. No footsteps. No voices. No screams or whimpers. Not even the sounds of nature filled his ears.

Will closed the space between him and Callie and whispered, "Fly, but stay close."

Callie shot into the sky without taking a running leap, sending a rush of air crashing down into Will and ruffling his tousled hair.

Will readied his sword, clasping the grip effortlessly. Multiple footprints lay among the snow, retreating from the tower. He passed under the archway, glancing up the spiral staircase lining the inside of the cold, damp stone tower. Inching up the wooden steps of the circular building, Will kept his senses on high alert, taking in every potential threat that might linger in the silence.

Plumes of mist fell from Will's mouth as he continued up, his bones rattling from the brisk temperatures within the tower. No heat radiated from the top floor. No crackling or smoke filled the area, only deafening silence and a bone-slicing chill wrapped around him.

His heart hammered in his chest as he drew in a slow steady breath, centering himself and regaining control. He did it again, in and out. Warmth filled his core as his trembling hands stilled. He wrapped his fingers tighter around the grip of the sword, preparing to fight, to defend if needed. His pulse slowed, his body calm and ready. Will continued to search the area, his brows pinched as he took in everything. He picked up his pace, his wide stride taking two steps at a time but still not making a sound under his heavy boots.

Will halted as a strong metallic tinge burned the inside of his nose, followed by a subtle trace of decay. Taking in a shuddering breath, Will shivered as a chill raced up his back.

"Karramis," he said under his breath as he raced up the stairs, no longer worried about who lay beyond the landing at the top of the stairs.

Will burst through the threshold as he reached the top, sword ready to strike. But it was empty.

He scanned the room, his eyes stopping on a mix of blood splatters and drips across the floor, observing multiple scorch marks as well along the stones.

Will bolted down the stairs, ignoring all his instincts to stay quiet as his footfalls pounded against the wooden steps, amplifying within the stone building. Jumping the last few stairs, he hurried under the archway and slid to a stop in the slick snow.

He whistled, a loud, piercing whistle that might have alerted anyone nearby, but Will did not care.

He had to find her.

Callie crashed her hooves to the ground, sending the snow flying through the air as a loud boom rattled beneath Will's feet. Realizing he still had the sword in his hand, he sheathed it in one fell swoop before jumping onto the winged horse's back. Her wings of solid white stretched out in a beautiful display of elegance, her wingspan stretching ten feet in both directions as Will grasped her black mane. Galloping away from the tower, Callie flapped in one swift beat before she was airborne.

Will gently tugged on Callie's mane, directing her upward and south over the wall of the castle and high above the trees, aiming for the high peaks of the mountain. Maybe she had portaled herself out. Maybe she had actually managed to escape.

Fog rolled down from Maevis Mountains, a thick gray haze filling the sky and obscuring both Will's and the winged horse's vision. Will urged her lower, closer to the trees just over the exterior walls, outside the murkiness consuming the sky above them.

Callie threw out her wings and came to a lurching stop in midair, and Will's stomach squeezed at the abrupt halt, the emptiness and churning emotions forcing bile to rise in his throat. He panicked as he swallowed it down. He searched the sky for any threat, but he saw nothing. He squinted, his eyes blinded by the bright snow down below. Callie sprang forward and swooped downward, soaring into a graceful free fall to the ground.

There. Among the forest was the reason for Callie's sudden halt and shift in direction.

Will's heart sank as his eyes fixed on a body lying motionless on the white ground among the trees. He leaned in as Callie sent a rush of wind flapping in one heaving motion and plunged faster.

It was Karramis.

~

Visions danced in her mind, memories playing in fast-forward in disjointed flashes with a bright orange glow flickering behind them. Images of the mother she never knew, the moment her magic surfaced, flames rising from her body as she slept, her first intimate experience with Will, the birth of her children, and each one of her family members smiling back at her. The orange light faded in the blink of an eye and shifted to darkness as the ominous words spoken moments ago echoed in her ears, distant and distorted. Her mind floated inward, reliving the last few hours through a haze of shadows. Emptiness and rage and power and pleasure burned in the eyes of those around her as a blade rammed into her, thrusting in without hesitation. Coldness and delight rose across a spiteful grin glaring down at her before fangs pierced her neck and wrist, sucking with ferocity and draining the life from her body before the blood from her stomach spilled out onto the floor.

Her mind drifted further away as her body grew weaker. But a sudden jolt halted her in place, her life clinging to the string tugging against her soul. A voice. A voice echoed in the distance, calling her name. The voice warmed her to the core and drove hope into her body, bringing her back to life.

Will.

Karramis fought, forcing her mind, body, and soul back together as Will's presence emerged next to her. His hands slid under her, and pain shot outward from her as he lifted her off the ground and cradled her in his lap. The warmth from his body covered her like a blanket, comforting and peaceful.

"Bloody hell," he said, his voice quiet and troubled. "What the hell did they do to you?"

Her face was bruised along the left side. Blood soaked her shirt as varying shades of red stained the ripped material next to two puncture wounds along the collar, the deep fang marks lining her neck as dry blood caked against her pale skin. Another set of bite marks dug into her wrist, the wounds jagged, as if the teeth had pulled and torn the skin.

Slight plumes of condensation flowed with her shallow breaths as he inspected her midsection, carefully lifting her shirt and searching for the injury. A single thin wound appeared along her lower stomach, but very little blood continued to flow from the deep laceration as he sat holding her, the snow around them painted with smears of crimson.

Karramis's eyes flickered open, her voice weak and raspy. "Will?"

"Yes, I'm here," he answered, his throat tight as he smiled down at her. "I'm here, darling. You did it. You got us both out."

Her watery eyes peered up at him, but they were distant. "You . . . You made it."

"Yes." Will wiped away the tears pooling along her eyelids. "Thanks to you."

"You came back."

"I told you I would."

Her body sagged in his arms as her eyes closed.

"No. No, you don't." Sadness and hopelessness strained his voice as he held her closer, shaking her awake. "Open your eyes. Open your eyes, darling."

Karramis fought against the heaviness of her eyelids, the raw pain and exhaustion washing over her like a powerful wave.

"You're going to be all right." Will kissed her forehead as he gave into the grief, the tears falling down his face. "You hear me? You are not dying on me." Lifting her up as he rose to his feet, he quickly halted as she winced and gasped in pain. "I'm sorry." He lowered them back down. "I'm so sorry. I know it hurts, but I need to get you out of here. I need to get you some help."

"Will," Karramis said with a shuddering exhale, fighting to keep her eyes open, "I'm . . . sorry."

"No." Will shook his head as tears slid down his cheeks. "I'm the one who's sorry. I should've saved you, not the other way around."

"But . . ." Streaks of warmth trailed along her cold cheeks. "You already saved me twice." Karramis winced as she struggled to form the words snagging within the pain searing through her body. "It was . . . my turn . . . to save you."

Will gave her a gentle grin as confusion drew his brows together. "Twice?"

"With the . . . dragon blood." She swallowed, but the pale task was difficult as the dryness rubbed in her throat. "And the day you . . . you told me you loved me."

Resting his hand against her cheek, he said softly, "No, you saved me the day you found me. I was lost and lonely, and you found me."

"There's no way I found you on my own." Another set of tears slid down her bruised face as she lifted one corner of her mouth. "I was meant to find you."

Will's throat bobbed. "You can't leave me."

Her body went taut as she winced.

"I . . . I'm sorry," she said again in a low, raspy whisper, her eyes laced with pain.

"No, you're not." His voice was shaken with denial. "You're not sorry because you aren't leaving me." Holding her close, he whispered in her ear, the warmth from his breath making her shiver, "I just got you back." He glanced down at her pale face and slightly blue lips. "No, you're not dying today. I won't allow it."

Tears swelled in the corners of her eyes as they fluttered open and closed. Raising a shaky, bloody hand, Karramis rested it against his warm cheek.

Will shivered at her icy touch.

"It's okay . . ." Karramis said, her words slurred as her eyes closed.

"Darling? Don't close your eyes," he pleaded, his voice cracking. "Stay awake. Fight it!"

She went soft and limp in his arms.

"Dammit, Karramis, you can't die on me again."

Karramis gasped, and the crisp air made her cough, droplets of blood spitting from her mouth before she declared through swallow breaths, "I'm cold. I want . . . to go home."

Home. Not to the cabin, but somewhere else.

"All right, darling." Will kissed her forehead as he lifted her into his arms, carrying her over to Callie. "I'll take you to them. Just stay with me."

Callie lowered herself down to the ground as Will flung a leg over her backside. Resting Karramis against the winged horse, he pressed her into his chest and straddled the creature, squeezing his legs and holding tight with his thighs. He held Karramis with one arm as he gripped Callie's mane, and she took to the sky without so much as a nudge.

"Will . . ." Karramis said, barely loud enough for him to hear, the cold air whipping through her chestnut-brown waves.

Will lowered his ear to her mouth, his skin brushing against her lips.

She kissed him gently, every fiber of her wanting just one final embrace. "I'm not cold anymore."

"No." He jerked his head back, peering down at her with her glossy eyes staring up at him. "No, this isn't happening. Not again. Not now."

"I love you . . ." She closed her eyes and forced herself to swallow, the dryness and lump in her throat making it difficult. "All of you."

Her body went limp in his arms.

"Karramis." Taking his hand off Callie's mane, he cupped her cheek. "Karramis?"

The world around him was silent as his heart pounded in his ears. He trembled as he held her tight, her cold body making him shiver. A pain pierced through him as disbelief and heartache drowned him, pulling him deeper into the depths of his soul. His eyes welled with tears as he held his breath, lowered his head, and closed his eyes, hoping it was all a nightmare.

~

"Dad!" voices called out, echoing as Callie landed.

Will shifted his eyes upward and spotted James and Rhiannon running toward him across the field by the infirmary.

The winged horse slid to a stop, billows of condensation huffing from her nose.

"Get help!" Will pleaded frantically, the words lodging in his throat as tears chilled along his face.

Rhiannon bolted back over to the infirmary, the snow crunching under her feet. "Aidan! Nina! Alfina!"

Keeping his eyes on Karramis, he lifted her into his arms and slid off Callie, crashing to his knees. "Please. Open your eyes."

He leaned back onto his heels, pulling her closer to him. She was so cold through the two layers of clothes. And her lips were so blue.

"Not yet, darling," he whispered into her ear. "You hear me? I'm not ready to let you go. Please. Please stay. Don't leave me."

"Dad," James said softly, kneeling in the snow. "Dad?"

Will lifted his teary gaze up to his son. "I'm so sorry. I didn't get back to her in time."

Shuffling to a stop, Rhiannon panted as Aidan's footsteps pounded behind her.

"No," Rhiannon said with a heavy breath, staring down at her mother. "No."

James's face was lined with shock as he knelt beside his parents. He stared down at his mother, his hand taking on a mind of its own as it traced over her cold blue-tinged skin, stopping against her wrist.

Kneeling beside him, Rhiannon took hold of her brother's other hand and squeezed.

James held his breath as he pressed his index and middle finger against the inside of Karramis's uninjured wrist.

Moments passed as everyone waited for something that would never happen.

Aidan reached down and placed a hand on James's shoulder. "James, she's gone."

James stared down at his mother, the realization washing over him like a powerful wave.

Aidan was right. Karramis was dead.

Chapter 32

Fate of the Unknown

Covering her mouth, Rhiannon unleashed herself. Heavy sobs rose in her chest, the pain constricting around her heart and squeezing every bit of oxygen from her lungs. Her muffled cries hid behind her hand as sorrow and hopelessness trailed down her cheeks, the warmth of each tear slicing into her cold skin.

Emptiness filled James's insides, a deep hole of vast nothingness leaving his body hollow. But the hole quickly filled with a crushing surge of emotions that swelled up and over the edges with anger, disbelief, and guilt. They all stormed together as the world around him turned to chaos, and the walls of his mind rushed open, unable to control the forces surging through him.

Rage charged, sending a surge of electric energy through him, firing off and igniting his blood as it flowed between him and his sister. Anger and sadness churned together, whipping up a storm inside them, sending the powerful burst outward. Wind ripped through the air as the snow around them began to melt.

The twins' emotions crashed together in a thunderous explosion, rippling out like a raging charge. Electricity shot through them as fire burned in their veins. Their bodies quaked with waves of power that flowed through them like an earth-shattering gust of wind. Their pulses raged, the blood shifting back and forth between blazing hot and ice-cold.

Then the world around them exploded.

The ground rumbled, shaking everything. The building behind them creaked, and the trees swayed, shaking the snow from the branches.

Callie took to the sky in one quick flap of her wings, joining the dragons in the sky high above as the clouds thickened overhead and a bolt of lightning streaked across darkened clouds.

"What the hell is goin' on?" Aidan yelled over the rumbling of the earth.

Wind swirled and swept through the trees as it twisted the branches. The windows of the infirmary shattered, and glass clattered as it fell to the ground.

"It's them!" Will said, matching his tone. "It's their powers!"

Aidan stumbled. "We have to stop them before they destroy everythin'!"

Will lifted Karramis's lifeless body into his arms.

A fissure opened up a few feet away, the dirt and snow crumbling into the crack in the ground as flames burst out with a loud boom.

Aidan fell back as the earthquake intensified. "Shit!" He hurried to his feet, rushing in front of Rhiannon, who was still kneeling on the ground, and gripping her shoulders.

"Rhiannon!" There was nothing but pain and distance in her eyes. "Rhiannon!"

Thunder cracked overhead, the loud boom sending the dragons and Callie arching midair and flying away as the dark gray clouds overhead shifted to violet and amethyst. Thunder roared again and lingered with a rumbling echo. Streaks of purple and blue lightning flashed above them, striking the ground like an explosion. Another bolt erupted and struck the flames reaching toward the sky, sending sparks flying. Fire and magma spewed from the small, narrow opening in the earth, melting the snow and setting the dead grass below ablaze.

Will ran away from the fiery crack in the earth and carefully lowered Karramis to the ground before racing back to his children and dropping to his knees beside Aidan. "James! Rhiannon!"

Moisture burst from the sky, the downpour of rain exploding with unwavering power before turning to snow as a blizzard consumed them. Funnel clouds formed overhead, swirling around and making the dark gray and purple sky dance with the pouring rain. Flowers rose from beneath the snow-covered ground—lilacs, sunflowers, roses, and daisies blooming and ripping from their stems, no match for the ravaging winds.

"James!" Will said again, grasping his son's shoulder.

Aidan pulled Rhiannon into his chest and rubbed her back, his words pleading as he leaned into her ear. "Rhiannon, come back. Focus on my voice."

Oblivious to the events unfolding simultaneously around them, the twins had awoken the powers of the four elements hidden deep inside them.

Will stared into his son's watery eyes, the same eyes as his wife, and cupped his cheek in his hands. "James, listen to me."

The wind around them whipped harder, swirling faster as the snow slammed into them.

"Son, control it." His voice was calm. "Control the power inside of you. Don't let it take over."

James blinked, and the wind and shaking slowed.

He blinked again, his brown eyes meeting his father's.

The flurries crashed to the ground, and the earth rattled to a stop.

"Rhiannon?" Aidan said calmly, matching Will's actions. "Listen to my voice. Come back."

Rhiannon blinked multiple times before meeting his gaze as the flames around them disappeared and the storm overhead halted.

The twins blinked at each other, regaining awareness and control.

The thunder and lightning stopped as the clouds evaporated, and the flames and magma sucked back into the ground as the earth sealed shut.

The twins stood without saying a word and took each other's hands. Strolling over to their mother, they stared down at her as she lay on the ground. Rhiannon dropped to her knees and clutched her mother's bloody hand. It was so cold and limp.

With her eyes closed, Karramis seemed like she was sleeping, but the hint of blue on her ashen skin was more pronounced against the white snow, reassuring the others the life in her was gone. Rhiannon refused to let go of her mother as she leaned into her brother, who now knelt beside her. Wrapping his arm around his sister, James pulled her closer. Together, the twins' grief-stricken cries changed to quiet gut-wrenching sobs as they held each other.

Will sat on the other side of Karramis and tucked her hair behind her ears before taking hold of his children's hands. Aidan placed his hand on Will's back and bowed his head, his own eyes filling with tears.

All four of them remained quiet behind silent whimpers as they each accepted Karramis's final fate.

~

The snow was falling again minutes later, this time the light flurries not being controlled by the twins.

"We can't keep her here," Aidan said somberly as he laid the blanket Rhiannon had dropped on the porch out across the ground.

"I know." Will lifted her into his arms and lowered her stiff body onto the blanket, gently wrapping it around her. "I'll take her inside and clean her up."

"No, Will, I can do that for you," Aidan offered softly.

"No, it's all right. I'll do it."

"We're coming too," the twins said in unison, both voices low and hoarse.

Will's eyes were red and puffy as he met their gazes. "All right."

They all headed over to the infirmary.

Spotting the broken windows, Rhiannon asked, the regret and guilt clear in her tone, "Is everyone inside okay?"

"Yes," Aidan answered. "Just a few broken things, but nobody was hurt."

Rhiannon halted as she started to cry. "I'm so sorry." Her bloodshot gaze dropped to the ground.

Aidan reached out his arms to Will. "Here, I'll take her."

Will gently handed Karramis's body to his best friend and rushed over to his daughter, pulling her into his chest and wrapping his arms around her. "What could you possibly be sorry about?"

"She . . ." Her voice shuddered. "She's gone because of us."

"No." Will framed her face with his hands. "This is not your fault." He locked eyes on James. "Neither of you are to blame for this." Returning his attention to Rhiannon, he said tenderly, "Listen to me. Your mum gave her life to protect you—to make sure you two would see another day. And she would do it again and again if she could. Her choices have always been to keep you both safe."

"He's right," Aidan added. "This is not yer fault. Yer mom has—"

His words cut off.

Will tilted his gaze over at Aidan and noticed his friend's blanched expression as he stared down at Karramis. "What's wrong?"

Aidan lifted his eyes, his face tight with confusion. "She's warm."

"What?" Will and the twins blurted.

"She's warm."

"What do you mean?" Rhiannon said in a hurried tone.

The coldness under Aidan's arms from the snow had faded as Karramis's body radiated heat, and she was getting warmer under the blanket. The warmth spread across his arms, beads of sweat pooling and soaking into the blanket.

"Ouch!" Aidan snapped as he lowered Karramis to the ground, the snow thinning beneath her.

Smoke rose from the wrapped body, thicker and darker with each passing second.

"What're you doing?" James asked his sister, unnerved.

"It's not me," Rhiannon stated, both shocked and terrified.

Smoke billowed higher from the blanket as a unique blend of burned cotton, cinnamon, spiced honey, and smoked cedar filled the air.

"What's happening?" Rhiannon asked frantically, shuffling away from her mother's body with the others.

The blanket burst into flames.

"Holy shit!" Aidan yelped.

Will shouted, "Bloody hell!"

Both pulled James and Rhiannon with them as they backed away.

The flames rose higher and burned hotter, raging as they stretched a few feet into the air. Orange, red, and yellow danced together, a mesmerizing mix of danger and comfort.

"Get back!" Aidan yelled, urging Will away from the smoldering inferno as he inched back over.

The four of them stared awestruck as they retreated away, the heat becoming unbearable as the ground burst into flames, the fire consuming the body and creating a huge fireball along the mud and grass.

"What the hell is happening?" James demanded.

The fire exploded, burning bright in an outward burst with blinding orange and yellow as the flames hummed a thunderous tune.

"I think it's her fire magic," Rhiannon answered loudly over the noise. "It happened to her mother."

"What do you mean?" James asked.

"Grandpa said that he never understood why Karramis didn't die in the same fire as her mother. But he thought maybe Keya had died somehow in the forest by accident, and when her magic released from her, it caused the fire to start."

"But why didn't it kill Mom too?"

"Because she, too, was a Fire Witch, and her own magic protected her."

The fire popped and crackled, creating a larger explosion of blinding light. Flames reached twenty feet into the air, stretching along the ground within a contained circle reaching outward ten feet.

The inferno flashed again, and everyone jerked their heads sideways, averting their eyes from the extraordinary brightness. Blinking multiple times, they all waited for the spots to disappear from their vision. As their sight returned, the four of them gawked out into the open field, standing in complete shock at the sight in front of them. They could not move, frozen in place as all eyes opened wide and each mouth parted in disbelief.

A figure stood in the inferno, the fire flowing across its body in a gentle wavelike motion, elegantly rolling and swaying in a flawless upward motion, the small flickers of fiery wisps floating off it. The figure rose off the ground as the raging fire roared around it. Fiery tresses swirled above its head, waves of molten fire drifting upward in a fluid motion as if the figure were in a liquid fire, aimlessly floating among the watery blaze.

The figure's eyes shot open, glaring through the flames with glowing white eyes, small flickers of fire dancing among them. Closing them again, the figure landed, its feet pressing against the dry ground, no traces of snow remaining, and the fire along the ground vanished, sucking into the body standing before them.

Flames rose from beneath the naked body, covering every inch of it as fiery hair turned a chestnut brown with golden hues highlighted among it. Features appeared as the fire pulled inward under the skin, revealing a familiar face with only the scar remaining on her now-healed ivory skin.

It was Karramis.

The fire continued to disappear from her naked body, inching closer to her skin as each soft curve came into view.

Aidan quickly removed his jacket and handed it to Will. "Here."

Will rushed over and shielded his wife from exposing herself to the others. He watched in pure amazement as every familiar inch of her came into view, the sheer sight of her sending him into a state of astonishment and longing.

Every ember faded, and only Karramis remained—motionless, completely exposed . . . and alive.

Will closed the distance between him and Karramis and wrapped the oversized jacket around her, but she did not move.

"How?" James asked, surprise hanging on the word.

Will chuckled under his breath as he continued holding her. "Born among ashes and soot."

James glanced at him. "What?"

Karramis's eyes shot open, the same rich brown peering up in a blank stare. She gasped, inhaling a deep breath before collapsing into Will's arms as he held the jacket around her.

"She's been reborn," Aidan asked, the shock plastered on his face.

"Reborn?" Rhiannon asked, her voice tight in her throat. "Into what?"

"The eternal flame." Will brushed back her hair as her knees weakened, and he carefully lowered her to the ground. "She's a phoenix."

Karramis blinked up at him, golden specks now glimmering within her beautiful chocolate gaze.

"Hello, darling," he said, smiling down at her with tears in his eyes. "You really need to stop dying on me."

Her dry lips parted, and she cleared the tightness from her throat. "No promises."

He chuckled at the light in her eyes fully present. "How are you feeling?"

"Cold." Her voice was hoarse. "And wet."

He could not help but laugh. "Well, you *are* lying naked on the ground."

"Why am I naked?"

"Well, I reckon it has something to do with your clothes not being fireproof." He ran the back of his hand over her cheek before running his finger along her scar. "But honestly, how are you feeling?"

"A bit dizzy." Her eyes remained on him, taking in every inch of his face. "And tired. Really tired."

"I can imagine."

Her gaze focused on the bruises and split lip. "What happened?"

"To be honest, I'm not quite sure. You tell me."

Reaching up, she traced a finger over the bruise on his face. "They hurt you."

"Yes, they did," he said, realizing her question was regarding his injuries and not what had happened to her.

"They were hurting you. They made me watch."

He nodded and cradled her cheek.

"And I . . . I died." The final word came out with an uneven breath.

Will held back his emotions. "Yes, darling, you did."

Tears filled her eyes. "I was dead."

"I know."

Fire burned in her veins as she stared up at Will, remembering every single moment that had led to her dying in his arms.

Born among ashes and soot, a savior will set the journey afoot. The words of the prophecy rang true, for Karramis was reborn among the flames. A phoenix. Created with the gift of resurrection, she was a true immortal. Powers stronger than the average folk, she was now the eternal flame—generating life with a smallest ember.

She was life and death.

And now she would stop at nothing to bring hell upon those who had threatened her and what she loved most—her family.

"I'm going to slaughter them," Karramis promised with unyielding conviction as rage ignited in her lethal gaze. "All of them. Starting with the son of a bitch who stabbed me."

To be continued in:

The Shadow of Darkness
Magic of the Realm ~ Book Four

Andralae: ANN-DR-UH-LAY
Lescan: LUH-SCAN
Nikolai: NEE-KO-LIE
Racentu: RAY-SIN-TOO
Stoweward: STOW-WORD

Refer to Book One and Book Two for more pronunciations

Mon amour – My love
Mon dieu – My god / My goodness / Good heavens
Oui – Yes
Piuthar beag – Little sister
S'il te plaît – Please

Content Warning

This book contains the following:

Death

Violence

Abuse

Mature Language

Suggestive Language

Mature Situations

Suggestive Situations

Depression

Anxiety

Recommended for a mature audience

Ages: 14+

Acknowledgements

To my children, Isabelle and Ian, you are my heart, my soul, my life. You are my everything, and I promise, with every fiber of my being, I will be the best mother and person I can be. I will always stand and fight everything that tries to push me down. And I will do it all, not only for myself, but for you. I love you both so much.

A huge thank you to Nathan Marraffino, Anna Gough, Jennifer Gonzales, and Stephanie Kittleson for your never-ending support and always being there for me.

I would also like to thank my alpha readers, Christine Hutton and my daughter, Isabelle (my biggest fan), and my beta readers, Isaac Marraffino and Jennifer Gonzales.

A special thanks to my amazing audiobook narrators Nichole James and Keval Shah. You two are amazing and working with you has been an amazing experience. I cannot wait to work on the rest of this series with you both.

Also, thank you to Tati B. Alvarez, Stefanie Saw, Natalia and Greg with Enchanted Ink Publishing, Dennis Doty, Beth Gilbert, Julia Blake, Megan Bradley, Sierra Clark, Madison Cooper, Rebecca Kaufman, Julia Lawrence, Bella Nox, Kaley Ruta, and Jesse Shimmin.

And lastly, to my readers. Thank you. This is truly a dream of mine to bring this story to life, and I hope you are enjoying it and are excited to see where this adventure goes. Thank you for supporting my author journey.

---

*Only the characters and creatures previously introduced in the
series are listed below in order of appearance or mention.
No new characters or creatures from Fate of the Unknown are
listed in this section.*

Will – *William Drolnogard Cassil*

Father to James and Rhiannon. Husband to Karramis.
Best friend to Aidan. Brother-in-law to Pavian,
Kavana, and Meadow. Drolnogard (Dragon telepath).

Terramina

Earth Dragon.

Raeth

Earth Dragon.

Oakley

Earth Dragon.

Ignara

Fire Dragon.

Quinian

Member of Zarrius's guard. Weapons master, blacksmith, and combat instructor. Dwarf.

Raina – *Raina Richards Ward*

Wife to Pavian. Mother to Liam. Aunt to James and Rhiannon. Sister-in-law to Kavana, Karramis, and Meadow. Astral Traveler.

Liam – *Liam Ward*

Son to Pavian and Raina. Cousin to James and Rhiannon. Nephew to Kavana, Karramis, and Meadow.

Callie

Will's companion. Winged horse.

James – *James Cassil*

Main male protagonist. If you do not know who this is, you have not been paying attention.

Rhiannon – *Rhiannon Llewellyn Cassil*

Main female protagonist. If you do not know who this is, you really should go back and reread Book One and Book Two.

Alfina

Medical specialist. Member of Zarrius's guard. Elf.

Nina – *Nina Reade*

Family friend to the Wards and Cassils. Younger sister to Aidan. Shapeshifter.

Aidan – *Aidan Reade*

Family friend to the Wards and Cassils. Boyfriend to Kavana. Best friend to Karramis and Will. Older brother to Nina. Shapeshifter.

Karramis – *Karramis Llewellyn Ward Cassil*

Mother to James and Rhiannon. Wife to Will. Sister to Pavian, Kavana, and Meadow. Daughter to Zarrius and Keya (deceased). Fire Witch and Guardian.

Merrick – *Cillian Merrick Elldon Devlin*

Main male antagonist. If you do not know who this is, I am positive you have not read the first two books.

Pavian – *Pavian Liam Ward*

Uncle to James and Rhiannon. Brother to Kavana, Karramis, and Meadow. Father to Liam. Husband to Raina. Son to Zarrius and Vivian (deceased). Member of Zarrius's guard. Guardian.

Kavana – *Kavana Aurora Ward*

Aunt to James and Rhiannon. Sister to Pavian, Karramis, and Meadow. Girlfriend to Aidan. Daughter to Zarrius and Vivian (deceased). Member of Zarrius's guard. Guardian.

Meadow – *Meadow Ward Cannington*

Aunt to James and Rhiannon. Sister to Pavian, Kavana, and Karramis. Daughter to Zarrius and Randolyn. Water Witch and Guardian.

Ryan – *Ryan Hillvec*

Best friend to Rhiannon. Friend to James. Volunteers at the library with Randolyn. Werewolf and Celestial Witch.

Viktor

Member of Zarrius's guard. Gargoyle.

Zarrius – *Zarrius Ward*

Grandfather to James and Rhiannon. Father to Pavian, Kavana, Karramis, and Meadow. Husband to Randolyn. Head Guardian and the one in charge of the guard.

Randolyn – ***Randolyn Natomna Ward***

Step-grandmother to James and Rhiannon. Wife to Zarrius. Step-mother to Pavian, Kavana, and Karramis. Mother to Meadow. Water Witch and Kiluemar's librarian.

Tressa

Friend and advisor to Merrick. Celestial Witch.

Cami – ***Camille De la Rue Beaumont***

Found in France by Lucas to use her abilities to return to Kiluemar. Friend to Lucas, Leif, Haydrin, and Gastell. Echo. Killed by Merrick in The Evil Within.

Theseus

Companion and bodyguard to Tressa. Minotaur.

Leif – ***Leif Nyland***

Works for Merrick. Vampire.

Lucas – ***Lucas Fraye***

Works for Merrick. Ex-best friend to Karramis. Telematra (powerful telepath and magic tracker).

Haydrin – ***Haydrin Tevlak***

Works for Merrick. Werewolf.

Gastell

Works for Merrick. Ogre.

Niko – *Nikolai Lescan*

Companion to Tressa. Works for Merrick. Vampire.

Tiffasa – *Tiffasa Hernandez*

Childhood best friend to Karramis. Friend to Raina.
Neighbor to Raina and Pavian in Stoweward.
Illusionist.

Avery

Childhood best friend to Karramis. Telepath.

Sterling – *Sterling Andralae*

Daughter to Marie. Seer.

Marie – *Marie Andralae*

Seer who predicted the second verse of the prophecy.

Tenarick

Member of Zarrius's guard. Weapons master. Magic
and combat instructor. Elf.

Phosmeratae

Air Dragon.

<u>Mikel – *Mikel Dorrasa*</u>

Son to Sadora, the seer who predicted the first verse of the prophecy. Repeated the verse years later and drew the symbol of the prophecy. Seer.